The Essential Fictions

ISAAC BABEL

THE ESSENTIAL FICTIONS

*Edited and translated
from the Russian by*
Val Vinokur

Illustrations by
Yefim Ladyzhensky

NORTHWESTERN UNIVERSITY PRESS
EVANSTON, ILLINOIS

Northwestern University Press

www.nupress.northwestern.edu

Printed in the United States of America

10   9   8   7   6   5   4   3   2

Library of Congress Cataloging-in-Publication Data

Names: Babel', I. (Isaak), 1894–1940, author. | Vinokur, Val, editor,
    translator. | Ladyzhensky, Yefim, 1911–1982, illustrator.
Title: The essential fictions / Isaac Babel ; edited and translated from the Russian by Val
    Vinokur ; illustrations by Yefim Ladyzhensky.
Description: Evanston, Illinois : Northwestern University Press, 2017. | Includes
    bibliographical references.
Identifiers: LCCN 2017021506 | ISBN 9780810135956 (pbk. : alk. paper)
Subjects: LCSH: Babel', I. (Isaak), 1894–1940—Translations into English.
Classification: LCC PG3476.B2 A2 2017 | DDC 891.7342—dc23
LC record available at https://lccn.loc.gov/2017021506

CONTENTS

Red Cavalry

TRANSLATOR'S PREFACE

Having deprived me of seas, of running and flying away,
and allowing me only to walk upon the violent earth,
what have you achieved? A splendid result:
you could not stop my lips from moving.
>—Osip Mandelstam, *The Voronezh Notebooks*,
>trans. Richard and Elizabeth McKane

Babel . . . speaks of the stars and the clap in the same voice.
>—Viktor Shklovsky, "Babel: A Critical Romance"

Literary introductions have been compared to monsters in an illuminated medieval manuscript—monsters that, in Lewis Bagby's words, have "broken through the frame border, torn it open in such a way that they might step or gesture out into the text they accompany . . . Here the monster transgresses the space of the discourse, sometimes even producing in cartoon boxes the folio's first words as quoted speech from the mouth of the beast. And finally, there are frames that have wholly disappeared. The monster roams the page freely."[1] I will keep my monster on a leash. There is, of course, a simpler, if more unstable and equivocal, idea of what most preambles try to do: to convince you, the reader, that something of *mine* should be or, indeed, already *is*, something of *yours*. By writing this introduction, I claim that the translation you are going to read is, in some sense, *my* Babel—and that it should also be yours. Is it, in fact, already destined to be yours? I can only say that if this preface fails to persuade, then perhaps my translation will. And if not—well, there are other translations.

In 1929, Lionel Trilling read a book "about Soviet regiments of horse operating in Poland" that disturbed him, charged, as it was, with an "intensity, irony, and ambiguousness" he wished to avoid. Then again, wrote Trilling, "if we stop to think of the museum knowingness about art which we are likely to acquire with maturity, of our consumer's pride in buying only the very best spiritual commodities, the ones which are sure to give satisfaction, there may possibly be a grace in those moments when we lack the courage to confront, or the strength to endure, some particular work of art or kind of art."[2]

The disturbing book—a book that, like Samson in the temple of the Philistines, still moves the pillars of "museum knowingness"—was Nadia Helstein's 1929 translation of Isaac Babel's *Red Cavalry* (1926). Ernest Hemingway—who confessed that "Babel's style is even more concise than mine," proving that "even when you've got all the water out of them, you can still clot the curds a little more"—read the same edition.[3] Hemingway also owned the 1955 edition of Babel's *Collected Stories*, introduced by Lionel Trilling, edited and translated by Walter Morison. The generally ignored publisher's note on the first page of this edition—now out of print for more than two decades—complicates its provenance: "The stories in the section entitled *Red Cavalry*, with the exception of 'Argamak,' were originally published in Nadia Helstein's translation by Alfred A. Knopf, Inc., in 1929; they have been revised by Walter Morison for this edition. 'The Sin of Jesus' was translated by Mirra Ginsburg; 'First Love' by Esther and Joseph Riwkin; and 'Guy de Maupassant' by Raymond Rosenthal and Waclaw Soski. All the other stories have been translated by Walter Morison." Stranger still is the fact that Helstein's 1929 translation is apparently identical to a translation attributed to a John Harland, published in London the same year by the same publisher.

The Corporate Law division of Fine Jacobson took up the entire thirty-sixth floor of the CenTrust Tower, and that is where I first encountered Morison's Babel—immured in a windowless mail room of the downtown Miami law firm working as a sixteen-year-old Bartleby. I had emigrated from Moscow as a child in 1978, and a decade later I was vicariously experiencing my own glasnost and perestroika. Interrupted by the dull and regular crash of corporate minutes arriving on the dumbwaiter, Babel's words—full of horrified hopefulness, doleful and bespectacled Jewish comedy, sublime initiations into the bloody gyre of Russian history, Odessa gangsters in raspberry wingtips, long-legged Cossacks in their boxy black cloaks, thorns of "detached" prose that lodged in one's skin—accompanied me into adulthood. And ever since then, I have dreamed of retranslating his works. Not because Morison's 1955 edition was lousy. Indeed, it has a beautiful and coherent literary matrix—aurally and visually *right*, a fluid mix of high modernist lyricism and vernacular shape-shifting, prancing like *Dubliners* on horseback. But because, at the same time, it was littered with prominent but correctable errors: for example, overtranslations of names (Sashka becomes "Sandy," Matvei "Matthew"); overexplanatory titles ("The Crossing of the Zbruch" becomes "Crossing into Poland," even though Babel deliberately fudges the location, since whatever Poland was in 1920 began at the River Sluch); and, as Charles Timmer has pointed out, reliance on Soviet editions that were censored after Babel's death.[4] The two new translations that have appeared during the past two decades (David McDuff's in 1994 and Peter Constantine's in 2002) fixed many of these mistakes, but as Timothy Sergay and many a reviewer have noticed, they have added fresh ones.[5] Aside from Boris Dralyuk's new versions of *Red Cavalry* and *Odessa Tales*, published after I began my work, these were the only English versions of Babel in print, obliging me, and most of my colleagues who teach these stories, to use photocopies from out-of-print translations.

Born in Odessa in 1894, Babel was a Jew who became a Russian writer. For Jews, whether they admit it or not, to speak is to quote and to quote is to speak. As the rabbis of the Talmud write, "A person who quotes his source brings deliverance to the world, as it is written, 'And Esther spoke to the king, in the name of Mordechai'" (Pirkei Avot 6:6). Babel wrote and lived by this proverb. Just as his texts cite (or rather, much as the rabbis and Tevye the Dairyman did, slyly *misquote*) his precursors (i.e., Turgenev and Maupassant), so, too, did Babel's life (and especially his misleading "autobiographies") "quote" that of the young Tolstoy, whose early literary fame was, like Babel's, also based on his military service with Cossacks.

Given Babel's mystifying quotations and obfuscations, when Mike Levine and Northwestern University Press asked me to revise Morison's edition, I was grateful to add my uncertain name to its uncertain provenance, to a string of attributions that should also include several rather graceful translations by Max Hayward and Andrew McAndrew (published in the out-of-print collections *You Must Know Everything* and *Isaac Babel: The Lonely Years, 1925–1939*, both edited by Babel's daughter Nathalie Babel Brown). In the process, the "revisions" became a retranslated edition that included stories Morison had not included. According to the Talmud, when a sage is quoted after his death, his lips move even in the grave (PT Shekalim 2.7 47a). Perhaps the lips of Babel and his prior translators will move as you read this book—even at the risk (as the Talmud warns in Tanḥuma Ki Tissa 3) that such homage gives the dead masters no peace.

Babel himself was a translator, and one of his finest stories, "Guy de Maupassant," is about translation. Its narrator, a fictional Babel, has been hired by Raisa Bendersky, a rich Jewish Petersburg society wife, to help her with her attempts to transform Maupassant into Russian:

> In her translation there was no trace of Maupassant's free-flowing phrases with their drawn-out breath of passion. Mrs. Bendersky's

writing was tediously correct, lifeless and loud, the way Jews used to write Russian back in the day . . . I took the manuscript home with me, and . . . I spent all night hacking a path through someone else's translation. The work wasn't as bad as it sounds. A phrase is born into the world both good and bad at the same time. The secret lies in a barely discernible twist. The lever should rest in your hand, getting warm. You must turn it once, but not twice . . . In the morning I brought back the corrected manuscript. Raisa wasn't lying when she told me of her passion for Maupassant. She sat motionless, her hands clasped, as I read it to her: those satin hands melted to the floor, her forehead went pale, and the lace between her bound breasts strained and trembled . . . "How did you do that?" . . . So then I started talking of style, of the army of words, an army in which all manner of weapons are in play. Nothing of iron can breach the human heart with the chill of a period placed just in time. She listened, her head bowed, her painted lips unsealed. A black light glowed in her lacquered hair, smoothly pressed and parted. Her legs, with their strong tender calves, were bathed in stockings and splayed wide on the rug.

Translation can be a peculiar drug—and, at its heady best, it is indeed as exhilarating, intimate, crafty, and paramilitary as the hero's steam-punkish metaphor.

But the seduction—the hero's and the translator's—is inconclusive. After planting a drunken kiss, the hero stumbles into the bookcase, causing twenty-nine volumes of Maupassant—"twenty-nine petards stuffed with pity, genius, passion"—to come crashing down. The narrator returns home to his bohemian garret, where he ponders the fate of Maupassant in the pages of Maynial's biography:

That night I learned from Édouard de Maynial that Maupassant was born in 1850, the child of a Norman aristocrat and Laure de Poitevan, Flaubert's cousin. He was twenty-five when he had his first bout of congenital syphilis. His prolific joie de vivre resisted the onset of the disease. At first he suffered from headaches and fits of hypochondria. Then the specter of blindness rose before him. His sight grew weak. He became maniacally paranoid, unsociable, and querulent. He struggled furiously, dashed about the Mediterranean in a yacht, fled to Tunis, Morocco, Central Africa—and wrote constantly. Having achieved fame, in his fortieth year he cut his own throat, lost a lot of blood, but survived. They put him in a madhouse. There he crawled about on all fours and ate his own excrement. The last line on his medical chart read, "Monsieur de Maupassant va s'animaliser" (Mr. Maupassant has turned into an animal). He died when he was forty-two. He was survived by his own mother . . . I read the book to the end and got out of bed. The fog came up to the window and concealed the universe. My heart felt tight. I was brushed by a premonition of the truth.

A premonition of the truth. But what truth? Elif Batuman has noted that "according to contemporary Babel scholarship, 'neither Maynial nor any other biographer has Maupassant walking on all fours or eating his own excrement'; the image appears to be borrowed from either [Zola's] *Nana* (Count Muffat crawls at Nana's feet, thinking of saints who 'eat their own excrement') or *Madame Bovary* (a reference to Voltaire on his deathbed, 'devouring his own excrement') . . . Babel mentions neither Voltaire nor Zola nor Flaubert—except to claim that Maupassant's mother is Flaubert's cousin: a false rumor explicitly controverted by Maynial."[6]

Babel wrote "Guy de Maupassant" in 1922, and it appeared in 1932, but it describes the period in which he wrote "Odessa," in 1916, when he was living in Petrograd, dreaming about Odessa, while dreaming—and having "premonitions"—about being an Odessan who makes it big in Petrograd:

It is becoming axiomatic that Odessans do very well in Petrograd. They make money. They are brunettes—so naturally the city's soft blond ladies fall in love with them . . . I'm not setting up a joke here. No, sir. This is about something more profound. Quite simply, these brunettes bring a little sunshine and lightheartedness with them . . . Aside from gentlemen bringing a bit of sun and a lot of sardines in their original containers, I would also think that there will come—and come soon—the prolific, life-giving influence of the Russian south, of Russian Odessa, which may be (*qui sait?*) the only city in Russia where our very own and much-needed national Maupassant will be born. In fact, I perceive the tiniest slender wisps of a premonition—Odessan chanteuses . . . with small voices, but full of joy, joy artfully expressed in their very being, a fervent and light, charmingly sad yet touching feeling for a life that is good and bad and extraordinarily—*quand même et malgré tout*—interesting.

The tiniest slender wisps of a premonition, the small joyful voices of 1916 bringing sunshine through the Petersburg fog—by 1922 and surely by 1932, these congeal into the premonition of a truth caught tight in a heart shrouded by a world-concealing mist. The charmingly sad becomes—*quand même et malgré tout*—the crushingly tragic fate of all the mortal flesh that would marshal an army of immortal words.

Translations, according to one school of thought, are supposed to be mortal, because immortal *originals* deserve frequent and thus provisional retranslations. What then of the timely twist of the warm lever? I like to think there are a few such turns in my translation. I will give one example. In "The *Ivan & Marya*," from the deck of the river steamer that gives the story its name, a provincial singer named Seletsky lets loose a medley of classical and popular songs that had a bit of everything, including *Blokha Mussorgskogo, khokhot Mefistofelya*—literally and usually translated as "Mussorgsky's 'Flea,' Mephistopheles' (booming) laughter." Here, struck by the resonance between *blokha* and *khokhot*, I turned the lever once and arrived at "Mussorgsky's 'Flea,' Mephistopheles' glee."

In fact, I probably turned the lever more than once, just as Babel certainly turned the lever more than once, revising and pruning his stories, changing (or censoring) many of them in later editions. Perhaps the key is to make many turns look like one decisive twist—not *the truth*, but a *premonition*, a word that appears not only in "Guy de Maupassant" but also in "Pan Apolek," where the narrator is "brushed by a premonition of mystery." As Babel's friend and contemporary Osip Mandelstam said, poetry is "the consciousness of being right."[7] The emphasis here must be on the word *consciousness*, since that's where literary *rightness* dwells. Hemingway's curd can always be clotted tighter, more whey can always be squeezed out, but ultimately—as Babel reportedly complained when he was arrested in 1939 (to be tortured and executed shortly thereafter)—one is never "allowed to finish."

Notes

1. Lewis Bagby, *First Words: On Dostoevsky's Introductions* (Brighton, Mass.: Academic Studies Press, 2016), xix.

2. Lionel Trilling, introduction to *Isaac Babel: The Collected Stories*, ed. and trans. Walter Morison (New York: New American Library, 1955), 9–10.

3. Quoted in Cynthia Ozick, *Fame and Folly* (New York: Vintage, 1997), 138.

4. Charles B. Timmer, "Translation and Censorship," in *Miscellanea Slavica: To Honour the Memory of Jan M. Meijer*, ed. B. J. Amsenga et al., 443–68 (Amsterdam: Rodopi, 1983).

5. Timothy D. Sergay, "Isaac Babel's Life in English: The Norton *Complete Babel* Reconsidered," *Translation and Literature* 15, no. 2 (Autumn 2006): 238–53.

6. Elif Batuman, *The Possessed: Adventures with Russian Books and the People Who Read Them* (New York: Farrar, Straus and Giroux, 2010), 79.

7. Osip Mandelstam, "On the Addressee," in *Critical Prose and Letters*, trans. J. G. Harris and C. Link (Ann Arbor, Mich.: Ardis, 1990), 69.

Babel's narrator tells Mrs. Bendersky of the "army of words" and the chill of the "period placed just in time," but Babel's own sentences—like those of many Russian authors—often run on or end abruptly. Unlike several previous translations, mine tends to leave such sentences intact, except where they truly strain the sensibilities of English-language readers, even those who make allowances for Woolf or Joyce or Kerouac. Babel also often made changes in later editions of his work, in the early 1930s in particular, changes that include corrections of printing errors; stylistic adjustments; and the excision of words, phrases, and even entire paragraphs—omissions that very often reflect self-censorship to accommodate the political land mines and aesthetic prudishness of Stalin's regime. In a handful of instances, Babel adds words to later editions. I have tended to follow earlier versions, except where I detected a likely correction or improvement in a later edition published before Babel's death; I have mentioned all significant deviations and variants in the notes. In this endeavor, I have relied on Efraim Sicher's edition of Babel's stories, *Detstvo i drugie rasskazy* (Jerusalem: Biblioteka Aliya, 1979); Christopher Luck's edition of Babel's *Konarmiya* (London: Bristol Classical Press, 2001); I. Shurygina's two-volume edition, *Sochinenia v dvukh tomakh* (Moscow: Terra, 1996); and Igor Sukhikh's four-volume collected works, *Sobranie sochinenii v chetyrekh tomakh* (Moscow: Vremia, 2006). Any dates and locations at the bottom of each story are those the author included in at least one of the published versions; the dates in parentheses are the dates of first publication. Early in his career, Babel—who was born Isaac Manievich *Bobel*—signed several of his publications as "Bab-El," literally "Gate-of-God," evoking the etymology of Babel or Babylon.

My translation does not convert measurements into American units, in order to reflect Babel's own inconsistency—since the Soviet Union moved to the metric system in 1924. The mix of archaic Russian and Soviet metric units thus gives a sense of time and place.

I am immensely grateful to Carol Avins and Nick Paliocha for their incredibly attentive and insightful readings of this entire manuscript, and to Mike Levine, the editor who first suggested and then supported the project—as well as to Gianna Mosser, who, along with Maggie Grossman, has so capably brought it into print. Anne Gendler was an exemplary managing editor; Marianne Jankowski developed wonderful cover art based on David Stromberg's paintings of Babel's ubiquitous sun and moon; and J.D. Wilson has promoted the book with great care. I have also, on many occasions, consulted a small army of experts and amateurs of Russian letters who lent all manner of weapons to my largely peaceable campaign: Gregory Freidin, Andrei Malaev-Babel, Leonid Yanovskiy, Vika Adamenko, Mikhail Iossel, Galya Diment, Jarrod Tanny, John Haskell, Sasha Senderovich, Blue Montakhab, Thomas Campbell, Anna Ankova, Julia Murygina, Evalina Mustafinova, Anna Abutova, Kate Sosenkova, Kira Chesalina, Pavel Druy, Nikita Borintsev, Thomas Rozenblatt, Vlad Tulyakov, Kirill Kovalchuk, Amy Byron, Victor Korol, Igor (a cab driver from Tashkent), Barbara Henry, Rebecca Stanton, David Novack, Liz Hynes, Vlad Davidzon, Tony Anemone, Stanley Rabinowitz, and, of course, my mother, Faina Vinokurov. My research assistants Anna Katsman, Anna Furstenberg, and Owen Deutsch supported my work and provided excellent commentary on the manuscript as well. Mila Khononov generously permitted me to include illustrations drawn for *Red Cavalry* by the great Odessa-born painter Yefim Ladyzhensky (1911–1982). Finally, I must thank my wife, Rose Réjouis, and my son, Elia, who have put up with me and my Babel babble for years.

The Essential Fictions

OPENINGS

Odessa

Odessa is a nasty town. Everybody knows this. Instead of saying "what's the difference," over there it's "what's the differences," and on top of that they also say "thisaway and thataway." But still, it seems to me you could say a lot of good things about this important and most remarkable city in the Russian Empire. Just consider—a city where life is simple and easy. Half of the population consists of Jews, and Jews are a people who are sure about a few basic things. They get married so they won't be lonely, make love so they will live forever, save up money to have houses and buy their wives astrakhan jackets, love their offspring because, after all, it's very good and important to love one's children. Poor Jews in Odessa can get very confused by officials and official forms, but it isn't easy to shift them from their ways, their fixed and ancient ways. Shift they will not, and one can learn a lot from them. To a significant degree, it is thanks to their efforts that Odessa has such a simple and easygoing atmosphere.

An Odessan is the opposite of someone from Petrograd. It is becoming axiomatic that Odessans do very well in Petrograd. They make money. They are brunettes—so naturally the city's soft blond ladies fall in love with them. In general, an Odessan in Petrograd tends to settle on Kamennoostrovsky Prospect. I'm not setting up a joke here. No, sir. This is about something more profound. Quite simply, these brunettes bring a little sunshine and light-heartedness with them.

Aside from gentlemen bringing a bit of sun and a lot of sardines in their original containers, I would also think that there will come—and come soon—the prolific, life-giving influence of the Russian south, of Russian Odessa, which may be (*qui sait?*) the only city in Russia where our very own and much-needed national Maupassant will be born. In fact, I perceive the tiniest slender wisps of a premonition—Odessan chanteuses (I speak of Isa Kremer) with small voices, but full of joy, joy artfully expressed in their very being, a fervent and light, charmingly sad yet touching feeling for a life that is good and bad and extraordinarily—*quand même et malgré tout*—interesting.

I saw Utochkin, an Odessan *pur sang*, carefree and profound, fearless and absentminded, graceful and gangly-armed, brilliant and stuttering. They say he's been consumed by cocaine or morphine since he fell out of his airplane over some swamp in Novgorod Province. Poor Utochkin, he's lost his mind, but all the same it's clear to me that soon the time will come when Novgorod Province will walk itself over to Odessa.

Above all, this city simply has the material conditions necessary to nurture, let's say, the talents of a Maupassant. In the summer, its sunny bathing establishments gleam with the bronzed and muscled physiques of young sports enthusiasts, the powerful bodies of fishermen, who are not sports enthusiasts, the fat, round-bellied, amiable bulks of the "gentlemen of commerce," the pimply, scrawny dreamers, inventors, and brokers. And a small distance from the deep wide sea, there are factories puffing smoke, and Karl Marx is up to his usual business.

In Odessa there is a very poor and crowded, long-suffering Jewish ghetto, a very self-satisfied bourgeoisie, and a very Black Hundreds town council.

In Odessa, there are sweet and languorous spring evenings, the spicy scent of acacia, and the unwavering and irresistible light of the moon above the dark sea.

In Odessa, in the evening, out at their comical vulgar dachas, beneath the dark velvety sky, the fat comical bourgeois lie about on their daybeds in white socks, digesting their full dinners . . . Behind the bushes, their powdered wives, fat from idleness and naively corseted, are passionately squeezed by temperamental physicians and jurists.

In Odessa the "luftmenschen" root around the coffeehouses trying to make a ruble and feed the family, but there's nothing to be made, because what can a completely useless person—a "luftmensch"—really make?

In Odessa there is a port, and in the port—ships from Newcastle, Cardiff, Marseilles, and Port Said; Negroes, Englishmen, Frenchmen, and Americans. Odessa has known prosperity, and now knows its own decline—a poetic, rather carefree, and utterly helpless decline.

"Odessa," the reader will finally say, "is a city like any other city, and you are just unreasonably biased."

All right, so I'm biased, it's true, and maybe deliberately so, but *parole d'honneur*, there is something to it. And a truly human being will sense this something and will say, true enough, life can be sad and monotonous, but all the same—*quand même et malgré tout*—extraordinarily, most extraordinarily interesting.

From these thoughts about Odessa my mind turns to deeper things. If you think about it, doesn't it seem that in Russian literature one has yet to find a truly joyful and vibrant description of the sun?

Turgenev sang of the dewy morn, the stillness of the night. With Dostoevsky you can feel the uneven gray pavement along which Karamazov walks to the tavern, the heavy and mysterious Petersburg fog. Those gray roads and shrouds of fog have stifled people and, having stifled them, contort them in amusing and awful ways, giving birth to a rumble and jumble of passions, making people even more frantic amid the usual human bustle. Do you remember the bright and fructifying sun in Gogol, a man who came from the Ukraine? If there are such descriptions, they are but a passing phase. But "The Nose," "The Overcoat," "The Portrait," and "Diary of a Madman" are not just a phase. Petersburg defeated Poltava, Akaky Akakievich has modestly but with brutal efficiency overwritten Gritsko, and Father Matvei finished off what Taras had begun. The first person who started to talk about the sun in a Russian book, and to talk about it ecstatically, passionately, was Gorky. But the very fact that he talks about it ecstatically and passionately means that it's still not quite the real thing.

Gorky is a precursor, and the mightiest in our time. But he is not the singer of the sun, rather a herald of the truth: that if there is one thing worthy of song, you can be sure it is the sun. In Gorky's love of the sun there is something cerebral; it is only thanks to his enormous talent that he overcomes this obstacle.

He loves the sun because Russia is rotten and perverted, because in Nizhny and in Pskov and in Kazan people are flabby, thick, sometimes incomprehensible, other times pitiful, and sometimes just incredibly and stupefyingly boring. Gorky knows why he loves the sun, why one is supposed to love it. This awareness is in fact the reason why Gorky is a precursor, an often mighty and magnificent one, but a precursor.

As for Maupassant, maybe he doesn't know anything, and maybe he knows everything; a covered wagon clatters down a scorched road, in the carriage sit the fat and sly Polyte and a strapping clumsy peasant lass. What they're doing in there and why they are doing it—that's their business. The sky is hot, the earth is hot. Polyte and the lass are dripping with sweat, while the wagon clatters on the bright scorched road. And that's all.

Lately, there's been a lot of writing about how people live, love, kill, and elect local village councils in the province of Olonetsk, Vologda, or, say, Archangelsk. All of it is written in the most authentic dialect, exactly like they speak in Olonetsk and Vologda. People live there, it turns out, and it's cold, and there's a lot of rough stuff. An old story. And pretty soon people will get sick of reading about this old story. Actually, they're already sick of it. And what I think is, Russians will be drawn south, to the sea and the sun. *Will* be drawn? No, in fact, that's wrong. They *have* been drawn already, for many centuries. It is in Russia's persistent drive to the steppe, even perhaps "to the Cross of the Holy Sophia," that she will find her way.

People feel the blood should be refreshed. It's stifling here. The literary Messiah, awaited in vain for so long, will arrive from there—from the sunny steppe, washed by the sea.

Bab-El, 1916.

Shabbos Nahamu

It was morning, it was evening, the fifth day. It was morning, evening came, the sixth day. On the sixth day, on Friday evening, you have to pray; having prayed—you take a stroll through the shtetl in your best hat and come home in time for supper. At home a Jew will drink a little glass of vodka—neither God nor the Talmud prohibits two glasses—eats gefilte fish and raisin kugel. After supper he's jolly. He tells stories to his wife, then goes to sleep with one eye closed and his mouth open. He sleeps, but in the kitchen Gapka hears music—as though a blind fiddler had come from the shtetl and was playing under the window.

So it is with every Jew. But every Jew—that's not Hershele. Small wonder then that his fame has spread over all Ostropol, all Berdichev, all Vilyuisk.

Out of six Fridays, Hershele celebrated one. The other evenings—he and his family sat in the cold and the dark. The children would cry. The wife hurled reproaches. Each of them heavy as a cobblestone. Hershele would respond in verse.

One time—so the story goes—Hershele decided he would think ahead. On Wednesday he left for the fair, so that by Friday he'd have made some money. Where there is a fair there is a *pan*. Where there's a *pan*, ten Jews are bustling. From ten Jews, you won't make three pennies. Everybody listened to Hershele's jokes, but nobody was around when it came time to pay up.

Hershele trudged home, his stomach as empty as a wind instrument.

"What did you earn?" his wife asked him.

"I earned life everlasting," he replied. "Rich and poor alike promised it to me."

Hershele's wife had only ten fingers. One by one, she clenched them into fists. Her voice rumbled like thunder in the mountains.

"Every wife has a husband like a husband. But I'm the only wife with a husband who feeds her with punch lines. May God take his tongue and his arms and his legs by the New Year."

"Amen," replied Hershele.

"In other people's windows candles burn like they set oak trees ablaze inside the house. In my house the candles are thin as matches and smoke like columns up to heaven. Everybody else has fresh white bread prepared, but my husband brought firewood wet as a freshly washed braid . . ."

Hershele uttered not a single word in reply. Why throw more logs on a raging fire? That's first of all. And what do you say to an ill-tempered wife when she's right? That's second of all.

Eventually the wife got tired of shouting. Hershele withdrew, lay in his bed, and got to thinking.

"Maybe I should go to Rebbe Borukhl?" he asked himself.

(As everybody knows, Rebbe Borukhl suffered from black melancholy, and no medicine worked better for him than Hershele's words.)

"Maybe I should go to Rebbe Borukhl? The tsaddik's servants give me bones and keep the meat for themselves, that's true. Meat is better than bones, but bones are better than air. I'll go to Rebbe Borukhl."

Hershele got up and went to harness his horse. She looked at him sternly and sadly.

"That's fine, Hershele," her eyes said, "you gave me no oats yesterday, no oats the day before yesterday, and I got nothing today either. If you give me no oats tomorrow, I will have to consider whether I'm going to live."

Hershele couldn't bear her searching look, lowered his eyes, and stroked the horse's soft lips. Then he sighed loud enough for the horse to understand, and decided, "I'll go to Rebbe Borukhl on foot."

When Hershele set off, the sun was high in the sky. A long hot road stretched before him. White oxen pulled carts full of fragrant hay. Muzhiks sat high on the carts, dangling their legs and swishing their long whips. The sky was blue, the whips were black.

Having gone part of the way—about five versts—Hershele reached a forest. The sun was already rushing home. Frail fires kindled in the sky. Barefoot girls were bringing in the cows from pasture. Full pink udders swayed beneath each cow.

The forest met Hershele with cool, quiet twilight. Green leaves bowed and caressed one another with their flat hands, whispered softly in the canopy above, then returned to their quivering rustle.

Hershele paid no mind to their whispers. In his stomach played an orchestra big enough for a ball at Count Potocki's. He still had a long way to go. Dusk flooded over the horizon, closing in over Hershele's head, washing over the earth. Lanterns were set in the sky. The earth fell silent.

It was night by the time Hershele reached a tavern. A light burned in the little window. By the window in the warm room sat Zelda, the proprietress, sewing diapers. Her belly was so large it seemed for certain she was having triplets. Hershele took one look at her little red face and blue eyes and said hello.

"May I stop and rest here, madame?"

"You may."

Hershele sat down. His nostrils heaved like a blacksmith's bellows. A hot fire glowed in the stove. Water boiled in a large kettle, snow-white dumplings tumbling in the froth. A fat chicken pitched and tossed atop a golden broth. The scent of raisin cake wafted from the oven.

Hershele sat on a bench, writhing like a woman in labor. More schemes were born in his head in that single minute than King Solomon had wives.

The room was still, the water boiled, the chicken tossed atop the golden waves.

"Where is your husband, madame?" asked Hershele.

"My husband went to the *pan* to pay the rent," she replied and was quiet again.

Then her childlike eyes grew large. She asked suddenly, "I'm sitting here at the window and got to thinking. And I have a question for you, esteemed Jew. Probably you've wandered and seen much of the world, learned with the rebbe, and know much about our ways. I never learned with anyone. Tell me, esteemed Jew, will Shabbos Nahamu be coming soon?"

"Oho," thought Hershele. "That's a nice question. Seems all kinds of potatoes grow in God's garden."

"I ask because my husband promised that when Shabbos Nahamu comes, we'll visit my mama. And also, he says, I'll buy you a dress and a new wig, and we'll go to Rabbi Motale to ask him to pray for a son and not a daughter—everything when Shabbos Nahamu comes. So I'm thinking—surely this is a person from the world beyond?"

"You are not mistaken, madame," replied Hershele. "God Himself has put these words to your lips . . . You shall indeed have a son, as well as a daughter. For this Shabbos Nahamu is I myself, madame."

The diapers slipped off Zelda's knees. She got up and bumped her little head on a rafter, since Zelda was tall and thick, red and young. Her high breasts were like two sacks packed tight with grain. She opened her wide blue eyes like a child.

"This Shabbos Nahamu is I myself, madame," Hershele confirmed. "I have been traveling two months already, traveling and helping people. It has been a long journey—from heaven to earth. My boots are torn. I bring you regards from all your folks."

"From Aunt Pesya, too?" the woman cried, "and from Papa, and from Aunt Golda—do you know them?"

"Who doesn't know them?" replied Hershele. "I spoke to them just like you and I are speaking now."

"How are they doing over there?" asked the proprietress, folding her trembling fingers across her belly.

"They're doing poorly," Hershele intoned dolefully. "How do you expect a dead person to live? They're not exactly dancing over there . . ."

The woman's eyes filled with tears.

"They're cold up there," Hershele continued. "Cold and hungry. They eat like angels, after all. And nobody in the world beyond has the right to eat more than the angels eat. And what does an angel need? A sip of water is plenty for him. In a hundred years you'll never see a little glass of vodka up there."

"Poor Papa," she whispered, shaken.

"On Passover, he'll have one latke. One blintz will last an angel for days."

"Poor Aunt Pesya," she shuddered.

"I myself go around hungry," Hershele muttered, turning his face away as a tear rolled from his nose and disappeared into his beard. "I can't say anything about it, seeing as I'm one of them . . ."

Hershele didn't finish his speech.

With a patter of thick feet, the proprietress bustled and brought out plates, bowls, cups, bottles. Hershele started eating, and then the woman came to understand that this truly was a man from the world beyond.

For starters Hershele ate chopped liver jellied with translucent lard and garnished with chopped onions. Then he drank a glass of the *pan*'s vodka (this vodka had orange peels floating in it). Then he ate fish, mashing the sauce into the soft potatoes and pouring out half a jar of red horseradish such as would have made five *pans*, in all their robes and caftans, weep.

After the fish, Hershele gave the chicken its due and gulped down the hot soup together with the droplets of fat floating on its surface. Butter-bathed dumplings jumped into Hershele's mouth, like hares jumping from a hunter. And let's not mention what happened to the cake—after all, what could have happened when oftentimes a year might pass without Hershele's laying eyes on a cake? . . .

After supper, the proprietress gathered up things she wanted Hershele to take to the world beyond—for Papa, Aunt Golda, and Aunt Pesya. For her father she packed a new tallis, a bottle of cherry brandy, a jar of raspberry jam, and a pouch of tobacco. For Aunt Pesya she prepared a pair of warm gray stockings. Aunt Golda was to receive an old wig, a big comb, and a prayer book. In addition, she supplied Hershele with new boots, a loaf of bread, cracklings, and a silver coin.

"Give them our regards, Mr. Shabbos Nahamu, regards to all of them," she said in parting to Hershele, who set off with a heavy bundle. "Or maybe wait a little—my husband will be back soon."

"No," replied Hershele. "I must hurry. You think you're the only one I have to visit?"

Deep in the dark forest slept the trees and the birds and the leaves of green. The pale stars that watch over us slumbered in the sky.

When he had gone about a verst, Hershele stopped to catch his breath, threw down his bundle, sat down on it, and set to arguing with himself.

"You ought to know," he said to himself, "that there are many fools on this earth. The lady at the tavern was a fool. Her husband, however, might be a smart fellow, with big fists, fat cheeks, and a long whip. If he gets home and then catches up to you in the woods, then what? . . ."

Hershele wasted no time answering his own question. Straightaway he buried his bundle in the ground and marked the spot so he could find it again.

Then he ran in the other direction through the woods, stripped naked, put his arms around the trunk of a tree, and began to wait. He didn't have to wait long. At dawn Hershele heard the crack of a whip, the smacking of lips, and the beating of hooves. This was the innkeeper galloping after Mr. Shabbos Nahamu.

When he reached the naked Hershele with his arms around a tree, the innkeeper stopped his horse, looking dumb as a monk who just met the devil.

"What are you doing here?" he asked in an unsteady voice.

"I have come from the world beyond," replied Hershele dolefully. "I have been robbed, important papers I had for Rebbe Borukhl have been stolen from me . . ."

"I know who robbed you," yelled the innkeeper. "I have my own accounts to settle with him. Which way did he run?"

"Can't say which," Hershele muttered bitterly. "If you like, you can give me your horse and I'll catch him right now. And you can wait for me here. Take off your clothes, hold on to the tree like this, and don't budge until I return. This is a holy tree, and much in our world depends on it . . ."

Hershele never needed long to look at a person and figure him out. From the very first glance, he could tell that the husband wasn't much unlike his wife. And indeed the innkeeper stripped and grabbed the tree. Hershele got in the cart and rode off. He dug up his things, loaded them on the wagon, and rode to the edge of the forest.

There Hershele slung the bundle over his back again, let the horse go, and started walking toward the house of the holy Rebbe Borukhl.

It was already morning. Birds were singing with their eyes still shut. The innkeeper's horse, dejected, pulled her empty wagon back to the place where she had left her master.

He was waiting for her, gripping the tree, naked beneath the rays of the rising sun. The innkeeper was cold. He kept shifting from foot to foot.

(published March 16, 1918)

Elya Isaakovich and Margarita Prokofyevna

Hershkovich left the inspector's office with a heavy heart. He had been notified that if he didn't take the first train out of Orel, he'd be sent out with the convicts. But to leave now meant losing the deal.

Briefcase in hand, slim and unhurried, he walked along the dark street. At the corner, a tall female figure called out to him:

"Coming inside, kitten?"

Hershkovitch looked up at her through his shimmering eyeglasses, thought it over, and guardedly replied:

"I'll come inside."

The woman took his arm. They walked around the corner.

"So where are we going, a hotel?"

"I need the whole night," Hershkovitch replied, "let's go to your place."

"That'll cost you three bits, Pop."

"Two," said Hershkovitch.

"That won't cover it, Pop."

A bargain was struck at two and a half. They walked on.

The prostitute's room was small, clean, with torn curtains and a pink lantern.

When they came inside, the woman took off her coat, unbuttoned her blouse . . . and winked.

"Eh," Hershkovich grimaced, "that's silly."

"You're upset, Pop."

She sat down on his lap.

"I reckon," Hershkovich said, "you're, what, five poods?"

"Four thirty."

She passionately kissed his graying cheek.

"Eh," Hershkovich grimaced again, "I'm tired, I need sleep."

The prostitute stood up. She had a nasty look on her face now.

"You're a Jew?"

He looked at her through his glasses and replied:

"No."

"Listen here, old man," she said slowly, "that'll cost you ten."

He got up and went to the door.

"Five," the woman said.

Hershkovich returned.

"Make me a bed," said the exhausted Jew, as he took off his jacket and looked around for a place to hang it. "What's your name?"

"Margarita."

"Change the sheets, Margarita."

The featherbed was soft and wide.

Slowly Hershkovitch started getting undressed, removed his white socks, spread his sweaty toes, locked the door, put the key under the pillow, and went to bed. Margarita yawned, took off her dress without rushing, squinted as she squeezed a pimple off her shoulder, and started braiding her streaming hair for the night.

"What's your name, Pop?"

"Eli, Elya Isaakovich."

"And your business?"

"Our business . . ." Hershkovich answered ambiguously.

Margarita blew out the night-light and came to bed.

"I reckon," said Hershkovich, "you eat well."

Soon they fell asleep.

Next morning the room was flooded with bright sunshine. Hershkovich woke up, got dressed, went to the window.

"We've got the sea, you've the country," he said. "Very nice."

"Where are you from?" asked Margarita.

"From Odessa," Hershkovich replied. "A first-rate city, a real nice town." He broke into a sly smile.

"I can see it's nice for you most anyplace," said Margarita.

"True," replied Hershkovich. "Anyplace with people is nice."

"You're such a fool," muttered Margarita, propping herself up in bed. "People are mean."

"No," said Hershkovich, "people are kind. They've been taught to think they're mean, and so they believed it."

Margarita thought this over, then smiled.

"You are an interesting one," she proclaimed slowly and looked him over. "Turn around. I'll get dressed."

Then they had breakfast, drank tea with bagels. Hershkovich taught Margarita how to butter bread and arrange slices of salami on it in a special way.

"You try it, but right now I have to go."

As he left, Hershkovich said:

"Here's three rubles, Margarita. Believe me, there's not a kopeck to be made around here."

"You're such a cheapskate. Give me the three rubles. Will you come tonight?"

"I'll come."

That evening Hershkovich brought dinner—herring, a bottle of beer, salami, apples. Margarita wore a dark dress with a high neckline. They ate, they talked.

"You can't get by on less than fifty a month," Margarita was saying. "In this line of work, if you dress cheap, you won't make enough to eat soup. And mind you, I have to pay the fifteen for the room . . ."

"Where I live, in Odessa," Hershkovich mused, doing his best to cut the herring into equal parts, "for ten rubles you can get a room in the Moldavanka fit for a king."

"And you have to take into account, I get everybody, I can't avoid drunks . . ."

"Everybody's got their troubles," said Hershkovich and told her about his family, his ailing business, about his son who'd been drafted into the army.

Margarita listened with her head propped on the table, and her face was attentive, quiet, and thoughtful.

After dinner, having taken off his jacket and carefully wiped his glasses with a felt cloth, he sat down at the table, brought the lamp close, and began his business correspondence. Margarita was washing her hair.

Hershkovich wrote without haste, carefully, arching his brows, with an occasionally thoughtful expression, and, when dipping his pen, never once forgot to shake off the excess ink.

Having finished his letter, he had Margarita sit on the correspondence copybook.

"You, I reckon, are a lady of some heft. Keep sitting there please, do me the honor, Margarita Prokofyevna."

Hershkovich smiled, his glasses shimmered, and his eyes grew bright, narrow, jolly.

He set off the next day. Walking up and down the train platform a few minutes before departure, he noticed Margarita briskly walking toward him with a small bundle in her hands. Inside the bundle there were meat pies, and grease stains on the wrapping paper.

Margarita's red face was a sorry sight, her breast heaved from walking so fast.

"Give my regards to Odessa," she said, "my best regards . . ."

"Thanks," replied Hershkovich, took the pies, raised his brows, thought of something, and shrank.

The third bell rang. They shook hands.

"Good-bye, Margarita Prokofyevna."

"Good-bye, Elya Isaakovich."

Hershkovich boarded. The train began to move.

(published 1916)

Mama, Rimma, and Alla

The day had been trouble since early that morning.

Last evening the maid decided to quit on a whim. Varvara Stepanovna had to do everything herself. The second thing that happened early that morning was the electric bill came. Third, the Rastokhin brothers, students renting a room, presented a completely unexpected demand. That night they had supposedly received a telegram stating that their father had taken ill and that they had no choice but to go to him. And so they were vacating the room and requesting the return of the sixty rubles they had advanced Varvara Stepanovna.

Varvara Stepanovna replied that it was awkward to vacate a room in April, when no one would be looking to rent it, and that it would be difficult to return the money since it was not given to her as an advance but as payment for rent, albeit payment made up front.

The Rastokhin brothers did not agree. The discussion became drawn out and less than friendly. The students were stubborn and bewildering block-heads in neat, floor-length frock coats. They acted like their money was weeping. Then the older one proposed that Varvara Stepanovna set aside the sideboard in the dining room and a dressing table for them.

Varvara Stepanovna turned purple and objected, replying that she would not be spoken to in such a tone, that the Rastokhins' proposal was pure trash, that she knew the law, that her husband happened to be a member of the district court in Kamchatka, and so on. The younger Rastokhin replied in a rage that he could spit from a tall tree on the fact that her husband was a member of the district court in Kamchatka, that it was clear that you couldn't pry a kopeck from her claws, that they would never forget their stay at Varvara Stepanovna's—the dirt, the muddle and mess—and that the district court in Kamchatka was far, but the magistrate in Moscow was near . . .

And that was how the discussion came to a close. The Rastokhins left in a huff, dumb with spite, while Varvara Stepanovna went to the kitchen to make coffee for her other lodger, a student named Stanislav Markhotsky. A sharp and prolonged ringing had been coming from his room for several minutes already.

Varvara Stepanovna stood in front of the spirit stove in the kitchen, on her nose sat a nickel pince-nez, wobbly from age, her graying hair was disheveled, her pink morning coat full of stains. She made coffee and thought how these boys would never have spoken to her in such a tone if there hadn't been that eternal lack of money, that unfortunate need to constantly snatch, hide, and cheat.

When Markhotsky's coffee and scrambled eggs were ready, she brought his breakfast to his room.

Markhotsky was a Pole—tall, bony, light blond, with sleek nails and long legs. That morning he was wearing a foppish gray jacket with Brandenburg buttons.

Varvara Stepanovna was met with displeasure.

"I'm tired of there never being a maid around," he said, "so that I have to ring for a whole hour and then I'm late for lecture."

It's true that all too often the maid wasn't there, and that Markhotsky had to ring and ring, but this time there was a different reason for his displeasure.

The evening before, he had been sitting on the living room sofa with Rimma, Varvara Stepanovna's older daughter. Varvara Stepanovna could see how they kissed about three times with their arms around each other in the darkness. They sat there until eleven or even twelve, then Stanislav put his head on Rimma's breast and dozed off. Who in his youth hasn't sat in a sofa corner and dozed atop the breast of a gymnasium girl met by chance along the way? No great harm in that, and usually no consequences either, but all the same one must take into account the circumstances—namely, that it's quite possible the girl has school the next morning.

It was only at half past one that Varvara Stepanovna announced rather sourly that it was time to show a little consideration. Markhotsky, full of Polish "honor," pursed his lips and took offense. Rimma shot her mother a look full of indignation.

So the matter was concluded. But Stanislav, evidently, still remembered everything the following morning. Varvara Stepanovna served him breakfast, salted his omelet, and left.

It was eleven in the morning. Varvara Stepanovna opened the curtains in her daughters' room. Feathery, gleaming rays of cool sunlight alighted on the untidy floor, on the clothes strewn everywhere, on the dusty bookcase.

The girls were already awake. The older one, Rimma, was slim, petite, sharp-eyed, black-haired. Alla was a year younger—only seventeen—larger than her sister, blond, languid, with skin like soft dough, and a sweet dreamy expression in her blue eyes.

After her mother left the room, she began to speak. Her plump bare arm lay on the blanket, the fingers barely twitching.

"I had a dream, Rimma," she said. "Just imagine—some strange little town, a Russian one, I'm not sure . . . The light-gray sky was very low and you could touch the horizon. The dust on the little streets was also gray, smooth, serene. It was dead quiet. Not a sound, not a single person anywhere. And it seemed I was walking along unfamiliar lanes past quiet little wooden houses. Sometimes I'd walk down a dead end, other times I would find myself on a road where I could see only ten steps ahead of me but I walk on it forever. Somewhere up ahead I can see wisps of dust swirling. I come closer and I see wedding carriages. In one of them I see Mikhail and his bride. The bride was wearing a veil, and her face was happy. I walk beside the carriages, I feel like I'm above them all, and my heart aches. Then they all notice me. The carriages come to a halt. Mikhail comes up to me, takes my hand, and slowly leads me down the lane. 'Alla, my friend,' he says in a monotone, 'this is sad, I know. There's nothing to be done, for I do not love you.' I walk beside him, my heart keeps shuddering, new gray paths open up before us."

Alla stopped talking.

"A bad dream," she added. "Who knows? Maybe because it was no good, things will turn out well and I'll get a letter from him."

"Like hell," Rimma replied. "You should've been smarter before instead of running off on dates. But you know what, today I'm going to have it out with Mama . . ." she said suddenly.

Rimma got up, dressed, and went to the window.

Spring was upon Moscow. Warm dew glistened on the long, dreary fence that stretched across from the post office along the entire length of the alley.

In the front yard of the church, the grass was damp and green. Soft sunlight lay like gold over the faded vestments, shimmering over the dark countenance of the icon mounted on the crooked column at the entrance to the churchyard.

The young ladies went to the dining room. There sat Varvara Stepanovna, eating a great deal with great care, peering intently through her glasses, first at the biscuits, then the coffee, then the ham. She drank her coffee with loud, rapid gulps, while the biscuits were devoured quickly, greedily, almost furtively.

"Mama," Rimma addressed her sternly and turned up her proud little face, "I want to talk to you. Don't get worked up. Everything will be calm, once and for all. I can't live with you anymore. Set me free."

"As you wish," Varvara Stepanovna replied calmly, gazing at Rimma with her colorless eyes. "This is because of yesterday?"

"Not because of yesterday, but it has something to do with it. I'm suffocating here."

"And what do you plan to do?"

"I'll take courses, learn stenography, nowadays there's a demand . . .

"Nowadays stenographers are like fish in the sea. As if they need you . . ."

"I will not come running to you, Mama," Rimma squeaked, "I will not come running to you. Set me free."

"If you wish," Varvara Stepanovna said once more, "don't let me hold you back."

"And give me a passport."

"I'm not giving you a passport."

The conversation had been unexpectedly quiet. Now Rimma felt that one could begin yelling on account of the passport.

"Oh, I like that," she laughed sarcastically, "and where am I supposed to go without a passport?"

"I'm not giving you a passport."

"Then I'll shack up with somebody," Rimma screamed hysterically, "with a policeman . . ."

"Who's going to take you?" Varvara Stepanovna examined her daughter's trembling figure and smoldering face. "A policeman could do better . . ."

"I'll go out on Tverskaya," Rimma shouted, "and walk up to some old man. I don't want to live with her, with this stupid, stupid, stupid . . ."

"Oh, so that's how to talk to your mother." Varvara Stepanovna rose from the table with great poise. "We're living hand to mouth, everything's going to pot, there's nothing in the house, I just want to give up, and now you . . . Papa will be hearing about this . . ."

"I'll write to Kamchatka myself," Rimma screamed in a frenzy. "I'll get a passport from Daddy . . ."

Varvara Stepanovna left the room. Rimma paced the room excitedly, looking small and disheveled. Wrathful, disconnected phrases from the as-yet-unwritten letter to her father were racing through her brain.

"Dear Pop," she would write, "I realize you're busy with your own affairs, but I have to tell you everything . . . This allegation that Stasik fell asleep on my chest should weigh on Mama's conscience. He was sleeping on the embroidered sofa pillow, but that's not the real issue. Mama is your wife, so you're biased, but I can't live at home anymore—she's a difficult person . . . If you like, I'll live with you in Kamchatka, but I need a passport, Pop . . ."

Rimma was pacing around, while Alla sat on the couch staring at her sister. Sad, quiet thoughts settled on her soul.

"Rimma's stewing," she thought, "but I'm the unhappy one. It's all so hard, so confusing . . ."

She went to her room and lay down. Varvara Stepanovna walked past in a corset, thickly and naively powdered, all red, bewildered, and pathetic.

"I just remembered," she said, "the Rastokhins are moving out today. We have to return the sixty rubles. They're threatening to sue. There are eggs on the shelf. Make some for yourself, I'm going to the pawnshop."

When Markhotsky came home from class at six, he found packed suitcases in the front hallway. There was noise coming from the Rastokhins' room: they were arguing, apparently. Also in the hallway, a desperately determined Varvara Stepanovna borrowed ten rubles from him, quick as lightning. Only upon finding himself in his room did Markhotsky realize how stupid he had been.

Markhotsky's room did not resemble the other quarters in Varvara Stepanovna's apartment. It was kept tidy, lined with knickknacks, and hung with rugs. Drafting implements, fancy smoking pipes, English tobacco, ivory-white paper knives were neatly arranged on the desks.

Stanislav hadn't had time to change out of his street clothes when Rimma quietly came into his room. She got a cold welcome.

"You're angry, Stasik?" the girl asked.

"I'm not angry," the Pole replied, "I only ask to be spared the need to witness your mother's excesses."

"It'll all be over soon," said Rimma. "Soon I'll be free, Stasik . . ."

She sat down next to him on the little couch and embraced him.

"I am a man," Stasik began, "this kind of platonic stagnation is really not for me, I have my career ahead of me . . ."

He spoke these words with irritation, words typically addressed, in the end, to certain kinds of women. With them there's nothing to talk about, whispering tender nothings gets boring, and they don't want to move on to anything more substantial.

Stasik said that he was consumed with desire; that this interfered with his work and caused considerable consternation; that it should be resolved one way or the other—whatever the decision, it was all the same to him, so long as the matter was decided.

"Why are you talking like this now?" Rimma said pensively. "What's all this 'I am a man' and everything 'should be resolved'—why the mean, cold face? Can't we talk about something else? It's just too hard to talk about. Spring is here, it's so lovely outside, and look how we're fighting . . ."

Stasik did not respond. Both of them were silent.

A smoldering sunset waned on the horizon, filling the distant sky with a crimson radiance. The other end was draped gently by the slowly thickening darkness. The room was illuminated by the last blush of daylight. On the couch, Rimma inclined all the more tenderly toward the student. They were doing what they usually did at that most lovely hour of the day.

Stanislav kissed the girl. She laid her head on the throw pillow and closed her eyes. Their fires were kindled. After several minutes Stanislav was kissing her without interruption and, in a fit of spiteful, unquenchable passion, began to toss her thin, burning body about the room. He tore her blouse and bodice. Rimma, her lips parched and rings under her eyes, consented to be kissed and defended her maidenhood with a sad, crooked grimace. Soon enough someone knocked on the door. Rimma whirled across the room, clutching the hanging scraps of her shredded blouse to her breast.

They took their time opening the door. It was a friend of Stanislav's, it turned out. He watched with an ill-concealed sneer as Rimma squeezed past him. She crept off to her room, changed her blouse, and stood beside the frigid windowpane to cool down.

Varvara Stepanovna got only forty rubles for the family silver from the pawnbroker. She had borrowed ten rubles from Markhotsky, the rest she got from the Tikhonovs, running on foot all the way from Strastny Boulevard to Pokrovka. She was so preoccupied that she completely forgot she could have taken a tram.

At home, besides the raging Rastokhins, she found Mirlitz, the barrister's assistant, waiting for her on urgent business; he was a tall young man with rotten stumps instead of teeth and moist, sheepish gray eyes.

Some time ago, Varvara Stepanovna had been forced to consider borrowing against a cottage her husband owned in Kolomna. Mirlitz had brought over the mortgage agreement. Varvara Stepanovna thought something wasn't right, that she ought to get advice from someone before signing anything, but she told herself she had too many problems to deal with all on her own . . . Enough already with all of it—the lodgers, the daughters, the disrespect.

After talking business, Mirlitz uncorked a bottle of Crimean Muscat Lunel that he had brought—he knew Varvara Stepanovna's weakness. They each drank a glass and prepared to have another. Their voices rang out a little louder, Varvara Stepanovna's fleshy nose grew red, every bone in her corset strained and bulged. Mirlitz was telling a funny story and cracking up. Rimma sat quietly in the corner wearing a fresh blouse.

After they had finished the Muscat Lunel, Varvara Stepanovna and Mirlitz went for a walk. Varvara Stepanovna felt a little drunk—she was embarrassed and at the same time didn't care because life was too hard and the heck with it.

Varvara Stepanovna returned sooner than planned because the Boykos hadn't been home when she came calling. Upon arrival she was struck by the silence that prevailed in the apartment. Usually this was the time for fooling about with the students, giggling, running around. The only sounds to be heard were coming from the bathroom. Varvara Stepanovna went to the kitchen, which had a little window through which one could see what was going on in the bathroom . . .

She went to the window and witnessed a strange, quite unusual scene—namely this:

The water stove was red-hot. The bathtub was filled with boiling water. Next to the stove, Rimma was on her knees. In her hands she had curling tongs. She was heating them over the fire. Alla was standing naked by the bath. Her long braids were loose. Tears were rolling from her eyes.

"Come here," she said to Rimma. "Listen, I think maybe it's kicking . . ."

Rimma put her head against the tender, barely swollen belly.

"It's not kicking," she replied. "Doesn't matter. There's no doubt about it."

"I'll die," Alla whispered. "The water's going to burn me alive. I won't be able to stand it. We don't need the tongs. You don't know how they do it."

"Everybody does it like this," Rimma declared. "Stop whining, Alla. It's not like you can have a baby."

Alla was about to sit in the tub when she heard the soft and unforgettable croak of her mother's voice:

"What are you doing, children?"

Two hours later, Alla lay tucked, coddled, and wept over in Varvara Stepanovna's wide bed. She told her everything. It was easy. She felt like a little girl who had a silly childish misfortune.

Without a word or a sound, Rimma went around the room cleaning up, made tea for her mother, made her eat something, did everything to make the room tidy. Then she lit the lamp that no one had bothered to fill for the past two weeks, undressed as quietly as possible, and lay down beside her sister.

Varvara Stepanovna was sitting at the table. She could see the lamp, its smooth, dark-red flame casting a dim light on the Virgin Mary. A light, somewhat peculiar intoxication still wandered around in her head. The girls were soon asleep. Alla's face was pale, large, and peaceful. Rimma clung to her, gasping in her sleep and shuddering.

Around one in the morning, Varvara Stepanovna lit a candle, placed a sheet of paper before her, and wrote a letter to her husband:

"Dear Nikolai. Today Mirlitz came by, a very decent Jew, and tomorrow I'm expecting a gentleman to bring the money for the house. I think I'm doing what should be done, but I worry all the more because I cannot rely on myself.

"I know you have your own troubles, your own work, and it would be better if I weren't writing about all this, but things at home, Nikolai, aren't getting any better. The children are growing up, today's world demands a lot—courses, stenography—the girls want more freedom. They need a father, to yell at them a little, maybe, but I can't rely on myself at all. It still seems to me that it was a mistake for you to go to Kamchatka. If you were here we could move to Starokolenny Lane—there's a very bright little apartment for rent there.

"Rimma lost weight and doesn't look good. For a whole month, we were getting cream from the dairy across the street, the children got better, but then we stopped doing it. Sometimes my liver hurts, other times it doesn't. Write more. After I get your letters I take better care of myself, I stop eating herring, and my liver doesn't bother me. Come visit, Kolya—we could all use a rest. Regards from the children. Big kiss. Your Varya."

(published 1916)

Through a Crack

There's a woman I know—Madame Kebchik. In her day, Madame Kebchik insists, she would never accept less than five rubles—"not for anything in the world." Now, she has a family residence, and in the family residence there are two girls—Marusya and Tamara. Marusya gets picked more often than Tamara.

One window in the girls' room looks out on the street, the other—a transom just under the ceiling—into the bathroom. I realized this, and said to Fanny Osipovna Kebchik:

"In the evening you'll put a ladder up to the little window in the bathroom. I'll go up the ladder to take a peek in the room at Marusya. I'll give you five rubles."

Fanny Osipovna said:

"Oh, what a rotten man you are!" And we had a deal.

She would get my five rubles not infrequently. I'd make use of the little window whenever Marusya had guests. Everything had always come off without a hitch, until one day I had a stupid accident.

I was standing on the ladder. Fortunately, Marusya hadn't turned off the light. This time the caller was a nice, unassuming, cheerful fellow with a long and harmless type of mustache. He was getting undressed just as he would at home: takes off his collar, looks in the mirror, finds a pimple under his mustache, examines it thoroughly, and squeezes it out with his hanky. He pulls off a boot and examines that too: could be something wrong with the soles.

They kissed, got undressed, and each had a cigarette. I was just going to climb down again. And at that moment I felt the ladder slipping and swaying beneath me. I grab the window frame and break through the glass. The ladder comes crashing down. I'm hanging beneath the ceiling. The apartment was in an uproar. In rush Fanny Osipovna, Tamara, and an official I'd never seen before in the uniform of the Finance Ministry. They help me down. I was in a pitiful state. Marusya and her gangly guest come into the bathroom. The girl stares me up and down, stiffens, and quietly declares:

"Scum, oh what scum . . ."

She falls silent, blankly looks around at us all, goes over to the gangly guy, and kisses his hand and starts crying. Weeping and kissing, she says:

"Sweetheart, oh my God, sweetheart . . ."

The gangly guy stands there like a complete dope. My heart is pounding uncontrollably. I dig my nails into my palms and go to Fanny Osipovna's room.

A few minutes later Marusya knows everything. All is known, and all forgotten. But I'm still wondering: why was the girl kissing the gangly guy?

"Madame Kebchik," I say, "put the ladder up one last time. I'll give you ten rubles."

"You're cracked in the head, cracked like that ladder of yours," said the madame, and we had a deal.

And there I was again standing at the transom peeking once more, and I can see Marusya had put her slender arms around her guest, kissing him, slowly, and her eyes were flowing with tears.

"My sweetheart," she whispers, "oh God, my sweetheart," and gives herself to him with the passion of a woman in love. And her face suggests that she has only one person on earth to protect her—the gangly guy.

And the gangly guy busies himself in his bliss.

1915 (published 1917)

The Sin of Jesus

A rina had a room by the main staircase, while Seryoga, the junior janitor's
helper, lived by the back stairs. Between them there was shame. On Forgiveness Sunday Arina bore Seryoga twins. Water flows, stars shine, a man
ruts. Arina got into another interesting situation, her sixth month was slipping by—so slippery, a woman's months. Seryoga gets drafted, a fine mess. So
Arina goes and says:

"No sense in me waiting for you, Sergunya. Four years we'll be apart, and
in four years, one by one, I'll bring three more into the world. Cleaning rooms
is like hitching up your skirt. Whoever passes through, he's your master, be it
a Jew, be it anybody at all. By the time you're done with the service, my womb
will be spent, I'll be a washed-up woman, no match for you."

"Indeed," Seryoga nodded.

"There's plenty want to marry me: Trofimych the contractor, he's got no
class, and there's that little old man Isai Abramych, there's the warden of
Nikolo-Svyatsky Church, a feeble man—and your wicked power is wringing
the very life out of me, swear to God, chew me up and spit me out . . . I'll
spill my load three months from today, take the baby to the orphanage, and
go marry one of them . . ."

Seryoga heard this, took off his belt, grabbed Arina, aimed at her belly, like
a hero.

"Hey you," the woman says to him, "go easy on the belly, it's your stuffing,
after all, nobody else's . . ."

Then there came a flood—a flood of savage blows, a man's tears, a woman's
blood, though none of it solved anything. Then the woman comes to Jesus
Christ and says:

"So on and so forth, Lord Jesus. I'm Arina, the girl from the Hotel Madrid
and Louvre, the one on Tverskaya. Cleaning rooms is like hitching up your
skirt. Whoever passes through, he's your master, be it a Jew, be it anybody at
all. There's another servant of yours here walking the earth, the junior janitor,
Seryoga. Last year on Forgiveness Sunday I bore him twins . . ."

And she described everything to the Lord.

"And what if Seryoga didn't go into the army after all?" the Savior suggested.

"No doubt the cops will drag him there."

"The cops," the Lord bowed his head. "Didn't think of that . . . Listen, then maybe you could live clean for a while?"

"For four years?" replied the woman. "To hear you talk, nobody should live a life, that's you up to your old ways, but then who'll be going forth to multiply? Give me some real help to ease my lot . . ."

Then the Lord's cheeks were flushed red, the woman had cut to the quick, and there was nothing he could say. You can't kiss your own ear, even God knows that.

"I'll tell you what, servant of God, glorious sinner, Arina the maiden," proclaimed the Lord in his glory, "I got this little angel hanging around in heaven—they call him Alfred, he's gotten completely out of hand, keeps crying, 'What have you done, Lord, turned me into an angel in my twentieth year, when I was still a healthy young man.' I'll give you Alfred the angel as a husband for four years, you lucky girl. He'll be your blessing, your shield, and your lover boy too. And as for offspring, he can't conceive a duckling, let alone a baby, because there's a lot of fun in him but nothing serious . . ."

"That's just what I need," Arina the maiden wept gratefully. "Their seriousness kills me three times every two years."

"You shall have sweet rest, Arina, child of God, your prayer shall be light as a song. Amen."

And so it was decided. They brought over Alfred. Real puny fellow, delicate, two wings fluttering behind his pale-blue shoulders, flickering with pink fire like doves playing in heaven. Arina pawed at him, weeping from tenderness with her soft woman's heart.

"Alfie, my sweet consolation, my betrothed . . ."

Still, the Lord warned her that before going to bed she had to take off the angel's wings, since they've got latches, kind of like door hinges, so she had to take them off and wrap them in a clean sheet at night, for a wing could break if you tossed around—after all, it's made from the sighs of babes and nothing more.

The Lord blessed the union one last time; he brought in the cathedral choir for the occasion, and they gave thunderous song, there wasn't any food served, not a crumb, since that's not how they do, and then Arina and Alfred, their arms wrapped around each other, slid down a silken ladder straight back to earth. They reached Petrovka—that's right, only the best for this broad—where she took Alfred (who, by the way, not only had no pants but was also altogether in his natural state) and bought him patent-leather half boots, checked knit trousers, a Jaeger jersey, and a velvet vest of electric blue.

"The rest, my little friend," she says, "we'll find at home."

Arina took some time off and didn't clean rooms that day. Seryoga arrived to make a scene, but she didn't come out and said to him through the door:

"Sergey Nifantyich, I'm washing my feet at the moment and kindly request that you get lost without making a scene."

He didn't say a word and left. This was the angel's power already starting to reveal itself.

In the evening Arina prepared a supper fit for a merchant—oh, she was devilishly vain. A half-bottle of vodka, plus wine, Danube herring with potatoes, tea from a samovar. As soon as Alfred had partaken of this earthly bounty, he keeled over. Right away, Arina took his wings off the hinges, packed them away, and carried him to bed.

There he lies on the down pillows of her tattered, sin-filled bed, the snowy miracle, an unearthly radiance emanates from him, shafts of moonlight and crimson wander the room swaying on radiant feet. While Arina weeps and rejoices, sings and prays. You have been granted something unheard of in this battered world, Arina, blessed art thou among women!

They drank up the half-bottle to the last drop. And it took effect. Soon as they fell asleep, she went and rolled her scorching, six-month, Seryoga-filled stomach on top of Alfred. Not enough for her to sleep with an angel, not enough that there was nobody next to her who spat at the wall or snored or snorted, that wasn't enough for the raging, rutting wench—no, she had to warm her burning bloated belly, too. And so she smothered the angel of God in her drunken slumber and delight, smothered him like a week-old babe, went and crushed him, and he died for good, and his wings, wrapped up in the sheet, wept pale tears.

Come dawn—the trees bowed low. In the distant forests of the north each fir tree turned into a priest, each fir tree bent down at the knee.

Once more the woman stands, mighty and broad in the shoulder, before the throne of the Lord, the young corpse draped across her huge red arms.

"Behold, O Lord . . ."

But here the gentle heart of Jesus could endure no more; he cursed the woman with great anger.

"Just as it is on earth, so shall it be with you, Arina . . ."

"How's that, O Lord?" replied the woman most quietly. "Was it I who made my body heavy, was it I that brewed vodka, was it I that invented a woman's soul, lonely and foolish?"

"I don't want to deal with you anymore," the Lord Jesus exclaimed. "You've smothered my angel, you brute."

And a foul wind blew Arina back to earth, down to Tverskaya Street, back to her just deserts at the Hotel Madrid and Louvre. And there the water was up to here. Seryoga was living it up, since he was about to ship off. The contractor Trofimych had just come from Kolomna, took one look at Arina, all big and red-cheeked.

"Ooh, you bubble belly," he said, and other things besides.

Isai Abramych, the old coot, having heard about this bubble belly, likewise started proclaiming through his nose:

"I cannot wed you lawfully, after all that happened," he said, "but for that same reason, I can still sleep with you . . ."

He ought to be lying in cold mother earth instead of thinking of such things, but no, he, too, must take his turn spitting in her soul. It was like they had all slipped the chain—kitchen boys, merchants, and foreigners. A man away on business—he likes to have his fun.

And here's the end of my tale.

Before she was about to give birth, for three months had rolled by in the meantime, Arina went out into the backyard, behind the janitor's rooms, raised her awful enormous belly to the silken sky, and in a stupor uttered:

"See, Lord, here's a belly for you. They play my drum with their peashooters. And what and why I don't know. But I don't want any more."

And Jesus answered Arina, and, washed with his tears, the Savior fell to his knees.

"Forgive me, Arinushka, forgive your sinful God for all that I have done to you . . ."

"I got no forgiveness for you, Jesus Christ," replied Arina, "none at all."

(published August 29, 1921)

Line and Color

The first time I saw Alexander Fyodorovich Kerensky was on December 20, 1916, in the dining hall of the Ollila Sanatorium. We were introduced to each other by the barrister Zatzareny from Turkestan. What I knew of Zatzareny was that he had circumcised himself at the age of forty. Grand Duke Pyotr Nikolaevich, the disgraced madman exiled to Tashkent, cherished his friendship with Zatzareny. This grand duke used to walk the streets of Tashkent stark naked, had married a Cossack woman, lit candles before the portrait of Voltaire as though it were an image of Jesus Christ, and had drained the boundless floodplain of the Amu Darya. Zatzareny was his friend.

So then—the Ollila. Ten kilometers away we could see the deep-blue granite of Helsingfors. O Helsingfors, love of my heart. O sky, flowing over the esplanade and flying away like a bird.

So then—the Ollila. Northern flowers smoldered in their vases. Deer antlers sprawled along the somber ceiling panels. The dining hall smelled of pine, of Countess Tyszkiewicz's cool breast, and the silken underwear of English officers.

At the table next to Kerensky sat a polished convert from the Police Department. To his right was Nikkelsen the Norwegian, owner of a whaler. On the left—Countess Tyszkiewicz, lovely as Marie Antoinette.

Kerensky had three desserts and went off with me into the woods. Fröken Kirsti swept past us on skis.

"Who's that?" asked Alexander Fyodorovich.

"That's Nikkelsen's daughter Fröken Kirsti," I told him. "She's really something . . ."

Then we saw old Johann on his sleigh.

"Who's that?"

"That's old Johann," I said. "He brings fruit and cognac to Helsingfors. Don't you know Johann the sleigh driver?"

"I know everybody here," replied Kerensky, "but I can't see anybody."

"You're nearsighted, Alexander Fyodorovich?"

"Yes, I'm nearsighted."

"You need glasses, Alexander Fyodorovich."

"Never."

Then, in my youthful fervor I said to him:

"Just think, you're not merely blind, you're almost dead. Line—that divine trait, ruler of the world—she slips past you forever. We walk through this enchanted garden, this indescribable Finnish forest. For the rest of our lives, we shall never come to know anything better. And yet you can't see the frozen pink edges of the waterfall over there by the stream. The weeping willow leaning over the waterfall like a Japanese carving—you cannot see it. The red pine trunks speckled in snow. The granular radiance swarming over the snow. It begins as a lifeless line draped along the tree, rippling on the surface like a line by Leonardo, wreathed in reflections of the flaming clouds above. And what about Fröken Kirsti's silk stocking, and the line of her already ripe leg? Buy a pair of glasses, Alexander Fyodorovich, I implore you . . ."

"Child," he replied, "don't waste your powder. A half ruble for glasses—that's the one coin that stays in my pocket. I don't need your line—base like reality is base. You live no better than some trigonometry teacher, while I am surrounded by wonders, even on the Klyazma. Why do I need to see Fröken Kirsti's freckles if, even though I can barely distinguish her, I can discern in her all I wish to discern? Why do I need clouds in this Finnish sky, when I can see a heaving ocean above my head? Why do I need line—when I have color? To me the whole world is a gigantic theater, and I am the only one in the audience without opera glasses. The orchestra plays the overture to the third act, the stage is far away, like in a dream, my heart swells with ecstasy, I see Juliet's carmine velvet, Romeo's lilac silk, and not a single false beard . . . And you want to blind me with half-ruble eyeglasses!"

That evening I left for the city. O Helsingfors, refuge of my dreams . . .

As for Alexander Fyodorovich, I saw him again six months later, in June 1917, when he was supreme commander of the Russian armed forces and master of our destinies.

That day the Troitsky Bridge was drawn. The Putilov workers were marching on the Arsenal. Trolley cars lay flat like dead horses in the street.

A meeting had been called at the House of the People. Alexander Fyodorovich gave a speech about Russia—Mother and Wife. The crowd was smothering him in the sheepskins of its passions. What could he see in these bristling sheepskins as the only one in the audience without opera glasses? I don't know . . .

But after him Trotsky came to the podium, twisted his lips, and declared, in a voice that eliminated all hope:

"Comrades and brothers . . ."

(published 1923)

Bagrat-Ogly and the Eyes of His Bull

B y the side of the road I saw a bull of remarkable beauty.
There was a boy bent over him, weeping.

"That is Bagrat-Ogly," said the snake charmer, eating his humble repast nearby. "Bagrat-Ogly, Kyazim's son."

I said: "He is as lovely as twelve moons."

The snake charmer said:

"Never will the green cloak of the Prophet cover the stubborn beard of Kyazim. He was a petulant man, left his son a pauper's hut, a few fat wives, and a bullock without peer. But great is Allah . . ."

"Allah il Allah," I said.

"Great is Allah," the old man repeated, setting aside his basket of snakes. "The bull grew up and became the mightiest bull in Anatolia. Mehmed-Khan, a neighbor, sick with envy, castrated him last night. No one will bring cows for Bagrat-Ogly to stand stud. No one will pay Bagrat-Ogly a hundred piastres for the love of his bull. He is a pauper—Bagrat-Ogly. He sobs on the side of the road."

The mountainous silence unfurled its lilac banners above our heads. Snow glittered on the peaks. Blood ran down the legs of the mutilated bull and seethed in the grass. And when I heard the moaning of the bull, I looked into the bull's eyes and saw his death and my own death and fell to the ground from immeasurable sorrows.

"Wanderer," cried the boy, his face rosy like the dawn, "you writhe, and foam bubbles at the corners of your lips. A black sickness binds you in the ropes of its convulsions."

"Bagrat-Ogly," I replied, exhausted, "in the eyes of your bull I found the reflection of the ever-roused wickedness of our neighbors, our Mehmed-Khans. In the moist depths of these eyes I found a mirror ablaze with the green bonfires of the treachery of our neighbors, our Mehmed-Khans. I saw my own youth, killed without issue, in the eyes of that mutilated bull, and the ripeness of my manhood crashing through the thorns of indifference. The trails of Syria, Arabia, and Kurdistan, which I have thrice traversed, these, too, I find in the eyes of your bull, O Bagrat-Ogly, and their plains of sand leave me without hope. All the hatred in the world creeps into the open sockets of your bull. You should flee the wickedness of our neighbors, our Mehmed-Khans, O Bagrat-Ogly, and let the old snake charmer take up his basket of boas and flee along with you . . ."

And with a groan that filled the mountain pass, I got to my feet. I felt the scent of eucalyptus and went on my way. The many-headed dawn took off like a thousand swans over the mountains. The wet steel of the Bay of Trebizond gleamed in the distance. And I glimpsed the sea and the yellow flanks of feluccas. The freshness of grass spilled over the ruins of Byzantine walls. Before me appeared the bazaars of Trebizond and the carpets of Trebizond. I came across a young man of the mountains as I turned into the city. His outstretched arm held a red-footed falcon on a tether. The mountaineer was light of foot. The sun floated over our heads. And an unexpected calm descended upon my wandering soul.

(published 1923)

My First Advance

To live in Tiflis in the springtime, to be twenty years of age, and to be unloved—this is a sorry thing indeed. Such a thing happened to me. I had a job as a proofreader in the printing works of the Caucasus Military District. The River Kura seethed beneath the windows of my garret. In the morning, the sun would rise behind the mountains, setting its muddy knots ablaze. I rented the garret from a newlywed Georgian couple. The man sold meat at the Eastern Market. On the other side of the wall the butcher and his wife, possessed by love, writhed like two large fish in a jar. The tails of these crazed fish thrashed against the partition. They rocked the whole attic—that attic blackened by the steep sun—they wrenched it from its timbers and bore it off into infinity. Their teeth, joined in vicious passion, could not be unclenched. In the morning, the bride, Miliet, would go down to buy lavash. She was so weak she had to hold on to the banister not to fall. Groping for the steps with her small feet, she had the faint, vacant smile of a convalescent. Palm on her modest breast, she would bow to everybody she met on the way—to the Assyrian, green with age, to the kerosene seller, and to the old hags who sold skeins of wool, hags with faces seared in deep wrinkles. At night the heaving and moaning of my neighbors was followed by a silence as shrill as the whine of a cannonball.

To be twenty years of age, to live in Tiflis, and to listen at night to the storms of other people's silence—this is a sorry thing. To get away from it, I rushed headlong out of the house down to the Kura, where I was overcome by the steam bath of the Tiflis spring. The heat overtook and stifled you. I wandered the humpbacked streets with a parched throat. The humid haze of spring drove me back to my attic, to that moonlit forest of blackened stumps. There was nothing left to do but look for love. Of course, I found it. For better or worse, the woman I chose turned out to be a prostitute. Her name was Vera. I shadowed her every night along the Golovinsky Prospect, not daring to open my mouth. I had no money for her, and no words either—those trite and tireless grubby words of love. From childhood all the strength of my being had been devoted to making up tales, plays, thousands of stories. They lay on my heart like a toad on a stone. Possessed by demonic pride,

I did not want to write them down too soon. I thought it was pointless to write worse than Lev Tolstoy wrote. My stories were supposed to survive oblivion. Daring thoughts, consuming passions are worth the effort spent on them only when they are arrayed in lovely garments. How does one sew such garments . . .

For someone caught in the coils of an idea, under the spell of its serpentine gaze, it is difficult to spew up a froth of meaningless, grubby words of love. Such a person is ashamed to weep from sorrow. He lacks the wit to laugh from happiness. I was a dreamer and hadn't mastered the senseless art of happiness. I would be forced, therefore, to give Vera ten rubles out of my meager earnings.

When I had made up my mind, I started to wait one evening outside the Sympatia tavern. Princes in blue Circassian tunics and soft leather boots sauntered past me. Picking their teeth with silver toothpicks, they eyed the carmine-painted women, Georgians with ample feet and narrow hips. The twilight flickered turquoise. The flowering acacias along the streets began to sigh in a low, faltering voice. A throng of officials in white tunics heaved down the boulevard: they were met by a balmy breeze wafting down from Mount Kazbek.

Vera came later, after dark. Tall and white-faced, she sailed ahead of the apish throng as the Mother of God rides the prow of a fishing boat. She drew level with the door of the Sympatia tavern. I swayed and moved toward her:

"Whither goest thou, pilgrim?"

Her broad, pink back moved before me. She turned around:

"What're you mumbling there? . . ."

She frowned, her eyes were laughing.

"Where does the Lord take you?"

The words crumbled in my mouth like dried-out logs. She shifted her feet and started walking beside me.

"Ten, would ten set you back?"

I agreed so quickly that she became suspicious.

"Do you actually have ten rubles?"

We went into a doorway and I gave her my wallet. Squinting her gray eyes and moving her lips, she counted twenty-one rubles in it. She stacked the gold coins with the gold and the silver with the silver.

"Ten for me," said Vera, returning the wallet, "five for us to walk around on, and five for you to live on. When is payday?"

I replied that payday was in four days. We left the doorway. Vera took me arm in arm and pressed her shoulder into me. We went up the street as it grew cooler. The pavement was littered in a carpet of wilted vegetables.

"I should really go to Borzhom and get away from this heat . . . ," she said.

Vera's hair was bound in a ribbon. Flashes of streetlamp lightning flowed and curved in the ribbon.

"So shove off to Borzhom . . ."

That's what I said: "shove off." For some reason this is what my mouth uttered—those actual words.

"Not enough pennies," Vera said with a yawn and forgot all about me. She forgot all about me because her day was made and because I was easy money. She knew I wouldn't turn her in to the police or rob her of her money and her earrings in the night.

We reached the foot of St. David's Mount. There, in a pub, I ordered lulya kebab for us. Without waiting for it to come, Vera went over and sat with some old Persians who were discussing business. Leaning on their polished sticks and nodding their olive-colored heads, they were trying to convince the owner it was time to expand the business. Vera butted into their conversation. She took the side of the old men. She was for moving the pub to Mikhailovsky Prospect. The publican, blinded by flabby caution, sniffled. I ate my kebab alone. Vera's bare arms flowed from the silk of their sleeves, she banged her fist on the table, her earrings swinging between the long, faded backs, orange beards, and painted fingernails. The kebab was cold by the time she came back to the table. Her face was flushed with concern.

"He won't budge, the donkey . . . I say you can do great things with Eastern cooking on Mikhailovsky . . ."

One after another, acquaintances of Vera's came past the table—princes in Circassian tunics, aging officers, shopkeepers in shantung jackets, and potbellied old men with tan faces and green acne on their cheeks. It was midnight by the time we got to the hotel, but Vera had a hundred and one things to do here as well. Some old woman was getting ready to go and see her son in Armavir. Vera ran off to help and started kneeling on her suitcase, tying pillows together, wrapping pies in wax paper. In her gauze cap, a ginger-colored handbag at her side, the broad-shouldered old woman went to each room to say good-bye. She shuffled along the corridors in her rubber shoes, sobbing and smiling with all her wrinkles. It took an hour—no less—to see her off. I waited for Vera in a musty room with three-legged armchairs, a clay stove, and corners covered in damp patches.

I had been tormented and dragged around town for so long that my love now seemed like an enemy, an enemy stuck to my back . . .

In the corridor outside, there was the shuffling and sudden cackling of another life altogether. Flies were dying in a round flask filled with a milky liquid. Each died in its own way. One would writhe in agony, the jerking of its death throes long and drawn out; another died quietly, with a barely noticeable quiver. Lying about next to the flask on the worn tablecloth was a book, Golovin's novel about the life of the boyars. I opened it at random. The letters lined up in a row and got mixed up. Rising before me, framed by the square of the window, was a stone-paved hillside, a crooked Turkish street. Vera came into the room.

"We've just said good-bye to Feodosya Mavrikeyevna," she said. "She was like family to us, you know. An old woman, and she's traveling all alone, got nobody to go with her . . ."

Vera sat down on the bed with her knees apart. Her eyes were far away, roaming over pure realms of care and friendship. Then she saw me in my double-breasted jacket. She clasped her hands and stretched herself.

"Waited long enough, I bet . . . Don't worry, we'll get to it . . ."

But exactly what Vera was going to do—I still couldn't fathom. Her preparations were like those of a doctor getting ready for an operation. She lit a kerosene stove and put a pot of water on it. She threw a clean towel over the headboard of the bed, and above it she hung an enema cup—the white tube dangled down the wall. When the water was warm, she poured it into the enema, threw a red crystal into it, and started taking off her dress, pulling it over her head. A large woman with drooping shoulders and a crumpled stomach stood before me. Her flabby nipples pointed blindly sideways.

"The water's getting ready," said my beloved, "get over here, my jumping bean."

I didn't budge. I was numb with despair. Why had I exchanged my loneliness for the misery of this sordid den, for these dying flies and three-legged furnishings? . . .

O, gods of my youth! How different it was, this dull concoction, from the love of my landlords on the other side of the wall, their long, drawn-out squeals . . .

Vera put her hands under her breasts and wobbled them.

"What's with you, sitting there all unhappy? Come here . . ."

I didn't budge. Vera pulled her petticoat up to her belly and sat down on the bed again.

"Or are you sorry about the money?"

"It's not the money . . ."

My voice cracked when I said this.

"What do you mean 'it's not the money'? Maybe you're a thief?"

"I'm not a thief."

"Thieves pimping you?"

"I'm a boy."

"I can see you're not a cow," Vera muttered. She could hardly keep her eyes open. She lay down, pulled me toward her, and started running her hands over me.

"A boy," I shouted, "a boy with the Armenians, don't you understand? . . ."

Oh, Gods of my youth! . . . Of my twenty years, five had been spent making up tales, thousands of tales, sucking on my brain. They lay on my heart like a toad on a stone. Dislodged by the force of loneliness, one of them had fallen to the ground. It was evidently a matter of fate that a Tiflis prostitute was to be my first reader. I went cold all over at the suddenness of my invention, and I told her my story about a boy with the Armenians. Had I been lazier and given less thought to my craft, I would have braided together some trite story about a rich official's son who had been driven from home, about a despot of a father and a martyr of a mother. I didn't make this mistake. There's no reason for a well-made story to resemble real life; real life wants nothing more than to resemble a well-made story. For this reason, and also because this was what my listener required—I was born in the small town of Alyoshki in Kherson Province. My father worked as a draftsman for a riverboat company. He slaved day and night at his drawing board to give us children a good education, but we all took after our mother, a frivolous pleasure-seeker. At ten I started stealing money from my father; when I was older, I ran away to Baku, to some relatives of my mother's. They introduced me to an Armenian, Stepan Ivanovich. I moved in with him and we lived together for four years . . .

"But how old were you then? . . ."

"Fifteen."

Vera was expecting to hear about the wickedness of the Armenian who had corrupted me. Then I said:

"We lived together for four years. Stepan Ivanovich was the most trusting and generous person I've ever met, the most noble and reliable. He believed every word his friends said to him . . . I ought to have learned a trade during those four years, but I didn't lift a finger . . . All I cared about was billiards . . . Stepan Ivanovich's friends ruined him. He gave them bronze promissory notes, and his friends presented them for payment . . ."

Bronze promissory notes—I myself have no idea how they got into my head. But I did right to bring them in. Vera believed everything after she heard about the bronze promissory notes. She wrapped herself in her shawl as it slipped off her shoulders.

". . . Stepan Ivanovich was ruined. He was thrown out of his apartment, and his furniture was sold at auction. He became a traveling salesman. I wasn't going to live with him now that he was poor, so I moved in with a rich old churchwarden . . ."

The churchwarden—that bit was filched from some writer, the invention of a lazy heart that had no wish to expend the effort to create a living person.

A churchwarden, I said—and Vera's eyes blinked and drifted out of my dominion. Then, to set things right, I installed asthma in the old man's yellow chest, attacks of asthma, hoarse gasps of suffocation in that yellow chest. He would jump out of bed at night and gulp the kerosene-choked air of Baku. He soon died. The asthma finished him off. My relatives kicked me out. So here I am in Tiflis with twenty rubles in my pocket—the very same rubles Vera had counted in the doorway on Golovinsky. The room attendant in the hotel where I was staying had promised to get me rich customers, but so far he had sent me only tavern keepers with bellies out to here . . . These people like their own country, their own songs, their own wine, but they trample all over other people's souls and over other women, like a village thief tramples his neighbor's garden . . .

And I started churning up what I had heard once somewhere about tavern keepers . . . My heart was breaking from self-pity. Doom was upon me. I writhed in tremors of sorrow and inspiration. Streams of ice-cold sweat started down my face like snakes moving over grass warmed by the sun. I stopped talking, began to cry, and turned away. The story was finished. The kerosene stove had long since gone out. The water had boiled and gone cold again. The rubber tube was hanging from the wall. The woman went silently up to the window. Her back moved before me, dazzling and sorrowful. In the window, light appeared behind the mountaintops.

"What people do . . ." Vera whispered, without turning around. "God, what people do . . ."

She stretched out her bare arms and threw open the shutters. In the street, the paving stones hissed as they grew cooler. There was a smell of dust and water coming from the road . . . Vera's head swayed back and forth.

"So you're a whore . . . our sister—another bitch . . ."

I hung my head.

"Your sister—a bitch . . ."

Vera turned around to face me. Her petticoat hung aslant on her body like a rag.

"What people do," she said again, in a louder voice. "God, what people do . . . Have you even been with a broad? . . ."

I pressed my pale lips to her hand.

"No, how could I? Who would let me?"

My head shook against her breasts rising freely above me. The taut nipples pushed against my cheeks. Opening their moist eyelids, they pushed like baby calves. Vera looked down at me from above.

Openings

"Little sister, . . ." she whispered, and sat down on the floor beside me. "My little sister, a whore like me . . ."

Now tell me, I want to ask you about this, tell me, have you ever seen village carpenters helping another fellow carpenter build his house, how thick and fast and merry the shavings fly as they plane a beam together? . . . That night a thirty-year-old woman taught me her science. That night I came to know secrets you will never know, I experienced a love you will never experience, I heard the words one woman says to another. I have forgotten them. We are not supposed to remember them.

We fell asleep at dawn. We were awakened by the heat of our bodies, heat that lay in the bed like a stone. When we woke up, we laughed to each other. I didn't go to the printing works that day. We drank tea in the *maidan*, in the bazaar of the Old City. A mild-mannered Turk came with a samovar wrapped in a towel and poured us tea, maroon like bricks and steaming like freshly shed blood. Sun fire smoldered in my glass. The drawn-out braying of donkeys blended with the hammering of boilermakers. Copper pitchers were arranged in rows on faded carpets under tents. Dogs nosed around in the entrails of oxen. A caravan of dust flew toward Tiflis—the city of roses and mutton fat. Dust speckled the raspberry fire of the sun. The Turk poured more tea for us and kept count of our bagels on an abacus. The world was lovely just to give us pleasure. When I was covered all over with fine beads of sweat, I turned my glass upside down. After I'd paid the Turk, I pushed two gold five-ruble pieces over to Vera. Her plump leg lay across mine. She pushed the money away and removed her leg.

"So it's spit and split, little sister? . . ."

No, I didn't want to spit and split. We agreed to meet in the evening, and I put the two gold pieces back into my wallet—my first advance.

Many years have passed since then. During that time I have often received money from editors, from learned men, from Jews trading in books. For victories that were defeats, for defeats turned into victories, for life and for death they paid me trifling sums, much smaller than the one I received in my youth from my first reader. But I am not bitter. I'm not bitter, because I know I shall not die before I have snatched one more gold piece—this time, my last—from the hands of love.

1922–1928 (published 1963)

Guy de Maupassant

In the winter of 1916 I found myself in Petersburg with a forged passport and not a penny to my name. I found shelter with a teacher of Russian literature—Alexey Kazantsev.

He lived in Peski on a yellow, frozen, foul-smelling street. He supplemented his meager salary by doing translations from the Spanish; at the time, Blasco Ibáñez was just becoming famous.

Kazantsev had never even passed through Spain, but his love for that country filled his whole being—he knew all its castles, gardens, and rivers. Besides me there were many other people huddling around Kazantsev, all of them castaways from a proper life. We lived hand to mouth. From time to time the tabloids would publish our news commentary in small print.

Mornings I would hang around the morgues and police precincts.

Still, Kazantsev was happier than the rest of us. He had a motherland—Spain.

In November I was offered a post as a clerk at the Obukhov factory, not a bad job; it would have exempted me from military service.

I refused to become a clerk.

Even back then when I was twenty years old, I had told myself: better starve, go to jail, or roam the earth than sit ten hours a day behind a desk. There's nothing especially impressive about this resolution, but I didn't break it and never will. The wisdom of my grandfathers was fixed in my head: we are born to take pleasure in our work, in our fights, in our love; we are born for that and nothing else.

Kazantsev listened to my sermons, ruffling the short yellow fuzz on top of his head. The horror in his eyes was mixed with admiration.

At Christmastime we had a stroke of luck. Bendersky the barrister, who owned a publishing house called Halcyon, decided to publish a new edition of Maupassant's works. The barrister's wife, Raisa, tried her hand at the translation. Nothing came of this noble venture.

Kazantsev, who translated from Spanish, was asked whether he could recommend someone to assist Raisa Mikhaylovna. Kazantsev directed them to me.

The next day, dressed in someone else's jacket, I made my way to the Benderskys'. They lived at the corner of Nevsky and the Moyka, in a house built of Finland granite and adorned with pink columns, crenellations, coats of arms carved in stone. Bankers without family or tribe, converts who made money selling supplies to the army, had put up many such vulgar, pretentious castles in St. Petersburg before the war.

There was a red carpet on the stairs. On the landings, stuffed bears stood on their hind legs.

Crystal orbs burned in their gaping maws.

The Benderskys lived on the third floor. A high-breasted maid with a white cap on her head opened the door. She led me into a drawing room decorated in the Old Slavonic style. On the walls hung deep-blue paintings by Roerich—prehistoric stones and monsters. Antique icons were perched on stands in the corners. The high-breasted maid moved majestically across the room. She was shapely, nearsighted, and haughty. Her gray, wide-open eyes were hard with depravity. The maid moved slowly. I thought, when she makes love, she must toss and turn with brutal dexterity. The brocade curtain over the doorway stirred. Conveying her ample bosom, a black-haired woman with pink eyes entered the drawing room. I quickly recognized Mrs. Bendersky as one of those charming Jewesses who have come to us from Kiev and Poltava, from the sated towns of the steppes, planted over with chestnut trees and acacias. The money made by their resourceful husbands is transformed by these women into a pink layer of fat on the belly, the nape, and on their rounded shoulders. Their tender sleepy smiles drive the garrison officers mad.

"Maupassant is the single passion in my life," Raisa said to me.

Trying to control the swaying of her ample hips, she left the room and returned with a translation of "Miss Harriet." In her translation there was no trace of Maupassant's free-flowing phrases with their drawn-out breath of passion. Mrs. Bendersky's writing was tediously correct, lifeless and loud, the way Jews used to write Russian back in the day.

I took the manuscript home with me, and, in Kazantsev's attic, while the others slumbered, I spent all night hacking a path through someone else's translation. The work wasn't as bad as it sounds. A phrase is born into the world both good and bad at the same time. The secret lies in a barely discernible twist. The lever should rest in your hand, getting warm. You must turn it once, but not twice.

In the morning I brought back the corrected manuscript. Raisa wasn't lying when she told me of her passion for Maupassant. She sat motionless, her hands clasped, as I read it to her: those satin hands melted to the floor, her forehead went pale, and the lace between her bound breasts strained and trembled.

"How did you do that?"

So then I started talking of style, of the army of words, an army in which all manner of weapons are in play. Nothing of iron can breach the human heart with the chill of a period placed just in time. She listened, her head bowed, her painted lips unsealed. A black light glowed in her lacquered hair, smoothly pressed and parted. Her legs, with their strong tender calves, were bathed in stockings and splayed wide on the rug.

The maid, looking askance with her hard wanton eyes, brought in breakfast on a tray.

The glassy Petersburg sun lay on the faded and uneven carpet. Twenty-nine volumes of Maupassant stood on a shelf above the desk. The melting fingers of the sun touched the morocco spines of the books—a magnificent grave of the human heart.

Coffee was served in dark-blue cups, and we began translating "An Idyll." Everyone remembers the story of the hungry young carpenter who suckled on the plump wet nurse to relieve her of the milk that burdened her. It happened on a train going from Nice to Marseille, in the middle of a scorching day, in the land of roses, the birthplace of roses where flowering slopes reach down to the sea . . .

I left the Benderskys' with a twenty-five-ruble advance. Our crowd at Peski got sloshed that night like a drunken gaggle of geese. We shoveled spoons of unpressed caviar and then ate it with liver sausage. Quite drunk, I started ragging on Tolstoy.

"He got spooked, your count, chickened out . . . His religion—that was just fear. When he got scared of the cold, old age, death, the count sewed himself long undies out of his faith."

"And then what?" Kazantsev asked, swaying his avian head.

We fell asleep next to our own beds. I dreamed of Katya, a forty-year-old washerwoman who lived below us. We would get hot water from her every morning. I had never even managed to see her face really, but in my dream Katya and I did God knows what. We tormented each other with kisses. I could barely wait to go get my hot water from her the next morning.

When the door opened, I saw a withered woman, shawl across her chest, with loose ash-gray curls and prune hands.

From then on I had breakfast each day at the Benderskys'. In our attic there appeared a new stove, herring, chocolate. Twice Raisa took me out on drives to the islands. I couldn't resist and told her of my childhood. The story turned out rather grim, to my own surprise. From under her moleskin cap she looked at me with gleaming, frightened eyes. The russet fur of her eyelashes trembled with pity.

I met Raisa's husband, a yellow-faced Jew with a bald skull and a flat powerful body angled and ready for takeoff. There were rumors that he was close to Rasputin. The profits he made from the war made him look like he was possessed. His eyes would drift, he had been torn from the fabric of normal life. Raisa was embarrassed whenever she had to introduce new people to her husband. Because I was young, I noticed this a week later than I should have.

After the New Year, Raisa's two sisters arrived from Kiev. One day I stopped by with the manuscript of "The Confession" and, not finding Raisa at home, returned again that evening. They were at dinner. From the dining room there issued a sterling whinny of laughter and the din of overexcited male voices. In rich houses without tradition, dinners are noisy. It was a Jewish noise, rolling and rich with melodious finishes. Raisa came out to me in a ball gown with an open back. Her feet stepped awkwardly in their precarious shiny slippers.

"Sweetie, I'm drunk," she said, reaching out to me with her arms, loaded with chains of platinum and stars of emerald.

Her body swayed like the body of a snake charmed to the ceiling by music. She tossed her curled hair, jangling her rings, and suddenly collapsed into a chair with ancient Russian carvings. Scars glowed on her powdered back.

Behind the wall there was another explosion of feminine laughter. Out of the dining room came Raisa's sisters, wisps of mustaches on their lips, as tall and full-figured as Raisa herself. Their busts protruded and their black hair flipped back and forth. Both were married to their own Benderskys. The room was filled with disjointed, feminine vivaciousness, the vivaciousness of ripe women. The husbands wrapped the sisters in their sealskins and Orenburg shawls and shod them in black boots; beneath the snowy rims of their shawls, all you could see were rouged, smoldering cheeks, marble noses, and the nearsighted Semitic glint of their eyes. They made a little more noise and then left for the theater, to see Chaliapin in *Judith*.

"Let's work," Raisa lisped, reaching out with her bare arms, "we've skipped a whole week . . ."

She brought a bottle and two glasses from the dining room. Her breasts were unfettered inside the silken sack of her gown; the nipples rose, concealed by the silk.

"It's priceless," said Raisa, pouring out the wine. "Muscat '83. My husband will kill me when he finds out . . ."

I had never been introduced to a Muscat '83 before and so thought nothing of knocking back three glasses one after the other. They carried me swiftly down back alleys where an orange flame flickered and music could be heard.

"I'm drunk, darling . . . What do we have today?"

"Today we have *L'Aveu*. 'The Confession,' in other words. The sun is the hero of this story, *le soleil de France* . . ." Molten drops of the sun falling on the red-haired Céleste, turning into freckles. The sun burnished the face of Polyte the coachman with its steep rays, its wine and apple cider. Twice a week Céleste drove into town to sell cream, eggs, and chickens. She paid Polyte ten sous for herself and four for her basket. And on each trip Polyte would wink at the red-haired Céleste and ask, "When are we going to have some fun, *ma belle?*"—"What does that mean, Monsieur Polyte?" Bouncing up and down on the box, the coachman explained, "To have some fun—why, hell, just means to have some fun! A lad with a lass—no music necessary . . ."

"I do not care for such jokes, Monsieur Polyte," replied Céleste and moved her skirts away from the lad, skirts that covered her mighty calves in their red stockings.

But that devil Polyte kept right on chortling and coughing: "Someday we'll have our bit of fun, *ma belle*," while tears of delight rolled down his face the color of brick-red blood and wine.

I drank up another cup of the priceless muscat. Raisa touched glasses with me. The hard-eyed maid passed through the room and disappeared.

Ce diable de Polyte . . . Over two years Céleste had paid him forty-eight francs. That's two francs short of fifty. At the end of the second year, when they were alone in the carriage, Polyte, who had had some cider before setting out, asked her his usual question: "And won't we have some fun today, Mam'selle Céleste?" And she replied, lowering her eyes, "I am at your service, Monsieur Polyte . . ."

Raisa flung herself down on the table, laughing. *Ce diable de Polyte* . . .

The carriage was pulled by a white nag. The white nag, its lips pink with age, went at a walk. The lively French sun enveloped the ancient coach, screened from the world by a rusty old hood. A lad with a lass, no music necessary . . .

Raisa held out a glass to me. It was the fifth.

"To Maupassant, *mon vieux*."

"And won't we have some fun today, *ma belle* . . ."

I reached over to Raisa and kissed her on the lips. They quivered and swelled.

"Aren't you fun," she mumbled through her teeth and recoiled.

She pressed herself against the wall, spreading her bare arms. Spots began to glow on her arms and shoulders. Of all the gods ever nailed to a cross, this one was the most seductive.

"Be so kind as to sit down, Monsieur Polyte . . ."

She pointed to a sloping blue armchair done in Slavonic style. Its back consisted of carved wooden lacework with decorated tailpieces. I fumbled over there, tripping over myself.

Underneath my famished youth the night had slipped a bottle of Muscat '83 and twenty-nine books, twenty-nine petards stuffed with pity, genius, passion . . . I sprang up, knocked over the chair, banged against the shelf. The twenty-nine volumes crashed to the floor, their pages flew open, they stood on their sides . . . and the white nag of my fate went on at a walk.

"Aren't you fun," growled Raisa.

I left the granite house on the Moyka around midnight, before the sisters and the husband returned from the theater. I was sober and could have walked a plank, but it was much better to stagger, and I swayed from side to side, singing in a language I had just invented. Through the tunnels of the streets, lined by a chain of lamps, billowed mists of fog. Monsters roared behind the seething walls. The pavements severed any legs that walked them.

Kazantsev was asleep when I got home. He slept sitting up, his skinny legs stretched out in felt boots. A canary fluff rose over his head. He had fallen asleep by the stove bent over a volume of *Don Quixote*, the 1624 edition. On the title page of the book was a dedication to the duc de Broglie. I got into bed quietly so as not to wake Kazantsev, moved the lamp closer, and began to read a book by Édouard de Maynial, *The Life and Work of Guy de Maupassant*.

Kazantsev's lips stirred, his head kept tipping over.

That night I learned from Édouard de Maynial that Maupassant was born in 1850, the child of a Norman aristocrat and Laure de Poitevan, Flaubert's cousin. He was twenty-five when he had his first bout of congenital syphilis. His prolific joie de vivre resisted the onset of the disease. At first he suffered from headaches and fits of hypochondria. Then the specter of blindness rose before him. His sight grew weak. He became maniacally paranoid, unsociable, and querulent. He struggled furiously, dashed about the Mediterranean in a yacht, fled to Tunis, Morocco, Central Africa—and wrote constantly. Having achieved fame, in his fortieth year he cut his own throat, lost a lot of blood, but survived. They put him in a madhouse. There he crawled about on all fours and ate his own excrement. The last line on his medical chart read, "Monsieur de Maupassant va s'animaliser" (Mr. Maupassant has turned into an animal). He died when he was forty-two. He was survived by his own mother.

I read the book to the end and got out of bed. The fog came up to the window and concealed the universe. My heart felt tight. I was brushed by a premonition of the truth.

1920–1922 (published 1932)

The Road

I left the front as it was falling apart in November 1917. At home, my mother packed some clean underclothes and dry biscuits for me. I happened to arrive in Kiev the day before Muravyov began bombing the city. I had to get to Petersburg. We sat twelve days and nights in the basement of Chaim Tsirulnik's hotel in Bessarabka. I got my exit permit from the commander of Soviet Kiev.

In the whole world, there is no sadder spectacle than the Kiev train station. For many years now, temporary wooden barracks have defiled the approaches to the city. Lice crackled on the wet planks. Deserters, smugglers, Gypsies loitered about. Galician old ladies would stand and piss right on the train platforms. The low sky was furrowed with clouds full of rain and gloom.

Three days passed before the first train set off. At first it stopped every verst, then it got going, the warm wheels rattling in a mighty song. This made everyone in our freight car happy. Fast travel made people happy in 1918. Toward night our train jolted and came to a halt. The door of the freight car slid open, revealing a green glimmer of snow. The station telegraphist came inside wearing a belted fur coat and soft Caucasian boots. The telegraphist stretched out his hand and tapped the open palm with his finger.

"Papers . . ."

Right by the door an old woman was curled up quietly atop some bundles. She was traveling to Lyuban to see her son, a railwayman. Nodding off next to me sat a schoolmaster, Yehuda Veynberg, and his wife. The schoolmaster had gotten married a few days before and was taking his young bride to Petersburg. They had been whispering to each other the whole way about the "complex method" of teaching, then fell asleep. In their sleep their hands had become intertwined, one into the other's.

The telegraphist read their credentials, signed by Lunacharsky, reached into his coat, and took out a Mauser with a thin dirty muzzle and shot the teacher in the face. Behind the telegraphist there was a big, slouching muzhik in a hat with dangling earflaps. His boss gave him a wink, and the muzhik put down his lantern, undid the murdered man's buttons, sliced off his sexual organs, and began stuffing them into the wife's mouth.

"You couldn't stand *treyf*," said the telegraphist, "eat kosher, then."

51

The woman's soft neck swelled. She was silent. The train stood on the steppe. The undulating snow roiled in a polar sheen. They were throwing Jews off the train onto the tracks. Intermittent shots resounded like exclamations. The muzhik with the dangling earflaps took me behind a frozen stack of firewood and started searching me. We were lit by the darkling moon. The violet wall of the forest was shrouded in mist. Stiff lumps of frostbitten fingers crawled over my body. The telegraphist shouted from the footboard of the train car:

"A Yid or a Russian?"

"Russian," the muzhik muttered, digging into me, "though you could make a good rabbi out of him . . ."

He brought his wrinkled, weathered face close, tore out four gold ten-ruble coins my mother had sewn into my pants for the road, took off my boots and coat, spun me round, knocked the back of my head with the edge of his hand, and said in Yiddish:

"Ankloyf, Chaim . . ."

I took off, stepping barefoot through the snow. A target burned on my back, a bull's-eye piercing the ribs. The muzhik didn't shoot. Among the pillars of pines, under the covered cellar of the forest, a small light swayed in a wreath of scarlet mist. I ran to the lodge. It was shrouded in dung smoke. The forester groaned when I burst into the cabin. Wrapped in strips cut from furs and overcoats, he sat in a velvet-cushioned bamboo armchair, crumbling tobacco on his knees. Looming through the smoke, the forester groaned, then got up and bowed to me from the waist:

"You must leave, dear fellow . . . Leave, dear citizen . . ."

He took me to a trail and gave me a rag to wrap my feet. I reached a shtetl by late morning. There was no doctor at the hospital to cut off my frostbitten feet: a medical orderly ran the ward. Each morning he would race to the hospital on his short raven-black stallion, tie him to the hitching post, and greet us with an enflamed bright gleam in his eyes.

"Friedrich Engels"—the orderly's eyes burned like coals as he bent over my bed—"teaches your brothers that nations shouldn't exist, but we say the opposite—the nation must exist . . ."

Tearing the wrapping off my feet, he straightened up and asked me in a hushed voice, grinding his teeth:

"Where? Where are you running, all of you, that nation of yours . . . For what? . . . Why are you making trouble, roiling things up . . ."

That night, the local soviet picked us up in a wagon—those patients who didn't get on with the orderly and some old Jewish women in wigs, the mothers of shtetl commissars.

My feet healed. I pushed on along the hard road to Zhlobin, Orsha, Vitebsk.

A howitzer barrel gave me shelter on the stretch from Novo-Sokolniki to Loknya. We rode on exposed terrain. Fedyukha, my chance companion on the great deserter trail, was a keen wit, joker, and teller of tales. We slept beneath the mighty snub-nosed, turned-up muzzle and took warmth from each other in a canvas hollow that was lined with hay like the lair of an animal. Around Loknya, Fedyukha stole my little trunk and disappeared. The trunk had been issued by the shtetl soviet and contained two pairs of army underwear, crackers, and some money. As we approached Petersburg, we went two days straight without food. I arrived to hear the last shots fired at Tsarskoe Selo Station. The defense squad fired into the air as our train pulled in. The smugglers were brought to the platform and stripped. Liquor-filled rubber bodies tumbled onto the asphalt alongside the human ones. Toward nine in the evening, the station chucked me out of its howling mayhem onto Zagorodny Prospect. Across the street, on the wall of a boarded-up pharmacy, a thermometer read -24°C. The wind roared in the tunnel beneath Gorokhovaya; a spike of gaslight faded over the canal. A Venice of cooled lava stood motionless. I came out onto Gorokhovaya, which stretched like an icy field scarred with crags.

The Cheka was set up at Number 2, in the former municipal government building. Two machine guns, two hounds of steel with upturned snouts, stood in the lobby. I showed the commandant my letter from Ivan Kalugin, my NCO in the Shuysky Regiment. Kalugin had become an investigator in the Cheka; he had written that I should come see him.

"Go to Anichkov Palace," said the commandant, "that's where he's stationed now . . ."

"I won't make it," I replied with a little smile.

The Milky Way of Nevsky Prospect flowed into the distance. Dead horses marked the road like milestones. Their upturned legs held up the low-hanging sky. Their exposed bellies were shiny and clean. An old man who looked like an imperial guardsman passed me dragging a toy sled. He was straining as he cracked the ice with his leather feet, a Tyrolean hat on his skull, his beard bound with twine and tucked in a shawl.

"I won't make it," I said to the old man. He stopped. His pitted, leonine face was full of calm. He stopped to think for a bit and continued on his way with his sled.

"And thus, the need to conquer Petersburg disappears," I thought and tried to recall the name of the man trampled by the hooves of Arabian chargers at the end of his journey. It was Yehuda Halevi.

Two Chinese in bowler hats stood on the corner of Sadovaya with loaves of bread under their arms. They notched portions of bread with their chilled fingernails and displayed them to passing prostitutes. The women paraded silently past them.

At the Anichkov Bridge, I sat by the pedestal of one of Klodt's horses.

Elbow under my head, I stretched out against the polished stone, but the granite scorched my skin and shot me like a cannonball to the palace.

The door to the lingon-colored side wing was open. A spike of pale-blue gaslight glowed above a lackey sleeping in an armchair. A lip drooped on his wrinkled ink-battered face, his unbelted army tunic, drenched in light, was draped over his gold-trimmed livery pants. A sloppy ink arrow pointed the way to the commandant. I went upstairs and passed empty low-ceilinged rooms. Women painted in black somber tones danced in circles on the walls and ceilings. Metal grates stretched across the windows, broken latches hung on the casements. In the last suite, lit as if onstage, crowned in straw-colored peasant hair, sat Kalugin. On the table before him was a hill of children's toys, colorful rags, torn picture books.

"There you are," said Kalugin, looking up. "Great . . . We could use you here . . ."

I parted the toys that lay on his desk, lay down on his shining tabletop, and . . . I woke up—minutes or hours later—on a low sofa. A glass water-fall of chandelier beams played above my head. My rags had been cut and stripped from me and lay in a puddle on the floor.

"Time to wash up," said Kalugin, looming above me, then picked me up and carried me to the bathtub. It was an antique tub, with low-hanging sides. There was no water in the taps. Kalugin poured water on me from a bucket. Clothes had been laid out on pale-yellow satin poufs, on backless wicker chairs—a robe with buckles, a shirt and socks of double-weave silk. The long underwear went up to my neck, the robe was made for a giant, my feet were kicking at my sleeves.

"Making fun of old Alexander Alexandrovich?" said Kalugin, rolling up my sleeves. "The old boy was about nine poods . . ."

Somehow we cinched up the robe of Emperor Alexander III and returned to the room we had been in before. This had been Maria Fyodorovna's library, a perfume box wrapped in gilded walls and bound in raspberry cabinets.

I told Kalugin about the Shuysky Regiment—who had been killed, who chosen as commissar, who had left for the Kuban. We drank tea, stars swimming in our crystal cups. We ate horsemeat sausage, black and a little raw. We were removed from the world by thick curtains of light silk; the streaming sun beat and shimmered on the ceiling, a sultry heat rose from the steam pipes.

"Oh, what the heck," said Kalugin as we finished off the horsemeat. He went off someplace and returned with two boxes—gifts from Sultan Abdul-Hamid to the Russian sovereign. One of them was made of zinc; the other, a cigar box, was pasted with ribbons and paper medallions. "À sa majesté, l'Empereur de toutes les Russies" was the engraving on the zinc box, "with kind regards from his cousin . . ."

Maria Fyodorovna's library was filled with the fragrance it had grown accustomed to four centuries ago. Cigars twenty centimeters long and as thick as a finger were wrapped in pink paper; I don't know if anyone had ever smoked such cigars save the Russian autocrat, but I took one. Kalugin looked at me and smiled.

"Oh, what the heck," he said, "nobody counted them . . . The lackeys were telling me Alexander III was a die-hard smoker: he loved tobacco, kvass, champagne, too . . . But take a look at this, on his desk he's got five-kopeck clay ashtrays and there on his pants—patches . . ."

And indeed, the robe in which I had been dressed shone with grease stains and had been mended many times.

We spent the rest of the night going through the toys of Nicholas II, his drums and train sets, his christening shirts and notebooks with boyish scribbles. Photos of grand dukes who had died as infants, locks of their hair, diaries of the Danish princess Dagmar, letters from her sister, the queen of England, exuding perfume and decay, crumbled beneath our fingers. On the title pages of the Gospels and Lamartine, girlfriends and ladies-in-waiting—the daughters of burgomasters and state councillors—bade farewell in slanting and painstaking script to the princess who was leaving for Russia. Her mother, Louisa, queen of a modest kingdom, did her best to place her children well; she gave one daughter in marriage to Edward VII, emperor of India and king of England, another to a Romanov, and her son George was made king of Greece. In Russia, Princess Dagmar became Maria. The canals of Copenhagen, the chocolaty sideburns of King Christian—they went a long way. Having given birth to the last of the kings, this little woman, fierce like a fox, paced along the palisade of the Preobrazhenksy Grenadiers, but the blood of her childbirths was shed into the implacable, vindictive granite ground . . .

As dawn approached, we could not tear ourselves away from this outlandish and disastrous chronicle. The cigar of Abdul-Hamid had been smoked. In the morning, Kalugin took me to the Cheka at Gorokhovaya 2. He had a talk with Uritsky. I stood behind a curtain whose fabric rippled to the ground. Fragments of their words reached me.

"He's one of us," said Kalugin, "father's a shopkeeper, does business, but he broke with all that . . . Good with languages . . ."

The commissar of internal affairs for the Northern Region came lurching out of his office. His swollen eyelids, seared and loose from lack of sleep, were spilling out of his pince-nez.

I was made translator in the Foreign Division. I received a military uniform and meal tickets. In a corner designated to me in the grand hall of the former Petersburg Governorate, I set about translating testimony given by diplomats, provocateurs, and spies.

It had hardly been a day, and I had everything—clothing, food, work, and comrades faithful in friendship and in death, comrades not to be found anywhere on earth except in our country.

Thus began my splendid life thirteen years ago, a life full of thought and merriment.

1920–1930 (published 1932)

THE STORY OF MY DOVECOT (CHILDHOOD CYCLE)

Childhood. At Grandmother's

On Saturdays I would come home late after six classes. Walking down the streets never seemed like a waste of time to me. The walk was surprisingly good for daydreams, and every single thing was so familiar. I knew each and every sign, shop window, and stone in each and every house. I knew them in a special way that was just for me, and I was quite certain that I could see in them what was most important, mysterious, what we grown-ups call the essence of things. All of it was lodged firmly in my soul. If someone were to mention a particular store, I would recall the sign, its faded gold lettering and the scratch on the left corner, the lady at the cash register with the tall hairdo, and I would remember the air that stirs only near this store and no other. And it was from these shops, people, breezes, theater posters that I would compose my hometown. I remember it till this day, I feel it, I love it; I know it the way we know our mother's smell, the smell of tenderness, of her words and her smile; I love it because it's where I grew up, where I was happy, sad, full of dreams, passionately, incomparably full of dreams.

I always walked along the main street, which had the most people.

The Saturday I want to tell you about was at the beginning of spring. At that time of year we don't get that soft mild air, so sweet in central Russia, over some quiet river or modest valley. Here we get a light shimmering chill, just a hint of passion blowing on a cool breeze. I was just a little kid then and didn't understand much about anything, but I could feel spring in the air, and the chill made my cheeks bloom and blush.

The walk took me a while. I gazed for a long time at the diamonds in the jeweler's window, and read the theater posters from A to Z, and at the same time had a look at the long-laced, pale-pink corsets in Madame Rosalie's shop. Just as I was about to move on, I bumped into a tall student with a big black mustache.

He smiled and asked, "Studying hard?" I got all mixed up. Then he solemnly slapped my shoulder and sneered, "Keep up the good work, colleague. Well done. All the best!" He chortled, turned around, and left. I was quite embarrassed, trudged home, and never looked at Madame Rosalie's storefront again.

This Saturday I was supposed to spend the afternoon with Grandmother. She had her own room at the very end of the apartment, behind the kitchen. A stove stood in the corner: Grandmother always felt cold. The room was hot and stuffy, and this always made me miserable, I wanted to get out, to break free.

I dragged my supplies over to Grandmother's—my books, music stand, violin. The table was set for me. Grandmother sat down in the corner. I ate. We didn't speak. The door was locked. We were alone. For lunch I had cold gefilte fish with horseradish (a dish that could make one take up Judaism), a rich tasty soup, meat fried with onions, salad, compote, coffee, cake, and apples. I ate all of it. I was a dreamer, it's true, but I had a big appetite. Grandmother cleared the table. The room became tidy. Stunted flowers sat on the windowsill. The only living things Grandmother loved were her son, her grandson, her dog, Mimka, and flowers. Mimka also came over, curled up on the sofa, and immediately fell asleep. She was a terrible sleepyhead, but a grand dog, sweet, reasonable, small and lovely. Mimka was a pug. She had light-colored fur. In her old age she didn't grow fat and flabby but remained slim and trim. She lived with us for a long time, from cradle to grave, the whole span of her fifteen dog years, and she loved us, obviously, and loved our stern and utterly merciless grandmother most of all. I will save the story of their silent and secretive friendship for another time. It's a very good story, touching and tender.

And so there were three of us—me, Grandmother, and Mimi. Mimi was sleeping. Grandmother was feeling kind, sitting in the corner in her good silk dress, and I was supposed to study. This was a difficult day for me. I had six periods at the gymnasium, and now I was waiting for Mr. Sorokin, the music teacher, and for Mr. L., the Hebrew teacher, who was supposed to come for a makeup lesson, and later perhaps Peysson, the French teacher, and I had to do homework as well. I could deal with L., we were old friends, but music, scales—what misery! First, I began my homework. I spread out my notebooks and began to solve problems with great concentration. Grandmother did not interrupt me, God forbid. She was so tense, so full of reverence for my work, that her face looked dumbstruck. She could not tear her round translucent yellow eyes away from me. Whenever I turned a page—they slowly followed the movement of my hand. Anybody else would have been uncomfortable under the relentless scrutiny of her fixed gaze, but I was used to it.

Then Grandmother would listen to me go over my lessons. It should be said that she spoke Russian badly, mangling the words in her own special way, mixing up Russian with Polish and Yiddish. She couldn't read Russian, obviously, and would hold a book upside down. But that didn't get in the way of me reciting the entire lesson to her from beginning to end. Grandmother would listen, not understanding a thing, but the music of the words sounded sweet to her, she was in awe of learning, she believed me, believed in me and wanted me to become a *bogatyr*—a Russian epic hero—which is what she called a *bogatyi* or wealthy man. I finished the homework and turned to my reading—namely, Turgenev's *First Love*. I liked everything about it, the clear words, the descriptions, the dialogue, and I was strangely excited by the scene in which Vladimir's father strikes Zinaida across the cheek with his whip. I heard the swish of the whip, its supple leather suddenly, painfully, and sharply digging into my flesh. I was gripped by an inexplicable excitement. I had to stop reading and started pacing the room. But Grandmother continued to sit motionless, and even the hot, stupefying air did not stir and surely would not dare to interrupt me while I was studying. The room kept getting hotter. Mimka started snoring. But before that, there had been silence, a ghostly silence—I hadn't heard a sound. Everything seemed extraordinary at that moment, and I wanted to run away and never come back. The darkening room, Grandmother's yellow eyes, her figure wrapped in a shawl, silent and hunched up in the corner, the heat, the closed door, and the crack of the whip, its penetrating swish—only now do I understand how strange this was, how much it meant to me. My agitation was interrupted by the doorbell. It was Sorokin. I hated him right then, hated those scales, all that incomprehensible, pointless, squawking music. I must admit that Sorokin himself was a splendid fellow, with cropped black hair, large red hands, and beautiful full lips. That day he was supposed to work a whole hour under Grandmother's watchful eye, and, what's more, he had to put everything into it. None of this earned him any recognition. His every movement was observed by my grandmother's cold, tenacious eyes—the eyes of a stranger that remained indifferent to him. Outsiders were of no interest to Grandmother. She required that they fulfill their duties with respect to us and that was all. We began our lesson. I wasn't afraid of Grandmother, but for a whole hour I had to endure poor Sorokin's excessive devotions. He felt very out of place in this remote room, with its peacefully sleeping dog and the hostile old woman eyeing him coldly. At last he took his leave. Grandmother, full of indifference, offered him her tough, large, wrinkled hand without even making the slightest movement with it. He bumped into a chair as he left.

I survived the next hour as well—Mr. L.'s lesson—counting the minutes until the door closed behind him.

Evening came. Faraway specks of gold were lit in the sky. The deep enclosure of our courtyard was blinded by moonlight. At the neighbors' a woman's voice began to sing, "Why do I love so madly?" My folks had gone to the theater. I grew sad. I was tired. I had read so much, studied so much, seen so much. Grandmother lit the lamp. Her room was suddenly still; the dark, heavy furniture glowed softly. Mimi woke up, walked around the other rooms, came back, and waited for dinner. The maid brought in the samovar. Grandmother loved to drink tea. A piece of gingerbread had been saved for me. We drank tea, a lot of it. Sweat began to glisten in the deeply etched seams of her face. "Sleepy?" she asked. "No," I replied. So we started talking. And once again I listened to Grandmother's stories. Many years ago, there was a Jew who kept a tavern. He was poor, married, burdened with children, and he sold unlicensed vodka. The inspector kept coming over and giving him a hard time. It became impossible for him to make a living. He went to the tsaddik and said, "Rabbi, this inspector is a plague upon my very life. Beseech God on my behalf." "Go in peace," the tsaddik said to him. "The inspector will calm down." The Jew left. At the front steps of his tavern he found the inspector. There he was, lying dead with his face all purple and swollen.

Grandmother fell silent. The samovar hummed. The neighbor kept singing. The moon was blinding. Mimi wagged her tail. She was hungry.

"In the old days, people believed," said Grandmother. "Life in this world was simpler. When I was a girl, the Poles rebelled. A Polish count had his estate not far from us. The tsar himself used to visit him. They used to make merry there for seven days straight. At night I would run to the count's palace to look in the brightly lit windows. The count had a daughter and the finest pearls in the world. Then the uprising came. Soldiers came and dragged him into the square. "All of us were standing around crying. The soldiers had dug a hole in the ground. They wanted to blindfold the old man. 'Not necessary,' he said and stood before the soldiers and gave the order, 'Fire!' The count was a tall man, with gray hair. The muzhiks loved him. As they began to bury him, a courier charged into the square. He was carrying a pardon from the tsar."

The samovar was going out. Grandmother drank up the last, already cold, glass of tea, sucking on a piece of sugar in her toothless mouth.

"Your grandfather," she started again, "he knew lots of stories, but he didn't believe in anything, only believed in people. He gave all his money to his friends, but when he came to them, they threw him down the stairs, and he became touched in the head."

And now Grandmother tells me stories about my grandfather, a tall man, sarcastic, passionate, and a despot. He played the violin, wrote essays at night, and knew all languages. He was ruled by an inextinguishable thirst for knowledge and for life. A general's daughter had fallen in love with their eldest son, and he wandered around a lot, played cards, and died in Canada when he was thirty-seven. Grandmother had only one son left, and me. All is in the past. The day wanes toward evening, and slowly death draws near. Grandmother stops speaking, lowers her head, and weeps.

"Study!" she suddenly erupts, "study, and you will have everything—wealth and glory. You must know everything. Everyone will fall and grovel before you. Everyone should envy you. Do not believe people. Do not have friends. Do not give them money. Do not give them your heart."

Grandmother doesn't say anything else. It's quiet. Grandmother ponders the years and sorrows gone by, ponders my destiny, and her solemn covenant presses firmly—and forevermore—upon my weak little shoulders. In a dark corner the cast iron stove glows and smolders. It's stifling, I can't breathe, I need fresh air, have to break free, but I don't even have the strength to lift my head.

There's a crash of dishes in the kitchen. Grandmother goes over there. We were about to have supper. Soon I hear her wrathful and metallic voice. She is yelling at the maid. I feel awkward and hurt. After all, only a second ago she had been full of such peace and sadness. The maid replies scornfully. And then I hear an unbearably shrill voice full of uncontrollable fury: "Get out of here, you wench! I am the mistress here. You are destroying my things. Out!" I can't bear these deafening metallic outbursts. I can see Grandmother through the open door. Her face is tense, her pitiless lips twitching slightly, her throat swollen, bloated. The maid puts up some kind of protest. "Get out," Grandmother said. It was quiet again. The maid cowered and crept out of the room, afraid to offend the silence.

We don't speak at supper. We eat well, heartily, taking our time.

Grandmother's translucent eyes are motionless, and I do not know what they are staring at. After supper she . . . [break in the text]

I see nothing more because I am fast asleep, slumbering like a babe beneath seven seals in my grandmother's stuffy room.

Saratov, November 12, 1915 (published 1965)

The Story of My Dovecot

TO M. GORKY

As a child I really wanted to have a dovecot. Never in all my life have I desired a thing more. But not till I was nine did Father promise the money to buy the wood to make one and three pairs of pigeons to stock it. This was in 1904. I was studying for the entrance exams to the preparatory class of the Nikolaev gymnasium. My family lived in the town of Nikolaev, in Kherson Province. This province no longer exists, our town having been incorporated into the Odessa Region.

I was only nine, and I was scared of the exams. Now, after two decades, it's very difficult to express how horribly scared I was. In both subjects, Russian language and arithmetic, I couldn't afford to get less than 5's. At our school the quota was stiff: a mere five percent. Out of forty boys only two Jews could get into the preparatory class. The teachers used to put trick questions to these boys; no one except us was asked such intricate questions. So when Father promised to buy the pigeons, he demanded a 5-plus in both subjects. He utterly tormented me, threw me into an endless waking dream, a long despondent childish stupor, and I went to the exam deep in this stupor and nevertheless did better than everybody else.

I had a knack for book learning. Though the teachers tried their tricks, they could not rob me of my clever mind and insatiable memory. I had a knack for book learning and got top marks in both subjects. But then everything went wrong. Khariton Ephrussi, the corn dealer who exported wheat to Marseille, slipped someone a five-hundred-ruble bribe. My grade was changed from a 5 to a 5-minus, and little Ephrussi got my place. This really killed my father. From the time I was six he had been cramming me with every possible subject. The matter of the minus drove him to despair. He wanted to beat up Ephrussi, or at least bribe two teamsters to beat up Ephrussi, but Mother talked him out of it, and I started studying for the second exam the following year, the one for the lowest class. Behind my back my family got the teacher to take me in one year through the preparatory and first year courses at the same time, and since we were thoroughly desperate, I memorized three whole books by heart. These were Smirnovsky's *Russian Grammar*, Yevtushevsky's *Problems*, and Putsykovich's *Manual of Early Russian History*. Children no longer use these books, but I learned them by heart, line by line, and the following year in the Russian language exam the teacher, Karavaev, gave me an unrivaled 5-plus. Our little town would long whisper of my extraordinary success, and my father was so pathetically proud of it that I couldn't bear to think about his unstable and erratic life, and about how helplessly susceptible he was to its every twist and turn, each of which would cause him either to exult or to wilt.

The teacher, Karavaev, was better than a father to me. Karavaev was a red-faced, irritable fellow, a product of Moscow University. He was hardly more than thirty. Crimson glowed in his manly cheeks as it does in the cheeks of peasant children who do no heavy labor, an inoffensive wart sat perched on one cheek, and from it sprouted a tuft of ash-colored cat's whiskers. At the exam, besides Karavaev, there was the assistant curator Pyatnitsky, who was reckoned an important figure in the gymnasium and throughout the province. The assistant curator asked me about Peter the Great, and I experienced a feeling of total oblivion, the sensation that the end, the abyss, was near, an arid abyss lined with ecstasy and despair.

Of Peter the Great I knew things by heart from Putsykovich's book and Pushkin's verses. I recited these verses, sobbing, the florid human faces suddenly streaming and jumbling in my eyes, like cards from a new deck. They shuffled at the bottom of my eyes, and meanwhile, shivering, straightening, galloping headlong, I was shouting Pushkin's stanzas at the top of my voice. On and on I shouted them, and no one interrupted my squealing flood of words. Through crimson blindness, through total freedom, I saw only Pyatnitsky's old face bent toward me with its silver-touched beard. He didn't interrupt me and merely whispered to Karavaev, who was rejoicing for my sake and Pushkin's.

"What a nation," said the old man. "Your little Yids, there's a devil in them."

And when at last I could shout no more, he said:

"Very well, run along, my little friend."

I went out from the classroom into the corridor, and there, leaning against an unpainted wall, I began to awaken from the convulsions of my exhausted dreams. Russian boys were playing around me, the school bell hung not far away under the staff staircase, the caretaker was dozing on a chair with a broken seat. I looked at the caretaker and gradually woke up. Boys were creeping toward me from all sides. They wanted to give me a jab, or perhaps just wanted to play, but Pyatnitsky suddenly loomed in the corridor. As he passed me, he halted for a moment, the frock coat flowing down his back in a slow, arduous wave. I saw perturbation in that large, fleshy, lordly back and moved near the old man.

"Children," he said to the students, "don't touch this boy," and he laid a fat, gentle hand on my shoulder.

"My little friend," he said, turning to me, "tell your father that you are admitted to the first grade."

An opulent star flashed on his chest, medals jingled on his lapel, his great black uniformed body started to move away on unbowed legs. Hemmed in by the shadowy walls, moving between them as a barge moves through a deep canal, it disappeared in the doorway of the headmaster's study. The little serving man took in a tray of tea, clinking solemnly, and I ran home to the shop.

In our shop, a peasant customer, tortured by doubt, sat scratching himself. My father saw me and abandoned the peasant, and without a moment's hesitation believed everything I recounted to him. He told the assistant to start closing up and dashed out into Cathedral Street to buy me a school cap with a badge on it. My poor mother could barely tear me away from this crazy person. She was pale at the moment and was experiencing destiny. She kept caressing me and pushing me away in horror. She said there was always a notice in the paper about those who had been admitted to the school and that God would punish us and people would laugh at us if we bought a uniform too soon. My mother was pale, she was experiencing destiny in my eyes and looked at me with bitter compassion, as you would at a cripple, because she alone knew how unlucky our family was.

All the men in our clan tended to trust people and were quick to ill-considered actions, we had no luck in anything. My grandfather had been a rabbi somewhere in Belaya Tserkov. He had been thrown out for sacrilege and lived noisily and meagerly for another forty years, teaching foreign languages, and began to lose his mind in the eightieth year of his life. My uncle Lev, my father's brother, had studied at the Volozhin Yeshiva; in 1892 he ran away to avoid military service, eloping with the daughter of a quartermaster in the Kiev military district. Uncle Lev took this woman to California, to Los Angeles, abandoned her there, and died in a flophouse among Negroes and Malays. After his death, the American police sent us an inheritance from Los Angeles, a large trunk bound with brown iron hoops. In this trunk there were dumbbells, locks of women's hair, Uncle's tallis, horsewhips with gilt tips, herbal tea in lacquered boxes trimmed with cheap pearls. Of all the family there remained only crazy Uncle Simon, who lived in Odessa, my father, and I. But my father trusted people and would offend them with the raptures of first love; people could not forgive him for this and would cheat him. So my father believed that his life was guided by an evil fate, an inexplicable being that pursued him and that was in every respect unlike him. And so, I was all my mother had left in our entire family. Like all Jews, I was short, feeble, and suffered headaches from studying. All this my mother saw, my mother, who had never been blinded by her husband's pauper pride, by his incomprehensible belief that our ancient family would at some point become stronger and grander than everyone else in the world. She expected no success for us, was scared of buying a school jacket too soon, and the only thing she allowed was for me to get my picture taken at the photographer's for a large portrait.

On September 20, 1905, a list of those admitted into first grade was hung up at the school. In the list my name figured too. All our relatives kept going to look at this paper, and even Grandfather Shoyl, my great-uncle, went along. I loved that boastful old man, for he sold fish at the market. His fat hands were moist, covered with fish scales, and reeked of worlds that were cold and beautiful. Shoyl also differed from ordinary folk in the lying stories he used to tell about the Polish Uprising of 1861. Years ago Shoyl had been a tavern keeper at Skvira. He had seen the soldiers of Nicholas I shooting Count Godlevski and other Polish insurgents. But perhaps he hadn't. Now I know that Shoyl was just an old ignoramus and a naive liar, but his tall tales are not forgotten—they were good stories. Well, now, even silly old Shoyl went along to the gymnasium to read the list with my name on it, and that evening, not afraid of anyone, not fearful that nobody in the world liked him, he pranced and stomped at our meager ball.

My father put on the ball to celebrate my success and invited all his comrades—grain dealers, real estate brokers, and traveling salesmen who sold agricultural machinery in our parts. These salesmen would sell a machine to anyone. Peasants and landowners feared them—you couldn't break loose without buying something or other. Of all Jews, salesmen are the most worldly and the most fun. At our party they sang Hasidic songs consisting of only three words but which took an awfully long time to sing, songs performed with endless comical intonations. The beauty of these intonations may be recognized only by those who have had the good fortune to spend Passover with Hasidim or who have visited their noisy Volhynian synagogues. Besides the salesmen, old Lieberman, who had taught me the Torah and ancient Hebrew, honored us with his presence. In our circle he was known as Monsieur Lieberman. He drank more Bessarabian wine than he should have, the ends of his traditional silk tassels poked out of his red vest, and in ancient Hebrew he made a toast in my honor. In this toast the old man congratulated my parents and said that I had defeated all my foes at the examination, I had defeated the Russian boys with their fat cheeks, as well as the sons of our own vulgar rich. So, too, in ancient times David, the Judean king, had defeated Goliath, and just as I had triumphed over Goliath, so, too, would our indomitable people by the strength of their intellect conquer the foes who had encircled us and were after our blood. Monsieur Lieberman started to weep as he said this, drank more wine as he wept, and shouted, "Vivat!" The guests formed a circle and danced an old-fashioned quadrille with him in the middle, like at a wedding in a Jewish shtetl. Everyone was happy at our ball—even mother had a drop of wine, though vodka she did not like nor did she understand how anyone else could; because of this she considered all Russians crazy and couldn't imagine how women could live with Russian husbands.

But our happy days came later. For mother they came when, of a morning, before I set off for school, she got accustomed to the happiness of preparing sandwiches for me before school and when she went shopping for my presents—a pencil case, money box, satchel, new books in cardboard bindings, and notebooks in glossy covers. No one in the world has a stronger feeling for new things than children. Children tremble at this smell like a dog when it picks up the scent of a hare, and they experience that madness which later, when we become grown-ups, is called inspiration. And this pure childish feeling of ownership, for that subtly moist and cool smell of new things, my mother felt it too. It took us a month to get used to the pencil box, to the unforgettable morning twilight when I drank my tea on the corner of the large, brightly lit table and packed my books in my satchel; it took us a month to get used to our happy life, and it was only after the first half term that I remembered the pigeons.

I had everything prepared for them—a ruble fifty and a dovecot made from a crate by Grandpa Shoyl. The dovecot was painted brown. It had nests for twelve pairs of pigeons, different kinds of planks on the roof, and a special grate I had come up with to lure new birds more easily. Everything was ready. On Sunday, October 20, I set out for Hunters Square, but along the way there were unexpected obstacles.

The story I am recounting—that is, my admission to first grade at the gymnasium—took place in the autumn of 1905. Tsar Nicholas was granting a constitution to the Russian people; orators in shabby coats were clambering onto pedestals in front of the town hall and giving speeches before the crowd. At night shots had been heard in the streets, and Mother didn't let me go to Hunters Square. From early morning on October 20 the neighborhood boys were flying a kite right by the police station, and our water carrier, his duties forgotten, was walking around with pomade in his hair, red in the face. Then we saw the baker Kalistov's sons drag a leather vaulting horse out into the street and start doing gymnastics in the middle of the thoroughfare. No one interfered with them, the policeman Semernikov even kept daring them to jump higher. Semernikov was girt with a homemade silk belt, and his boots that day had been polished bright as they had never been polished before. The policeman, not wearing his uniform, frightened my mother most of all; because of him she didn't let me outside, but I sneaked out the back and ran to Hunters, which was behind our train station.

At Hunters, sitting in his customary place, was Ivan Nikodimych, the pigeon fancier. Besides the pigeons, he had rabbits for sale, too, and a peacock. The peacock, spreading his tail, sat on a perch moving a dispassionate head from side to side. A twine cord was tied to his foot, the other end of the cord lay pinched beneath Ivan Nikodimych's wicker chair. Right away I bought from the old man a pair of cherry-colored pigeons with luxuriant tousled tails and a pair of crowned pigeons, and hid them in a sack against my breast. After these purchases I had only forty kopecks left, but for this price the old man was not prepared to let me have a male and female pigeon of the Kryukov breed. What I loved about Kryukov pigeons was their beaks—short, grainy, and amicable. Forty kopecks was the right price, but the fancier insisted on haggling, averting from me a yellow face scorched by the unsociable passions of bird catchers. As business wound down, seeing that there were no other customers, Ivan Nikodimych called me over. Everything went my way, and everything went badly.

Around noon, or perhaps a bit later, a man in felt boots passed across the square. He stepped lightly on swollen feet, and lively eyes glittered in his worn-out face.

"Ivan Nikodimych," he said, as he passed the bird fancier, "pack up your gear. Back in town the Jerusalem gentry are being served a constitution. On Fish Street the Babels' old grandpa got served to death."

He said this and stepped lightly between the cages like a barefoot plowman between fields.

"What for," murmured Ivan Nikodimych in his wake. "For what!" he cried more sternly, collecting his rabbits and his peacock, and shoved the Kryukov pigeons at me for forty kopecks. I hid them against my bosom and watched as people ran away from Hunters Square. The peacock on Ivan Nikodimych's shoulder was the last to depart. It sat there like the sun in a damp autumn sky. It sat as July sits on a pink riverbank, a scorching July in the long cool grass. I watched the old man go with his cobbler's bench and the precious cages wrapped in colorful rags. No one was left in the market, and not far off shots thundered. Then I ran to the station, cut across the square, which looked to me like it had been flipped upside down, and flew down a deserted lane of trampled yellow earth. At the end of the lane, in an armchair on little wheels, sat the legless Makarenko, who rode about town in his chair selling cigarettes from a tray. The boys from our street used to buy cigarettes from him, children loved him; I dashed toward him down the lane.

"Makarenko," I gasped, panting from my run, and stroked the legless one's shoulder, "you haven't seen Shoyl, have you?"

The cripple did not reply; his coarse face, composed of red fat, fists, iron, was transfused with light. He fidgeted anxiously on his chair, while his wife, Katyusha, turning her padded rear, sorted through things scattered on the ground.

"How many did you count?" asked the legless man, shifting his bulk away from the woman, as though he knew her answer would be unbearable.

"Fourteen pairs of gaiters," said Katyusha, still bending over, "six blanket cases, now I'm counting the bonnets . . ."

"Bonnets," cried Makarenko, choking down a sob. "Looks like God's found me out, Katerina, looks like I must answer for all . . . People are carting off whole rolls of cloth, people have everything that people ought to have, but we get bonnets . . ."

And indeed a woman, her beautiful face ablaze, ran past us down the lane. She clutched a stack of fezzes in one arm and a roll of fabric in the other. She was calling in a joyfully desperate voice for her children who had strayed; a silk dress and a blue blouse dragged behind her as she flew past, and she didn't listen to Makarenko, who was rolling his chair in pursuit of her. The legless man couldn't catch up, his wheels clattering as he turned the handles for all he was worth.

"Little lady," he cried in a deafening voice, "where did you get that striped stuff, little lady?"

But the woman with the fluttering dress was already gone. At the corner a rickety cart lurched in her path. A peasant lad rode standing in the cart.

"Where are people going?" asked the lad, raising a red rein above the nags jerking in their collars.

"Everybody's on Cathedral Street," said Makarenko pleadingly, "everybody's there, dear fellow; anything you find, bring everything to me, I buy everything."

The lad wasted no time when he heard about Cathedral Street. He leaned forward and lashed his piebald nags. The horses bounded like young calves on their dirty rumps and galloped away. The yellow lane was once more yellow and deserted. The legless man then turned his extinguished eyes upon me.

"God's found me out, I reckon," he said lifelessly. "Look upon me, I'm a Son of Man, I reckon . . ."

And Makarenko stretched a hand spotted with leprosy toward me.

"What's that you've got in the feed bag?" he demanded, and took the sack that had been warming my heart.

With his fat hand the cripple fumbled among the startails and took out a cherry-colored hen. Tucking back its feet, the bird lay still in his palm.

"Pigeons," said Makarenko, and came even closer, scraping his wheels. "Pigeons," he repeated, like an inexorable echo, and struck me on the cheek.

He swung and struck me with the palm clutching the bird, Katyusha's padded rear turned around in my pupils, and I fell to the ground in my new overcoat.

"Their seed must be wiped out," Katyusha then said, straightening up over the bonnets. "I can't stand their seed and their stinking men . . ."

She said more about our seed, but I couldn't hear any more. I lay on the ground, and the innards of the crushed bird trickled from my temple. They flowed down my cheek, wriggling, splashing and blinding me. The pigeon's tender gut slid down my forehead, and I closed my last unblinded eye so as not to see the world spreading out before me. This world was small and horrible. A little stone lay before my eyes, a little stone, chipped, like the face of an old woman with a large jaw, a piece of string lay not far away and a clump of feathers, still breathing. My world was small and horrible. I closed my eyes so as not to see it, and pressed myself into the ground that lay soothingly mute beneath me. This trampled earth in no way resembled our life, nothing like the worrying about exams in our life. Somewhere far away woe rode across it on a great steed, but the hoofbeats grew weaker, died away, and silence, the bitter silence that sometimes overwhelms children in their misfortune, suddenly erased the boundary between my body and this earth moving nowhere. The earth smelled of raw depths, graves, flowers. I heeded its smell and started crying without any fear whatsoever. I walked along an unknown street cluttered with white boxes, walked in a garment of bloody feathers, alone between the pavements swept clean like on a Sunday, and wept so bitterly, fully, and happily as I never wept again in all my life. Bleached wires hummed above my head, a stray dog ran ahead of me, in a side lane a young muzhik in a vest was smashing a window frame in the house of Khariton Ephrussi. He was smashing it with a wooden mallet, striking out with his whole body, and, sighing, he smiled broadly, a kind smile, drunken, sweaty, full of spiritual power. The whole street was filled with a splitting, a snapping, a song of flying wood. The muzhik swung out with his mallet as if he lived to bend, to sweat, to shout bizarre words in some unknown, non-Russian language. He shouted the words and sang, his blue eyes bursting out of him, until in the street there appeared a procession with the cross moving from the town hall. Old men with dyed beards bore aloft the portrait of the well-groomed tsar, banners with graveyard saints swayed above the procession, inflamed old women surged in front. Seeing the procession, the muzhik in the vest pressed his mallet to his chest and dashed off in pursuit of the banners, while I, waiting till it passed, found my way to our house. It was empty. Its white doors were open, the grass by the dovecot trampled down. Only Kuzma was still in the yard. Kuzma the caretaker was sitting in the shed taking care of dead Shoyl.

"The wind bears you like a bad splinter," said the old man when he saw me. "You ran off ages ago . . . And here—see how they whacked our grandpa . . ."

Kuzma wheezed, turned away, and started pulling a pike perch out of a rent in Grandpa's pants. There were two of them stuck into Grandpa: one in his pants, the other in his mouth, and though Grandpa was dead, one perch was still alive and struggling.

"They whacked our grandfather, nobody else," said Kuzma, tossing the perch to the cat. "He sent them and their mothers packing all good and proper, damned their mothers to the very end, grand he was . . . Maybe you could fetch a couple of five-kopeck coins to put on his eyes."

But back then, at ten years of age, I didn't know what need the dead had of five-kopeck coins.

"Kuzma," I said, whispering, "save us . . ."

And I went over to the caretaker, hugged his crooked old back with the one shoulder sticking up, and behind that back I saw Grandfather. Shoyl lay in the sawdust with his chest caved in, his beard pulled up, battered shoes on his bare feet. His legs, thrown wide apart, were dirty, lilac-colored, dead. Kuzma fussed over them, he tied his jaw together and kept trying to see what else he could do for the deceased. He fussed as though someone had brought home a new dress, and cooled down only after he had combed the dead man's beard.

"Sent them and their mothers packing, every one of them," he said, smiling, and looked over the corpse with love. "Even if it was Tatars crossed his path he'd have sent them packing, but Russians came, and their women with them, Russian dames. Russian dames don't like to forgive, I know Russian dames . . ."

The caretaker spread some more sawdust beneath the body, threw off his carpenter's apron, and took me by my hand.

"Let's go to Father," he mumbled, squeezing me tighter. "Your father's been searching for you since morning, sure as fate you was dead."

And so with Kuzma I went to the home of the tax inspector, where my parents had hidden, escaping the pogrom.

(published 1925)

First Love

When I was ten years old, I fell in love with a woman by the name of Galina Apollonovna. Rubtsov was her last name. Her husband, an officer, went off to the Japanese War and returned in October of 1905. He brought a lot of trunks back with him. These trunks contained Chinese objects: screens, collectible weapons, all together weighing thirty poods. Kuzma told us that Rubtsov had bought all these things with money he had accumulated while serving as a chief engineer in the Manchurian Army. Kuzma wasn't the only one who said so. It was hard for people not to gossip about the Rubtsovs, for the Rubtsovs were happy. Their house adjoined our place, and their glass terrace went onto our property, but Father didn't make a fuss about it. Rubtsov's old man was a tax inspector and had a reputation in our town for being fair, and he had Jewish friends. And when the officer, the old man's son, returned from the war, all of us could see how well he and his wife got on together. Galina Apollonovna would hold her husband's hand all day long. She wouldn't take her eyes off him, since she hadn't seen her husband in a year and a half, but I was terrified of her gaze, would turn away and tremble. In her jubilant eyes I perceived that astonishing, shameful life led by every person on the planet; I longed to fall into a strange sleep so I could forget about this life that surpassed my wildest dreams. Galina Apollonovna would sometimes glide through her house with her braid undone, wearing red shoes and a Chinese robe. Beneath the lace of her low-cut slip one could see the descent and commencement of her white swollen, pushed-down breasts, while her robe had dragons, birds, tree hollows embroidered in pink silk.

All day long she sauntered about with a dazed smile on her moist lips, bumping into the unpacked trunks, the exercise ladders strewn about the floor. Galina would bruise herself doing this, she would then pull her robe above her knee, and say to her husband:

"Kiss baby better . . ."

And the officer would bend his long legs in their dragoon breeches, spurs, tight shiny boots, would get on the dirty floor, smile, crawl on his knees, and kiss the bruised spot, the spot right at the swollen crease from the garter.

I saw those kisses from my window. They made me suffer. I was tormented by unbridled fantasies, but there's no point talking about them, because the love and the jealousy of ten-year-old boys are exactly like the love and jealousy of grown men, only in children these feelings are more secretive, exalted, ardent. For two weeks I stopped going near the window and avoided Galina, until a certain occasion brought us together. That occasion was the pogrom against the Jews that broke out in 1905 in Nikolaev and other towns in the Jewish Pale of Settlement. A mob of hired murderers plundered my father's store and killed Grandpa Shoyl. All this happened when I was out on that sad morning I had bought pigeons from Ivan Nikodimych the fancier. For five of my ten years I had dreamed with my whole soul about pigeons. But when I finally bought them, Makarenko the cripple smashed them against the side of my head. Then Kuzma took me to the Rubtsovs'. A cross had been chalked on the Rubtsovs' gate, nobody touched them, they hid my parents in their house. Kuzma brought me to the glass terrace. My mother sat there with Galina in the green rotunda.

"Now we must wash," Galina said. "We must wash up, my little rabbi. Our face is all covered with feathers, and the feathers are all bloody."

She put her arms around me and led me down a hallway full of pungent odors. My head leaned on Galina's hip, her hip moved and breathed. We reached the kitchen, and Mrs. Rubtsov put my head under the tap. A goose was frying on the tiled stove, glowing pots and pans hung on the walls, and next to the dishes, in the cook's corner, hung Tsar Nicholas decorated with paper flowers. Galina washed what was left of the pigeon caked on my cheeks.

"You'll make a nice bridegroom, my pretty boy," she said, kissing me on the mouth with her full lips, and quickly looked around.

"Little rabbi," she suddenly whispered, "see, your pop is getting into trouble, walking the streets all day long for no good reason—go bring him home."

And through the window I saw the empty street and an enormous sky above, and my redheaded father walking on the road. He was walking without his hat, the soft red hair on his head standing on end, his paper shirtfront askew and attached somehow but on the wrong button. Vlasov, a drunken workman dressed in a soldier's tattered rags, was stubbornly following him.

"Look here," he said in a hoarse, passionate voice and laid two tender hands on my father, "we don't need freedom for the Yids to be free to do business . . . You oughta shine a little light upon the life of the working man, upon his sweat and tears, his awful burden . . . That's what you oughta do, my friend, know what I'm saying?"

The worker was begging my father for something, grabbing at his arm. Streaks of pure drunken inspiration on his face alternated with dejection and drowsiness.

"We oughta live like the Molokans," he mumbled and swayed on his buckling legs. "We oughta live like the Molokans, only without their God, without that Old Believer God of theirs—only the Jews get anything out of him, nobody else . . ."

And Vlasov yelled in wild desperation about the God of the Old Believers who took pity only on the Jews. Vlasov wailed, stumbled, and chased after his unknown God, but just then a Cossack patrol cut him off. An officer with stripes on his trousers and a silver ceremonial belt rode in front of the patrol, a tall peaked cap perched on his head. The officer rode slowly and didn't look left or right. He rode as though through a gorge, where you can only look straight ahead.

"Captain," my father whispered when the Cossacks came alongside him, "Captain," my father said, grasping his head in his hands and kneeling in the mud.

"Do what I can," the officer replied, still looking straight ahead and raising his hand in its lemon-yellow suede glove to his visor.

Right in front of them, at the corner of Fish Street, the mob was looting and smashing up our store, throwing out into the street crates filled with nails, equipment, and the new portrait of me in my school uniform.

"Look," my father said, still on his knees, "they are destroying everything dear to me, Captain—what for?"

"Yessir," the officer mumbled, put his lemon glove to his cap, and touched the reins, but the horse did not move. My father crawled before the horse on his knees, rubbing up against its short, kindly, slightly disheveled legs and its thick, patient, hairy muzzle.

"Yessir," said the captain once again, tugged at the reins, and rode off, the Cossacks following. They sat dispassionately in their tall saddles, they rode through their imaginary gorge and disappeared as they turned onto Cathedral Street.

Then Galina again nudged me to the window.

"Tell your pop to come home," she said, "he's had nothing to eat since morning."

So I leaned out the window.

"Papa," I said.

My father turned when he heard my voice.

"My sonny boy," he stuttered with immeasurable tenderness and trembled out of love for me.

And together he and I went onto the Rubtsovs' terrace, where my mother lay in the green rotunda. Dumbbells and gym equipment were strewn near her bed.

"A few lousy coins," my mother said when she saw us. "Human life, the children, our unhappy happiness—you gave it all up for that . . . Lousy coins," she shouted in a deep-throated croak that didn't sound like her real voice, jerked on the bed, and fell silent.

And then in the silence you could hear my hiccups. I was standing by the wall with my cap pulled down over my face and couldn't stop hiccupping.

"Shame on you, pretty boy." Galina smiled with that disdainful smile of hers and flicked me with her stiff robe. She went to the window in her red shoes and began to hang Chinese curtains on the outlandish window eaves. Her bare arms were drowning in silk, and the living braid of her hair stirred over her hip, and I stared at her in rapture.

I was a nervous, bookish little boy, and I looked at her as at a distant stage flooded in limelight. And then I imagined that I was Miron, son of the coal man who sold on our corner. I imagined myself to be a member of the Jewish Self-Defense, and there I was, just like Miron, wearing torn shoes tied together with string. On my shoulder a lousy rifle hangs by a green cord, I am kneeling by a wooden fence shooting back at the killers. Behind my fence there's an empty lot, heaped with dusty coal, the lousy rifle shoots badly, the murderers with their beards and white teeth keep coming closer; I experience the proud sensation of impending death, and high up above, in the deep blue of the world, I see Galina. I see an embrasure cut through the wall of a gigantic house built of myriad bricks. This carmine house looms over the alley where the gray earth had been poorly flattened, in the topmost embrasure stands Galina, flush with unforgiving winter glee, like a rich girl at the skating rink. She smiles disdainfully from her unattainable window; her husband, the half-dressed officer, stands behind her kissing her neck . . .

I imagined all this as I tried to relieve my hiccups so that I might love Mrs. Rubtsov all the more bitterly, ardently, hopelessly—maybe because, for a ten-year-old, the full measure of sorrow is small. Foolish dreams helped me forget the death of the pigeons and Shoyl's death, and I might have forgotten about those murders had Kuzma not come to the terrace with that awful Jew, Aba.

It was dusk when they came. On the terrace a flimsy lamp was burning, bent sideways somehow, a blinking little lamp, my fitful fellow traveler in misery.

"I got Grandpa together," Kuzma said as he entered. "He looks real good all laid out now—and here I've brought the caretaker along, he can say something over the old man."

Kuzma pointed to the bored shammes, Aba.

"Let him wail awhile," the caretaker pronounced amiably. "Stuff his gut and he'll pester God all night long . . ."

He was standing in the doorway—Kuzma—with his kindly beat-up nose twisted in all directions, and he wanted to tell us with as much heart as possible how he had tied the dead man's jaw together, but my father interrupted old Kuzma.

"Please, Reb Aba," my father said, "I ask that you pray over the deceased, I will pay you . . ."

"And I am afraid you won't pay," Aba replied in a tedious voice, and put his bearded, squeamish face on the tablecloth. "I am afraid you'll take my earnings and go off with it to Argentina, to Buenos Aires, and open a wholesale business there with my earnings . . . A wholesale business," said Aba, chomping his scornful lips and dragging the newspaper *Son of the Fatherland* across the table to him. There was something in the paper about the tsar's manifesto of October 17 and about freedom.

". . . Citizens of free Russia," Aba spelled out, chewing on a mouthful of his beard, "citizens of free Russia, greetings on this blessed Easter Sunday . . ."

The old shammes held the swaying paper sideways: he read in a somnolent singsong, laying stress on the most unexpected syllables in the Russian words unfamiliar to him. Aba's pronunciation resembled the obscure speech of a Negro come to a Russian port from his native land. It made even my mother laugh.

"I am committing a sin," she cried, leaning out from her rotunda. "I'm laughing, Aba . . . Better you should tell me how you're doing and how the family's doing."

"Ask me about something else," Aba growled, without releasing his beard from his teeth, and he went back to reading the paper.

"Ask him about something else," my father said, echoing Aba, and walked to the middle of the room. His eyes, smiling at us through tears, suddenly rolled in their sockets and focused on a point that no one could see.

"Oy, Shoyl," my father proclaimed in a flat, false, preparatory voice, "oy, Shoyl, my dear man . . ."

Father's face, shrouded in spasms, was torn apart with triumph, and he was preparing to scream, the way Jewish widows scream at funerals or old women in Morocco, old women who have come to grief. We could see he was about to scream horribly, but mother alerted us.

"Manus," she cried, her hair instantly disheveled, and she started tearing at her husband's breast. "Look how badly our boy is doing, why can't you hear how he's hiccupping, why, Manus?"

And Father became quiet. His failing eyes were ringed with tears.

"Rakhil," he said timidly, "I cannot convey to you, Rakhil, how sorry I am about Shoyl."

He went to the kitchen and came back with a glass of water.

"Drink, artiste," said Aba, coming over to me. "Drink this water, which will help you as incense helps the dead."

And it's true, the water didn't help me. I hiccupped even more. A growl ripped through my breast. A lump, pleasant to the touch, swelled on my throat. The lump breathed, expanded, spread across my gullet, and bulged out of my collar. My ragged breath gurgled inside. It gurgled like water boiling. And when, come nightfall, I was no longer the lop-eared lad I had been all my life, but a writhing ball, rolling in my own green vomit—then Mother wrapped herself in a shawl and, grown taller and shapelier, approached the petrified Galina.

"My dear Galina," said my mother in her strong, melodious voice, "look how we're disturbing you and dear Nadezhda Ivanovna and your whole family . . . I'm so ashamed of myself, dear Galina."

With burning cheeks, Mother pressed Galina toward the door, then she rushed to me and stuffed her shawl in my mouth to muffle my moans.

"Try to bear it, my son," she whispered, "try to bear it, my poor Babel, try, for Mother's sake."

But even if I could bear it, I wouldn't have tried, for I no longer felt any shame. I tossed on the bed, falling onto the floor, and I didn't take my eyes off Galina. The woman was shaking and squirming in terror—I growled in her face to prolong my power over her, and, as I growled in triumph and exhaustion, in the final exertions of love, I retched a river of green at her feet that came straight from the heart.

So began my illness. I was ten years old then. In the morning they took me to the doctor. The pogrom continued, but nobody touched us. The doctor, a fat man, found I had a nervous disorder.

"This disorder," he said, "occurs only among Jews, and among Jews affects only women."

Thus the doctor was surprised to find that I suffered from this strange disorder. He told us to go to Odessa as soon as possible to consult experts, and to wait there for the warm weather and sea bathing.

And that's what we did. A few days later I left with Mother for Odessa, to be with Grandpa Levi-Iztkhok and Uncle Simon. We left in the morning on the steamer, and already by noon the brownish waters of the Bug had given way to the heavy green swell of the sea. Life at crazy Grandpa Levi-Itzkhok's awaited me, and I bade farewell forever to Nikolaev, where ten years of my childhood had passed. And now, remembering those sad years, I find in them the beginning of the afflictions that torment me, and the causes of my untimely and terrible decline.

(published 1925)

Awakening

All the people in our circle—brokers, shopkeepers, clerks in banks and steamship offices—used to have their children taught music. Our fathers, seeing no way out for themselves, came up with a lottery. They established it upon the bones of these little individuals. Odessa was seized by this madness more so than other towns. And in fact, over several decades our town supplied the concert halls of the world with wunderkinds. From Odessa came Mischa Elman, Zimbalist, Gabrilowitsch—Jascha Heifetz got his start there.

When a boy turned four or five, his mother took this tiny, puny creature to Mr. Zagursky. Zagursky ran a factory of wunderkinds, a factory of Jewish dwarfs in lace collars and patent leather shoes. He hunted them out in the slums of the Moldavanka, in the foul-smelling courtyards of the Old Bazaar. Zagursky set the course, then the children were shipped off to Professor Auer in Petersburg. A mighty harmony dwelled in the souls of these stunted creatures with their swollen blue hands. They became renowned virtuosi. And so, my father decided to catch up with them. Though I was past the age limit for wunderkinds—I was already fourteen—I was sufficiently short and frail to pass as an eight-year-old. Therein lay all hope.

I was taken to Zagursky's. Out of respect for my grandfather, Mr. Zagursky agreed to take me for a ruble a lesson—a cheap price. My grandfather Levi-Itzkhok was the town laughingstock, its ornament. He used to roam the streets in a top hat and what was left of his boots and would dispel people's doubts in the most obscure matters. He would be asked what a Gobelin was, why the Jacobins betrayed Robespierre, how you made artificial silk, what a cesarean section was. My grandfather could answer these questions. Out of respect for his great learning and madness, Zagursky charged us only a ruble a lesson. And so he really went to work on me, dreading my grandfather, for with me there was nothing to work with. The sounds slithered from my fiddle like iron filings. The sounds cut into my very heart, but Father wouldn't let it be. At home there was talk only of Mischa Elman, exempted from military service by the tsar himself. Zimbalist, Father would have us know, had been presented to the king of England and had played at

Buckingham Palace; Gabrilowitsch's parents had bought two houses in St. Petersburg. Wunderkinds brought wealth to their parents. My father could have reconciled himself to poverty, but he could not do without fame.

"It's not possible," people dining at his expense would insinuate, "it's not possible that the grandson of such a grandfather . . ."

But I had other ideas. While I played my violin exercises, I would have books by Turgenev or Dumas on my music stand—and, as I sawed at the instrument, would devour page after page. By day, I would tell tall tales to the neighborhood boys, at night I would commit them to paper. Making things up was a hereditary occupation in our family. Levi-Itzkhok, who had become touched in the head in his advancing years, spent his whole life writing a tale titled "The Headless Man." I took after him.

Three times a week, lugging my violin case and music, I would drag myself to Zagursky's on Witte Street (formerly Dvoryanskaya). There, along the wall, Jewish girls full of fire and hysteria sat awaiting their turn. They pressed their violins against their weak knees, violins that surpassed the size of those who were to perform at Buckingham Palace.

The door to the sanctum would open. From Mr. Zagursky's study there would stagger bobble-headed, freckled children with necks thin as flower stems and an epileptic flush on their cheeks. The door would slam and swallow up the next dwarf. Behind the wall, with his bow tie, ginger curls, and spindly legs, the teacher strained and sang and conducted his charges. Director of a monstrous lottery, he populated the Moldavanka and the dark blind alleys of the Old Market with ghostly pizzicati and cantilenas. Later on, these strains would be burnished to a devilish brilliance by old Professor Auer.

There was nothing I could do in this sect. Though I was a dwarf just as they were, in the voice of my forebears I discerned inspiration of another sort.

My first step came with difficulty. One day I left home laden like a beast of burden with the case, the violin, sheet music, and twelve rubles in cash— payment for a month's lessons. I was going along Nezhin Street, and to get to Zagursky's I should have turned onto Dvoryanskaya, but instead I went up Tiraspolskaya and found myself at the port. The allotted three hours flew by at Practicheskaya Harbor. So began my liberation. Zagursky's waiting room saw no more of me. Matters of greater importance came to occupy my thoughts. My schoolmate Nemanov and I got into the habit of slipping aboard the *Kensington* to see an old sailor named Mr. Trottyburn. Nemanov was a year younger than me, and since the age of eight had been arranging the most sophisticated deals you can imagine. He had a real genius for deals and would deliver what he promised. Now he is a New York millionaire, an executive at General Motors, a company no less mighty than Ford. Nemanov took me along with him because I silently obeyed all his orders. He used to buy pipes smuggled in by Mr. Trottyburn. These pipes were carved in Lincoln by the old sailor's brother.

"*Gentlemen*," Mr. Trottyburn would say to us, "the little fellows must be done by hand. Smoke a factory pipe? . . . Might as well stick an enema in your mouth. Know who Benvenuto Cellini was? Now that was a master. My brother in Lincoln could tell you about him. My brother never bothers nobody. Only he's convinced that you have to make the little fellows by your own hand and no one else's. We cannot but agree with him, *gentlemen* . . ."

Nemanov used to sell Trottyburn's pipes to bank managers, foreign consuls, well-to-do Greeks. He made a hundred percent profit on them.

The pipes of the Lincolnshire master breathed poetry. Each of them was invested with thought, a drop of eternity. A little yellow eye glowed in their mouthpieces, their cases were lined with satin. I tried to picture Matthew Trottyburn living in Old England, the last of the master pipe makers, swimming against the tide.

"We cannot but agree, *gentlemen*, that the little fellows must be made by your own hand . . ."

The heavy waves by the seawall took me farther and farther away from our house, reeking of onions and Jewish fate. From Practicheskaya Harbor I migrated to the other side of the breakwater. There, on a tiny spit of sand, dwelled the boys from Primorskaya Street. Trouserless from dawn to dusk, they dived under barges, stole coconuts for dinner, and waited for the boats from Kherson and Kamenka to pull in with watermelons, watermelons that could be split against moorings.

Learning to swim became my dream. I was ashamed to confess to those bronzed lads that, born in Odessa, I had not seen the sea till I was ten, and at fourteen didn't know how to swim.

How late I came to learn the things one needs to know! As a child, nailed to the Gemara, I had led the life of a sage, and when I grew up—I started climbing trees.

Swimming proved beyond me. The hydrophobia of my ancestors—Spanish rabbis and Frankfurt money changers—dragged me to the bottom. The water wouldn't support me. Rinsed like a rag and full of salt water, I would return to shore—to my violin and sheet music. I was shackled to the implements of my crime and had to drag them with me. The rabbinic struggle with the sea continued until such time as the local water god—a proofreader at the *Odessa News*, Yefim Nikitich Smolich—took pity on me. In this man's athletic breast there dwelled pity for Jewish boys. He supervised a rabble of rickety starvelings. Nikitich would collect them from the bedbug-infested warrens of the Moldavanka, take them down to the sea, bury them in the sand, do calisthenics with them, dive with them, teach them songs, and, as he roasted under the vertical rays of the sun, tell them stories of fishermen and wild beasts. To grown-ups Nikitich would explain that he was a natural philosopher. The Jewish kids would die from laughter at Nikitich's tales, squealing and nuzzling up to him like pups. The sun would sprinkle them with creeping freckles, freckles the color of lizards.

Silently, out of the corner of his eye, the old man had been watching my duel against the waves. When he saw that it was hopeless and that I'd never learn to swim, he made room for me among those he held in his heart. That cheerful heart of his—it was always there with us, never ran off somewhere, was never jealous or troubled. With his copper shoulders, aging gladiator's head, and his bronzed, slightly crooked legs, he would lie among us behind the breakwater, among the last dregs of an undying tribe, master of these melony, kerosene waters. I came to love that man, with the love that only a boy beset by hysteria and headaches can feel for an athlete. I never left his side and tried my best to be of service to him.

He said to me:

"Don't you worry . . . You just get a grip on your nerves. The swimming will come of itself . . . What do you mean—the water won't hold you? . . . Why shouldn't it hold you?"

Seeing how drawn I was to him, Nikitich made an exception of me alone of all his pupils, invited me to visit his clean and spacious attic lined with straw mats, showed me his dogs, his hedgehog, tortoise, and pigeons. In return for these riches I brought him a tragedy I had written the day before.

"I was sure you did a bit of scribbling," said Nikitich. "You've got that look in your eye . . . You don't look at anything else that way . . ."

He read my writings, shrugged, passed a hand through his stiff gray curls, paced up and down the attic.

"One has to suppose," he said slowly, pausing after each word, "that there's a spark of the divine in you . . ."

We went out into the street. The old man stopped, firmly struck the pavement with his stick, and stared at me.

"Now what is it you lack? You're young, but the only cure for that is time . . . What you lack is a feeling for nature."

He pointed with his stick at a tree with a reddish trunk and a low crown.

"What kind of tree is that?"

I didn't know.

"What grows on that bush?"

I didn't know that either. We walked together along the park on Alexandrovsky Prospect. The old man poked his stick at every tree; he would grab my shoulder when a bird flew by and would make me listen to each call.

"Which bird sings like that?"

I couldn't answer any of these things. The names of trees and birds, their division into species, where birds were flying to, on which side the sun rises, when the dew falls thickest—all these things were unknown to me.

"And you dare to write! A person who doesn't live in nature, as a stone or an animal lives in nature, will never write two worthwhile lines in his entire life . . . Your landscapes are like descriptions of stage scenery. I'll be damned—what were your parents thinking about these fourteen years?"

What were they thinking about? About contested bills of exchange, Mischa Elman's mansions . . . I didn't say anything to Nikitich about that, I kept my mouth shut.

At home, over lunch, I couldn't touch my food. It just wouldn't go down.

"A feeling for nature," I thought. "How come that never entered my head? Where would I find someone who could explain birdcalls and tree names to me? What do I know about such things? I might perhaps recognize lilac, at least when it's in bloom—lilac and acacia. De Ribas and Greek Streets have acacias."

At lunch Father had a new story about Jascha Heifetz. Just before he got to Robinat's he ran into Mendelssohn, Jascha's uncle. Turns out the boy gets eight hundred rubles a performance. Go ahead and figure out how much that comes to at fifteen concerts a month.

I figured it out—it came to twelve thousand a month. Multiplying and carrying four in my head, I glanced out the window. Across the cement courtyard, his cloak lilting in the breeze, ginger ringlets poking out from under his soft hat, leaning on his cane, marched Mr. Zagursky, my music teacher. No one could accuse him of having caught on too soon. More than three months had passed since my violin had been abandoned on the sand by the breakwater . . .

Zagursky was approaching the front door. I dashed to the back door—it had been nailed up the previous day for fear of burglars. There was nowhere to run. So then I locked myself in the bathroom. After half an hour the whole family had gathered outside my door. The women were weeping. Bobka was grinding her fat shoulder against the door and exploding in sobs. Father was silent. Finally he began to speak, so quietly and distinctly as he had never spoken in his life.

"I am an officer," said my father. "I own property. I go hunting. Muzhiks pay me rent. I have entered my son in the Cadet Corps. I have no need to worry about my son . . ."

He was silent again. The women were sniffling. Then a terrible blow crashed upon the bathroom door, Father was smashing against it with his whole body, running and throwing himself.

"I am an officer," he wailed. "I go hunting . . . I'll kill him . . . End of story . . ."

The hook jumped off the door, there was still a bolt there, it was hanging by a single nail. The women were rolling on the floor, they grabbed Father by the legs; completely off his head, he was trying to break loose. The commotion drew the old lady—Father's mother.

"My child," she said to him in Yiddish, "our grief is great. It knows no bounds. Blood is the last thing we need in our house. I do not wish to see blood in our house . . ."

Father groaned. I heard his footsteps retreating. The bolt hung by its last nail.

I sat it out in my fortress till nightfall. When all had gone to bed, Aunt Bobka took me to Grandmother's. We had a long way to go. Moonlight curdled on unknown bushes, nameless trees . . . An invisible bird let out a whistle and was then quiet, perhaps gone to sleep . . . What bird was it? What was it called? Does dew fall in the evening? . . . Where is the constellation of the Great Bear? On which side does the sun come up? . . .

We were walking on Post Office Street. Bobka held me tight by the hand so that I wouldn't run away. She was right. I was thinking of running away.

1930 (published 1931)

In the Basement

I was a mendacious boy. This came of too much reading. My imagination was forever inflamed. I read during class, during breaks between classes, on my way home, at night under the table, concealed by the tablecloth that hung down to the floor. My nose in a book, I missed everything in the world that mattered—playing hooky at the harbor, learning billiards at the coffeehouses on Greek Street, going swimming at Langeron. I had no friends. Who would have wanted to have anything to do with a person like me?

One day I noticed that Mark Borgman, our top student, was holding a book on Spinoza. He had just read it and couldn't wait to tell the other boys about the Spanish Inquisition. The result was a stream of learned mumbo jumbo. Borgman's words lacked poetry. I couldn't help butting in. I told anyone willing to listen to me about old Amsterdam, about the twilight of the ghetto, about philosophers who cut diamonds. To what I had read in books I added much of my own. I couldn't do without that. My imagination heightened the dramatic scenes, tampered with the endings, wove more mystery into the beginnings. The death of Spinoza, his liberated lonely death, became more like a battle in my account. The Sanhedrin was trying to make the dying man repent, but he wouldn't break. I worked Rubens into the scene. I could see Rubens standing at the head of Spinoza's bed making a mask of the dead man's face.

My classmates listened mouths agape to this fantastical tale. It was told with great inspiration. When the bell rang, we dispersed reluctantly. During the next break Borgman came over, took me by the arm, and we started walking together. After a short time, we had come to terms. Borgman wasn't bad as top students go. To his powerful brain, schoolhouse wisdom looked like scribbles in the margin of the book. And it was the book itself that he avidly sought. Though we were silly twelve-year-olds, we could already tell that a learned and remarkable life awaited Borgman. He didn't study at home at all but just absorbed everything in class. This sober, self-possessed boy became attached to me for my special way of deliberately misinterpreting every last thing on the planet, such things as were impossible to imagine any simpler.

That year we moved up to the third class. My report card consisted of 3-minuses. I was such a bizarre babbler that the teachers thought twice and decided not to give me 2's. At the beginning of the summer Borgman invited me to his dacha. His father was the director of the Russian Bank for Foreign Trade. He was among the men who were turning Odessa into a Marseille or Naples. He was full of the yeast of the old-time Odessa merchant. He belonged to that company of suave, skeptical profligates. Borgman's father avoided speaking Russian, preferring to express himself in the rough, clipped speech of Liverpool sea captains. When the Italian Opera visited our city in April, a dinner for the members of the company was arranged at Borgman's house. The pudgy banker, last of the Odessa merchants, began a two-month affair with the large-bosomed prima donna. She departed with memories that did not strain her conscience and a necklace, selected with taste but not too expensive.

The old man was the Argentine consul and president of the stock exchange committee. He was very smart. It was to his house that I was invited. My aunt, whom we called Bobka, divulged this information to everyone on the block. She dressed me up as best she could. I took the steam tram to the Sixteenth Bolshoy Fontan stop. The dacha stood on a low red cliff right on the shore. On the cliff there was a flower garden with fuchsia and topiary balls of arborvitae.

I came from a poor and preposterous family. I was quite struck by the setup at the Borgman villa. Wicker armchairs dazzled white along green-shrouded promenades. The dining table was covered in flowers, the windows of the dining room were framed in green casements. A low wooden colonnade extended generously in front of the house.

In the evening the bank director came home. After dinner he placed a wicker armchair right at the edge of the cliff overlooking the heaving plain of the sea, put up his legs in their white trousers, lit a cigar, and started reading the *Manchester Guardian*. The guests, Odessa ladies, played poker on the veranda. A slender samovar with ivory handles rumbled on the corner of the table.

Gamblers and gourmands, sloppy mannequins and secretly loose ladies with perfumed underwear and full flanks—they snapped their black fans and staked their gold coins. The sun reached for them through a hedge of wild grapes. Its fiery disk was enormous. Glints of copper weighed down their black hair. Sparks of sunset in their diamonds—diamonds hanging everywhere: in the depths of parted bosoms, in painted ears, and on their puffy bluish she-wolf fingers.

Evening came. A bat rustled past. The blackening sea rolled against the red cliff. My twelve-year-old heart swelled with joy and lightness at the

wealth of others. My friend and I strolled arm in arm down a distant promenade. Borgman told me he was going to be an aircraft engineer. It was
rumored that his father was to be sent to represent the Russian Bank for
Foreign Trade in London—Mark would be able to receive his education in
England.

In our house, Aunt Bobka's house, no one ever talked of such things. I
had nothing to offer in return for all this uninterrupted magnificence. So
then I told Mark that, although everything at our place was quite different,
Grandpa Levi-Itzkhok and my uncle had traveled all around the world and
had thousands of adventures. I described these adventures one after the other.
At that moment, any recognition of the impossible abandoned me, I took
Uncle Wolf through the Russo-Turkish War to Alexandria, to Egypt . . .

Night straightened itself among the poplars, stars came to rest along the
sagging branches. I kept talking and gesticulating. The fingers of the future
aircraft engineer trembled in my hand. Struggling to awaken from his trance,
he promised to come to my place the following Sunday. With this promise
tucked away, I took the steam tram home to Aunt Bobka's.

For the whole week after my visit I kept picturing myself as a bank director. I crafted deals running into the millions, with Singapore and Port Said.
I bought a yacht and made solo voyages. On Saturday it was time to wake
up. Tomorrow young Borgman was coming to visit. Nothing I had told him
about really existed. What did exist was different, and much more surprising
than anything I had invented, but at the age of twelve I had no idea what to
do with the truth in this world. Grandpa Levi-Itzkhok, the rabbi expelled
from his shtetl for forging Count Branicki's signature on bills of exchange,
was reckoned crazy by the neighbors and the local boys. My uncle Simon
I just couldn't stand on account of his loud eccentricity, full of meaningless
and oppressive sound and fury. Aunt Bobka was the only sensible one. Bobka
was proud that a bank director's son was friends with me. She deemed this
friendship to be the beginning of a brilliant career, and she baked apple strudel with jam and poppy-seed cake for the guest. The entire heart of our tribe,
a heart so accustomed to struggle, was folded into those cakes. Grandfather,
with his tattered top hat and the rags on his swollen feet, we stowed away at
our neighbors' the Apelkhots, and I begged him not to show his face until
our visitor had left. Simon-Wolf was also dealt with. He went off with his
speculator friends to drink tea at the Bear tavern. At this tavern they used
to spike their tea with vodka, so you could count on Simon-Wolf taking
his time. Here it must be said that the family I came from did not resemble other Jewish families. We had drunkards among us, we had seducers of
generals' daughters who would abandon them just before they reached the

border, we had a grandfather who used to forge signatures and had composed blackmail letters for jilted wives.

I devoted all my efforts to making sure that Uncle Simon would stay away the whole day. I gave him three rubles I had saved up. Three rubles take some time to spend, Simon-Wolf would be back late, and the bank director's son would never learn that the tale of my uncle's kindness and strength was utterly false. To be perfectly honest, though, at heart it was actually true and not false, but if you found yourself looking at our dirty, loudmouthed Simon-Wolf for the first time, this incomprehensible truth would be difficult to discern.

On Sunday morning Aunt Bobka was decked out in a finely woven brown dress. Her kindly fat bosom spread in every direction. She put on a head scarf with a black floral print, the kind worn in the synagogue on the Day of Atonement and Rosh Hashanah. Bobka set the table with cakes, jam, pretzels, and waited. We lived in the basement. Borgman raised his brows as he went down the lumpy floor of the corridor. A barrel of water stood in the passageway. Borgman had hardly come inside when I began drawing his attention to all sorts of curiosities. I showed him an alarm clock that Grandfather had made down to the last screw. A lamp was attached to the clock; when the alarm clock struck the half hour or the hour, the lamp lit up. I also showed him a keg of shoe polish. The recipe for this polish had been invented by Levi-Itzkhok—he would never reveal the secret to anyone. Then Borgman and I read a few pages from Grandfather's manuscript. It was written in Yiddish on square yellow sheets of paper, huge as maps. The manuscript was titled "The Headless Man." It described all Levi-Itzkhok's neighbors over the course of seventy years: first in Skvira and Belaya Tserkov and later on in Odessa. Gravediggers, cantors, Jewish drunkards, cook maids at brisses, and the crooks who performed the ritual operation—that's who Levi-Itzkhok's heroes were. All of them were cantankerous individuals, tongue-tied, with lumps on their noses, pimples on their pates, and backsides askew.

While we were reading, Bobka appeared in her brown dress. She floated in with a samovar on a tray, cushioned by her fat, kindly bosom. I introduced them to each other. Bobka said, "Pleased to meet you," offered her stiff, sweaty fingers, and shuffled both feet. Everything was going wonderfully, couldn't be going better. The Apelkhots kept Grandfather busy. I dragged out his treasures one after the other: grammars in all languages and sixty-six volumes of the Talmud. Mark was dazzled by the keg of polish, the ingenious alarm clock, and the mountain of Talmud, all the things that could not be seen in any other home.

We each had two glasses of tea with strudel, then Bobka, nodding her head and retreating backward, disappeared. I grew light of heart, struck a pose, and started reciting my very favorite lines of verse. Antony, bending over Caesar's corpse, addresses the Roman crowd:

> Friends, Romans, countrymen, lend me your ears;
> I come to bury Caesar, not to praise him.

That's Antony's opening gambit. I choked up and pressed my hands to my breast.

> He was my friend, faithful and just to me:
> But Brutus says he was ambitious;
> And Brutus is an honourable man.
> He hath brought many captives home to Rome,
> Whose ransoms did the general coffers fill:
> Did this in Caesar seem ambitious?
> When that the poor have cried, Caesar hath wept:
> Ambition should be made of sterner stuff:
> Yet Brutus says he was ambitious;
> And Brutus is an honourable man.
> You all did see that on the Lupercal
> I thrice presented him a kingly crown,
> Which he did thrice refuse: was this ambition?
> Yet Brutus says he was ambitious;
> And, sure, he is an honourable man.

Before my eyes—in the mists of the universe—hovered the face of Brutus. It grew whiter than chalk. The Roman people closed upon me, grumbling. I raised my hand—Borgman's eyes dutifully followed it—my clenched fist trembled, I raised my hand . . . and through the window I saw Uncle Simon-Wolf crossing the courtyard accompanied by Leikakh the secondhand goods dealer. They were staggering beneath the weight of a clothes rack made of antlers and a red trunk with fittings shaped like lions' jaws. Bobka also saw them through the window. Forgetting our guest, she flew into the room and grasped me with her trembling hands.

"Oh my sweetheart, he's been buying furniture again! . . ."

Borgman rose in his school uniform and bowed to Bobka in some perplexity. Someone was forcing the door open. There was a crash of boots in the hall, the noise of the trunk being shunted. The voices of Simon-Wolf and the redheaded Leikakh thundered deafeningly. They were both tipsy.

"Bobka," shouted Simon-Wolf, "try and guess how much I paid for these antlers?!"

He was blaring like a trumpet, but there was uncertainty in his voice. Though he was drunk, he knew how we hated Leikakh the redhead, who instigated all his purchases and inundated us with outlandish and unnecessary pieces of furniture.

Bobka said nothing. Leikakh squeaked something at Uncle Simon. To drown out his serpentine hissing, to drown out my dismay, I began shouting Antony's lines:

> But yesterday the word of Caesar might
> Have stood against the world; now lies he there,
> And none so poor to do him reverence.
> O masters! If I were dispos'd to stir
> Your hearts and minds to mutiny and rage,
> I should do Brutus wrong, and Cassius wrong,
> Who, you all know, are honourable men.

Just then, there was a dull thud. That was Bobka falling, knocked off her feet by a blow from her husband. She must have made some bitter remark about the antlers. The day's performance had commenced. Uncle Simon's brazen voice caulked all the cracks in the universe. He was shouting his usual repertoire.

"You pull the glue out of me," my uncle complained, thundering, "pull the glue out of me to stuff your mongrel mouths. I've been unsouled by toil. I got nothing left to work with, I got no hands, I got no legs. You've put a stone around my neck, a stone is hanging from my neck . . ."

Cursing me and Bobka with Yiddish curses, he swore that our eyes would trickle out, that our children would rot and wither in their mother's womb, that we'd be unable to give one another a decent burial and would be dragged by the hair to a common grave.

Little Borgman rose from his chair. He was pale and kept looking around furtively. He couldn't understand the twists and turns of Yiddish blasphemy, but he was familiar with Russian swearing. Simon-Wolf didn't neglect the latter either. The bank director's son crumpled his little cap in his hands. He doubled in my eyes as I strained to outshout all the evil in the world. My dying despair and the already accomplished death of Caesar merged into one: I was dead, and I was shouting. A rattle rose from the depths of my being:

If you have tears, prepare to shed them now.
You all do know this mantle. I remember
The first time ever Caesar put it on.
'Twas on a summer's evening in his tent,
That day he overcame the Nervii.
Look, in this place ran Cassius' dagger through.
See what a rent the envious Casca made.
Through this the well-beloved Brutus stabb'd;
And as he pluck'd his cursed steel away,
Mark how the blood of Caesar follow'd it . . .

Nothing had the power to drown out Simon-Wolf. Bobka sat on the floor sobbing and blowing her nose. The imperturbable Leikakh was shoving the trunk around behind the partition. Just then, my madcap grandfather decided to come and help me out. He tore himself away from the Apelkhots, crept over to our window, and started sawing away on his fiddle, no doubt so that people passing by wouldn't hear Simon-Wolf's foul tongue. Borgman glanced out the window, which had been cut through at street level, and fell back in horror. My poor grandfather grimaced with his blue ossified mouth. He was wearing his dented top hat, a black padded frock coat with bone buttons, and what was left of his boots on his elephant feet. His tobacco-stained beard hung in clumps, swaying in the window. Mark made a run for it.

"It's quite all right," he mumbled as he made his escape. "Really, quite all right . . ."

His little uniform and cap with the turned-up edges flashed across the yard.

My worries departed with him. Serenity and determination took hold of me. I was waiting for evening. When Grandfather, having covered his square sheet of paper with Yiddish squiggles (he was describing the Apelkhots, with whom he had spent the day, thanks to me), had fallen asleep on his cot, I made my way out into the corridor. The corridor had a dirt floor. I moved through the darkness, barefoot, in my long patched shirt. Cobblestones shot blades of light through cracks in the boards. In the corner, as always, stood the water barrel. I lowered myself into it. The water sliced me in two. I plunged my head in, choked, and surfaced. From a shelf the cat looked down at me sleepily. The second time I stayed down longer, the water gurgled around me, absorbing my moans. I opened my eyes and saw the sail of my shirt and my two little feet squeezed together at the bottom of the barrel. Again my strength failed me, I surfaced. Grandfather stood by the barrel in a blouse. His lone tooth rang like a bell.

"My grandson," he uttered with clarity and contempt, "I am going to go take castor oil, so that I have something to lay on your grave . . ."

I started to shriek, completely beside myself, and splashed down into the water. I was pulled out by Grandfather's unsteady hand. Then for the first time that day I burst into tears, and the world of tears was so vast and beautiful that everything save tears vanished from my eyes.

When I came to, I was in bed, swaddled in blankets. Grandfather was stalking about the room whistling. Fat Bobka was warming my hands on her bosom. I let her have them.

"Look how he's shivering, our silly boychik," said Bobka. "Where does he find the strength to shiver like that . . ."

Grandfather tugged at his beard, whistled, and stalked off again. On the other side of the wall, I could hear the excruciating snores of Simon-Wolf. When he had his fill of war by day, he never woke up at night.

1929 (published 1931)

Di Grasso

I was fourteen years old. I belonged to the intrepid ranks of ticket scalpers. My boss was a swindler with a permanently screwed-up eye and an enormous silky mustache. Kolya Schwarz was his name. I came under his sway in that unhappy year when the Italian Opera flopped in Odessa. Having taken his lead from the newspaper critics, our impresario had decided not to bring Anselmi and Tito Ruffo as guest performers but to make do with a good ensemble. For this he would be sorely punished, ruined, and we with him. We were promised Chaliapin to straighten out our affairs, but Chaliapin demanded three thousand a performance. So instead we got the Sicilian tragedian Di Grasso and his troupe. They arrived at the hotel in carts crammed with children, cats, cages hopping with Italian birds. When he saw this band of gypsies, Kolya Schwarz said:

"Children, this is no kind of merchandise."

When he had settled in, the tragedian made his way to the bazaar with a grocery basket. In the evening—carrying a different grocery basket—he arrived at the theater. Hardly fifty people had turned up. We tried selling tickets at half price, but there were no takers.

That evening they staged a Sicilian folk drama, a tale as plain as day turning to night and night into day. The daughter of a rich peasant is engaged to a shepherd. She is faithful to him till one day there drives out from the city a young slicker in a silky vest. Keeping company with her out-of-town guest, the maiden giggled when she wasn't supposed to and was silent when she was. As he listened to them, the shepherd kept twisting his head like a startled bird. For the entire first act he kept flattening himself against walls, dashing off somewhere, pants flapping, looking around wildly when he returned.

"Call the undertaker," Kolya Schwarz said when the intermission came. "This might work . . . in some place like Kremenchug."

The intermission was designed to give the maiden time to ripen for betrayal. In the second act we couldn't recognize her—she was insufferable, scatterbrained, and quickly gave the shepherd back his engagement ring. Thereupon he led her over to a shabby painted statue of the Holy Virgin, and began in his Sicilian dialect:

"Signora," he said softly, turning away, "the Holy Virgin would like you to hear me out. To Giovanni from the city, the Holy Virgin will grant as many women as he wants; but I need none save you, signora. The Virgin Mary, our immaculate protector, will tell you exactly the same thing if you only ask her, signora."

The maiden stood with her back to the painted wooden statue. She listened to the shepherd, impatiently tapping her foot. In this world of ours—alas!—there has never been a woman who wasn't thoughtless at the very moment her fate is being decided . . . She is utterly alone in those moments, alone, without the Virgin Mary, and she won't be asking her about a thing.

In the third act Giovanni from the city met his fate. He was having a shave at the village barber's, his strong manly legs thrust across the proscenium; the pleats in his vest gleamed in the Sicilian sun. The scene depicted a village fair. In the far corner stood the shepherd. He stood there silently amid the carefree crowd. He hung his head, then raised it, and beneath the weight of his intense, searing gaze Giovanni began stirring and fidgeting in his chair, finally pushing the barber aside and leaping to his feet. He broke forth and demanded that the policeman should remove from the village square all persons of a gloomy and suspicious aspect. The shepherd—played by Di Grasso—stood there lost in thought, then he smiled, soared into the air, sailed across the stage of the city theater, plunged down on Giovanni's shoulders, and, having bitten through his throat, growling and squinting, began to suck blood from the wound. Giovanni collapsed, and the curtain—falling in ominous silence—hid the murdered man and the murderer from our view. Without a moment to lose, we dashed to the box office in Theater Lane, which was to open the following day. Kolya Schwarz ran ahead of everybody. As the sun rose, the *Odessa News* informed the few people who had been at the theater that they had seen the most remarkable actor of the century.

On this visit Di Grasso played *King Lear*, *Othello*, *The Outlaw*, Turgenev's *The Parasite*, his every word and gesture confirming that there is more hope and justice to be found in a frenzy of noble passion than in all the joyless rules of this world.

Tickets for these shows went for five times face value. Hunting for scalpers, buyers would find them at the tavern—yelling their heads off, faces purple, spewing harmless profanities.

Theater Lane was infused with a stream of rosy, dusty sultriness. Shopkeepers in felt slippers carried green bottles of wine and casks of olives out into the street. Macaroni seethed in foaming water in vats outside the shops, and the steam melted in distant skies. Old women in men's boots sold seashells and souvenirs, pursuing hesitant buyers with loud cries. Rich Jews with beards combed and parted down the middle would drive up to the Northern Hotel and tap discreetly on the doors of fat raven-haired women with little mustaches—Di Grasso's actresses. Everyone was happy on Theater Lane, everyone except for one person, and that person was me. In those days, for me, the end was near. Any minute now my father would miss the watch I had taken without his permission and pawned to Kolya Schwarz. But Kolya Schwarz had had the gold watch long enough to get used to it, and being the sort of person who drank Bessarabian wine in the morning instead of tea, even after he got his money back, he still could not bring himself to return the watch to me. Such was his character. My father's character was no different. Stuck between these two characters, I watched other people carry on happily. There was nothing left for me but to run away to Constantinople. I had made all the arrangements with the second engineer of the HMS *Duke of Kent*, but before setting off to sea I decided to bid farewell to Di Grasso. One last time he was playing the shepherd who escapes the bonds of earth by means of an incomprehensible power. The entire Italian colony was in attendance, led by the bald and fine-figured consul; also there were the fidgety Greeks; bearded externs gazing fanatically upon some point invisible to anyone else; and there was Utochkin with his long arms. Kolya Schwarz had even brought his wife in her fringed violet shawl, a woman fit to serve with the grenadiers, her body long like the steppe with a sleepy little crumpled face at the far end. When the curtain fell, this face was drenched in tears.

"Bum," she said to Kolya as they were leaving the theater, "now you see what love means."

Madame Schwarz lumbered along Langeron Street; tears rolled from her fishlike eyes, the fringe of her shawl trembled on her thick shoulders. She shuffled along on her manly feet, shaking her head, her deafening voice resounding through the street as she made an inventory of the women who got on well with their husbands.

" 'Chickadee' their husbands call them, 'precious,' 'baby doll' . . ."

Kolya trudged browbeaten beside his wife, gently puffing up his silky mustache. By force of habit I followed on behind, sniffling. When she became quiet for a moment, Madame Schwarz heard my sobs and turned around.

"Bum," she said to her husband, her fish eyes agoggle, "I shall die before my time if you don't give the boy his watch back!"

Kolya froze, mouth agape, then came to, gave me a vicious pinch, and shoved the watch at me sideways.

"What do I get from him?" the rough, tear-choked voice of Madame Schwarz wailed disconsolately as they left me. "Once an animal, always an animal. I'm asking you, you bum, how long can a woman wait?"

They reached the corner and turned onto Pushkin Street. I stood there clutching the watch, alone, and suddenly, with a clarity such as I had never before experienced, I saw the soaring columns of the City Hall, the gaslit foliage of the boulevard, Pushkin's bronze head touched by the dim glow of the moon—for the first time I saw everything around me as it really was, hushed and inexpressibly beautiful.

(published 1937)

ODESSA
STORIES

The King

The wedding was over; the rabbi slumped into an armchair, then went outside and saw the tables set across the entire length of the courtyard. There were so many of them that their tail-end poked out through the gates into Hospital Street. The velvet-covered tables wound their way down the yard like snakes covered in patches of every color, and they sang with viscous voices—those velvet patches of orange and red.

The living quarters had been turned into kitchens. A stout flame beat through the sooty doors, a drunk and swollen flame. Old women's faces, tremulous chins, and greasy bosoms baked in its smoky rays. Sweat, pink like blood, pink like the foaming mouth of a rabid dog, flooded over these bosoms of exorbitant, sweetly pungent human flesh. Three cooks, not counting the dishwashers, were preparing the wedding feast, and reigning over them was the eighty-year-old Reisl, traditional as a Torah scroll, tiny and humpbacked.

Before dinner a young man unknown to the guests wormed his way into the yard. He asked for Benya Krik. He took Benya Krik aside.

"Listen, King," said the young man, "I got a couple things to tell you. Aunt Hannah from Kostetskaya sent me . . ."

"Well, all right," replied Benya Krik, also known as the King. "What couple things?"

"New police chief arrived at the precinct yesterday, Aunt Hannah told me to tell you . . ."

"I knew that day before yesterday," replied Benya Krik. "Go on."

"The chief assembled the precinct and gave a speech."

"A new broom sweeps clean," said Benya Krik. "He wants to make a bust. Go on."

"And you already know when the bust will be made, I suppose, King?"

"It'll be tomorrow."

"King . . . it'll be today."

"Who told you that, boy?"

"Aunt Hannah told me. You know Aunt Hannah?"

"I know Aunt Hannah. Go on."

". . . The chief assembled the precinct and gave a speech. 'We've got to crush Benya Krik,' he said, 'because where there's a sovereign emperor there can be no king. Today, when Krik gives away his sister in marriage and all of them will be there, today is the day to make a bust.'"

"Go on."

"Then the cops began to get scared. They said, if we bust him today when he's celebrating, Benya will be cross, and a lot of blood will flow. So the chief said, self-respect is more precious to me . . ."

"Well, off you go," said the King.

"What do I tell Aunt Hannah about the bust?"

"Tell her Benya knows about the bust."

And he left, this young man. After him went three men, friends of Benya's. They said they'd be back in half an hour. And they were back in half an hour. And that's all.

At the table, the wedding guests did not sit according to their age. Foolish old age is no less pathetic than cowardly youth. Nor according to their wealth. Heavy purses are lined with tears.

At the table in the place of honor sat the bride and groom. This was their day. Next sat Sender Eichbaum, the King's father-in-law. Such was his right. The story of Sender Eichbaum is worth knowing, for it is no ordinary story.

How did Benya Krik, gangster and king of gangsters, become Eichbaum's son-in-law? Become son-in-law to a man who owned sixty milk cows minus one? It all happened because of a raid. Only a year before, Benya had written Eichbaum a letter.

"Monsieur Eichbaum," he had written, "I request that tomorrow morning you place twenty thousand rubles under the gate at 17 Sofievskaya. If you don't do this, something unheard of will happen to you, and you will be the talk of Odessa. Yours respectfully, Benya the King."

Three letters, each one more clear than the last, remained unanswered. Then Benya took measures. They came in the night—nine men with long sticks in their hands. The sticks had pitch and hemp wrapped around them. Nine flaming stars flared in Eichbaum's cattle yard. Benya knocked the locks off the door of the cowshed and began to lead the cows out one by one. They were met by a lad with a knife. He would overturn the cow with one blow and plunge his knife into her heart. Torches bloomed like roses of fire on the blood-drenched ground, and shots rang out. With these shots Benya scared away the workers who had come hurrying to the cowshed. After him the other gangsters began firing in the air, because if you don't fire in the air, you might kill someone. And when the sixth cow had fallen, mooing her last at the feet of the King, that's when Eichbaum ran out into the yard wearing nothing but long johns, asking:

"What's the point of this, Benya?"

"If I don't have my money, Monsieur Eichbaum, you won't have your cows. Simple as two times two."

"Come inside, Benya."

And inside they came to terms. The slaughtered cows were divided between them, and Eichbaum was guaranteed protection and issued a certificate with a seal. But the miracle came later.

During the raid, on that dread night when stuck cows bellowed and calves slipped in their mothers' blood, when the torches danced like Black Virgins and the dairymaids recoiled shrieking from the muzzles of amiable Brownings—on that dread night, wearing nothing but a low-cut shift, there ran out into the yard the daughter of old man Eichbaum—Tsilya. And the King's victory became his defeat.

Two days later, without warning, Benya returned all the money he had taken from Eichbaum, and afterward, in the evening, he made a social call. He wore an orange suit, beneath his cuff gleamed a diamond bracelet; he walked into the room, said hello, and asked Eichbaum for the hand of his daughter Tsilya. The old man had a little stroke, but he recovered. He was good for another twenty years.

"Listen, Eichbaum," said the King. "When you die, I will bury you in the First Jewish Cemetery, right by the entrance. For you, Eichbaum, I will put up a monument of pink marble. I will make you an elder of the Brody Synagogue. I will give up my own profession and enter yours as a partner. Two hundred cows we'll have, Eichbaum. I will kill all the other dairy farmers. No thief will walk the street that you live on. I will build you a dacha in the Sixteenth Station. And remember, Eichbaum, you were no rabbi yourself in your youth. Certain wills turned out to be forged, but why talk of such things? . . . And your son-in-law will be the King—not some snot nose, but the King, Eichbaum . . ."

And Benya Krik had his way, for he was passionate, and passion rules the universe. Three months the newlyweds lived off the fat of Bessarabia, amid the grapes, the rich food, and the sweat of love. Then Benya returned to Odessa to marry off his forty-year-old sister Dvoira, who suffered from goiter. And now, having told the story of Sender Eichbaum, we can return to the marriage of Dvoira Krik, sister of the King.

For dinner at this wedding they served turkey, roast chicken, goose, gefilte fish, fish soup in which lakes of lemon glistened like mother-of-pearl. A luxuriant plumage of flowers swayed above the lifeless heads of geese. But can it really be roast chicken that the spume and surf of the Odessa sea casts upon the shore?

On that star-filled, on that deep-blue night, all that was noblest of our contraband, each and every thing of glory from every corner of the earth, was busy with its destructive and seductive business. Otherworldly wines warmed the stomach, knocked the sweet legs out from under, intoxicated the brain, and called forth belching that resounded like trumpets of war. The black cook from the *Plutarch*, which had docked three days before from Port Said, crossed through customs with portly bottles of Jamaican rum, oily Madeira, cigars from the plantations of Pierpont Morgan, and oranges from just outside Jerusalem. That's what the spume and surf of the Odessa sea casts upon the shore, that's what sometimes comes the way of Odessa beggars at Jewish weddings. Jamaican rum came their way at the wedding of Dvoira Krik, and that's why, having sucked their fill like the *treyf* swine that they are, the Jewish beggars began to beat the ground with their crutches in a deafening din. Eichbaum, his waistcoat unbuttoned, squinted his eyes at the tumultuous gathering and hiccuped tenderly. The orchestra played a flourish. It was just like a divisional parade. A flourish—nothing but flourishes. The gangsters, sitting in closed ranks, were at first embarrassed by the presence of outsiders, but then they loosened up. Lyova Rooski broke a bottle of vodka on the head of his beloved. Monya Gunner fired in the air. But the revels reached their limit when, in accordance with ancient custom, the guests began bestowing presents upon the newlyweds. The synagogue shammosim would leap onto the tables and, to the accompaniment of roiling flourishes, sing out the amount of rubles and silver spoons presented. And then the friends of the King showed the true meaning of blue blood and the yet-to-be-extinguished chivalry of the Moldavanka. With nonchalant gestures, they cast gold coins, rings, strands of coral upon the silver platters.

Aristocrats of the Moldavanka, they were wrapped in raspberry waistcoats, orange jackets clasped their steely shoulders, and their fleshy feet strained in ivory-set leather of heavenly azure. Rising to their full height and thrusting out their bellies, the bandits clapped in time with the music, cried "Bitter!" and tossed flowers at the bride, while she, forty-year-old Dvoira, sister of Benya Krik, deformed by illness, with her overgrown goiter and her eyes bulging from their sockets, sat on a hillock of cushions beside the frail boy who had been bought with Eichbaum's money and was now mute with misery.

The ritual bestowal of gifts was drawing to a close, the shammosim grew hoarse, and the double bass fought with the fiddle. Suddenly over the courtyard there spread the faint smell of burning.

"Benya," said Papa Krik, the old drayman, renowned among draymen as a lout, "Benya, you know what kind of notion I got? I got a notion our chimney's on fire . . ."

"Papa, I insist," said Benya to his inebriated father, "please, eat and drink, and don't be bothered by such foolishness."

And Papa Krik followed his son's advice. Drink and eat he did. But the cloud of smoke grew more and more noxious. Portions of the sky were already turning pink. And suddenly a narrow tongue of flame shot up like a fencing foil. The guests, rising in their seats, began to sniff the air and their women squealed. The gangsters exchanged glances. And only Benya, not taking the slightest notice, was disconsolate.

"They're ruining my party," he cried, filled with despair. "Good friends, I beg you, eat and drink!"

But at that moment there appeared in the courtyard the same young man who had come earlier in the evening.

"King," he said, "I got a couple things to tell you . . ."

"Well, tell me," said the King. "You've always got a couple things tucked away . . ."

"King," said the unknown young man, and giggled. "It's hilarious, the precinct is burning like a candle . . ."

The shopkeepers were mute. The gangsters grinned. The sixty-year-old Manka, matriarch of the Slobodka bandits, put two fingers in her mouth and whistled so sharp that her neighbors jerked.

"Manya, you're not on the job," Benya remarked. "Keep your blood cool, Manya . . ."

The young man who had brought this astonishing news was still cracking up. He was giggling like a bashful schoolgirl.

"They came out of the precinct, like forty of them," he recounted, chewing vigorously, "to go and do the bust; they'd gone about fifteen paces before the whole place was already on fire. Hurry and take a look if you want . . ."

But Benya forbade his guests to go and see the fire. He set out himself with two comrades. All four corners of the precinct house were ablaze, as promised. The policemen, backsides jouncing, were rushing up smoky staircases and hurling trunks out of the windows. The prisoners snuck off. The firemen were full of enthusiasm, but it turned out that the nearest hydrant had no water. The police chief—the very broom that was to sweep clean—stood on the sidewalk across the street, biting the ends of the mustache that curled into his mouth. The new broom stood stock-still. As he passed the captain, Benya gave him a military salute.

"Good health, Your Excellency," he said, sympathetically. "What can one say about such a misfortune? It's just a nightmare!"

He stared at the burning building, shook his head, and smacked his lips: "Ai-ai-ai . . ."

* * *

And when Benya got back home, the lights in the courtyard were flickering out, and dawn began to work its way across the sky. The guests had departed, and the musicians were dozing, leaning their heads on the necks of their double basses. Only Dvoira gave no thought to sleep. With both hands she was pushing her tentative husband to the doors of their nuptial chamber and gazing at him carnivorously, as a cat with a mouse in her jaws tests it gently with her teeth.

(published 1921)

How It Was Done in Odessa

It was I that began.

"Reb Arye-Leib," I said to the old man, "let us talk of Benya Krik. Let us talk of his lightning-fast rise and his terrible fall. Three shades block the paths of my imagination. There is Froim the Rook. The hard steel of his deeds—can it really not bear comparison with the strength of the King? There is Kolka Pakovsky. The rabid fury of that man contained all that was necessary for him to wield power. And is it really possible that Chaim Drong failed to see the brilliance of a rising star? Why did Benya Krik alone climb to the top of the rope ladder, while all the rest hung swaying on the lower rungs?"

Reb Arye-Leib was silent, sitting on the cemetery wall. Before us stretched the green stillness of graves. A man who thirsts for answers must stock himself with patience. A man possessed of wisdom is arrayed in dignity. For this reason Reb Arye-Leib was silent, sitting on the cemetery wall. Finally he spoke:

Why him? Why not them, you wish to know? It's like this—forget for a while that you have glasses on your nose and autumn in your heart. Quit brawling at your desk and stuttering in front of people. Imagine for a moment that you brawl in the street and stutter on paper. You are a tiger, you are a lion, you are a cat. You spend the night with a Russian woman, and the Russian woman is satisfied. You are twenty-five. If hoops were fastened to heaven and earth, you would grasp them and pull heaven and earth together. And your old man is Mendel Krik the drayman. About what does such a papa think? He thinks about drinking a good glass of vodka, about smashing somebody's face, about his horses—and nothing more. You want to live, and he makes you die twenty times a day. What would you have done in Benya Krik's shoes? You wouldn't have done a thing. But he did something. That's why he's the King, while you give people the finger with your hand in your pocket.

He—Benchik—went to see Froim the Rook, who already in those days looked at the world out of only one eye and was already then what he is now. He said to Froim:

"Take me on. I want to hitch to your harbor. The harbor I hitch to wins."

The Rook asked him:

"Who are you, where are you coming from, and how do you live?"

"Try me, Froim," replied Benya, "and let's stop smearing porridge on a nice clean table."

"Let's not smear porridge," assented Rook. "I'll try you out."

And the gangsters had a conference to consider the matter of Benya Krik. I wasn't at that conference. But they say there was a conference. Chairman at that time would have been the late Lyovka Byk.

"This little Benchik, what goes on under his hat?" asked the late Byk.

And the one-eyed Rook offered his opinion:

"Benya says little, but what he says has flavor. He says little, but you want him to say something more."

"If so," exclaimed the late Byk, "then let's try him on Tartakovsky."

"Let's try him on Tartakovsky," the conference resolved, and all in whom conscience dwelled blushed when they heard this resolution. Why did they blush? This you shall learn if you go to the place I will show you.

We used to call Tartakovsky "Yid and a Half" or "Nine Holdups." "Yid and a Half" he was called because no single Jew could have had so much money and moxie as Tartakovsky. He was taller than the tallest cop in Odessa and weighed more than the fattest Jewess. And "Nine Holdups" he was called because the firm of Lyovka Byk and Co. had raided his office neither eight times, nor ten, but precisely nine. The honor of carrying out the tenth raid on Yid and a Half fell to Benya Krik, who was not yet the King. When Froim informed him of this, he said yes and went out, slamming the door. Why slam the door? This you shall learn if you go to the place I will show you.

Tartakovsky has the soul of a killer, but he is one of us. He came from us. He is our blood. He is our flesh, as though one mama had borne us. Half of Odessa works in his stores. And it was through his own Moldavanka lads that he suffered. Twice they held him for ransom, and once during a pogrom they buried him with a choir. The Sloboda thugs were beating up the Jews then on Bolshaya Arnautskaya. Tartakovsky got away from them and met a funeral procession with a choir going down Sofiyskaya. He asked:

"Who's that they're burying with a choir?"

The passersby replied that it was Tartakovsky they were burying. The procession got to the Sloboda Cemetery. Then our boys took out a machine gun from the coffin and started raining hell on the Sloboda thugs. But Yid and a Half had not foreseen this. Yid and a Half was scared to death. And what boss would not have been scared in his place?

A tenth raid on a man already once buried was a rude thing to do. Benya, who was not yet the King, understood this better than anyone. But he had said yes to the Rook and that same day wrote Tartakovsky a letter similar to all letters of this sort:

"Much esteemed Ruvim Osipovich: Be so kind as to place by Saturday under the rain barrel, et cetera. In case of refusal, such as you have allowed to occur before, you will be met with a great disappointment in your family life. Respects from your acquaintance Bentzion Krik."

Tartakovsky was no slouch and replied without delay:

"Benya! If you were an idiot I would write to you as I would to an idiot! But I do not know you as such, and God forbid I ever shall. It seems you want to behave like a little boy. Do you really mean you don't know that this year there is a crop in Argentina big enough to drown in, while here we sit with all our wheat and no customers? And I'll tell you, hand on my heart, that in my old age I am sick and tired of having to swallow such a bitter crust of bread and to experience such disagreeableness, having worked all my life like a beast of burden. And what do I have to show for all this endless convict labor? Ulcers, sores, troubles, insomnia. Let's drop this nonsense, Benya. Your friend (much more than you suppose)—Ruvim Tartakovsky."

Yid and a Half had done his part. He had written a letter. But the post didn't deliver it to the right address. Receiving no reply, Benya was cross. The next day he turned up with four friends at Tartakovsky's office. Four masked youths with revolvers poured in.

"Hands up!" they cried, and started waving their pistols about.

"Take it easy, Solomon," Benya remarked to one shouting louder than the rest. "Don't make a habit of being nervous on the job." And turning to the clerk, who was white as death and yellow as clay, he asked him:

"Is Yid and a Half on the premises?"

"They're not on the premises," replied the clerk, who went by the last name of Muginstein, first name Iosif, bachelor son of Aunt Pesya the poultry dealer on Seredinskaya Square.

"Well then, who's in charge in the boss's absence?" They started interrogating poor Muginstein.

"I'm in charge in the boss's absence," said the clerk, green as green grass.

"Then with God's help open up the cashbox!" Benya ordered, and so began an opera in three acts.

Nervous Solomon was packing cash, papers, watches, and monograms in a suitcase; the late Iosif stood before him with his hands up while Benya was recounting tales from the life of the Jewish people.

"Forever playing the Rothschild, that one," Benya was saying of Tartakovsky, "so let him roast on a slow fire. Explain this to me, Muginstein, as a friend: if he receives a business letter from me, why shouldn't he pay five kopecks to take a streetcar and come see me at my place and drink a glass of vodka with my family and have a bite and whatnot? What prevented him from opening his heart to me? 'Benya,' he might have said, 'so on and so forth, here's my balance sheet, give me a couple days to catch my breath and see how things shake out.' What can I say to that? A pig doesn't talk things out with a pig, but a human being can talk to a human being. Muginstein, you understand me?"

"I understand you," said Muginstein, but he was lying, for he hadn't the remotest idea why Yid and a Half, a respectable well-to-do personage, would want to take a streetcar to have a bite with the family of Mendel Krik the drayman.

And in the meantime misfortune traipsed beneath the window like a pauper at daybreak. Misfortune broke into the office with a racket. And though on this occasion it took the shape of the Jew Savka Butsis, said misfortune was drunk as a water carrier.

"Ho-hoo-ho," cried Savka the Jew, "forgive me, Benchik, I'm late." And he started stamping his feet and waving his arms. Then he fired, and the bullet landed in Muginstein's gut.

What can one say? A man was, and is no more. A blameless bachelor living his life like a bird on a twig—and now he has to die over some nonsense. Along comes a Jew dressed like a sailor and takes a potshot not at some carnival bottle with a prize inside but at a person's stomach. What is there to say?

"We're outta here," cried Benya, and ran out last. But as he departed he managed to say to Butsis:

"I swear on my mother's grave, Savka, that you will lie next to him . . ."

Now tell me, my young sir, you who snip coupons on other people's shares, what would you have done in Benya's place? You would not have known what was to be done. But he knew. That's why he's the King, while you and I sit on the wall of the Second Jewish Cemetery blocking the sun from our eyes with our palms.

Aunt Pesya's unfortunate son did not die right away. An hour after they had got him to the hospital, Benya showed up. He asked for the doctor in charge and the nurse to be sent out to him and, without taking his hands out of his cream-colored trousers, said to them:

"It is in my interest," he said, "that the patient Iosif Muginstein should recover. Let me introduce myself, just in case. Bentzion Krik. Camphor, air cushions, a private ward—provide all these things liberally. Otherwise any doctor I find, even a doctor of philosophy, will get no more than six feet of dirt."

But Muginstein died that night regardless. And only then did Yid and a Half cry out through all Odessa.

"Where do the police begin," he wailed, "and where does Benya end?"

"The police end where Benya begins," replied sensible folk, but Tartakovsky refused to take the hint, and he lived to see the day when a red automobile with a music box played its first march from the opera *Laugh, Clown* on Seredinskaya Square. In broad daylight the car flew up to the little house in which Aunt Pesya dwelled.

The automobile arrived on thundering wheels, spat fumes, shone brass, stank of gasoline, and played arias on its horn. Someone sprang out of the car and made his way into the kitchen, where little Aunt Pesya was flailing on the dirt floor. Yid and a Half was sitting in a chair waving his arms.

"You thug!" he cried when he saw the visitor. "You bandit, may the earth spit you up! A nice custom you've taken up, killing live people."

"Monsieur Tartakovsky," Benya Krik replied quietly, "it's been two days and nights now that I've been weeping for the dear departed as for my own brother. But I know that you don't give a damn for my young tears. Shame, Monsieur Tartakovsky. In what kind of safe have you locked up your sense of shame? You had the gall to send the mother of our deceased Iosif a measly hundred *karbovanets*. My brain stood on end with my hair when I heard the news."

Here Benya paused. He was wearing a chocolate jacket, creamy trousers, and raspberry wingtips.

"Ten thousand up front," he roared, "ten thousand up front and a pension till the day she dies, may she live to a hundred and twenty. Otherwise, Monsieur Tartakovsky, let's go outside and discuss this in my automobile . . ."

Then they barked at each other some. Yid and a Half barking at Benya. I wasn't present at this quarrel. But those who were there, they remember it. The men agreed to five thousand in cash and fifty rubles monthly.

"Aunt Pesya," Benya said to the disheveled old lady rolling on the floor, "if you need my life you may take it, but everyone makes mistakes, even God. A huge mistake has been made, Aunt Pesya. But wasn't it a mistake on God's part to settle Jews in Russia and let them be tormented worse than in hell? And would it have been so bad if the Jews lived in Switzerland, where they would be surrounded by first-class lakes, mountain air, and nothing but Frenchmen? Everyone makes mistakes, even God. Listen to me with your ears, Aunt Pesya. You'll have five thousand up front and fifty rubles a month till death—may you live to a hundred and twenty. Iosif will have a deluxe funeral: six horses like six lions, two carriages with garlands, the choir from the Brody Synagogue, Minkovsky himself will sing for your deceased son."

And the funeral was held the next morning. Ask the cemetery beggars about that funeral. Ask the caretakers from the Synagogue of Kosher Poultry Dealers, or ask the old ladies from the Second Almshouse. Odessa had never before seen such a funeral, and the world will never see one. On that day the cops wore cotton gloves. In the synagogues, decked with greenery, their doors thrown open, electric lights were burning. Black plumes swayed on the white horses harnessed to the hearse. A choir of sixty led the procession. The singers were boys, but they sang with the voices of women. The elders of the Synagogue of Kosher Poultry Dealers helped Aunt Pesya along. Behind the elders walked members of the Association of Jewish Store Clerks, and behind the Jewish store clerks were the lawyers, doctors of medicine, and certified midwives. On one side of Aunt Pesya were the women who sold chickens at the old bazaar, and on the other side, draped in orange shawls, were the honorable dairymaids of Bugayevka. They stamped their feet like gendarmes at a holiday parade. Their wide hips wafted breezes that smelled of the sea and of milk. And behind them all plodded Ruvim Tartakovsky's employees. There were a hundred of them, or two hundred, or two thousand. They wore black frock coats with silk lapels and new shoes that squeaked like piglets in a sack.

And now I will speak as the Lord God spoke on Mount Sinai from the Burning Bush. Put my words in your ears. All that I saw, I saw with my own eyes, sitting here on the wall of the Second Cemetery next to lisping Moiseyka and Shimshon from the undertaker's. I saw this, I, Arye-Leib, a proud Jew who lives beside the dead.

The hearse drove up to the cemetery synagogue. The coffin was placed on the steps. Aunt Pesya was trembling like a little bird. The cantor crawled out of the carriage and began the service. Sixty singers responded. Just then a red automobile flew around the bend. It honked, "Laugh, clown!" and came to a stop. People were silent as death. Trees, singers, beggars—all silent. Four men emerged from under the red roof and slowly approached the hearse carrying a wreath of roses such as was never seen before. And when the service ended, the four men placed their steel shoulders beneath the coffin and with burning eyes and heaving breasts walked side by side with the members of the Association of Jewish Store Clerks.

In front walked Benya Krik, whom no one as yet called the King. He was the first to approach the grave, climbed the mound of earth and raised his arm.

"What would you like to do, young man?" cried Kofman of the Burial Society, running over to him.

"I would like to make a speech," replied Benya Krik.

And a speech is what he made. It was heard by all who wished to listen. I, Arye-Leib, listened to it, and lisping Moiseyka, who was sitting on the wall next to me.

"Ladies and gentlemen," said Benya Krik. "Ladies and gentlemen," said he, and the sun rose above his head like a sentry with his rifle. "You have come to pay your last respects to an honest worker who perished over a copper penny. In my name, and in the name of all those not present here, I express my gratitude to you. Ladies and gentlemen! What did our dear Iosif get to see in his life? He saw nothing worth mentioning. How did he occupy himself? Counting other people's money. What did he perish for? He perished for the entire working class. There are people already condemned to death, and there are people who have not even begun to live. And here comes a bullet flying into a condemned breast and cuts down our Iosif, who in his whole life had seen nothing worth mentioning. There are people who know how to drink vodka, and there are people who don't know how to drink vodka but drink it all the same. And one kind gets pleasure from grief and from joy, and another suffers on account of all those who drink vodka without knowing how to drink vodka. And so, ladies and gentlemen, after we have said a prayer for our poor Iosif, I will ask you to accompany to his final resting-place a man unknown to you but already deceased, Savely Butsis . . ."

And having finished his speech Benya Krik descended from the mound. Silent were the people, the trees, and the cemetery beggars. Two grave-diggers bore an unpainted coffin to the next grave. The cantor stammered through his prayers. Benya tossed the first spadeful of soil and crossed over to Savka's grave. All the lawyers and all the ladies with brooches followed him like sheep. He made the cantor roll out the full funeral service over Savka, and the sixty choirboys sang in response. Savka never dreamed of such a funeral—take it from Arye-Leib, an old man who has seen a thing or two.

They say that on that day Yid and a Half decided to close up shop. I didn't witness this myself. But the fact that neither the cantor, nor the choir, nor the Burial Society charged anything for the funeral—this Arye-Leib did see with his own eyes. Arye-Leib—that's what they call me. And more than that I couldn't see, because the people crept quietly away from Savka's grave, then started running as if a house were on fire. They fled in carriages, carts, and on foot. And only the four who had driven up in the red automobile also drove off in it. The music box played its march, the car shuddered and away it went.

"A King," said lisping Moiseyka, watching the car disappear—Moiseyka, the very same one who takes all the best seats from me on the cemetery wall.

So now you know everything. You know who first uttered the word *King*. It was Moiseyka. You know why he didn't give that name to one-eyed Rook or crazy Kolka. You know everything. But what's the use, if you still have glasses on your nose and autumn in your heart? . . .

(published 1923)

The Father

Froim the Rook had been married once. That was a long time ago, twenty years had passed since then. Froim's wife had borne him a daughter then and died in childbirth. They called the girl Basya. Her maternal grandmother lived in Tulchin, that self-serving, weak-sighted little town. The old woman didn't like her son-in-law. She used to say, Froim is a carter by trade, and he's got raven horses, but Froim's soul is blacker than the raven hair of his horses . . .

The old woman didn't like her son-in-law and took the newborn home with her. She lived twenty years with the girl and then died. Then Baska returned to her father's. It all happened like this.

On Wednesday the fifth, Froim the Rook was hauling wheat from the warehouses of Dreyfus and Co. to the *Caledonia* down in the harbor. Toward evening he finished work and drove home. As he turned off Prokhorovskaya Street he ran into Ivan Fiverubles the blacksmith.

"Greetings, Rook," said Ivan Fiverubles. "Some woman is banging down the door of your establishment . . ."

The Rook drove on and saw in his yard a woman of gargantuan height. She had enormous hips and brick-colored cheeks.

"Pa," said the woman in a deafening bass, "I'm bored as hell. I've been waiting for you all day. See, Grandma died in Tulchin."

The Rook stood there on his cart and gaped at his daughter.

"Stop dancing around in front of the horses," he shouted in despair. "Grab the wheeler by the bridle, you'll wreck my horses . . ."

The Rook stood on his cart and cracked his whip. Little Basya took the wheeler by the bridle and brought the horses to the stable. She unharnessed them and went off to fuss in the kitchen. The girl hung her dad's foot cloths on a line, she scoured the sooty teapot with sand, and began to heat up *zrazy* in a cast-iron pot.

"Your place is unbearably dirty, Pa," she said, and took the curdled sheep-skins off the floor and tossed them out the window. "But I'll get rid of this here dirt," cried Baska and served her father supper.

The old man drank his vodka out of an enamel teapot and ate up the *zrazy*, which smelled of happy childhood. Then he took his whip and walked out the gate. And Baska came out after him. She was wearing men's boots and an orange dress, she was wearing a hat decked with birds and sat herself down on a bench. Evening sauntered past the bench, the gleaming eye of sunset was falling into the sea beyond Peresyp, and the sky was red like a red-letter day on the calendar. All business on Dalnitskaya had been wrapped up, and the gangsters drove down Glukhaya Street to Yoska Samuelson's brothel. They drove in lacquered carriages, dressed like hummingbirds in colorful jackets. Eyes bulging, one leg resting on the footboard, and an outstretched arm of steel clutching a bouquet wrapped in tissue paper. Their lacquered cabs moved at a walk, in each carriage sat one man with a bouquet, and the drivers, sticking out prominently on their high seats, were decorated with bows like the best man at a wedding. Old Jewesses in bonnets idly watched this customary procession flow past—they were indifferent to everything, those old Jewesses, and only the sons of the shopkeepers and shipwrights envied the kings of the Moldavanka.

Solomonchik Kaplun, the grocer's son, and Monya Gunner, the smuggler's son, were among those who tried to avert their eyes from the glint of another's good fortune. They both walked past Baska and gave her a wink. They walked past her, swooning like girls who had just come to know love, they exchanged whispers and used their arms to show how they might embrace Baska if only Baska should want it. And, indeed, Baska immediately did want it, for she was a simple girl from Tulchin, from that narrow-minded, nearsighted itty-bitty town. She weighed five poods plus a couple funts; all her life she had spent with the spiteful spawn of Podolian brokers, wandering book peddlers, and timber contractors, and never had she seen people like Solomonchik Kaplun. And so, when she did see him, she started shuffling her fat feet laced up in men's boots, and said to her father:

"Pa," she said in her thunderous voice, "look at that little gentleman. He has footsies like a doll, I could just about smother those footsies . . ."

"Eh-heh, Pani Rook," whispered an old Jew sitting next to them, an old Jew by the name of Golubchik, "I see your wee one wants to run on the grass . . ."

"Now, that'll muddle a mind," Froim replied, played a little with his whip, went off to bed, and calmly fell asleep, because he didn't believe the old man. He didn't believe the old man, and it turned out he couldn't have been more wrong. Golubchik was right. Golubchik did some matchmaking on our street, nights he read prayers over the richly departed, and he knew everything about life you could possibly know. Wrong was Froim the Rook. And Golubchik was right.

And indeed, from that day on Baska spent all her evenings outside the gate. She would sit on the bench and sew her trousseau. Pregnant women would sit next to her; mounds of linen slid across her mighty straddled knees; the pregnant ladies filled up on this and that, just as a cow's udder at pasture fills with the pink milk of spring, and that was also when, one after another, their husbands would come home from work. The husbands of nagging wives would wring out their matted beards under the tap and then make way for humpbacked old ladies. The old ladies would bathe fat babies in washtubs, slap grandkids on their gleaming rumps, and wrap them up in their worn-out skirts. And so Baska from Tulchin came to see the life of our most bountiful Mother Moldavanka, a life stuffed with suckling babes, rags hung out to dry, and nuptial nights full of purlieu chic and soldierly stamina. The girl wanted the same sort of life for herself, but now she learned that a daughter of the one-eyed Rook could not count on a worthy mate. That's when she stopped calling her father Father.

"Redheaded robber," she would shout in the evening, "come and get it, you redheaded robber, it's suppertime . . ."

And this went on until Baska had sewn herself six nightshirts and six pairs of drawers with lace ruffles. Having finished the ruffles she started crying, her voice thin and quite unlike her own, and through tears she said to the unshakable Rook:

"Every girl," she said to him, "every girl has her interest in life, and I alone live like a night watchman guarding someone else's warehouse. Either do something with me, Pa, or I'll do myself in."

The Rook did hear his daughter out. The next day he put on a sailcloth cloak and went to visit Kaplun the grocer on Import Square.

Above Kaplun's shop gleamed a golden sign. His was the first shop on Import Square. It smelled of the seven seas and of wonderful lives unknown to us. A boy was sprinkling the cool depths of the shop with a watering can and singing a song such as only grown-ups should sing. Solomonchik, the owner's son, stood behind the counter; on this counter there was a display of olives from Greece, oil from Marseille, coffee beans, Malaga from Lisbon, Philippe & Canot brand sardines, and cayenne pepper. Kaplun himself sat in his waistcoat basking in the sunroom, eating a watermelon—a red watermelon with black seeds, seeds that slanted like the sly eyes of Chinese women. Kaplun's gut lay on the table under the sun, and there was nothing the sun could do with it. But then the grocer saw the Rook in his sailcloth cloak and blanched.

"Good day, Monsieur Rook," he said, and pushed back his chair, "Golubchik warned me you'd be coming by, and I've prepared for you a pound of such tea, you've never had the like."

And he went on about a new variety of tea brought to Odessa on the Dutch steamers. The Rook listened to him patiently, but then interrupted, for he was a simple man without cunning.

"I am a simple man without cunning," said the Rook, "I stick to my horses and go on about my own business. I'll put up new linens for Baska and an old coin or two, and I will stand for Baska myself—if that's not enough for people, may they burn in flames . . ."

"Why should anyone burn?" Kaplun replied, the words rushing from his mouth, and stroked the carter's arm. "There's no need for such words, Monsieur Rook, after all, everyone knows that you are a man who is able to help another man and, what's more, that you're able to upset another man, and if you are not a Cracow rabbi, well, I didn't stand under the chuppah with the niece of Moses Montefiore either, but . . . but Madame Kaplun . . . There's the matter of Madame Kaplun, that grande dame, and God himself wouldn't know what she wants . . ."

"But I know," the Rook interrupted the shopkeeper with terrible calm, "I know that Solomonchik wants Baska, but that Madame Kaplun doesn't want me . . ."

"That's right, I don't want you," yelled Madame Kaplun, who had been eavesdropping at the door, and she entered the sunroom all ablaze, her breast heaving, "I don't want you, Rook, just like a person doesn't want death; I don't want you like a bride doesn't want pimples on her head. Don't forget that our departed grandfather was a grocer, that our departed papa was a grocer, and that we maintain our position . . ."

"By all means, maintain your position," the Rook replied to the blazing Madame Kaplun, and took himself home.

There Baska awaited him decked in her orange dress, but the old man didn't look her way; he spread his cover under the wagons, lay down to sleep, and slept till Little Basya's mighty hand yanked him out from under the wagons.

"You red robber, you," said the girl in a whisper unlike her usual whisper, "why must I endure your teamster ways, and why are you silent as a stump, you red robber, you? . . ."

"Baska," the Rook announced with terrible calm, "Solomonchik wants you, but Madame Kaplun doesn't want me . . . They're looking for a grocer over there."

And the old man fixed his cover and crept back under the wagons while Basya vanished from the yard . . .

All this happened on a Sabbath, a day no work is done. The carmine eye of sunset swept across the earth and lit on the Rook as he snored beneath his cart that evening. The impetuous ray poked the sleeping man with flaming reproach and pushed him out onto Dalnitskaya Street, dusty and glistening like young rye in the breeze. Tatars were walking up along Dalnitskaya, Tatars and Turks with their mullahs. They were returning from a pilgrimage to Mecca, going home to the Orenburg steppes and to Transcaucasia. A steamer had brought them to Odessa, and they were walking from the harbor to the inn of Lyubka Schneiweiss, nicknamed Lyubka the Cossack. Stiff striped robes covered the Tatars and flooded the pavement with the bronze sweat of the desert. White towels were wound around their fezzes, and these distinguished a man who had bowed to the dust of the prophet. The pilgrims reached the corner, they turned toward Lyubka's inn, but couldn't pass because a crowd had gathered at the gate. Lyubka Schneiweiss, purse hanging on her hip, was beating a drunk and pushing him out into the street. With her clenched fist she beat his face like a tambourine, and with her other hand she held the guy up so he wouldn't fall over. Rivulets of blood trickled between the muzhik's teeth and around his ear—he had a thoughtful expression and looked at Lyubka as if he'd never seen her before, then he fell on the cobbles and went to sleep. Lyubka gave him a kick and returned to her establishment. Her watchman, Yevzel, shut the gates behind her and waved to Froim the Rook, who was passing by.

"My respects, Rook," he said. "If you wish to observe something out of real life, come inside the courtyard, there's something to make you laugh . . ."

And the watchman led the Rook to the wall where the pilgrims who had arrived the evening before were sitting. An old Turk in a green turban, an old Turk green and light as a leaf, lay on the grass. He was covered in pearly sweat, breathing with difficulty. and rolling his eyes.

"There," said Yevzel, and straightened the medal on his worn jacket. "There's a real-life drama from the opera *The Turkish Sickness*. He's on his last legs, the old fellow, but you can't call the doctor because, for them, anyone who dies on the way home from visiting the god of Muhammad is reckoned happy and rich beyond measure . . . Halvash," cried Yevzel to the dying man, and burst out laughing, "here's a doctor come to fix you."

The Turk looked at the watchman with childlike fear and loathing, and turned away. Then Yevzel, pleased with himself, led the Rook across the yard to the wine cellar. Already in the cellar lamps burned and music played. Old Jews with heavy beards played Jewish and Romanian songs. Mendel Krik sat at one of the tables drinking wine from a green glass and recounting how his own sons—the elder Benya and the younger Lyovka—had beaten the crap out of him. He shouted his story in a hoarse and fearsome voice, displayed his shattered teeth, and let people feel the wounds on his stomach. Volhynian tsaddiks with porcelain faces stood behind his chair, transfixed by the bragging of Mendel Krik. They were amazed at all they heard, and the Rook despised them for it.

"The old braggart," he muttered, and ordered wine.

Then Froim called for the owner, Lyubka the Cossack. She was over by the door swearing and drinking vodka standing up.

"Speak," she shouted at Froim, and squinted her eyes in fury.

"Madame Lyubka," began Froim, making room for her to sit beside him, "you are a smart woman, and I come to you like you were my own mama. I place my hopes in you, Madame Lyubka—first in God, next in you."

"Speak," cried Lyubka, ran off across the whole cellar, and then returned to her place.

And the Rook spoke:

"In the colonies," he said, "the Germans have a rich harvest of wheat, while in Constantinople groceries are dirt cheap. A pood of olives you can buy in Constantinople for three rubles, and here they sell them at thirty kopecks a pound. Things are good for grocers now, Madame Lyubka, grocers go around with their stomachs out to here, and if a person approached them with a delicate touch, he might find favor. But I work all on my own, the departed Lyova the Bull has died, there's nowhere I can turn for help, and so I'm all by myself, like God in heaven."

"Benya Krik," Lyubka then said. "You tried him out on Tartakovsky, what's wrong with Benya Krik?"

"Benya Krik?" repeated the flabbergasted Rook. "And he's a bachelor, I believe?"

"He's a bachelor," said Lyubka. "Splice him with Baska, give him money, make introductions . . ."

"Benya Krik," the old man repeated himself like an echo, like an echo from afar, "I hadn't thought of him . . ."

He stood up, muttering and stuttering, Lyubka ran ahead, and Froim plodded along behind her. They went out into the yard and went upstairs to the second floor. There, on the second floor, lived the women that Lyubka kept for visitors.

"Our bridegroom's with Katyusha," said Lyubka to the Rook, "wait for me in the hallway," and she went into the room all the way at the end, where Benya Krik lay with a woman by the name of Katyusha.

"That's enough slobbering," said the innkeeper to the young man. "First you got to get fixed up with some type of occupation, Benchik, and then you can slobber . . . Froim the Rook is looking for you. He's looking for a man for a job and can't find one . . ."

And she told him all she knew about Baska and the affairs of the one-eyed Rook.

"I'll think about it," Benya replied, covering Katyusha's bare legs with the sheet. "I'll think about it, let the old man wait a little."

"Wait a little," Lyubka said to Froim, who was still in the hall. "Wait a little, he'll think about it."

The innkeeper gave Froim a chair, and he was plunged into boundless expectation. He waited patiently, like a muzhik at the council office. Beyond the wall Katyusha moaned and drowned with laughter. The old man nodded off for two hours outside her locked door, two hours and maybe more. Evening had long since turned to night, the sky had grown black, and its milky ways filled with gold, glitter, and chill breezes. Lyubka's cellar had already closed, drunkards lay strewn about the yard like broken furniture, and the old mullah in the green turban had died by midnight. Then music came from the sea, French horns and trumpets from the English ships, the music came from the sea and then faded, but Katyusha, meticulous Katyusha, was still heating up her thickly painted, ruddy, Russian paradise for Benya Krik. She moaned beyond the wall and drowned with laughter; Old Froim sat still at her door, he waited till one in the morning, and then knocked.

"Really, young man," he said, "are you making fun of me?"

Then Benya finally opened the door of Katyusha's room.

"Monsieur Rook," he said, embarrassed, radiant, and covering himself with a sheet, "when we're young, we think of women as goods, but they are but straw that burns from nothing . . ."

And having dressed he straightened out Katyusha's bed, fluffed her pillows, and went out into the street with the old man. They took a walk and reached the Russian cemetery, and there, by the cemetery, there was a meeting of minds between Benya Krik and the crooked Rook, that old gangster. They agreed that Baska should bring her husband a dowry of three thousand rubles, two thoroughbred horses, and a pearl necklace. They also agreed that Kaplun should pay two thousand rubles to Benya, Basya's betrothed. He was guilty of family pride—Kaplun of Import Square, he had grown rich on olives from Constantinople, he had shown no pity for Basya's first love, and for this reason Benya Krik took it upon himself to collect two thousand rubles from Kaplun.

"I will take it upon myself, Pa," he said to his future father-in-law, "God will help us, and we shall punish all the grocers."

This was spoken at dawn, when the night had already passed—and here begins another story, the story of the fall of the House of Kaplun, the tale of its slow ruin, of arson and shots fired in the night. And all this—the fate of the arrogant Kaplun and the fate of Baska the maiden—was decided on that night when her father and her abruptly betrothed strolled past the length of the Russian cemetery. That night boys were pulling girls behind the fences, and kisses resounded upon the tombstones.

(published 1924)

Justice in Brackets

My first run-in was with Benya Krik, the second was with Lyubka Schnei-weiss. Can you even understand these words? Can you sink your teeth into these words and actually taste them? Only Seryozhka Utochkin was missing on this road to ruin. I didn't run into him this time around, and that's why I'm still alive. Like a bronze monument he towers over the city—Utochkin with his red hair and gray eyes. All will be obliged to pass between his bronze legs.

. . . But I shouldn't lead my story down side streets. Shouldn't do it, even when acacia is blooming along those side streets and the chestnuts are about to flower. First Benya, then Lyubka Schneiweiss. We'll stop there. And all will say, there sits a period where it behooves a period to sit.

. . . I had become a broker. Having become an Odessa broker, I grew leaves and sprouts. Burdened with sprouts, I started feeling miserable. The reason? The reason is competition. Otherwise I wouldn't even blow my nose on this whole justice business. I've got no skills up my sleeve. Open air is before me. It shines like the sea beneath the sun, all that beautiful empty air. The sprouts want to eat. I've got seven of them, and my wife is the eighth sprout. I didn't blow my nose on justice. Justice blew its nose on me. The reason? The reason is competition.

The cooperative store was called Justice. There's nothing bad to say about it. Sin be upon him who should speak ill of it. It was run by six partners, *primo de primo*, specialists, one might say, in their vocation. The shop was full of merchandise, and the policeman they posted there was Motya from Golovkovskaya. What more do you need? Nothing, it would seem. The whole deal was suggested to me by the bookkeeper from the Justice. An honest deal, a sure deal, a plain deal. I scrubbed my body with a clothes brush and sent this body off to Benya. Benya made like he didn't notice my body. Then I coughed and said:

"This and that and the other, Benya."

The King was having a bite to eat. A carafe of vodka, a fat cigar, a wife with a belly in her seventh or eighth month—can't say for sure. The terrace was full of greenery and wild grapes.

"This and that and the other, Benya," I say.

"When?" he asks me.

"Seeing as you're asking me," I tell the King, "then I must give you my opinion. In my opinion, best of all would be between Saturday and Sunday. The guard, by the way, is none other than Motya from Golovkovskaya. You could even do it on a weekday, but why turn a simple deal into a not so simple deal?"

Such was my opinion. And the King's wife agreed with it.

"Baby," Benya then said to her, "you should go take a rest on the couch."

Then his fingers slowly tore the golden band off a cigar, and he turned to Froim Shtern:

"Tell me, Rook, are we busy Saturday or are we not busy Saturday?"

But Froim Shtern is a man who keeps his own counsel. He is a man with red hair and only one eye in his head. You're not going to get a straight answer from Froim Shtern.

"On Saturday," he says, "you promised to drop by the Mutual Credit Society . . ."

The Rook made like he had nothing else to say, and his one eye stared aimlessly at the farthest corner of the terrace.

"Excellent," Benya Krik continues, "remind me on Saturday about Tsudechkis, make a note of it, Rook. Go home to your family, Tsudechkis," the King turns to me, "on Saturday evening, in all likelihood, I'll come by the Justice. Take my words with you, Tsudechkis, and be on your way."

The King speaks little and he speaks politely. This scares people so much that they never ask him twice. I left his place, went down Hospital Street, turned on Stenovaya, and then stopped to consider Benya's words. I felt their texture and their weight, I tested them with my front teeth, and realized these were not the words that I needed at all.

"In all likelihood," said the King, as his slow fingers removed the gold band on his cigar. The King speaks little and he speaks politely. Who can ponder the meaning of the King's rare words? In all likelihood, I'll come by, or, in all likelihood, I won't come by? Between a yes and a no there's a five-grand commission. Not counting the two cows, which I keep around out of necessity, I've got nine open mouths to feed. Who gave me the right to take risks? After the Justice bookkeeper came to see me, didn't he go to Buntselman? And hadn't Buntselman, in turn, gone to see Kolya Shtift, and Kolya is an impossible hothead. The words of the King lay like a boulder in the road upon which I had wagered hunger, multiplied by nine mouths. Put more simply, I may have given Buntselman a little heads-up. He was coming to see Kolya just as I was leaving Kolya. It was hot, and he was sweating. "Slow down, Buntselman," I told him, "no point rushing, and no point sweating. This one's my meal ticket. *Und damit Punktum*, as the Germans say."

And it was the fifth day. And it was the sixth day. The Sabbath came to the streets of the Moldavanka. Motya was already at his post, I was already sleeping in my bed, and Kolya got busy at the Justice. He had filled half a cart, and he aimed to fill another half a cart. That's when there was a racket in the alley, a rumble of ironbound wheels; Motya from Golovkovskaya grabbed the telegraph pole and asked, "Should I let it drop?" Kolya replied, "Not yet." (The thing is that the pole could be made to fall if need be.)

The wagon crept down the alley up to the store. Kolya believed the police had come, and his heart was ripped to pieces over the thought he'd have to give up the fruits of his labor.

"Motya," he said, "when I fire, drop the pole."

"Say no more," replied Motya.

Shtift returned to the store and all his helpers with him. They stood along the wall with guns drawn. Ten eyes and five revolvers were pointed at the door, and that's not to mention the notched telegraph pole. The boys could barely contain themselves.

"Beat it, cops," whispered someone who couldn't control himself. "Beat it, or we'll crush you."

"Silence," proclaimed Benya Krik, jumping down from the loft. "Where do you see cops, you mutt? This is the King."

Another minute and there could have been a misfortune. Benya knocked Shtift off his feet and took away his gun. Men started dropping from the loft like rain. It was so dark you couldn't make out anything.

"Well now," Kolka screamed, "Benya wants to kill me, now how do you like that? . . ."

This was the first time in his life that Benya had been taken for a deputy. That was worth a laugh. The gangsters roared with laughter. They turned on their flashlights, clutching their guts, rolling on the floor, gasping with laughter.

Only the King did not laugh.

"In Odessa they will say," he began gravely, "in Odessa they will say, the King was tempted by the earnings of his friend."

"They'll say it once," replied Shtift. "Nobody will say it twice."

"Kolya," the King continued in a solemn and quiet voice, "do you believe me, Kolya?"

And that's when the gangsters stopped laughing. Each of them still had a flashlight glowing in his hand, but all the laughter had skulked out of the Justice cooperative store.

"Believe what, King?"

"Do you believe me, Kolya, that I had nothing to do with this?"

And he sat down in a chair, the downcast King, he covered his eyes with a dusty sleeve and wept. Such was the man's pride, may he burn. And all the gangsters, every single one saw how their King wept from injured pride.

Then they stood before one another. Benya stood, and Shtift stood. They hailed one another in greeting, they made their apologies, they kissed on the lips, and each shook the hand of his fellow like he wanted to rip it off. The dawn was already clapping with its sleepy eyes, Motya already left for the precinct to be relieved, two full carts had already carted away everything of which the Justice cooperative had once consisted, while the King and Kolya were still anguished, still bowing, and now putting their arms around each other's necks and kissing each other tenderly, like drunks.

Whom did Fate seek out that morning? She was seeking me, Tsudechkis, and find me she did.

"Kolya," the King at last inquired, "who sent you to the Justice?"

"Tsudechkis. And who sent you, Benya?"

"Tsudechkis sent me, too."

"Benya," Kolya then exclaimed, "can it really be that we would let him live?"

"Surely not." Benya turns to the one-eyed Shtern, who was standing off to the side giggling, because he and I had had a falling out. "Order a brocade coffin, Froim, and I'll go get Tsudechkis. And you, Kolya, since you started something, you've got to finish it, and I implore you on my behalf and on my wife's behalf to come visit with me in the morning for a bite to eat with my family."

It was five in the morning, or maybe four in the morning, and then again maybe it wasn't four just yet, when the King came into my bedroom, took me, if you will, by the back, removed me from my bed, lay me on the floor, and placed his foot on my nose. Hearing various sounds and so forth, my wife sprang up and asked Benya:

"Monsieur Krik, what are you upset with my Tsudechkis for?"

"What for?" Benya replied, his foot still firmly on the bridge of my nose, as his eyes began to drip with tears, "he has cast a shadow over my name, he has disgraced me before my comrades, you may bid farewell to him, Madame Tsudechkis, for my honor is worth more to me than happiness and he cannot remain among the living . . ."

He continued weeping as he trampled me with his feet. My wife, who could see that I was in great distress, began to scream. This happened at half past four, she finished around eight o'clock. But she really gave it to him good, oho, she really did! It was something splendid!

"Why be angry at my Tsudechkis," she cried, standing on the bed while I writhed on the floor and gazed at her with delight, "why beat up my Tsudechkis? Because he wanted to feed nine hungry nestlings? You're so high and mighty, you're the King, you're son-in-law to a rich man and you're a rich man yourself, and your father's a rich man. To you everyone gives and everything's given, what's one deal gone wrong to Benchik when next week will bring seven deals gone right? How dare you beat up my Tsudechkis? How dare you?"

She saved my life.

When the children woke up, they started screaming together with my wife. Benya nevertheless damaged my health to the extent he felt it needed damaging. He left two hundred rubles for medical costs and left. I was taken to the Jewish Hospital. Sunday I was dying, Monday I got better, and on Tuesday my condition was critical.

So that's my first story. Who is to blame, and why? Is Benya really to blame? Let's not pull the wool over each other's eyes. There is no king like Benya. He exterminates lies and looks for justice, justice in brackets and justice without brackets. But all the rest of them are as cold as aspic—they don't like to look, they're not going to look, and that is worse.

I recovered. And only to fall out of Benya's hands into Lyubka's. First Benya, then Lyubka Schneiweiss. We'll stop there. And anyone can say: there sits a period where it behooves a period to sit.

(published 1921)

Lyubka the Cossack

In the Moldavanka, on the corner of Dalnitskaya and Balkovskaya, there stands the house of Lyubka Schneiweiss. Her house contains a wine cellar, an inn, an oat shop, and a dovecot for a hundred pairs of Kryukov and Niko-laev pigeons. These establishments, together with Section Number 46 of the Odessa quarries, belong to Lyubka Schneiweiss, known as Lyubka the Cos-sack, and only the dovecot is the property of her watchman, Yevzel, a retired soldier with a medal. On Sundays Yevzel makes his way to Hunters Square and sells pigeons to government officials from town and to neighborhood boys. Apart from the watchman, at Lyubka's there lives a Pesya-Mindl, cook and procuress, and the manager, Tsudechkis, a little Jew of the same build and beard as our Moldavanka rabbi, Ben-Zkharya. I know a lot of stories about Tsudechkis. First among them is the story of how he got to be man-ager at the inn of Lyubka, nicknamed the Cossack.

Some ten years ago Tsudechkis brokered the sale to a landowner of a horse-powered threshing machine, and that evening he took the landowner to Lyubka's to celebrate the deal. His client had a mustache with side whis-kers and went around in patent leather boots. Pesya-Mindl served him gefilte fish for his supper, and later on a very nice young lady by the name of Nastya. The landowner spent the night, and in the morning Yevzel roused Tsudech-kis, who had curled up in a ball on the doorstep of Lyubka's room.

"There you go," said Yevzel, "you were bragging yesterday evening how the landowner bought from you a thresher, so you're likely aware that after he spent the night here he ran off at dawn like a son of a . . . And now do pres-ent me with two rubles for the food and four rubles for the young lady. I can tell you're an old man who's seen a thing or two."

But Tsudechkis wouldn't give up the money, so Yevzel shoved him into Lyubka's room and locked him in.

"There you go," said the watchman, "you'll keep here, and later Lyubka will come home from the quarry, and then, by God, she'll rip the soul out of you. Amen."

"Damn ex-convict," replied Tsudechkis to the soldier, and took in his new quarters. "You don't know a thing, you ex-convict, aside from your pigeons, but I still believe in God, who will lead me out of here as he led all the Jews—first out of Egypt, and then out of the wilderness . . ."

The little broker had a lot more he wanted to say to Yevzel, but the soldier took the key and walked off, his boots rumbling on the ground. Then Tsudechkis turned around and saw Pesya-Mindl by the window, sitting and reading a book called *The Miracles and the Heart of the Baal-Shem*. She was reading the gilt-edged Hasidic book and rocking an oak cradle with her foot. In the cradle lay Lyubka's son, Davidka, and he was crying.

"I see there's a fine state of affairs on this Sakhalin Island of yours," said Tsudechkis to Pesya-Mindl. "Here's a child lying and ripping his lungs apart so that it's sad to look at, and you, you whale of a woman, sit there like a stone in the forest and can't give him something to suck . . ."

"You give him something to suck," Pesya-Mindl replied without looking up from her book, "provided he'll take it from you, you old charlatan, 'cause he's a big boy now, big as a Roosky, and all he wants is his mama's milk, and his mama is careering around her old quarries, drinking tea with Jews at the Bear tavern, buying contraband at the harbor, and thinking as much about her son as about last year's snow."

"Yes," the little broker then said to himself, "you're in the hands of Pharaoh, Tsudechkis," and he went over to the eastern wall, mumbled the entire morning prayer, plus supplements, and then took the crying infant in his arms. Davidka looked at him in amazement and wiggled his little raspberry legs bathed in infant sweat, and the old man started walking around the room and, swaying like a tsaddik at prayer, singing a song that went on and on.

"Ah-ah-ah," he sang, "other boys get pinches, but Davidka will get a cake, so that day and night he'll go right back to bed if he should wake. Ah-ah-ah, other boys get punches . . ."

Tsudechkis showed Lyubka's little son a little fist covered with gray hairs and kept repeating the business about pinches and punches until the child fell asleep and the sun had reached the middle of the gleaming sky. It reached the middle of sky and hung there quivering like a fly overcome by the heat. Wild muzhiks from Nerubaysk and Tatarka who had stayed at Lyubka's inn crawled under their wagons, a wild slumber lapping over them, a drunken workman staggered to the gate and, casting off his plane and his saw, collapsed to the ground, collapsed and began to snore unto the very foundation of the world, covered in the golden flies and pale-blue flashes of July. Not far from him, wrinkled German colonists, who had brought Lyubka wine from the Bessarabian border, settled down in the shade. They lit their pipes, and the smoke from their curved stems went tangling through the silvery bristles on their unshaved elderly cheeks. The sun hung down from the sky like the pink tongue of a thirsty dog, the colossal sea rolled against faraway Peresyp, and the masts of distant vessels swayed on the emerald waters of Odessa Bay. Day sat in a brightly painted galley, day sailed on toward evening, and to greet the evening, at almost five o'clock, Lyubka returned from town. She arrived on a little roan nag with a big belly and an overgrown mane. A fat-legged lad in a cotton print shirt opened the gate for her, Yevzel held her horse by the bridle, and then Tsudechkis cried out to Lyubka from his imprisonment:

"My respects to you, Madame Schneiweiss, and good day. Here you've been gone three years on business and abandoned a hungry child in my arms."

"Shut your mug," Lyubka replied to the old man, and dismounted. "Who's that opening his big mouth in my window?"

"That's Tsudechkis, an old man who's seen a thing or two," the soldier with the medal informed his boss, and he started telling her the whole business about the landowner, but he didn't finish his tale, for the broker interrupted and started shrieking with all his might:

"Oh, the nerve," he shrieked, and threw down his yarmulke. "Oh, the nerve, throwing your child into a stranger's arms and then disappearing for three years. Come over and give him the tit."

"Oh, I'm coming over, all right, you swindler," muttered Lyubka, running to the stairs. She came inside the room and pulled a breast out of her dusty blouse. The boy stretched toward her, bit at her monstrous nipple, but got no milk. A vein swelled on the mother's forehead, and Tsudechkis said to her, shaking his yarmulke:

"You want to grab everything for yourself, greedy Lyubka; you drag the whole world to yourself, like children drag a tablecloth that's got bread crumbs; the first wheat you want and the first grapes, too; you want to bake white loaves in the full hot sun, but your little wee one, your little star of a wee one, has to knock around with no milk."

"What milk," cried the woman, squeezing her breast, "what milk is there going to be when the *Plutarch* arrived at port today and I covered fifteen versts in this heat? . . . And you've started singing a song that doesn't end, you old Jew—better pay the six rubles instead . . ."

But again Tsudechkis wouldn't pay up. He loosened his sleeve, bared his arm, and shoved his thin and grimy elbow into Lyubka's mouth.

"Choke, you jailbird," he said and spat in a corner.

Lyubka held the unfamiliar elbow in her mouth, then took it out, locked the door behind her, and went into the yard. Expecting her there was a Mr. Trottyburn, a man like a pillar of orange meat. Mr. Trottyburn was chief engineer on the *Plutarch*. He had brought two sailors with him to Lyubka's. One of the sailors was an Englishman, the other a Malay. The three of them dragged the contraband from Port Said into the courtyard. Their crate was heavy, they dropped it to the ground, and out of the crate tumbled cigars tangled in Japanese silk. A multitude of females ran over to the box, and two visiting Gypsies, swaying and jangling, began to sidle over.

"Out, you crumb pickers!" Lyubka shouted at them, and led the sailors to the shade beneath the acacia.

There they sat down at a table, Yevzel served them wine, and Mr. Trottyburn spread out his wares. Out of his parcel he produced cigars and fine silks, cocaine and sanding files, loose tobacco from the state of Virginia, and black wine procured from the island of Chios. Each ware had its own price—they drank to each figure with Bessarabian wine that smelled of sunshine and bedbugs. Dusk rushed across the yard, dusk rushed like an evening swell along a broad river, and the drunken Malay, full of wonder, touched Lyubka's breast with his finger. Touched it with one finger, then with all his fingers in turn.

His tender yellow eyes hung suspended above the table like paper lamps in a Chinese alley; he started singing a song you could barely hear and fell to the ground when Lyubka pushed him with her fist.

"Look at this classy gent," Lyubka said to Mr. Trottyburn. "I'll lose my last drop of milk because of that Malay, and that Jew there has already chewed me out over the milk . . ."

And she pointed at Tsudechkis, who was standing at the window washing his socks. The little lamp smoked in the room behind him, his basin foamed and hissed, and he poked his head out the window, sensing that people were talking about him, and shouted with despair.

"People, rescue me!" he cried, and waved his arms.

"Shut your mug!" Lyubka burst out laughing. "Shut up!"

She threw a stone at the old man, but missed at first. Then the woman grabbed an empty wine bottle. But Mr. Trottyburn, the chief engineer, took the bottle from her, took aim, and managed to chuck it through the open window.

"Miss Lyubka," said the chief engineer, standing up and gathering his drunken legs together, "many worthy persons come to me for goods, Miss Lyubka, but I don't let anyone have them, not Mr. Kuninzon, nor Mr. Bat, nor Mr. Kupchik, nor nobody except you, because I find your conversation a pleasure, Miss Lyubka . . ."

And having planted himself firmly on his shuddering legs, he took his sailors by the shoulders, one an Englishman and the other a Malay, and went dancing with them across the yard that was now cool. The men from the *Plutarch*, they danced in profoundly thoughtful silence. An orange star that had slid to the very edge of the horizon gaped at them. Then they got their money, linked arms, and went out into the street, swaying like a hanging lamp sways in a ship. From the street they could see the sea, the black waters of Odessa Bay, toy flags atop plunging masts, and piercing lights burning deep below deck. Lyubka saw her dancing guests to the crossing; she remained alone in the empty street, laughed at her own thoughts, and returned home. The sleepy lad in the cotton print shirt locked the gate behind her, Yevzel brought his boss that day's receipts, and she made her way upstairs to bed. There dozed Pesya-Mindl, the procuress, and Tsudechkis was rocking the oak cradle with his bare feet.

"How you have tormented us, shameless Lyubka," said he, and took the child from the cradle. "Now watch and learn, you mother most foul . . ."

He placed a fine-toothed comb against Lyubka's breast and laid her son beside her in bed. The child stretched toward his mother, pricked himself on the comb, and started to cry. Then the old man pushed a nursing bottle at him, but Davidka spurned the bottle.

"What kind of sorcery are you working on me, you old crook?" mumbled Lyubka as she fell asleep.

"Be silent, mother most foul!" replied Tsudechkis. "Be silent and learn, may you drop dead . . ."

The baby again pricked himself on the comb, then hesitantly took the bottle and began to suck.

"There," said Tsudechkis and laughed. "I've weaned your child for you—look and learn, may you drop dead . . ."

Davidka lay in the cradle, sucking the bottle and dribbling blissful drool. Lyubka woke up, opened her eyes, and closed them again. She had seen her son—and the moon breaking through her window. The moon skipped among black clouds like a stray calf.

"Very well then," Lyubka said, "open the door for Tsudechkis, Pesya-Mindl, and let him come by tomorrow for a pound of American tobacco . . ."

And on the next day Tsudechkis came for his pound of loose tobacco from the state of Virginia. He got it, plus a quarter pound of tea to boot. And a week later, when I called on Yevzel to purchase some pigeons, I saw the new manager in Lyubka's yard. He was tiny, like our Rabbi Ben-Zkharya. The new manager was Tsudechkis.

He remained in his new job some fifteen years, and during this time I heard many a tale about him. And if I can, I will tell them all in order, for they are very interesting tales.

(published 1924)

Sunset

One time Levka, the younger Krik, saw Lyubka's daughter Tabl. Tabl is the Yiddish for "dove." He saw her and then disappeared for three days and nights. He took joy from the dust of unfamiliar streets and the geraniums in unfamiliar windows. After three days and nights Levka returned home and found his father in the garden. His father was taking supper. Madame Gorobchik was sitting next to her husband and staring daggers.

"Go away, wicked son," said Papa Krik when he saw Levka.

"Papa," Levka replied, "take a tuning fork and tune up your ears."

"Get to the point."

"There's this girl," he said, "she's got blond hair. Her name is Tabl. Tabl is the Yiddish for 'dove.' I got my eye on this girl."

"You got your eye on filth," said Papa Krik, "and her mother's got a whorehouse."

Hearing his father's words, Levka pulled up his sleeves and lifted an ungodly hand against his father. But Madame Gorobchik sprang up and got between them.

"Mendel," she shrieked, "knock his lights out! He ate up eleven of my cutlets . . ."

"You ate up eleven of your mother's cutlets!" Mendel shouted and went for his son, but Levka got loose and ran from the yard, his older brother, Benchik, on his heels. They roamed the streets into the night, seething like the yeast of vengeance, and at last Levka said to his brother, Benya, who was destined in a few months' time to become Benya the King:

"Benchik," he said, "let's take over, and people will come and kiss our feet. We should kill Pop, who isn't even called Mendel Krik anymore in the Moldavanka. Mendel Pogrom, the Moldavanka calls him. We should kill Pop, for can we really wait any longer?"

"The time hasn't come," replied Benchik, "but the time is coming. Listen for its footsteps and make way. Stand aside, Levka."

And Levka stood aside to make way for time. And it began to make its way—time, that ancient bookkeeper—and along the way it crossed paths with the King's sister, Dvoira, with Manasseh the driver, and with Marusya Yevtushenko, a Russian girl.

Ten years ago, I still knew people who had wanted Dvoira, daughter of Mendel Pogrom, but now Dvoira's got a goiter dangling under her chin and eyes drooping from their sockets. Nobody wants Dvoira. And here's this elderly widower with grown daughters. He had need of a dray and a pair of horses. When Dvoira learned of this, she washed her green dress and hung it out to dry in the yard. She intended to go see the widower and see just how old he was, what kind of horses he needed, and whether she could have him. But Papa Krik had no use for widowers. He took the green dress, hid it in his cart, and drove off to work. Dvoira got the iron ready to press the dress, but she couldn't find it. That's when Dvoira fell to the ground and had a seizure. Her brothers dragged her to the pipe faucet and poured water over her. People, do you not recognize the hand of their father, otherwise known as the Pogrom?

Then there was Manasseh, the old driver who drove Maid of Honor and Solomon the Wise. To his own downfall, he learned that Butsis and Froim the Rook and Chaim Drong had their horses shod in rubber. When he saw that, Manasseh went to Fiverubles and put rubber shoes on Solomon the Wise. Manasseh loved Solomon the Wise, but Papa Krik told him:

"I'm no Chaim Drong and no Nicholas II that my horses should work in rubber."

And he took Manasseh by the collar, lifted him into his cart, and drove out of the yard. Manasseh hung from his outstretched arm like a man on a gallows. The setting sun boiled in the sky, a sunset thick like jam, bells tolled at the Alexeyev Church, the sun was setting behind Blizhniye Melnitsy, and Levka, the owner's son, trailed the cart like a dog trailing his master.

A teeming throng ran after the Kriks as though they were an ambulance, as Manasseh hung implacably from the iron hand.

"Papa," Levka said then to his father, "in your outstretched hand you have crushed my heart. Throw it down and let it roll in the dust."

But Mendel Krik didn't even turn his head. The horses galloped, the wheels thundered—a regular circus for children of all ages. The cart rolled onto Dalnitskaya Street to Ivan Fiverubles the blacksmith. Mendel scoured the smithy wall with Manasseh and tossed him into a pile of scrap metal. Then Levka ran to fetch a bucket of water and threw it over old Manasseh the driver. People, do you now recognize the hand of Mendel, father of the Kriks, otherwise known as the Pogrom?

"The time is coming," Benchik had said once, and his brother, Levka, had stood aside to make way for time. And so Levka stood aside, until Marusya Yevtushenko got knocked up.

"Marusya got knocked up," people started whispering, and Papa Krik laughed when he heard them.

"Marusya got knocked up," he would say, laughing like a little kid. "Woe unto Israel, who is this Marusya?"

Just then, Benchik came out of the stable and put a hand on his father's shoulder.

"I have a fondness for women," Benchik said sternly, and gave his father twenty-five rubles because he wanted to get her scraped out by a doctor at a clinic and not at home.

"I'll give her the money," the father said, "and she'll get scraped, else I shan't live to see the happy day."

And the next morning, at the usual hour, he rode out on Marauder and My Better Half, but around lunchtime Marusya Yevtushenko turned up in the Kriks' yard.

"Benchik," she said, "I loved you, goddamn it."

And she flung ten rubles in his face. Two notes of five was never more than ten.

"Let's kill Pop," Benchik then said to his brother, Levka, and they sat down on the bench by the gate, and beside them sat the son of Anisim the caretaker, Semyon, who was seven years of age. And, indeed, who is to say what a seven-year-old nothing has already learned to love and to hate. Who knew that this nothing loved Mendel Krik, and yet that was who it loved.

The brothers sat on the bench and tried to calculate how old Papa must be and how long a tail trailed after his sixty years, and Semyon, son of Anisim the caretaker, sat beside them.

At that hour the sun hadn't yet reached Blizhniye Melnitsy. It poured into the clouds like blood from a gutted boar, and on the streets old Butsis's carts thundered as they returned from work. The milkmaids were milking the cows for the third time already, and Madame Parabellum's workers were hauling pails of evening milk onto her porch. And Madame Parabellum stood on the porch clapping her hands.

"Ladies," she shouted, "ladies near and ladies far, Berta Ivanovna, ice creamers and butter milkers! Get your evening milk here."

Berta Ivanovna, the German teacher, who would get two quarts of milk for each lesson, got her portion first. Next was Dvoira Krik, who came to see how much water Madame Parabellum poured into her milk and how much soda she sprinkled.

But Benchik took his sister aside.

"This evening," he said, "when you see the old man killing us, come up to him and bash his head in with the colander. And let that be the end of Mendel Krik and Sons."

"Amen, in good time," Dvoira replied and went out the gate. And she saw that Semyon, Anisim's son, was no longer in the yard and that all Moldavanka was coming to visit the Kriks.

The Moldavanka came in droves, as if there were an exclusive engagement in the Kriks' yard. Residents came like people go to Fairground Square on Easter Monday. Ivan Fiverubles the blacksmith dragged his pregnant daughter-in-law along with the grandkids. Old Butsis brought his niece, who had come downriver from Kamenetz-Podolsk. Tabl came with a Russian guy. She leaned on his arm and twirled the ribbon on her braid. Last of all was Lyubka galloping on her roan stallion. And only Froim the one-eyed Rook came all by himself, red as rust, in his sailcloth cloak.

People sat down in the front garden and took out things to eat. Factory workers removed their shoes, sent the kids for beer, and laid their heads on their wives' bellies. And that's when Levka told his brother, Benchik:

"Mendel Pogrom may be our father," he said, "and Madame Gorobchik our mother, but people—people are dogs, Benchik. We're working for dogs."

"We need to think," Benchik replied, but barely had he uttered these words when thunder rumbled on Golovkovskaya Street. The sun soared and started spinning like a red chalice on the sharp end of a spear. The old man's cart was racing to the gates. My Better Half was in a lather. Marauder tore at the harness. The old man cracked his whip over the crazed horses. His enormous legs were spread, raspberry sweat seethed on his face, and he was singing songs in a drunken voice. And that's when Semyon, son of Anisim, slithered like a snake between somebody's legs, sprang into the middle of the street, and shouted at the top of his lungs:

"Turn back the cart, Uncle Krik, your sons wanna whoop you . . ."

But it was too late. Papa Krik stormed into the yard on his lathered horses. He raised his whip, he opened his mouth, and . . . was silent.

The people sitting in the garden feasted their bulging eyes on him. Benchik stood stage left by the dovecot. Levka stood stage right by the caretaker's shed.

"People, neighbors!" Mendel Krik said faintly and lowered his whip. "Behold, how my own blood rises against me."

The old man sprang down from the cart, threw himself at Benya and tarnished the bridge of his nose with his fist. Then Levka rushed over and did what he could. He shuffled his father's face like a new deck of cards. But the old man was sewn from the devil's own hide and the stitches reinforced with cast iron. The old man twisted Levka's arms and threw him to the ground next to his brother. He sat on Levka's chest, and women closed their eyes not to see the old man's broken teeth and his face streaming blood. And at that very moment, the residents of the indescribable Moldavanka heard the swift footsteps of Dvoira and her voice cry out:

"This is for Levka," she said, "this is for Benchik, this is for me, Dvoira, and for everybody," and she bashed her daddy's head in with a colander. People sprang up and ran to him, waving their arms. They dragged the old man to the water pipe, as Dvoira was dragged once, and turned on the faucet. Blood ran in the trough like water and water like blood. Madame Gorobchik squeezed sideways through the crowd, skipping like a sparrow.

"Mendel, say something," she whispered, "shout, anything, Mendel . . ."

But when she heard the silence in the yard, when she saw that the old man had returned from work but the horses weren't unharnessed and nobody was pouring water on the warm wheels, she lurched and started running around the yard like a three-legged dog. And then the honorable neighbors gathered around. Papa Krik lay with his beard sticking up.

"Curtains," said Froim the Rook and turned away.

"Kaput," said Chaim Drong, but Ivan Fiverubles the blacksmith wagged a forefinger under his very nose.

"Three against one," said Fiverubles, "a disgrace for all the Moldavanka, but it ain't evening yet. I've yet to see the lad who could finish off old Krik . . ."

"Evening has come," Arye-Leib cut him off out of nowhere, "evening has come, Ivan Fiverubles. Do not say no, my Russian friend, when life is rumbling yes."

And Arye-Leib squatted down, took out a handkerchief, and wiped the old man's lips, kissed his head, and told him about King David, about the king of all the Jews, who had many wives, much land and treasure, and who knew when the time to weep was nigh.

"Enough with the lamentations, Arye-Leib," cried Chaim Drong and began shoving Arye-Leib from behind, "don't read us the funeral service, we're not at your cemetery!"

And turning to Papa Krik, Chaim Drong said:

"Get up, you old drayman, gargle out your gullet, give us a couple curses like only you know how, you old lout, and get a couple carts ready by morning—I've got scrap to haul . . ."

And everybody waited to hear what Mendel would say regarding the carts. But he said nothing for some time, then opened his eyes and then his mouth, matted with dirt and hair, and blood oozed out between his lips.

"I got no carts," said Papa Krik, "my sons have murdered me. My sons can take over."

Now there's no need to envy anybody who has to take over the bitter legacy of Mendel Krik. There's no need to envy them, for all the mangers in the stables had rotted, half the wheels needed retreading. The sign over the gate was falling apart, you couldn't make out a single word on it, and all the drivers were down to their last putrid pair of underwear. Half the town owed Mendel Krik money, but when the horses picked stray oats from the mangers, they'd also lick the numbers chalked on the stable walls. All day the dumbfounded heirs would be visited by all kinds of muzhiks demanding money for barley and chaff. All day there would be women coming to get their gold rings and nickel-plated samovars out of pawn. There was no peace in the Krik home, but Benya, who in several months' time was destined to become Benya the King, refused to give up and ordered a new sign made: MENDEL KRIK AND SONS COMMERCIAL HAULING COMPANY. This was to be painted in gold lettering on a sky-blue background, intertwined with bronze-colored horseshoes. He also bought a length of striped ticking cloth to make linens for the drivers and a veritable forest of lumber to repair the carts. He hired Fiverubles for an entire week and started giving receipts to each customer. And, let me tell you, by the next day, come evening, he was more worn out than if he'd made fifteen trips between Odessa Port and Odessa Freight. And let me tell you, come evening, he could not find one bread crumb nor one clean plate in the entire house. Try and wrap your mind around the sheer barbarism of Madame Gorobchik. Trash lay unswept in every room, a veal aspic like you've never tasted had been thrown to the dogs. And Madame Gorobchik was perched by her husband's bedside, like a slop-soaked crow on an autumn branch.

"Watch them closely, those two," Benchik said then to his younger brother, "keep them under a microscope, that pair of newlyweds there, because I got the idea, Levka, that they'll be coming after us."

Thus said Benchik to his brother, Levka—thus said Benchik, who could see right through anybody with the eyes of Benya the King, but he, Levka the undershepherd, didn't believe it and went to sleep. His dad was likewise already snoring and rattling the bed boards, while Madame Gorobchik was tossing to and fro. She spat at the wall and coughed phlegm on the floor. Her noxious disposition got in the way of her sleep. But at last she, too, fell asleep. Outside the window, stars were scattered like soldiers relieving themselves, green stars against the midnight-blue. Across the way, Petka Ovsyanitsa's gramophone started playing Jewish songs, then stopped. The night went about its own business, and the air, the rich air, flooded into young Levka's window. He loved the air, Levka did. He lay there and breathed and drowsed and played with the air. He felt like he was on top of the world, until he heard a shuffling and a scraping coming from his father's bed. So the lad closed his eyes and pricked up his ears. Papa Krik poked out his head like a mouse sniffing the air, and crept out of bed. The old man took a satchel of coins from under his pillow and slung his boots over his shoulder. Levka let him leave, for where could he really go, the old hound dog? Then the lad snuck after his father and saw Benchik creeping from the other side of the yard, flat against a wall. The old man silently tiptoed over to the drays, stuck his head in the stable, and whistled to the horses, who ran over to nuzzle against Mendel's head. Night filled the yard with stars, blue air, and silence.

"Sh-sh," Levka put a finger to his lips, and Benchik, who was creeping from the other side of the yard, likewise put a finger to his lips. Papa Krik was whistling to the horses like they were little children, then he ran between the carts and out to the driveway.

"Anisim," he said in a low voice and knocked on the caretaker's window, "Anisim, my old friend, open the gates for me."

Anisim emerged from his shed, bestraggled like hay.

"Old master," he said, "I beg you from the bottom of my soul, don't demean yourself before me, a simple man. Go back to bed, master . . ."

"You'll open the gate for me," Papa Krik whispered even more softly, "I just know you will, Anisim, old friend . . ."

"Go back inside, Anisim," Benchik then said as he went to the caretaker's shed and put his hand on his papa's shoulder. And Anisim then saw before him the face of Mendel Pogrom, pale as paper, and he turned away for he could not look upon his master's face in such a state.

"Don't hit me, Benchik," said old Krik, backing away—"when will your father's torments cease . . ."

"Oh you lowdown father," Benchik replied, "how could you say a thing like that?"

"I could!" cried Mendel and punched himself in the head. "I could. Benchik!" he cried at the top of his lungs and started swaying like an epileptic. "Look at this yard where I spent half my life on earth. This yard saw me when I was a father to my children, a man to my wife, and master of my horses. It saw me in my glory with my twenty stallions and my twenty ironbound carts. It saw my legs, steadfast like pillars, and my hands, my vicious hands. And now, dear sons, open the gate and let me have my wish today, let me depart from this yard that has seen too much . . ."

"Papa," Benya replied, looking down, "return to your wife."

But there was no need to return to Madame Gorobchik. She herself raced to the driveway and started rolling on the ground, kicking her old yellow legs in the air.

"Aiee," she wailed, rolling on the ground, "Mendel Pogrom, my sons, my bastards . . . What have you done to me, my bastards, what have you done to my hair, my body, my teeth, where are they, where is my youth . . ."

The old woman shrieked, tore the shirt off her shoulders, got to her feet, and started spinning in place like a dog trying to bite its own tail. She clawed at her sons' faces, kissed them, tore at their cheeks.

"You old thief," Madame Gorobchik bellowed and skipped around her husband, twirling and pulling his whiskers, "you old thief, my old Mendel . . ."

All the neighbors were roused by her yelling, and everyone in the yard came running to the driveway, and the bare-bellied children tooted on their fifes. The Moldavanka streamed toward the scene of the scandal. And Benya Krik, who had gone gray from disgrace before everyone's eyes, barely managed to chase his newlyweds back inside the house. He drove everyone out with a stick, herding them toward the gate, but Levka, the younger brother, grabbed him by the collar and shook him like a pear tree.

"Benchik," he said, "we're tormenting the old man . . . My tears are burning, Benchik . . ."

"Your tears are burning," replied Benchik, collected a wad in his mouth, and spat in Levka's face. "Oh lowdown brother," he muttered, "contemptible brother, let go of my hands and don't get tangled in my legs."

And Levka let go of his hands. The lad spent the night in the stables till daybreak and then vanished. He took joy from the dust of unfamiliar streets and the geraniums in unfamiliar windows. The boy saw the full length of the road of sorrows, disappeared for two full days, and, when he returned on the third, saw a light-blue sign blazing over the Krik house. The blue sign made his heart jump, the velvet tablecloths knocked Levka's eyes off their feet, the velvet tablecloths were spread out on tables, and a multitude of guests roared with laughter in the garden. Dvoira walked around among the guests wearing a white headdress, starched ladies glittered in the grass like enamel teapots, and staggering factory men, who had already thrown off their jackets, grabbed Levka and brought him inside. There sat the scar-faced Mendel, oldest of the Kriks, while the owner of the Chef D'oeuvre establishment, Usher Boyarsky, his hunchbacked tailor Efim, and Benya Krik all bustled around the disfigured patriarch.

"Efim," Usher Boyarsky was telling his tailor, "would you be so kind as to come measure Monsieur Krik for one of our deluxe striped suits, treat him like family, and do be so bold as to inquire what fabric they would prefer—English double-breasted navy, English single-breasted army, Lodz *demi-saison*, or Moscow slim . . ."

"What kind of outfit you prefer?" Benchik asked Papa Krik. "Make your confession before M. Boyarsky."

"Whatever is in your heart for your father," replied Papa Krik, squeezing a tear from his eye, "make a suit of that."

"Since Papa is no navy man," Benya cut his father off, "the single-breasted army makes more sense. Let's start with a suit for everyday."

Monsieur Boyarsky leaned in and cupped his ear.

"What do you have in mind?" he said.

"This is what I have in mind," Benya replied, "here is a Jew who went his whole life naked and barefoot and muddy like a convict sentenced to Sakhalin Island . . . And now that, thanks be to God, he has reached a ripe old age, it's time to put an end to this interminable sentence, it's time the Sabbath was a Sabbath . . ."

1924–1925 (published 1964)

Froim the Rook

In 1919 Benya Krik's crew ambushed the rearguard of the White Volunteer Army, carved out the officers, and seized part of the supply convoy. As a reward, they demanded that the Odessa soviet grant them three days of "peaceful insurrection," but they didn't get permission and therefore went down Alexandrovsky Prospect and relieved all the shops of their dry goods. Then they redirected their activities to the Mutual Credit Society. Letting the customers go in first, they entered the bank and turned their attention to the porters to request that they load the bags of money and valuables into the car waiting outside. It took a month before they started getting rounded up and shot. At the time, some people said that their capture and arrest had something to do with Aron Peskin, who ran a workshop. As for the manner of work done in this workshop—that was as yet undetermined. His apartment contained a workbench—a long contraption with a bent leaden roller; the floor was littered with sawdust and cardboard for book bindings.

One spring morning, Peskin's pal Misha Yablochko knocked at the door of his workshop.

"Aron," the guest said to Peskin, "the weather outside is divine. I daresay I'm the type of fellow who could grab a half-bottle and a homemade snack and go for a ride to Arcadia with the top down . . . Laugh if you must, but I'm a man who loves to cast his earthly cares aside from time to time . . ."

Peskin got dressed and left for Arcadia with Misha Yablochko in a Steiger touring car. They drove around till evening came; at dusk Misha Yablochko entered the room where Madame Peskina was bathing her fourteen-year-old daughter in a washtub.

"Salutations," said Misha, doffing his hat, "we had a most marvelous time. All that fresh air—simply unbelievable, though I can only talk to that husband of yours on a stomach full of peas . . . Such a tiresome character."

"You're telling me?" proclaimed Madame Peskina, clutching her daughter by the hair and spinning her every which way. "Where is he, the old grifter?"

"He's resting in the front garden."

Misha tipped his hat once more, excused himself, and drove off in his Steiger. Madame Peskina wouldn't wait for her husband and went to find him out front. He was sitting in his panama hat, elbows on the garden table, grinning.

"Grifter!" Madame Peskina said to him, "you're still laughing . . . I'm going to have a fit on account of your daughter—she doesn't want to wash her hair . . . Come and have a talk with your daughter . . ."

Peskin was silent and kept grinning.

"Gorilla!" Madame Peskina began, then she looked at her husband under his panama hat and started screaming.

The neighbors came running when they heard her screams.

"He isn't living," Madame Peskina said to them. "He's dead."

That was incorrect. Peskin was shot in the chest in two places and his skull was bashed in, but he was still alive. They took him to the Jewish Hospital. None other than Dr. Zilberger operated on the wounded man, but Peskin was out of luck—he died under the knife. That very night the Cheka arrested a person nicknamed the Georgian and his friend Kolya Lapidus. One of them was Misha Yablochko's driver, the other was waiting for the buggy in Arcadia, along the shore where the road turned away toward the steppes. They were shot after an interrogation that didn't take very long. Only Misha Yablochko evaded the ambush. There was no trace of him, and after several days an old woman came to Froim the Rook's yard selling sunflower seeds. She was carrying her goods in a basket. One of her brows was arched like a bushy coal-black hedge, the other, barely discernible, curved above her temple. Froim the Rook was sitting outside the stable with his legs spread, playing with his grandson, Arkady. Three years ago, the boy had dropped from the mighty womb of his daughter, Baska. The grandfather gave his finger to Arkady, who grabbed it and started swinging like he was on a high bar.

"You're so silly . . ." said Froim to his grandson, gazing at him with his solitary eye.

Along came the old woman with the bushy brow and the men's top boots laced with twine.

"Froim," she said, "I tell you these people aren't human beings. They don't say nothing. They smother us in the cellar like dogs in a ditch. They don't let us say a word before we die . . . They should be chewed up and spat out, these people, and their hearts should be ripped from their chests . . . Nothing to say, Froim?" added Misha Yablochko, "the boys are waiting for you to say something . . ."

Misha rose, put the basket around his other arm, and left, arching his black brow. Three girls with their hair in braids met him on Alexeevsky Square by the church. They were strolling with their arms around each other's waists.

"Young ladies," Misha Yablochko said to them, "afraid I can't invite you for tea and sesame bagels . . ."

He poured a glassful of sunflower seeds into their dress pockets and disappeared behind the church.

Froim the Rook remained alone in his yard. He sat motionless, peering into the distance with his one eye. Mules, taken from the colonialist forces, were crunching their hay in the stable, plump mares grazed in the meadow with their foals. In the shade beneath the chestnut tree, the drivers were playing cards and slurping wine from broken cups. Hot gusts of wind assaulted the chalky walls, the sun poured from its pale-blue stupor over the yard. Froim got up and went out into the street. He crossed Prokhorovskaya, its fumes filling the sky with the modest melting smoke of its kitchens, and the square of Tolkuchy Market, where people wrapped in drapes and curtains tried to sell them to one another. He reached Catherine Street, turned at the monument of the empress, and went inside the Cheka building.

"I'm Froim," he said to the commandant. "I need to see the boss."

At that time the chairman of the Cheka was Vladislav Simen, from Moscow. When he learned that Froim was there, he called over his investigator, Borovoi, to find out about the visitor.

"A grand fellow," Borovoi replied, "the living embodiment of all Odessa is in your presence . . ."

And the commandant brought in the old man—dressed in sailcloth overalls, big as a building, red-haired, with a patched eye and a scarred cheek.

"Boss," he said as he was led in, "who are you killing? . . . You're killing off the eagles. Who will you be left with, boss, the absolute dregs? . . ."

Simen reached for his desk drawer and began to open it.

"I'm clean," Froim said, "I got nothing in my hands and nothing in my boots, and I don't have anyone waiting outside . . . Let my boys go, boss, name your price . . ."

The old man was settled into an armchair and offered cognac. Borovoi left the room and called over the investigators and commissars from Moscow.

"Let me show you this guy," he said, "he's an epic unto himself—you'll never find the like . . ."

And Borovoi told them about how it was the one-eyed Froim, not Benya, who was the real ringleader of the forty thousand Odessa thieves. He kept it close to the vest, but everything that happened happened according to his plan—the attack on the factories and the Treasury in Odessa, the ambushes on the White Volunteers and the Allied forces. Borovoi was waiting for the old man to come out in order to have a talk with him. Froim didn't turn up. The investigator got tired of waiting and went looking for him.

He searched the whole building and then finally glanced in the backyard. Froim the Rook was lying there stretched out under a tarp by the ivy-covered wall. Two Red Army men were smoking hand-rolled cigarettes over his body.

"That guy was a bear," said the older one when he saw Borovoi, "strong like you wouldn't believe . . . Can't just kill an old man like that one, couldn't even wear him down . . . Ten rounds in the guy and he still keeps coming at you . . ."

The Red Army man went red in the face, eyes gleaming, his cap slipped to the side.

"You're talking out of your ear," said the other soldier, "he died like the rest . . ."

"Not like the rest," the older one protested, "this one begs and screams, that one doesn't say a word . . . What do you mean, like the rest?"

"As far as I'm concerned, just like the rest," the younger soldier repeated stubbornly, "every one of them is the same, I can't tell the difference . . ."

Borovoi bent down and pulled up the tarp. The old man's face was frozen in a grimace.

The investigator returned to his room. It was a circular hall lined with satin wallpaper. They were holding a meeting there about new work rules. Simen was presenting a report about irregularities he had found, poorly written verdicts, interrogation records that were unintelligible. He was insisting that investigators split up into groups and start working with legal advisers and conducting their business according to the rules and regulations laid down by the Chief Directorate of the Cheka in Moscow.

Borovoi listened sitting in the corner. He sat by himself, far away from the others. Simen went up to him after the meeting and held his hand.

"You're upset with me, I know," he said, "but we're the ones in charge now, Sasha, the only ones—the government's in charge, you've got to remember that . . ."

"I'm not upset," Borovoi replied and turned away, "you're not an Odessan, there's no way you would know how there's a whole history here with this old man . . ."

They sat side by side, the Cheka chairman, who had just turned twenty-three, and his subordinate. Simen held Borovoi's hand in his own hand and kept squeezing it.

"Tell me, as a Chekist," he said after a moment of silence, "tell me as a revolutionary—what use would this man be in the society to come?"

"I don't know." Borovoi didn't budge and looked straight ahead. "Probably none . . ."

He pulled himself together and drove away the memories. Later, when he had recovered, he began once again to tell the Chekists from Moscow of the life of Froim the Rook, of his resourcefulness, his elusiveness, his contempt for his fellow man, all the remarkable tales of bygone days.

1933 (published 1963)

The End of the Poorhouse

During the famine nobody lived better in Odessa than the residents of the poorhouse by the Second Jewish Cemetery. Kofman, the dry goods merchant, had at some point erected, in memory of his wife, Isabella, a poorhouse next to the cemetery wall. This location generated much amusement at the Café Fanconi. But Kofman was proven right. After the Revolution the old men and women sheltered by the cemetery were able to take over the responsibilities of the gravediggers, cantors, and corpse washers. They got themselves an oak coffin with a pall and silver tassels and rented it out to the poor.

Timber at the time was not to be had in Odessa. The rented coffin did not stand idle. The deceased lay in the oak box at home and at the service; he was lowered into the grave in nothing but a shroud. This was done according to a forgotten Jewish law.

The sages taught that the worms must not be hindered from joining with the carrion, for it was unclean. "From earth you came and to earth you shall return."

Thanks to the revival of the old law, in addition to their rations the old folk got such victuals as no one dreamed of in those years. Evenings they caroused in Zalman Krivoruchka's wine cellar and supplied their neighbors with the scraps.

Their well-being went undisturbed until the rebellion in the German colonies. The Germans killed the garrison commander in battle, Hersh Lugovoy.

He was buried with full honors. The troops arrived at the cemetery with brass bands, field kitchens, and machine guns on *tachanka*s. Speeches were given and oaths pledged before the open grave.

"Comrade Hersh," cried Lyonka Broitman the division chief, straining his voice, "Comrade Hersh entered the RSDLP of the Bolsheviks in 1911, where he worked as a propagandist and liaison agent. Comrade Hersh was subjected to repressive measures together with Sonya Yanovskaya, Ivan Sokolov, and Monoszon in 1913 in the town of Nikolaev . . ."

Arye-Leib, the poorhouse elder, stood ready with his comrades. Lyonka had barely concluded his farewell words when the old men began turning the coffin on its side so as to dump the banner-draped corpse. Lyonka gave Arye-Leib a discreet poke with his spur.

"Get lost," he said, "get lost, I told you. Hersh earned his keep for the Republic."

Before the eyes of the stunned old men, Lugovoy was interred together with the oak box, the tassels, and the black pall that had shields of David and a verse from the Hebrew prayer for the dead stitched in silver.

"We are dead men," said Arye-Leib to his comrades after the funeral, "we are in the hands of Pharaoh."

And he ran to Broidin, the man in charge of the cemetery, to request that lumber should be issued for a new coffin and cloth for a pall. Broidin promised but did nothing. His plans did not include enriching old men. At the office he said:

"My heart aches more for the unemployed municipal workers than for these old speculators . . ."

Broidin promised but did nothing. At Zalman Krivoruchka's wine cellar, Talmudic curses rained down upon Broidin's head and upon the heads of the members of the Union of Municipal Workers. The old men cursed the marrow in Broidin's bones and in the bones of the union members, cursed the fresh seed in the wombs of their wives, and wished each one his own particular type of ulcer and paralysis.

Their income was reduced. The ration now consisted of a blue broth with fish bones. The second course was barley porridge without butter.

An old man from Odessa can eat any kind of broth, whatever it consists of, so long as it contains a bay leaf, garlic, and pepper. In this case there were none of these things.

The Isabella Kofman Poorhouse shared in the common fate. The outrage of the famished elderly increased. It came crashing down upon the head of a person who least expected it. This person turned out to be Dr. Judith Shmeiser, who had come to the poorhouse to give smallpox injections.

The Provincial Executive Committee had issued a decree for compulsory smallpox inoculation. Judith Shmeiser laid out her instruments on the table and lit her alcohol lamp. Outside the windows stood the emerald walls of the cemetery bushes. The little blue tongue of flame mingled with the lightning flashes of June.

Right next to Judith stood Meyer the Endless, a skinny old man. He observed her preparations sullenly.

"Just a little prick," said Judith, and flicked her tweezers. She began to pull the blue whip of his arm out of its rags.

The old man jerked his arm back.

"I got nothing to prick."

"It won't hurt," cried Judith, "it won't hurt in the fleshy part."

"I got no fleshy part," said Meyer the Endless. "I got nothing to prick . . ."

He was seconded by dull sobbing from the corner of the room. The sobbing came from Doba-Leah, who used to cook at circumcisions. Meyer twisted his decrepit cheeks.

"Life is a dung heap," he mumbled, "the world a bordello, the people—all swindlers."

The pince-nez on Judith's little nose wavered, her bosom bulged from her starched gown. She opened her mouth to explain the benefits of smallpox inoculation, but she was interrupted by Arye-Leib, the poorhouse elder.

"Young lady," said Arye-Leib, "we were borne by a mother just as you were. This woman, our mama, gave birth to us so we could live, not so we could be tortured. She wanted us to live well, and she was right, the way a mother is right. A person satisfied with what Broidin lets him have, that person isn't worth the material from which he was made. Your goal, young lady, consists of inoculating smallpox, and you, with God's help, inoculate it. Our goal consists in living out the remainder of our life and not torturing it, and we are not accomplishing that goal."

Doba-Leah, a bewhiskered old woman with the face of a lion, heard these words and sobbed louder still. Her sobbing resounded in the bass clef.

"Life is a dung heap," Meyer the Endless repeated, "people are swindlers . . ."

The paralyzed Simon-Wolf seized the steering rod of his wheelchair and moved squeaking toward the door, twisting his hands. His yarmulke slipped from his swollen raspberry-colored head.

In Simon-Wolf's wake, all thirty old men and women swooped out onto the main alleyway, snarling and grimacing. They shook their crutches and brayed like hungry donkeys.

Seeing them, the guard slammed the cemetery gates shut. The gravediggers picked up their shovels with the soil and grass roots sticking to them and stopped in bewilderment.

When he heard the noise, bearded Broidin emerged in his gaiters and cycling cap and his cropped jacket.

"Swindler," Simon-Wolf shouted at him, "there's nowhere to prick us . . . there's no meat on our arms . . ."

Doba-Leah bared her teeth and growled. She started to drive the paraplegic's wheelchair into Broidin. Arye-Leib began, as always, with allegories, parables that crept up from afar and toward a target not all could see.

He began with the parable of Rabbi Hosea, who gave his property to his children, his heart to his wife, his fear to God, his taxes to Caesar, and kept for himself only a place beneath the olive tree where the setting sun shone longest. From Rabbi Hosea, Arye-Leib passed on to the subject of lumber for a new coffin and the question of rations.

Broidin planted his gaitered legs wide apart and listened, without lifting his eyes. The brown barricade of his beard lay motionless on his new army jacket; he looked like he had given himself over to sad and tranquil thoughts.

"You will forgive me, Arye-Leib," Broidin sighed, addressing the cemetery sage, "you will forgive me if I say that I cannot help but detect in you an ulterior motive and a political agenda . . . Behind your back, I cannot help but see people who know exactly what they are up to, just as you know what you are up to . . ."

Here Broidin lifted his eyes. In an instant they had filled with the white water of fury. The quivering mounds of his eyes were fixed on the old folk.

"Arye-Leib," said Broidin in his powerful voice, "go read the telegrams from the Tatar Republic, where great numbers of Tatars are mad with hunger . . . Read the appeals of the Petersburg proletariat, who toil and wait hungry by their work benches . . ."

"I have no time to wait," Arye-Leib interrupted the boss. "I've got no time left . . ."

"There are people," Broidin thundered, hearing nothing, "people who live worse than you, and there are thousands of people who live worse than those who live worse than you . . . You are sowing trouble, Arye-Leib, and you will reap the whirlwind. You will be dead men, if I turn away from you. You'll all die if I go my own way and you go yours. You'll die, Arye-Leib. You'll die, Simon-Wolf. You'll die, Meyer the Endless. But before you die, tell me—I am interested to know—are we under Soviet rule, perchance, or aren't we? If we aren't and I'm mistaken, then take me to Mr. Berzon on the corner of De Ribas and Yekaterininskaya, where I toiled as a waistcoat maker all the years of my life. Tell me I'm mistaken, Arye-Leib . . ."

And the cemetery boss came up to the cripples. His quivering eyeballs bulged right at them. They swept over the petrified, groaning herd like the beams of a searchlight, like tongues of flame. Broidin's gaiters crackled, sweat seethed on his plowed-up face, he got into Arye-Leib's face and demanded an answer—had he been mistaken in thinking Soviet rule had already arrived?

Arye-Leib was silent. This silence might have been his downfall had the barefooted Fedka Stepun not appeared in his sailor shirt at the end of the alleyway.

Fedka had been shell-shocked outside Rostov at some point, he lived as a convalescent in a hut next to the cemetery, carried a police whistle on an orange string and a revolver that had lost its holster.

Fedka was drunk. Curls of stone rested over his forehead. Beneath the curls was a bony face twisting in spasms. He went over to Lugovoy's grave, which was wreathed in faded garlands.

"Where were you, Lugovoy," Fedka said to the deceased, "when I stormed Rostov?"

The sailor gnashed his teeth, blew on his police whistle, and pulled the revolver from his belt. The burnished muzzle flashed.

"They crushed the tsars," cried Fedka, "the tsars are no more. They should all be lying without coffins."

The sailor squeezed his revolver. His chest was bare. There was a tattoo on it with the word *Riva* and a dragon whose head curved toward Fedka's nipple.

The gravediggers crowded around Fedka with their shovels raised. The women who washed the deceased emerged from their cells and got ready to wail together with Doba-Leah. Howling waves beat against the closed cemetery gates.

Relatives, who had brought their dear departed on wheelbarrows, demanded to be let inside. Paupers banged their crutches against the railings.

"They crushed the tsars." The sailor fired at the sky.

People came bounding and skipping down the alleyway. Broidin was slowly turning pale. He raised his hand, agreed to everything the poorhouse demanded, and, turning on his heel like a soldier, went to his office. The gates swung open that very instant. The relatives of the dead, pushing their little carts before them, trundled smartly down the paths. Self-proclaimed cantors sang "El moley rachim" in piercing falsettos over open graves. That evening they celebrated their victory at Krivoruchka's. Fedka was stood three quarts of Bessarabian wine.

"*Hevel havolim*," said Arye-Leib, clinking glasses with the sailor, "you're a true soul, one can get along with such a man . . . *Kuloi hevel*."

The owner, Krivoruchka's wife, was rinsing glasses behind the partition.

"If a Russian happens to be a person of good character," Madame Krivoruchka observed, "it is truly a thing of splendor . . ."

Fedka was helped outside close to two in the morning.

"*Hevel havolim*," he mumbled the devastating, incomprehensible words as he picked his way along Stepovaya Street. "*Kuloi hevel . . .*"

The next day the old people at the poorhouse were given four lumps of sugar apiece and some meat to make borscht. In the evening they were taken to the City Theater for a production arranged by the Department of Social Security. It was *Carmen*. For the first time in their lives the old crocks and cripples saw the gilt tiers of the Odessa theater, the velvet of its partitions, the buttery glow of its chandeliers. During the intermissions everybody got liver-sausage sandwiches.

Then they were taken back to the cemetery in an army truck. It belched and thundered its way along the frozen streets. The old folk fell asleep with bulging bellies. They belched in their sleep and twitched with satisfaction like dogs after a good chase.

In the morning Arye-Leib got up before the others. He turned to the east to pray, and saw a notice on the door. On it Broidin had announced that the poorhouse was being closed for repairs, and that all pensioners were to appear on this date at the Provincial Department of Social Security to register for work reassignment.

The sun floated over the treetops of the green cemetery grove. Arye-Leib brought his fingers to his eyes. He squeezed a tear from the extinguished hollows.

The gleaming chestnut avenue led toward the mortuary. The chestnuts were in bloom, the trees carried tall white flowers in their outspread paws. An unfamiliar woman with a shawl bound tight over her breast was busy in the mortuary. There everything had been redone—the walls decorated with fir trees, the tables scrubbed. The woman was washing an infant. She turned it deftly side to side: the water flowed in a brilliant stream down the sunken, blotchy little back.

Broidin in his gaiters sat on the steps of the mortuary. He had the look of a man at rest. He took off his cap and wiped his forehead with a yellow handkerchief.

"That's what I told Comrade Andreychik at the union," the unknown woman said in a melodious voice, "we don't shy away from hard work . . . They can ask about us in Yekaterinoslav . . . Yekaterinoslav knows how we work."

"Make yourself at home, Comrade Blyuma, make yourself at home," Broidin said peaceably, tucking away his yellow handkerchief in his pocket. "I'm very easygoing . . . Very easygoing," he repeated himself, and turned his flashing eyes on Arye-Leib, who had dragged himself to the mortuary steps, "so long as you don't spit in my porridge . . ."

Broidin didn't finish his speech: a cab drawn by a tall black horse pulled up at the gates. The Public Services director climbed out of the buggy in his Eton shirt. Broidin helped him down and led him to the cemetery.

The old tailor's apprentice showed his boss a hundred years of Odessa history resting beneath the granite flagstones. He pointed out the monuments and vaults of the wheat exporters, ship brokers, and businessmen who had built the Russian Marseille atop the settlement of Khadjibey. They all lay there facing the gates, Ashkenazis, Gessens, and Ephrussis—polished misers, philosophical philanderers, creators of wealth and Odessa humor. There they lay beneath the monuments of pink marble and labradorite, protected by chains of chestnuts and acacias from the plebs pressed up against the walls.

"When they were living, they wouldn't let you live," said Broidin, tapping his boot against a monument. "When they were dead, they wouldn't let you die . . ."

He became animated as he told the Public Services director about his plans for redesigning the cemetery and his campaign against the Burial Brotherhood.

"And get rid of those, too," said the director, pointing to the paupers crowding at the gate.

"It's getting done," replied Broidin, "getting done, one step at a time . . ."

"Well, keep at it," said the director Mayorov. "You got this under control, chief, keep at it . . ."

As he stepped onto the footboard of the buggy, he remembered Fedka.

"And what's that Punch and Judy all about? . . ."

"The guy's shell-shocked," said Broidin, lowering his eyes, "sometimes gets out of hand. But we explained things to him now and he's sorry."

"Everything's cooking," said Mayorov to his companion as they drove off, "purring along."

The tall horse drove Mayorov and the head of the Public Works Department toward town. Along the way they passed the old men and women who had been evicted from the poorhouse. Limping, bowed beneath their bundles, they plodded along in silence. Sprightly Red Army men were keeping them in line. The wheelchairs of the paraplegics squeaked. An asthmatic hiss, an abject rasping erupted from the breasts of cantors emeriti, wedding jesters, circumcision cooks, and retired sales clerks.

The sun was high. The heat tore into the heap of rags trailing along the ground. Their path lay along a cheerless, parched, and stony highway, past huts of packed clay, past stone-choked fields, past bombed-out houses, past the plague mound. In Odessa, an inexpressibly sad road once led from the town to the cemetery.

1920–1929 (published 1932)

You Missed the Boat, Captain!

The steamer *Halifax* had come to Odessa. It had come from London to load Russian wheat.

On the twenty-seventh of January, the day of Lenin's funeral, the colored crew—three Chinese, two Negroes, and a Malay—asked the captain to come on deck. In town the bands were thundering and a blizzard was blowing.

"Captain O'Nearn," said the Negroes, "there's no loading today, let us go into town till evening."

"Keep at your stations," replied O'Nearn. "There's a nine-point gale and it's blowing stronger: the *Beaconsfield* is stuck in the ice by Sanzheyka, and you don't want to look at the barometer. In such weather the crew's place is on board. Keep at your stations."

And having said this, Captain O'Nearn left to see the second mate. He and the second mate cracked jokes, smoked cigars, and kept pointing at the city, where, amid uncontrollable grief, the blizzard blew and the bands howled.

The two Negroes and the three Chinese slouched aimless about the deck. They blew on their benumbed palms, stamped their rubber boots, and kept looking in through the half-open door of the captain's cabin. From there issued a nine-point gale of velvet sofas, warmed by cognac and fine tobacco smoke.

"Bosun!" cried O'Nearn, upon seeing the sailors. "The deck's not a promenade. Send those boys to the hold."

"Aye, sir," replied the bosun, a pillar of red meat thick with red hair, "aye, sir," and he took the disheveled Malay by the scruff of the neck. He took him to the seaward side and chucked him out onto the rope ladder. The Malay scrambled down and ran off across the ice. The three Chinese and two Negroes ran behind him.

"Did you send the men to the hold?" asked the captain, sitting in the cabin warmed by cognac and fine tobacco smoke.

"Send them I did, sir," replied the bosun, that pillar of red meat, and then stood by the gangway like a sentinel in a storm.

The wind blew from the sea—a nine-point gale like nine shells discharged by the frozen batteries of the sea. White snow raged above the clumps of ice.

And flying frantically shoreward across the petrified waves, to the moorings, were five crouched commas with charcoal faces and billowing jackets. Scraping their hands, they scrambled ashore up the ice-covered posts, ran through the harbor, and flew into the city that shivered in the wind.

A squad of longshoremen with black banners was marching into the square, to the place reserved for Lenin's statue. The two Negroes and the Chinese marched beside the longshoremen. They were panting for breath and shaking people's hands and rejoiced with the joy of escaped convicts.

At that moment in Moscow's Red Square, Lenin's body was being lowered into the crypt. By us, in Odessa, the sirens wailed, the blizzard blew, and the crowds marched on in rows. While aboard the *Halifax* the impenetrable bosun stood at the gangway like a sentinel in a storm. Behind his equivocal protection, Captain O'Nearn drank cognac in his smoke-filled cabin.

He had relied on the bosun, O'Nearn had—and the captain missed the boat.

Bab-El (published 1924)

Karl-Yankel

Throughout my childhood Yonah Brutman had the blacksmith's shop at Peresyp. Horse dealers, teamsters—in Odessa they're called draymen—and butchers from the city slaughterhouses would all get together there. The smithy was near Balta Road. If you chose it as an observation post you could watch muzhiks carting oats and Bessarabian wine to the city. Yonah was a fearful little man, but he was accustomed to wine, and the soul of an Odessa Jew abided in him.

Back then he was raising three sons. You couldn't find a dovecot better than theirs in the whole city. The blacksmith's sons used to come to the Alexandrovsky Market with hundreds of pigeon pairs. Just before the war they started to breed homing pigeons. It was a veritable factory of birds; they took up as much space as the smithy itself. You wouldn't even dream of taking down Yonah's sons. There were three of them. The father reached up to their waists. It was on the shore at Peresyp that I first pondered the mighty powers that secretly dwell in nature. Three fattened bullocks with burgundy shoulders and feet like shovels—they used to carry the shriveled Yonah down to the water like you'd carry an infant. And yet all the same, it was he and nobody else who begat them. There were no doubts in that regard. The blacksmith's wife was devout, fanatically devout. Her native Volhynian shtetl of Medzhibozh was the birthplace of the teachings of Hasidism. The old woman went to the synagogue twice a week—on Friday evening and Saturday morning. It was a Hasidic synagogue—at Passover they would dance to the point of ecstasy, like dervishes. Yonah's wife used to donate to the emissaries sent out into the southern provinces by the Galician tsaddiks. The blacksmith did not interfere in his wife's relations with God—after work he used to go off to a wine cellar near the slaughterhouses and there, swilling cheap rosé, he would meekly listen to what people were talking about—the price of livestock and politics.

In strength and build the sons took after their mother. Two of them, when they grew up, went and joined the partisans. The eldest was killed at Voznesensk, the other Brutman, Semyon, went over to Primakov—into a Red Cossack division. They chose him to command a Cossack regiment, and later, when the division was expanded into a corps, he became a divcom. Out of him and a few other shtetl boys arose that unexpected breed of Jewish warriors, raiders, and partisans.

The third son went into his father's trade and became a blacksmith. He is now working at the Ghen plow factory in the old town. He never married and fathered no children.

Semyon's children roamed around with his division. The old woman needed a grandson to whom she could tell stories about the Baal-Shem. This grandson she would get from her youngest daughter, Polya. She was the only one in the family to take after little Yonah. She was easily spooked, nearsighted, and soft-skinned. She had lots of suitors. Polya chose Ovsey Belotserkovsky. We could never understand why. Even more amazing was the news that the young couple was quite happy together. A woman's household is her own business: outsiders don't see how the pots get broken. But in this case it was Ovsey Belotserkovsky breaking the pots. A year after the wedding he sued his mother-in-law, Brana Brutman. Taking advantage of Ovsey's absence on official business somewhere and of the fact that Polina was in the hospital with mastitis, the old woman had kidnapped her newborn grandson, carried him off to a small-time operator named Naftula Gerchik, and there, in the presence of ten wrecks, ten ancient and impoverished old men, regulars at the Hasidic synagogue, the ceremony of circumcision had been performed upon the infant.

All this Ovsey Belotserkovsky learned after his return. Ovsey had his name down for admission to the party. He decided to seek advice from Bychach, the party secretary of the local State Trade Commission.

"You've been morally sullied," Bychach told him. "You got to do something about this . . ."

The Odessa Prosecutor's Office decided to hold a show trial at the Petrovsky Factory. The small-time operator Naftula Gerchik and the sixty-two-year-old Brana Brutman found themselves in the dock.

In Odessa Naftula was just as much a city landmark as the statue of the Duc de Richelieu. He used to pass by our windows on Dalnitskaya with his tattered, grimy obstetrical bag in hand. In this bag he kept his very basic instruments. He would pull a little knife out of it, or a bottle of vodka and a piece of gingerbread. He would sniff the gingerbread before taking a drink and, having drunk, would draw out his prayers. He was redheaded, Naftula was, like the first redheaded man on earth. When he was cutting off what was his to cut, he didn't drain the blood through a little glass tube but sucked it away with his turned-out lips. The blood would be smeared on his unkempt beard. When he came out to the guests, he would be tipsy.

His bearlike eyes were shining merrily. Redheaded like the first redheaded man on earth, he would intone the blessing over the wine through his nose. With one hand he would tip the vodka into the overgrown, crooked, and fire-breathing pit of his mouth, in his other hand would be a plate. On it lay the little knife crimson with infant blood and a piece of gauze. As he collected his money, Naftula would make his away around the guests with this plate, he would push his way through among the women, falling over them, grabbing bosoms, and yelling for the whole street to hear.

"Fat mamas," the old man would yell, his coral eyes flashing, "make little boys for Naftula, thresh wheat on your bellies, do your best for Naftula . . . make little boys, you fat mamas . . ."

The husbands threw money on his plate. Wives would wipe the blood from his beard with napkins. The courtyards of Glukhaya and Hospital Streets faileth not. They seethed with children as estuaries seethe with roe. Naftula used to trudge along with his bag like a tax collector. Prosecutor Orlov put an end to Naftula's wanderings.

The prosecutor thundered from the podium, striving to prove that the small-time operator was in the service of a cult. The shaggy nut of Naftula's head dangled down somewhere near the guards' legs. The genius of the race spoke in the old man—in court he withered, curled, contracted implausibly.

"Do you, in fact, believe in God?" Naftula was asked.

"Let him believe in God who has won two hundred thousand," replied the old man.

"Were you not surprised by the arrival of Citizen Brutman at a late hour, in the rain, with a newborn child in her arms? . . ."

"I am surprised," said Naftula, "when a person behaves like a person, but when a person is playing crazy tricks, then I am not surprised."

The answers did not satisfy the prosecutor. He pressed Naftula even more fiercely. The question of the little glass tube came up. The prosecutor tried to prove that by sucking the blood with his lips the accused was exposing children to the risk of infection. Naftula's head—the shaggy nut of his head—was now bobbing somewhere near the floor. He was sighing, closing his eyes, and wiping his sunken mouth with his little fist.

"What are you mumbling, Citizen Gerchik?" the presiding chair of the court asked him.

Naftula fixed his extinguished gaze on Prosecutor Orlov.

"The late Monsieur Zusman," he said, sighing, "your late papa, had such a head on him such as you wouldn't find another like it in all the world. And, thank God, he had no apoplexy when thirty years ago he called me to your bris. And now we see that you have grown up to be a big man in the Soviet government, and that Naftula didn't take away, along with that little bit of nothing, anything that would later be useful to you . . ."

He blinked his bear eyes, shook his ginger nut of a head, and fell silent. He was answered by cannons of laugher, thunderous salvos of cackling. Orlov, born Zusman, waving his arms, was shouting something that could not be heard over the bombardment. He was demanding that it should go on the record . . . Sasha Svetlov, columnist for the *Odessa News*, sent him a note from the press box: "You're stubborn as a ram, Syoma," ran the note, "slay him with irony, only comedy kills . . . Yours, Sasha."

The gallery was hushed when they called in the witness Belotserkovsky.

The witness repeated his written testimony. He was lanky, dressed in breeches and cavalry boots. In Ovsey's words, the Tiraspol and Balta district party committees were fully cooperating in the preparation of oilcake. In the very middle of this preparation, he had received a telegram announcing the birth of a son. Upon consulting the chairman of the Balta committee, he had decided, in order not to interrupt the preparation, to restrict himself to a telegram of congratulations and would return home only after two weeks. Throughout the region sixty-four thousand poods of oilcake in all had been collected. At the apartment, aside from the witness Kharchenko, a neighbor who was a laundress by profession, and his son, he could find no one. His spouse had admitted herself into a clinic, while the witness Kharchenko, who rocked the child's cradle (an obsolete practice), was singing a lullaby. Knowing the witness Kharchenko to be an alcoholic, he had not considered it necessary to take note of the words she was singing, but was only surprised that she was calling the infant Yasha, whereas he had instructed that his son was to be named Karl, in honor of our teacher Karl Marx. Upon unswaddling the child he was confronted with the evidence of his misfortune.

The prosecutor asked a few questions. The defense stated that it had no questions. The bailiff brought in the witness Polina Belotserkovskaya. She walked up to the bar, swaying. The bluish spasm of recent maternity twisted her face, drops of sweat covered her forehead. She glanced at the little blacksmith, dressed in his holiday best with a bow tie and new boots, and at the bronze, gray-whiskered face of her mother. Witness Belotserkovskaya did not reply when asked what she knew about the matter under consideration. She said that her father was a poor man, had worked forty years at the smithy on Balta Road. Her mother had borne six children, three of them dead, one was a Red Army commander, the other works at the Ghen factory . . .

"My mother is very devout, as anyone can see, she always suffered because her children were not believers and could not bear the thought that her grandchildren would not be Jews. You have to understand the sort of family my mother was brought up in . . . Everybody knows about the shtetl of Medzhibozh—the women there still wear wigs . . ."

"Tell us, witness," a sharp voice interrupted her. Polina became silent, the sweat drops on her forehead turned red, like blood seeping through her delicate skin. "Tell us, witness," repeated a voice that belonged to the former barrister Samuel Lining.

Had the Sanhedrin existed in our day, Lining would have been presiding over it. But there is no Sanhedrin, and Lining, who learned to read Russian at the age of twenty-five, had in his fourth decade begun to write appeals to the Senate that were in no way different from Talmudic tractates.

The old man had been sleeping through the whole trial. His jacket was covered with tobacco ash. He woke up at the sight of Polina Belotserkovsky.

"Tell us, witness," the fishy row of his loose blue teeth began to rattle, "did you know of your husband's decision to call your son Karl?"

"Yes."

"What did your mother call him?"

"Yankel."

"And you, witness, what did you call your son?"

"I called him sweet cheeks."

"Why precisely sweet cheeks? . . ."

"I call all children sweet cheeks . . ."

"Let us continue," said Lining, his teeth fell out, he caught them with his lower lip, and stuck them back in his jaw. "Let us continue. On the evening when the child was taken to the defendant Gerchik, you were not home, you were at the clinic. Is that correct?"

"I was at the clinic."

"At what clinic were you being treated?"

"On Nezhin Street, by Doctor Drizo."

"Treated by Doctor Drizo?"

"Yes."

"You are quite sure of that?"

"How could I not be?"

"I have a document to submit to the court." Lining's lifeless face loomed over the table. "From this document the court can see that in the period in question Doctor Drizo was away attending the Pediatric Congress at Kharkov."

The prosecutor raised no objection to admitting the document.

"Let us continue," said Lining, rattling his teeth.

The witness leaned her whole body against the bar. Her whisper was barely audible.

"Maybe it wasn't Doctor Drizo," she said, slumped against the bar. "I can't remember everything, I'm worn out . . ."

Lining scratched his yellow beard with a pencil, rubbed his stooping back against the bench, and jiggled his false teeth.

When asked to present her health insurance card, the witness replied that she had lost it . . .

"Let us continue," said the old man.

Polina passed her hand over her forehead. Her husband was sitting on the edge of a bench away from the other witnesses. He was sitting up straight, his long legs tucked under him in their cavalry boots . . . The sun fell on his face, a face that was densely reinforced with thin, harsh bones.

"I'll find the card," whispered Polina, and her hands slipped off the bar.

At that moment a child began to scream. A child was weeping and groaning next door.

"What are you thinking, Polina?" the old woman shouted in a thick voice. "The child hasn't been fed since morning, the child's crying its lungs out."

The Red Army men woke with a start and grabbed their rifles. Polina slipped lower still, her head jerked back and lay on the floor. Her arms flew up, threshed the air, and collapsed.

"Recess!" cried the presiding chair.

The gallery exploded. His green sunken eyes gleaming, Belotserkovsky stepped like a crane toward his wife.

"Feed the child," people shouted from the back rows, cupping their hands into megaphones.

"They'll feed him," replied a female voice from afar. "They were just waiting for you . . ."

"The daughter's mixed up in this," said a workman sitting next to me. "The daughter's in on it . . ."

"That's family, brother," said his neighbor. "Deep, dark stuff. Things get tangled at night, can't untangle them by day."

The sun split the hall with slanted beams. The crowd milled about thickly, breathing fire and sweat. Working my way through with my elbows, I made it out into the corridor. The door to the red corner had been cracked open. That was where the groaning and champing of Karl-Yankel had been coming from. In the red corner hung a picture of Lenin, the one where he's speaking from the armored car on the square at Finland Station; the picture was surrounded by color diagrams produced at the Petrovsky Factory. Along the wall there were banners and rifles in wooden stands. A working woman with a Kirghiz face, her head bent, was feeding Karl-Yankel. He was a chubby little fellow of five months, with knitted booties and a white tuft on his head.

Sucking tight at the Kirghiz woman, he was rumbling, beating his nurse on the breast with his clenched little fist.

"What a ruckus," said the Kirghiz woman. "He'll always find someone to feed him."

Also hanging around the room was a girl of about seventeen in a red kerchief, with cheeks sticking out like pinecones. She wiped Karl-Yankel's diaper until it was dry.

"He'll be a military man," said the girl. "Look how he's fighting!"

The Kirghiz, pulling gently, took her nipple from Karl-Yankel's mouth. He started growling in despair and jerked back his head—with the little white tuft . . . The woman freed her other breast and presented it to the little boy. He looked at the nipple with bleary little eyes; something flashed in them. The Kirghiz woman gazed down at Karl-Yankel, squinting a dark eye.

"Why military?" she asked, straightening the boy's bonnet. "He'll be an aviator, you'll see, and fly beneath the sky."

In the courtroom the case had been resumed.

The battle was now being waged between the prosecutor and the experts, who offered evasive opinions. The public prosecutor, rising in his seat, was banging the desk with his fist. I could also see the first rows of the public: Galician tsaddiks, with their beaver caps on their knees. They had come to see the case in which, according to the Warsaw newspapers, the Jewish religion was on trial. The faces of the rabbis sitting in the front row hung suspended in the stormy, dusty glow of the sun.

"Down with 'em!" cried a Komsomol member who had forced his way up to the stage.

The battle flared even hotter.

Karl-Yankel, staring at me for no reason, sucked at the Kirghiz woman's breast.

From the window flew the straight streets that I walked in my childhood and in my youth—Pushkin Street stretched its way to the train station, Malo-Amautskaya reached to the park by the sea.

I had grown up on these streets, now it was Karl-Yankel's turn, but they hadn't fought over me as they were fighting over him; not many cared about me.

"It can't be," I whispered to myself, "it cannot be that you won't be happy, Karl-Yankel . . . It cannot be that you won't be happier than I . . ."

(published 1931)

RED
CAVALRY

The Crossing of the Zbruch

The divchief six reported Novograd-Volynsk was taken at dawn today. The staff had left Krapivno, and our convoy was spread out in a noisy rearguard upon the high road, the legendary high road from Brest to Warsaw built by Nicholas I upon the bones of peasants.

Fields flower around us, purple with poppies, the midday breeze plays in the yellowing rye, virginal buckwheat emerges on the horizon like the wall of a distant monastery. Peaceful Volhynia curves away, Volhynia recedes into the pearly haze of the birch groves, creeps through flowery slopes, entangling its weary arms in a wilderness of hops. The orange sun rolls down the sky like a lopped-off head, gentle light glows from the gorges in the clouds, the standards of sunset trail above our heads. The smell of the blood and slaughtered horses from yesterday drips into the evening chill. The blackened Zbruch roars and twists into knots of foam at the rapids. The bridges are destroyed, and we wade across the river. A majestic moon rests on the waves. The water laps at the horses' backs, noisy torrents gurgle among hundreds of horses' legs. Someone sinks and resoundingly curses the Mother of God. The river, patched with the black squares of wagons, is full of rumbling, whistling, and songs that thunder over moon snakes and gleaming hollows.

Far on in the night we reach Novograd. In the quarters assigned to me, I find a pregnant woman and two redheaded, scraggy-necked Jews; the third, huddled against the wall with his head covered up, is already asleep. I find turned-out wardrobes in the room assigned to me, scraps of women's fur coats on the floor, human excrement, and shards of the dishware Jews keep hidden and use once a year, at Eastertime.

"Clean this," I say to the woman. "People, how can you live in all this dirt? . . ."

Two of the Jews get up. Jumping on their felt soles, they clear the mess from the floor. They jump around quietly, monkey fashion, like circus Japanese, their necks swelling and twisting. They put down a disemboweled featherbed for me, and I lie down by the wall next to the third, already sleeping Jew. Fainthearted poverty covers my place of rest.

All is dead silence, with only the moon, her blue hands clasping her round, bright, carefree head, wandering outside the window.

I rub my numb legs, lie down on the ripped-open mattress, and fall asleep. I have a dream about the divchief six. He's chasing the brigcom on a heavy stallion, and then puts two bullets in his eyes. The bullets pierce the brigcom's head, and both his eyes fall to the ground. "Why did you turn back the brigade?" Savitsky, the divchief six, shouts to the wounded man—and that's when I wake up, for the pregnant woman is groping my face with her fingers.

"Panie," she says, "you're screaming in your sleep and you're tossing about. I'll make you a bed in another corner, because you're pushing my papa."

She lifts her thin legs and rounded belly from the floor and takes the blanket off the sleeper. A dead old man lay there on his back. His throat was torn out, his face cleft in two, in his beard blue blood clotted like a lump of lead.

"Panie," says the Jewess, shaking up the featherbed, "the Poles cut his throat while he begged them, 'Kill me in the yard so that my daughter won't see how I die.' But they did as they saw fit. He met his end in this room and was thinking of me. And now I wish to know," said the woman with sudden and terrible power, "I wish to know where in the whole world you could find another father like my father . . ."

Novograd-Volynsk, July 1920 (published 1924)

The Church at Novograd

I set out yesterday with my report to the military commissar, who was staying in the house of a Polish priest who had fled. In the kitchen I was met by Pani Eliza, the Jesuit's housekeeper. She served me sponge cakes and tea the color of amber. Her sponge cakes smelled like a crucifix. A cunning nectar was concealed in them, along with the aromatic fury of the Vatican.

Next to the house, in the church, there was a roar of bells, set pealing by a crazed bell ringer. The evening was full of July stars. Her attentive gray head atremble, Pani Eliza kept slipping me cookies, and I enjoyed the food of the Jesuits.

The old Polish woman addressed me as *pan*; in the doorway gray old men with ossified ears stood at attention, and somewhere in the serpentine twilight a monk's cassock flashed. The priest had fled, but he had left behind his assistant, Pan Romuald.

A eunuch with a nasal voice and a giant's body, Romuald honored us with the title of "comrades." He drew a yellow finger over the map, tracing the circles of the Polish debacle. Rasping with enthusiasm, he tallied his country's wounds. May mild oblivion swallow up the memory of Romuald, who would later betray us without hesitation and fall to a stray bullet. But that evening his slender cassock stirred every door curtain, swept every path in a fury, grinning at anyone who wanted vodka. That evening the monk's shadow trailed me unremittingly. He would have made bishop, this Pan Romuald, had he not been a spy.

I drank rum with him, an unseen order breathing, glimmering beneath the ruins of the priest's house, and its soothing seduction unmanned me. O crucifixes, tiny like a courtesan's talismans, the parchment of papal bulls and the satin of women's letters decomposing in the blue silk of waistcoats! . . .

I can see you from here, faithless monk in a lilac robe, your swollen hands, your soul delicate and pitiless like the soul of a cat, I see the wounds of your god oozing semen, a fragrant poison to intoxicate virgins.

We drank rum, expecting the military commissar, but he had yet to return from headquarters. Romuald slumped in a corner and fell asleep. He sleeps fitfully, while outside the window in the garden the black passion of the sky floods the garden path. Thirsty roses sway in the darkness. Green lightning glows amid the cupolas. An undressed corpse sprawls at the bottom of the slope. And moonlight gleams on the dead, open legs.

Here lies Poland, here lies the proud distress of the Rzecz Pospolita! A violent interloper, I spread out a louse-ridden mattress in a temple abandoned by its priest and placed beneath my head folios printed with hosannas to the Most Excellent and Illustrious Chief of the Pans, Józef Piłsudski.

Impoverished hordes roll toward your ancient cities, O Poland, and above them a thundering chorus of all the enslaved, and woe unto you, Rzecz Pospolita, woe unto you, Prince Radziwiłł, and unto you, Prince Sapieha, risen for an hour!

My commissar still isn't here. I look for him at headquarters, in the garden, at the church. The church gates are open, I enter, I find two silvery skulls gleaming on the lid of a broken coffin. Frightened, I dash down into the crypt. From there an oak staircase leads to the altar. And I see a multitude of lights darting about, high up in the cupola itself. I see the military commissar, the chief of the Special Section, and Cossacks with candles in their hands. They respond to my feeble cry and lead me out of the basement.

The skulls, which turned out to be carvings on a catafalque, no longer frighten me, and together we continue our search of the premises—for a search is what it was—begun after the discovery of piles of army uniforms in the priest's house.

Flashing the horse heads embroidered on our cuffs, whispering to one another, and clanging our spurs, we go around the echoing edifice, candles flickering in our hands. Holy Virgins studded with precious stones follow our steps with their pupils, pink like the eyes of mice, flames flutter in our fingers, and square shadows writhe on the statues of Saint Peter, Saint Francis, Saint Vincent, on their little rosy cheeks and curly beards tinted carmine.

We go around searching. Bone buttons spring beneath our fingers, icons that have been split down the middle come apart to reveal underground tunnels into caverns blossoming with mold. The temple is ancient and full of mysteries. Its glossy walls conceal secret passages, niches, trapdoors that open without making a sound.

O foolish priest, hanging the brassieres of your parishioners upon the nails of the Savior! Behind the sanctuary doors we found a suitcase with gold coins, a morocco-leather bag with banknotes, Parisian jewelers' cases filled with emerald rings.

Later, in the commissar's room, we counted the money. Piles of gold, carpets of money, a gusty wind blowing on the candles, the ravening madness in

Pani Eliza's eyes, Romuald's thunderous guffaws, and the incessant roaring of the bells set pealing by Pan Robacki, the crazed bell ringer.

"Away!" I told myself. "Away from these winking Madonnas deceived by soldiers!"

Novograd-Volynsk, July 1920 (published 1923)

A Letter

Here is a letter home dictated to me by Kurdyukov, one of the boys in our expeditionary group. It ought not be consigned to oblivion. I've copied it without embellishment and transmit it here word for word for the sake of accuracy.

"Dearest Mama, Evdokia Fyodorovna. In the first lines of this letter I hasten to inform you that, thank the Lord, I am alive and well and would wish to hear the same from you. And likewise I bow low to you all, white face to wet ground . . . (Next there's a long list of relatives, godparents, kith, and kin. Let's leave that be and go to the second paragraph.)

Dearest Mama, Evdokia Fyodorovna Kurdyukova. I hasten to write that I am in Comrade Budenny's Red Cavalry Army, and here, too, is your kinsman Nikon Vasilyich, who is at the present moment a Red Hero. They took me into the Politsection expeditionary group, where we distribute literature and newspapers—the *Izvestia* of the Moscow Central Executive Committee, the Moscow *Pravda*, and our own ruthless newspaper the *Red Trooper*, which every fighting man on the front line wants to read, and after that he gets heroic and cuts down the vile *szlachta*, and I am living with Nikon Vasilyich in grand style.

Dearest Mama Evdokia Fyodorovna, send me whatever may be in your power to send. I'm asking you to slaughter that speckled little hog and send me a package to Comrade Budenny's Politsection addressed to Vasily Kurdyukov. Every day I lie down to rest without anything to eat and without spare clothing, so it's real cold. Write me a letter about my Styopa, if he's living or not, I'm asking you to look after him and write to me about him—is he still scalping his hooves, or has he stopped doing that now, and also what about the mange on his front legs, has he been shod or not? I'm asking you, dearest Mama, Evdokia Fyodorovna, don't forget to wash his front legs with the soap I left behind the holy images, and if Papa used up the soap, then buy some more in Krasnodar and God won't ever abandon you. I can also tell you that the country around here is all poor, the muzhiks take their horses into the woods and hide from our Red eagles, you won't find much wheat and what's there is so short you have to laugh. They sow rye and oats, too. Hops grow on sticks here so that it comes out very even; they make moonshine with it.

In the second lines of this letter I hasten to tell you about Papa, that they killed brother Fyodor Timofeyich Kurdyukov back then a year ago. Our Red brigade was advancing under Comrade Pavlichenko on the town of Rostov when treason happened in our ranks. While Papa then was with General Denikin, commanding a company. People that saw them said they wore medals like under the old regime. And seeing as we'd been betrayed, they took us all prisoner and Papa caught sight of brother Fyodor Timofeyich. And Papa began cutting him up, saying—mangy hide, Red dog, son of a bitch, and other things, and went on cutting until it grew dark and Fyodor was done for. I wrote you a letter then about how your Fedya lies in the ground without a cross. But Papa caught me with the letter and said, you, your mother's children, sprouts from her root, the slut, I knocked your mama up and will keep knocking her up until the day I die, I'll wipe out my seed for the sake of the truth, and other things on top of that. I bore suffering from him like the Savior Jesus Christ. Only I soon ran away from Papa and managed to get to my unit under Comrade Pavlichenko. And our brigade got the order to go to the town of Voronezh for reinforcements, and we got reinforcements there, and also horses, packs, revolvers, and everything we ought to have. As far as Voronezh, I can tell you, dearest Mama Evdokia Fyodorovna, that the town is just grand, a little bigger than Krasnodar, the people in it are very good-looking, and you can swim in the river. They gave us two pounds of bread a day, half a pound of meat, and a good amount of sugar so that we drank sweet tea when we got up and the same in the evening and forgot about hunger, but for lunch I used to go to brother Semyon Timofeyich's to eat pancakes or goose and afterward I used to lie down for a rest. At that time the whole regiment wanted to have Semyon Timofeyich as commander because of his daring, and Comrade Budenny ordered that this should be done, and he got two horses, decent clothes, and his own wagon for all his stuff and the Order of the Red Banner, and everyone knew I was his brother when I was with him. So now if a neighbor tries any kind of whatnot with you—Semyon Timofeyich can pretty much take care of him for good. Then we began to chase General Denikin, cut them down by the thousands, and drove them into the Black Sea, only Papa was nowhere to be seen, and Semyon Timofeyich looked everyplace for him because he missed brother Fedya very much. But, dearest Mama, you know all about Papa and his stubborn character, so what did he do—he dyed his beard shamelessly from red to black and was staying in the town of Maikop in civvies so that none of the inhabitants knew that he was the same as was a cop under the old regime. But truth will out, your kinsman Nikon Vasilyich happened to see him in the house of one of the inhabitants and wrote a letter to Semyon Timofeyich. We got on our horses and did two hundred versts—me, brother Senka, and a few boys from our settlement who volunteered.

So what did we see in the town of Maikop? We saw there that the rear has no sympathy for the front and that there was treason everywhere and it was full of Yids just like under the old regime. And Semyon Timofeyich got into a mighty argument with the Yids in Maikop, for they had Papa under lock and key in prison and weren't letting him out, saying—an order had come from Comrade Trotsky not to cut down prisoners and saying we'll judge him ourselves, don't start getting all angry, he'll get his. Only it was Semyon Timofeyich who got his and proved he was in command of the regiment and that Comrade Budenny gave him all the Orders of the Red Banner, and he threatened to cut down any and all who wanted to argue and refuse to turn over said person, and the boys from the settlement threatened, too. Only Semyon Timofeyich got Papa all right and began to whip Papa and had all the troops line up in the yard at attention. Then Senka splashed water on Papa's beard, and the dye came off. And Senka asked Timofey Rodionych:

'You good, Pa, in my hands?'

'No,' Pa says, 'bad.'

Then Senka said, 'And Fedya, when you was carving him up, was it good for him in your hands?'

'No,' says Pa. 'It went bad for Fedya.'

Then Senka asked:

'And did you think, Pa, that it would go bad for you?'

'No,' says Papa, 'I didn't think it would go bad for me.'

Then Senka turned to the people and said:

'And what I think is that if I got caught by one of yours, there would be no quarter for me. And now, Pa, we're going to finish you off . . .'

And Timofey Rodionych started to swear at Senka something awful, mother this and mother of God that, and he hit Senka in the face, and Semyon Timofeyich sent me out of the yard so I can't describe to you, dearest Mama Evdokia Fyodorovna, how they finished Papa, since I was sent out of the yard.

Afterward we were stationed in the town of Novorossiysk. About that town it can be said that there isn't any dry land on the other side of it but only water, the Black Sea, and we stayed there right up until May, when we left for the Polish front, and now we're giving the *szlachta* a hard time of it.

I remain your dearest son, Vasily Timofeyich Kurdyukov. Ma, do look after Styopka and God won't ever abandon you."

Such is Kurdyukov's letter; not a single word has been changed. When I finished it, he took the written sheet and tucked it under his shirt against his bare breast.

"Kurdyukov," I asked the boy, "was your father a bad man?"

"Father was a dog," he replied grimly.

"And your mother was better?"

"Mother was fine. If you'd like to see, here's our family . . ."

He handed me a broken photograph. It showed Timofey Kurdyukov, a broad-shouldered policeman sporting a uniform cap and a beard combed down the middle, an immovable figure with high cheekbones and a gleam in his colorless and senseless eyes. Next to him, in a little bamboo armchair, sat a tiny peasant woman wearing a loose blouse, her features clear, timid, and drawn. And against the wall, against that sad provincial photographer's background of flowers and doves, towered two lads—monstrously tall, dull, broad-faced, goggle-eyed, ramrod ready for inspection, the two brothers Kurdyukov, Fyodor and Semyon.

Novograd-Volynsk, June 1920 (published 1923)

Chief of the Remount Service

Groaning breaks out over the village. The cavalry is ruining crops and changing horses. In exchange for their own tired hacks, the cavalrymen confiscate workhorses. Nobody to blame. Can't have an army without horses.

But knowing this doesn't make things any easier for the peasants. They keep crowding around the headquarters building, persistent.

They drag their stubborn nags on ropes, the horses slipping from exhaustion. Deprived of their breadwinners, the muzhiks, feeling a surge of bitter courage and aware that the courage won't last, rush to rail in utterly hopeless despair against the authorities, against God and their own wretched lot.

The chief of staff, Zh., is standing on the porch in full uniform. Shielding his swollen eyelids, he listens with apparent attentiveness to the muzhiks' complaints. But this attentiveness is more like a device. Like every well-trained and overworked employee, he knows how to stop all mental activity during the idle moments of existence. It is in these rare moments of blissful bovine vacancy that our staff commander unwinds his worn-out mechanism.

That's how he was now with the muzhiks.

To the soothing accompaniment of their desperate and disjointed drone, Zh. takes passing note of that gentle bustle in the brain that heralds a certain purity and energy of thought. Waiting for the inevitable lull, he snatches up the last muzhik teardrop, snarls authoritatively, and goes back inside headquarters to work.

This time, he didn't even have to snarl. Dyakov was here, the former circus athlete, now chief of the Remount Service—red-skinned and gray-whiskered, in a black cloak and silver stripes down his wide red trousers—galloping up to the porch on his fiery Anglo-Arabian.

"Blessings from the nun for honest whores and everyone!" he shouted, reining in his steed at a gallop, and at that very moment, just below his stirrup, there was a mangy little horse rolling about, one of those that had been given in exchange by the Cossacks.

"There, Comrade Chief," a muzhik wailed, slapping his trousers, "there, that's what your brothers give our brothers. See what they give us? You try and farm on that."

"For such a horse, let me tell you," Dyakov began distinctly and gravely, "for such a horse, my esteemed friend, you are fully entitled to receive fifteen thousand rubles from the Remount Service, and if that horse were a little livelier, in that sort of a case, you, dear friend, would receive twenty thousand from the Remount Service. As for the horse keeling over—doesn't mean nothing. If a horse falls and gits up again, then that's a horse. If, on the other hand, it doesn't gittup, then that's not a horse. But I tell you this, this nice little filly will most surely gittup for me . . ."

"O Lord, sweet merciful mother of mine!" The muzhik waved his arms about. "How's the poor orphan going to get up? She'll drop dead, the poor orphan!"

"You're insulting the horse, brother," replied Dyakov with profound conviction. "Now that's just like blasphemy, brother." And he swung his stately athlete's body skillfully out of the saddle. Splendid and supple, like a performer onstage, he straightened his perfect legs and gartered knees and approached the dying animal. It stared mournfully at Dyakov with its deep, broad eyes, licked some sort of invisible command from his raspberry palm, and all of a sudden the exhausted horse felt the skill and power flowing from this graying, blooming, and altogether dashing Romeo. Straightening its head and sliding on unsteady legs at the impatient and imperious tickle of the whip on its belly, slowly, carefully, the nag got up. And then we all saw a delicate hand in a wide, flowing sleeve pat the dirty mane and a whip keen and cling against the bloodstained flanks. Her whole body trembling, the nag stood on all four legs, her eyes fixed on Dyakov like a dog, frightened and smitten with love.

"Now that's a horse," said Dyakov to the muzhik, adding gently, "and here you were complaining, my dear friend."

Throwing the reins to his orderly, the chief of the Remount Service bounded up the four porch steps in a single stride and, with a flash of his opera cloak, disappeared into headquarters.

Belyov, July 1920 (published 1923)

Pan Apolek

The wise and wonderful life of Pan Apolek went to my head like an old wine. In Novograd-Volynsk, among the twisted ruins of that swiftly crushed town, fate threw at my feet a gospel hidden from the world. Surrounded by the simple-hearted glow of halos, I then made my vow to follow Pan Apolek's example. And the sweet spite of daydreams, my bitter scorn for the curs and swine of mankind, the fire of silent and intoxicating revenge—all this I sacrificed to my new vow.

In the house from which the Novograd priest had fled, an icon hung high up on the wall. It had an inscription: THE DEATH OF JOHN THE BAPTIST. I had no difficulty recognizing in that John the likeness of a man I had once seen.

I remember: The spiderweb stillness of a summer morning stretched between the straight, bright walls. The sun cast a straight shaft of light at the foot of the painting. It swarmed and sparkled with dust. Out of the blue depths of the niche, the lanky figure of John descended and came straight at me. A black cloak hung majestically about that implacable, repulsively emaciated body. Drops of blood flashed on the round clasps of the cloak. John's head had been cut crookedly off his tattered neck. It lay upon a clay platter gripped tight between the large yellow fingers of a warrior. The dead man's face seemed familiar to me. I was brushed by a premonition of mystery. Upon the clay platter lay the dead head, copied from Pan Romuald, assistant to the priest who had fled. The tiny body of a snake, its florid scales aglitter, looped from his gaping mouth. Its lively little head, a delicate pink, stood out magnificently against the deep background of the cloak.

I marveled at the painter's art, at his grim invention. All the more astonishing was my discovery the following day of a red-cheeked Holy Mother hanging above the matrimonial bed of Pani Eliza, the old priest's housekeeper. Both canvases bore the marks of the same brush. The beefy face of the Holy Mother was a portrait of Pani Eliza. And here was where I came closer to solving the riddle of the Novograd icons. The riddle led me to Pani Eliza's kitchen, where on fragrant evenings the shades of old feudal Poland assembled, a holy fool of a painter presiding over them. But was he really a holy fool, this Pan Apolek who had peopled the neighboring villages with angels and raised the lame convert Yanek to sainthood?

He had come here on an ordinary summer day with blind Gottfried, thirty years ago. The companions—Apolek and Gottfried—went up to Schmerel's tavern, which stands on the Rovno high road two versts from the center of town. In his right hand Apolek carried a paint box, with his left he guided the blind accordion player. The song of their German boots rang out with peace and hope. From Apolek's thin neck dangled a canary-colored scarf, three chocolate feathers fluttered on the blind man's Tyrolean hat.

The newcomers spread out paints and accordion upon the tavern window-sill. The painter unwound his scarf, endless as the ribbon of a magician at the fair. Then he went out into the yard, stripped naked, and poured frigid water over his rosy, narrow, puny body. Schmerel's wife brought the guests raisin vodka and a bowl of *zrazy*. When he had eaten his fill, Gottfried laid his accordion on his pointy knees. He sighed, threw back his head, and set his thin fingers dancing. The songs of Heidelberg echoed around the walls of the little Jewish tavern. Apolek sang along in his tremulous voice. It was as though someone had brought the organ from Saint Indeghilda Church to Schmerel's and at that organ the Muses had settled themselves down side by side in dappled cotton scarves and hobnailed German boots.

The guests sang on till dusk, then they stowed the accordion and the paints in canvas sacks, and Pan Apolek, with a low bow, handed a sheet of paper to Brayna, the tavern keeper's wife.

"Gracious Pani Brayna," he said, "accept this portrait of you from a wandering painter christened with the name of Apollinarius, as a token of our most humble gratitude, as a testament to the magnificence of your hospitality. If the Lord Jesus prolongs my days and strengthens my art, I shall return to copy this portrait in colors. Pearls would be right for your hair, and we shall pencil in an emerald necklace on your breast . . ."

On the small sheet of paper, in red pencil—red and soft, like clay—was portrayed the laughing face of Pani Brayna, ringed with copper curls.

"My money!" cried Schmerel when he saw the portrait of his wife. He took a stick and set off in pursuit of his lodgers. But on the way Schmerel recalled Apolek's rosy body streaming with water, the sunshine in his little yard, and the soft hum of the accordion. The tavern keeper's soul became confused; dropping his stick, he returned home.

The next morning Apolek presented his Munich Academy diploma to the Novograd priest and spread out before him twelve holy images. These were painted in oils on thin sheets of cypress wood. The pater saw on his table the blazing carmine of mantles, the brilliance of emerald fields, and the flowery veils cast over the plains of Palestine.

Pan Apolek's saints, that entire rustic and jubilant assembly of elders, gray-bearded and rosy-cheeked, were wedged into the flowing streams of silk and majestic evenings.

That very same day Pan Apolek received a commission to paint the new Catholic church. And over the benediction, the pater said to the artist:

"Santa Maria," he said, "my dearest Pan Apollinarius, from what wondrous realm have you brought down upon us so radiant a blessing!"

Apolek worked zealously, and after only a month the new sanctuary was filled with the bleating of flocks, the gold dust of sunsets, and the pale-yellow udders of cows. Buffaloes with chapped hides plodded beneath the yoke, dogs with pink snouts ran before the flock, and cherubic babes swung in cradles suspended from the upright trunks of palm trees. The brown rags of Franciscan monks surrounded a cradle. The throng of Magi was gashed with gleaming bald spots and blood-red wrinkles, like wounds. Among the throng of Magi gleamed the crone-faced Leo XIII, grinning like a fox, and the Novograd priest himself, fingering a carved Chinese rosary in one hand while blessing the newborn Jesus with the other.

Confined for five months in his wooden seat, Apolek crept along the walls, around the dome, and in the choir loft.

"You are partial to familiar faces, my dearest Pan Apolek," said the priest one day, recognizing himself in one of the Magi and Pan Romuald in the decapitated head of John the Baptist. He smiled, the old pater, and sent a goblet of cognac to the painter at work beneath the dome.

Afterward, Apolek completed the Last Supper and the Stoning of Mary Magdalene. One Sunday he unveiled his frescoes. The eminent citizens who had been invited by the priest recognized Yanek, the lame convert, in Saint Paul, and in Mary Magdalene a Jewish girl named Elka, daughter of unknown parents and mother of numerous stray children. The eminent citizens ordered the sacrilegious portraits to be covered up. The priest hurled threats upon the blasphemer. But Apolek did not cover up his frescoes.

Thus began an unprecedented war between the almighty body of the Catholic Church on the one hand and the heedless god-painter on the other. It lasted three decades—a war that was merciless like a Jesuit's passion. Chance nearly made the humble merrymaker the founder of a new heresy. He would then have been the most baffling and ridiculous opponent of all those whom the Roman Church has known in her tortured and turbulent history, an opponent wandering the earth in a state of drunken bliss, two white mice tucked in his bosom and a set of the finest brushes in his pocket.

"Fifteen zlotys for a Mother of God, twenty-five for a Holy Family, and fifty zlotys for a Last Supper depicting all the customer's relatives. The customer's enemy can be depicted as Judas Iscariot, and that comes to ten zlotys extra," was Apolek's announcement to the local peasants after he had been driven away from the church under construction.

He encountered no shortage of orders. And when the commission summoned by the Novograd priest's raging messages arrived a year later from the bishop of Zhitomir, it found in the most squalid and foul-smelling huts these monstrous family portraits—sacrilegious, naive, and picturesque like blossoms in a tropical garden. Josephs with gray hair parted down the middle, pomaded Jesuses, ever-pregnant village Marys with knees spread—these images hung in icon corners, festooned with paper flowers.

"He has made saints of you in your lifetime!" exclaimed the vicar of Dubno and Novokonstantinov in response to the crowd defending Apolek. "He has surrounded you with the ineffable attributes of sainthood, you who have thrice fallen into the sin of disobedience, moonshiners, merciless usurers, makers of false weights, and dealers in your own daughters' innocence."

"Your Holiness," then said the limping Vitold, who fenced stolen goods and looked after the cemetery, "who can tell the ignorant folk where the all-merciful Pan God sees truth? And isn't there more verity in Pan Apolek's pictures, which suit our pride, than in your words, full of reproach and lordly wrath?"

The shouts of the multitude put the vicar to flight. The general mood in the area threatened the safety of the servants of the Church. The painter who had been invited to replace Apolek did not dare paint over Elka and lame Yanek. They can still be seen today, in one of the side chapels of the Novograd church: Yanek as Saint Paul, a frightened lame man with the ragged black beard of a village apostate; and her, the harlot of Magdala, feeble and crazed, her body writhing and her cheeks sunken.

The struggle with the priest lasted three decades. Then the Cossack flood drove the old monk from his aromatic nest of stone, and Apolek—O the twists of fate!—made himself at home in Pani Eliza's kitchen. And here am I, a passing guest, drinking the evening wine of his conversation.

What sort of conversation? About the romantic age of the Polish gentry, about the fierce fanaticism of the womenfolk, about the artist Luca della Robbia, and about the family of the carpenter from Bethlehem.

"I have something to tell Pan Scribe," Apolek informs me mysteriously before supper.

"Yes," I reply. "Yes, Apolek, I'm listening . . ."

But the church caretaker, Pan Robacki, stern and gray, bony and big-eared, is sitting too close. He hangs before us the faded linen of silence and hostility.

"I must tell you, Pan," whispers Apolek, and leads me aside, "that Jesus son of Mary was married to Deborah, a Jerusalem maiden of obscure birth."

"O *ten chlovek!*" Pan Robacki cries in despair. "*Ten chlovek* won't die in his bed. People will tear *ten chlovek* apart."

"After supper," Apolek rustles, lowering his voice, "after supper, if it suits you, Pan Scribe . . ."

It suits me. Set ablaze by the beginning of Apolek's story, I pace up and down the kitchen awaiting the appointed hour. And beyond the window night has fallen, like a black column. Beyond the window, the dark and vibrant garden has grown stiff. The milky, luminous road to the church flows beneath the moon. The earth is enveloped in dusky radiance, glowing necklaces of fruit hang from the bushes. The scent of lilies is pure and strong like alcohol. This fresh poison bites into the fat roiling breath of the stove, overpowering the stale resin of the spruce logs strewn around the kitchen.

With his pink bow tie and pink threadbare trousers, Apolek putters in his corner like a gentle and graceful animal. His table is smeared with glue and paint. The old man works in slight and frequent movements, a faint melodious cadence can be heard from his corner. Old Gottfried taps along with his shaky fingers. The blind man sits motionless in the yellow, oily glow of the lamp. Bowing his bald head, he listens to the endless music of his blindness and the mumbling of Apolek his eternal friend.

". . . And that which the priests and the Evangelist Mark and the Evangelist Matthew tell you—that is not the truth. But the truth may be revealed to you, Pan Scribe, of whom for fifty marks I will paint a portrait in the image of the Blessed Francis, on a background of green and sky. He was a most simple saint, Pan Francis. And if you, Pan Scribe, have a bride in Russia, women love the Blessed Francis, though not all women, Pan . . ."

And so, in a corner smelling of spruce, began the story of the marriage of Jesus and Deborah. This girl had a bridegroom, according to Apolek. Her groom was a young Israelite who traded in elephant tusks. But Deborah's wedding night ended in bewilderment and tears. The woman was overcome by fear when she saw her husband approaching her bed. A hiccup distended her throat. She spewed forth all she had eaten at the wedding feast. Shame fell on Deborah, on her father, her mother, and all her kin. Her groom left her, jeering, and summoned all the guests. Then Jesus, seeing the anguish of the woman who thirsted for her husband and feared him, placed upon himself the groom's wedding clothes and, full of compassion, was joined with Deborah, who lay in her vomit. Then she went forth to the guests, loud, triumphant and shifty-eyed, like a woman taking pride in her fall. And only Jesus stood to the side. A deathly perspiration had broken out on his body, the bee of sorrow had stung his heart. No one noticed him as he departed from the banquet hall and made his way to the wilderness east of Judaea, where John awaited him. And Deborah bore her first child . . .

"So where is he?" I cried.

"He was hidden by the priests," Apolek proclaimed with significance, lifting a cold, light finger to his drunkard's nose.

"Pan Painter," cried Robacki, suddenly emerging from the shadows, his gray ears twitching, "*Tso vy muvite?* That is unthinkable."

"*Tak, tak.*" Apolek hunched himself up, grabbing Gottfried. "*Tak, tak,* Pan . . .*"

He dragged the blind man toward the door but lingered on the threshold and beckoned me with his finger.

"Blessed Francis," he whispered, winking, "with a bird on his sleeve, a dove or a goldfinch, whatever suits Pan Scribe."

And he vanished with his blind and eternal friend.

"Oh, folly!" then cried Robacki the beadle. "*Ten chlovek* won't die in his bed."

Pan Robacki opened his mouth wide and yawned like a cat. I bade farewell and left to spend the night at home with my plundered Jews.

The homeless moon wandered around town. And I went along with her, hopeless dreams and discordant songs growing warm in my breast.

Novograd-Volynsk, June 1920 (published 1923)

The Sun of Italy

Yesterday I sat once more in Pani Eliza's living quarters, beneath a warm garland of green spruce branches. I sat awhile beside the warm, living, growling stove, and afterward returned home in the dead of night. Below, in the ravine, the noiseless Zbruch rolled in a dark and glassy wave. My soul, filled with the tormenting stupor of a dream, smiled at nobody in particular, and my imagination, that blind and blissful lady, swirled before me like haze in July.

The scorched town—broken columns and hooks sticking out of the ground like a witch's pinky fingers—seemed to levitate in the air, cozy and chimerical, like a dream. Naked moonlight poured down over it with inexhaustible power. The damp mold of the ruins bloomed like the veined marble of opera seats. And my troubled soul waited for Romeo to appear from the clouds, a satin Romeo singing of love, while in the wings a dreary electrician waits with his finger on the moon switch.

Blue roads flowed past me like streams of milk spurting from many breasts. On my way home I dreaded meeting Sidorov, my neighbor, who would, each night, lay upon me the hairy paw of his ennui. Fortunately, on this night shredded by the milk of the moon, Sidorov did not utter a word. Surrounded by books, he was writing. On the table a hunchbacked candle gave off smoke—that sinister fire of dreamers. I sat on the other side, dozing, dreams leaping about me like kittens. And not till late at night was I roused by an orderly summoning Sidorov to headquarters. They left together. Then I hurried over to the table where Sidorov had been writing and went through his books. There was an Italian-language guide, a print of the Roman Forum, and a map of Rome. The map was covered with little crosses and dots. My vague stupor fell away like scales from a shedding snake. I leaned over a written sheet and, with sinking heart and twisted fingers, read another man's letter. Sidorov, that world-weary killer of men, tore the pink stuffing of my imagination to shreds and dragged me down the corridors of his sensible madness. The letter began on the second page—I dared not look for the first:

". . . Punctured my lung and kind of went nuts, or, as Sergei would say, *flew* out of my mind. After all, he can't simply *go* out of his stupid mind . . .

Anyway, tail out of the way and all joking aside, let us return to today's agenda, my friend Victoria . . .

"I finished a three-month campaign with Makhno—a tiresome scam and nothing more. And only Volin is still there. Volin dresses up in apostolic vestments and is scrambling to make himself the Lenin of anarchism. Awful. And the Old Man would listen to him, stroke the dusty wire of his locks, and let the long snake of his peasant grin get past his rotten teeth. And now I don't know if there isn't a weed seed of anarchy in all of this, and if we'll be wiping your prosperous noses, you self-proclaimed Tsekists from your self-proclaimed *tsekh* 'made in' Kharkov, that self-proclaimed capital. Nowadays your jolly good fellows don't like to recall the sins of their anarchist youth and laugh at them from the height of their government wisdom—to the devil with them! . . .

"And then I ended up in Moscow. How did I end up in Moscow? The boys were giving somebody a hard time with the requisitioning and whatnot. Driveler that I am, I got between them. Well, they sure set me straight—and rightly so. The wound was nothing, but in Moscow, ah, in Moscow, Victoria, I went dumb from misery. Every day the nurses brought me grain porridge. Bridled with awe, they dragged it in on a big tray, and I came to loathe that shock-brigade porridge, the supplies off the plan, and Moscow on the plan. Afterward I came across a handful of anarchists in the Soviet. They were all posers or half-senile old farts. I got into the Kremlin with a plan for some real work. They patted me on the head and promised to make me a deputy if I reformed. I didn't reform. What happened next? The front, the Red Cavalry, and troops reeking of fresh blood and human ashes . . .

"Save me, Victoria. Government wisdom is driving me crazy, I'm bored drunk. If you don't help, I shall drop dead completely off-plan, and who would want to see a worker croak in such an unorganized fashion—surely not you, Victoria, the bride who will never be wife. Look at me, all sentimental now—oh, to hell with this mother! . . .

"Now let's get down to business. I'm bored in the army. I can't ride because of my wound, and that means I can't fight either. Use your influence, Victoria—let them send me to Italy. I'm learning the language, and in two months I'll be able to speak it. The ground is smoldering in Italy. Things there are all set to go. You only need a couple of bullets. I can shoot one of them. The king must be sent to join his ancestors. That's the key thing. Their king is a grand old fellow, he plays to the crowd and gets himself photographed along with tame socialists for the family magazines.

"At the Tseka, at the Narkomindel, you don't talk about shootings or kings. They'll pat you on the head and mumble: 'A romantic.' Just say, 'He's ill, angry, drunk, and weary. He wants the sun of Italy and bananas.' Haven't I earned it after all, or even if maybe I haven't earned it? Just to get well—and *basta* . . . But if not, then let them send me to the Cheka in Odessa. The work makes sense there, and . . .

"How stupid—how wrong and stupid—my writing to you like this, Victoria, my friend . . .

"Italy has gotten inside my heart like an obsession. The thought of that country I have never seen is sweet to me, like the name of a woman, like your name, Victoria . . ."

I finished reading the letter and began to arrange myself on my sagging, unclean bed, but sleep would not come. On the other side of the wall the pregnant Jewess was crying in earnest, her lanky husband mumbled and groaned in response. They talked about their looted possessions and blamed each other for their misfortune. Then, before dawn, Sidorov returned. The dwindling candle was flickering out on the table. Sidorov took another candle stub from his boot and, with unusual pensiveness, used it to crush the guttering wick. Our room was dark, gloomy, everything in it breathed the dank odor of night, and only the window, full of moon fire, shone forth like deliverance.

He came and hid the letter, my tiresome neighbor. He slumped and sat down at the table and opened a picture album of Rome. The magnificent gilt-edged volume lay before his expressionless olive face. Over his rounded back gleamed the gap-toothed ruins of the Capitoline and the arena of the circus lit up by the sunset. A photograph of the royal family was wedged between the large glossy pages. On a scrap of paper torn from a calendar there was a picture of the amiable, puny King Victor Emmanuel with his black-haired wife, his heir, Prince Umberto, and a whole brood of princesses.

. . . And now it was night, full of the distant and wearisome ringing of bells, a square patch of light in the damp darkness, and in it Sidorov's deathly face, a lifeless mask, hanging above the yellow flame of the candle.

Novograd, June 1920 (published 1923)

The Sun of Italy   187

Gedali

On Sabbath eves I am afflicted by the dense melancholy of memories. On evenings such as these, my grandfather would stroke the tomes of Ibn Ezra with his yellow beard. The old woman in her lace cap would trace fortunes with gnarled fingers over the Sabbath candles and sob sweetly. On such evenings my child's heart pitched and tossed like a little ship upon enchanted waves. O the moldering Talmuds of my childhood! O the dense melancholy of memories!

I roam through Zhitomir in search of a shy star. By the ancient synagogue, by its yellow and indifferent walls, old Jews sell chalk, wicks, bluing—Jews with prophets' beards and passionate rags on their sunken chests . . .

Before me lies the bazaar and the death of the bazaar. The fat soul of plenty has been slaughtered. Mute padlocks hang upon the booths, and the granite paving is clean like the bald head of a corpse. She blinks and fades—my shy star . . .

Success came to me later, success came just before sunset. Gedali's little shop was hidden away in a row of others, all sealed tight. Dickens, where was your ghost that evening? In that little old curiosity shop you would have seen gilt slippers and ships' cables, an ancient compass and a stuffed eagle, a Winchester with the date 1810 engraved upon it and a broken saucepan.

Old Gedali meanders around his treasures in the rosy emptiness of evening—a little proprietor in smoked glasses and a green frock coat down to the ground. He rubs his small white hands, he plucks at his little gray beard, and listens, head bowed, to invisible voices wafting down to him.

This shop was like the box of an earnest and inquisitive boy who will grow up to be a professor of botany. In this shop you could find buttons as well as a dead butterfly. Its little owner went by the name of Gedali. Everyone left the bazaar, Gedali remained. He wound in and out of a labyrinth of globes, skulls, and dead flowers, waving a bright feather duster of cock's plumes and blowing dust from the dead flowers.

And here we are, sitting on beer kegs. Gedali twisting and untwisting his thin beard. His top hat swaying like a little black tower. Warm air flows past us. The sky changes colors. Delicate blood pours from an overturned bottle up there, and a whiff of decay covers me.

"The Revolution—we will say yes to it, but are we to say no to the Sabbath?" So Gedali begins and weaves around me the silken cords of his smoke-hidden eyes. "Yes, I cry to the Revolution. Yes, I cry to it, but it hides from Gedali and brings forth only shooting . . ."

"Closed eyes don't let sunlight in," I reply to the old man. "But we will unstitch those closed eyes . . ."

"A Pole closed my eyes," whispers the old man, in a voice that was barely audible. "The Pole is a mean dog. He takes the Jew and tears out his beard, the cur! And now he is being beaten, the mean dog. That is splendid, that is the Revolution. And then the one who beat the Pole says to me, 'Turn over your phonograph for registration, Gedali . . .' 'I like music, Pani,' I reply to the Revolution. 'You don't know what you like, Gedali. I'll shoot at you and then you'll know, and I cannot do without shooting because I am the Revolution.'"

"She cannot do without shooting, Gedali," I say to the old man, "because she is the Revolution."

"But the Pole, my gentle Pan, shot because he was the Counterrevolution. You shoot because you are the Revolution. But the Revolution—that's supposed to be pleasure. And pleasure does not like orphans in the house. A good man does good deeds. The Revolution is the good deed of good men. But good men do not kill. So then bad people are making the Revolution. But the Poles are bad people, too. So who can tell Gedali where is the Revolution and where is the Counterrevolution? I used to study Talmud—I love Rashi's commentaries and the books of Maimonides. And there are yet other understanding folk in Zhitomir. And here we are, all of us learned people, falling on our faces and crying out in a loud voice, 'Woe unto us, where is the sweet Revolution?'"

The old man fell silent. And we saw the first star breaking through across the Milky Way.

"The Sabbath has come," Gedali stated solemnly. "Jews should be going to the synagogue. Pan Comrade," he said, rising, his top hat like a little black tower swaying on his head, "bring a few good people to Zhitomir. Oh, there's a shortage of good people in our town, oh, such a shortage! Bring us kind people and we will hand over all the phonographs to them. We are not ignoramuses. The International—we know what the International is. And I want an International of kind people. I would like every soul to be registered and given first-category rations. There, soul, please eat and enjoy life's pleasures. Pan Comrade, the International—you don't know what it's eaten with . . ."

"It is eaten with gunpowder," I answered the old man, "and spiced with the best blood . . ."

And there she was, the young Sabbath appearing out of the blue darkness to take her throne.

"Gedali," I said, "today is Friday, and it's already evening. Where can one get Jewish biscuits, a Jewish glass of tea, and a little of that discharged God in the glass of tea?"

"Haven't got any," Gedali replied, hanging the padlock on his little booth. "Haven't got any. Next door is a tavern, and good people used to run it, but nobody eats there now—people weep there."

He buttoned his green frock coat on three bone buttons. He brushed himself with the cock's feathers, splashed a little water on his soft palms, and departed, a tiny, lonely dreamer in a black top hat, a large prayer book under his arm.

The Sabbath is coming. Gedali, founder of an unattainable International, has gone to the synagogue to pray.

Zhitomir, June 1920 (published 1924)

My First Goose

Savitsky, the divchief six, rose when he saw me, and I was struck by the beauty of his giant body. He rose and—with the carmine of his breeches, the raspberry of his tilted cap, the medals pressed onto his chest—split the cottage in half like a standard splits the sky. He smelled of perfume and the sickly sweet freshness of soap. His long legs were like girls sheathed to the shoulders in shining riding boots.

He smiled at me, struck his whip on the table, and drew toward him an order that the chief of staff had just finished dictating. It was an order for Ivan Chesnokov to advance on Chugunov-Dobryvodka with the regiment entrusted to him, to make contact with the enemy and destroy said enemy.

". . . For which destruction," the divchief six began to write, smearing the whole sheet, "I make this same Chesnokov fully responsible, up to and including the supreme penalty, and will if necessary strike him down on the spot; which you, Chesnokov, who have been working with me on the front for some months now, cannot doubt . . ."

The divchief six signed the order with a flourish, tossed it to his orderlies, and turned upon me gray eyes that danced with merriment.

"Speak!" he shouted and split the air with his whip. Then he read the order with my appointment to the staff of the division.

"So ordered!" said the chief. "So ordered, and see to his every refreshment, except full frontal. You read and write?"

"I read and write," I replied, envying the flower and iron of that youthfulness. "Graduated in law from Petersburg University."

"Well don't you stink of baby powder!" He burst out laughing. "Glasses on his nose, too. Look at the mangy little fellow! They send us your kind without asking, but here glasses get you killed. Think you'll manage with us, eh?"

"I'll manage," I said, and went off to the village with the quartermaster to find lodging. The quartermaster carried my trunk on his shoulder, the village street lay before us; round and yellow as a pumpkin, the dying sun in the sky gave up its pink ghost.

We went up to a hut painted over with garlands. The quartermaster stopped and suddenly said, with a guilty smile:

"A real hassle over here if you got glasses, and there's nothing you can do about it, either. Over here a person of the highest distinction is done for. But go ruin a lady, a real proper lady, too, then the troops will adore you . . ."

He hesitated, my little trunk on his shoulder, then he came quite close to me, only to dart away again in despair and run to the nearest yard. Cossacks were sitting there on the hay, shaving one another.

"Look here, troops," said the quartermaster, setting my little trunk down on the ground. "Comrade Savitsky's orders are that you're to take this man into your quarters, so no nonsense about it, because this man's been through a lot in the learning line."

The quartermaster, purple in the face, left us without looking back. I raised my hand to my cap and saluted the Cossacks. A lad with long, straight flaxen hair and a lovely Ryazan face went over to my little trunk and tossed it out the gate. Then he turned to me with his rear end and, employing remarkable skill, emitted a series of shameful noises.

"Double-zero ordnance!" an older Cossack shouted at him and burst out laughing. "Run and cover!"

His guileless art exhausted, the lad made off. Then, crawling on the ground, I began to gather together the manuscripts and tattered garments that had fallen out of the trunk. I picked them up and carried them to the other end of the yard. Next to the hut, perched on bricks, there was a cauldron simmering with pork, the smoke rising like the distant smoke of home in the village, mingling hunger with untold loneliness in my head. Then I covered my little broken trunk with hay, turning it into a pillow, and lay down on the ground in order to read from *Pravda* Lenin's speech at the Second Congress of the Comintern. The sun fell upon me from behind the toothed hillocks, the Cossacks trod on my feet, the lad made fun of me relentlessly, the beloved phrases came toward me along a thorny path and could not reach me. Then I put aside the newspaper and went out to our host, who was spinning yarn on the porch.

"Hey, you, lady," I said, "Food! . . ."

The old woman raised the diffused whites of her half-blind eyes and lowered them again.

"Comrade," she said, after a moment's silence, "all this business makes me want to go hang myself."

"Why you goddamn mother—" I muttered, annoyed, and pushed the old woman in the chest with my fist. "I have to spell it out for you . . ."

And turning around I saw somebody's sword lying within reach. A stern-looking goose was waddling about the yard, inoffensively preening its feathers. I overtook it and pressed it to the ground—the goose's head cracked beneath my boot, cracked and oozed. The white neck lay stretched out in the dung and the wings settled over the slaughtered bird.

"Why you goddamn mother—" I said, digging into the goose with the sword. "Go on, roast him for me, lady."

Her blind eyes and glasses glistening, the old woman picked up the bird, wrapped it in her apron, and took it over to the kitchen.

"Comrade," she said to me, after a moment's silence, "I'd like to hang myself." And she closed the door behind her.

The Cossacks in the yard were already sitting around their cauldron. They sat motionless, backs straight like high priests, and disregarded the goose.

"The lad will do," one of them said about me, winking and scooping up the sour cabbage soup with his spoon.

The Cossacks commenced their supper with the elegant restraint of peasants who have respect for one another, while I wiped the sword with sand, went out the gate and came back in, sick at heart. The moon hung over the yard like a cheap earring.

"Little brother," Surovkov, the oldest of the Cossacks, said suddenly, "sit and partake with us until your goose is done."

He took out a spare spoon from his boot and handed it to me. We slurped up the soup they had made and ate the pork.

"What's in the newspaper?" asked the flaxen-haired lad, making room for me.

"In the paper Lenin writes . . . ," I said, pulling out *Pravda*. "Lenin writes that there's a shortage of everything."

And loudly, like a triumphant man hard of hearing, I read Lenin's speech to the Cossacks.

Evening wrapped the quickening moistness of her dusky sheets about me; evening laid her motherly hands upon my burning brow.

I read and gloried, and in all my glory tried to track the mysterious curve of Lenin's straight line.

"Truth tickles everyone's nostrils," said Surovkov when I had come to the end. "But how do you pull it from the heap? Now, this one, he hits it straight like a hen pecks grain."

This is what was said of Lenin by Surovkov, platoon commander of the staff squadron, and then we went to bed in the hayloft. We slept, all six of us warming one another, our legs intermingled, beneath a tattered roof that let in the stars.

I had dreams and saw women in my dreams—and only my heart, imbrued with slaughter, oozed and groaned.

July, 1920 (published 1923)

The Rebbe

"All is mortal. Only the mother is destined for life eternal. And when the mother is not among the living, she leaves behind a memory none yet has dared to defile. The memory of the mother nourishes in us a compassion like the ocean, a boundless ocean that feeds the rivers dissecting the universe."

Such were Gedali's words. He uttered them with great solemnity. The dying evening surrounded him with the rose-tinted haze of its sadness. The old man said:

"In the passionate edifice of Hasidism the doors and windows have been smashed, but it is immortal, like the soul of the mother . . . With oozing eye sockets Hasidism still stands at the crossroads of the raging winds of history."

Thus spoke Gedali, and having prayed in the synagogue, he took me to Rebbe Motale, the last rebbe of the Chernobyl dynasty.

We went up the main street, Gedali and I. White churches gleamed in the distance like fields of buckwheat. The wheel of a gun carriage groaned around a corner. A couple of pregnant *khokhlushki* came out of a gateway, jingling their coin necklaces, and sat down on a bench. A shy star was kindled in the orange strife of the sunset, and peace, Sabbath peace, rested upon the crooked roofs of the Zhitomir ghetto.

"Here," whispered Gedali, and pointed out a long building with a broken pediment.

We entered a room—stony and empty, like a morgue. Rebbe Motale was sitting at a table surrounded by the liars and the possessed. He wore a sable hat and a white robe cinched with a cord. The rebbe sat with closed eyes and dug his thin fingers into the yellow fluff of his beard.

"From where does the Jew come?" he asked and opened his eyes a little.

"From Odessa," I replied.

"A God-fearing town," the rebbe suddenly said with remarkable force, "the star of our exile, our unwished well of sorrows. What is the Jew's occupation?"

"I am putting into verse the adventures of Hersh of Ostropol."

"A great undertaking," whispered the rebbe, and closed his eyelids. "The jackal whines when he is hungry, every fool has folly enough for despondency, and only a sage can tear the veil of being with laughter. What has the Jew studied?"

"The Bible."

"What is the Jew seeking?"

"Merriment."

"Reb Mordkhe," said the tsaddik and shook his beard, "let the young man take a seat at the table, let him eat on this Sabbath eve with the other Jews, let him rejoice that he is alive and not dead, let him clap his hands when his neighbors dance, let him drink wine if he is given wine . . ."

And Reb Mordkhe darted over to me—a jester of old, a hunchbacked geezer with turned-out eyelids, no taller than a boy of ten.

"Oh, my dear and so very young man," said the ragged Reb Mordkhe, winking at me, "oh, how many rich fools I used to know in Odessa, how many penniless sages I used to know in Odessa! Do sit down at the table, young man, and drink the wine you won't be given . . ."

We all sat side by side—the possessed, the liars, and the slackjaws. In a corner some broad-shouldered Jews who looked like fishermen and apostles were moaning over their prayer books. Gedali, in his green frock coat, was dozing by the wall like a colorful little bird. And suddenly I caught sight of a youth behind Gedali, a youth with the face of Spinoza, the mighty brow of Spinoza, the wan face of a nun. He was smoking and shivering like an escaped man caught and returned to his cell. Ragged Reb Mordkhe crept up behind him, tore the cigarette from his mouth, and ran away to me.

"That's the rebbe's son, Ilya," he croaked, the bloodshot flesh of his turned-out eyelids drawing close to my face, "the cursed son, the last son, the unruly son."

And Mordkhe shook his fist at the youth and spat in his face.

"Blessed is the Lord," rang out the voice of Rebbe Motale Bratslavsky, and he proceeded to break bread with his monkish fingers. "Blessed is the God of Israel, Who hath chosen us from among all the nations of the earth . . ."

The rebbe blessed the food and we began our meal. Beyond the window horses were neighing and Cossacks shouting. Beyond the window yawned the wasteland of war. The rebbe's son smoked one cigarette after another amid the silence and prayers. When the supper came to an end, I was the first to rise.

"My dear and so very young man," Mordkhe muttered behind my back, tugging at my belt, "if there were no one in the world besides the wicked rich and the poor vagabonds, how then would the holy ones live?"

I gave the old man some money and went out into the street. Gedali and I parted, I made my way back to the station. There, at the station, in the agitprop train of the First Cavalry, I was greeted by the flare of hundreds of lights, the magic brilliance of the radio station, the persistent churn of printing presses, and my unfinished article for the *Red Cavalryman*.

July 1920 (published 1924)

The Way to Brody

I mourn for the bees. They are tormented by warring armies. There are no more bees in Volhynia.

We defiled untold hives. We fumigated them with sulfur and blasted them with gunpowder. The smell of singed rags reeked in the sacred republic of the bees. Dying, they flew around slowly and you could barely hear them buzzing. Deprived of bread, we extracted honey with our sabers . . . There are no more bees in Volhynia.

The chronicle of our everyday offenses oppresses me unremittingly, like a heart defect. Yesterday was the first day of carnage near Brody. Having lost our way upon this sky-blue earth, we hadn't suspected it would happen like this—not I, nor Afonka Bida, my friend. The horses had their oats in the morning. The rye was tall, the sun resplendent, and the soul, undeserving of these blazing, fleeting skies, longed for drawn-out agonies. And so I forced Afonka's unflinching lips to bend to my sorrows.

"The womenfolk of the Cossack settlements tell of the bee and its goodly soul," the platoon commander, my friend, responded, "all sorts of tales. Whether people offended Christ or if there was no such offense, we'll get to know about all that in due time. But imagine, as the womenfolk of the settlements tell it, Christ all lonesome on the Cross. And all kinds of gnats fly up to Christ to persecute him. And his eyes looked on the gnat and his heart fell. Only the innumerable gnat couldn't see those eyes of his. And the bee was flying around Christ, too. 'Strike him,' cries the gnat to the bee. 'Strike him and we'll answer for it!' 'Can't do it,' says the bee, lifting her wings over Christ. 'Can't do it—he's in the carpenter trade.' Got to understand the bee," concluded Afonka, my platoon commander. "And the bee has got to make it through this now. We're digging it all up for her sake, aren't we . . ."

And waving his arms Afonka struck up a song. It was a song about a dun-bay stallion. Eight Cossacks—Afonka's platoon—sang along, and even Grishchuk, dozing on his coach box, shifted his cap to the side.

The dun-bay stallion called Djigit belonged to a Cossack captain loaded up on vodka on the Day of the Beheading. Thus sang Afonka, drowsy, stretching his voice like a string. Djigit was a faithful steed, but on holidays the

Cossack captain's desires knew no bounds. He had five bottles all told on the Day of the Beheading. After the fourth, the captain mounted his steed and started for heaven. The ascent was slow, but Djigit was a faithful steed. They arrived in heaven, and the Cossack captain reached for the fifth bottle. But it had been left behind on earth, that fifth bottle. Then the Cossack captain wept over the futility of his labors. He wept, and Djigit flicked his ears and watched his master . . .

Thus sang Afonka, caroling and drowsing. The song floated like smoke. And we moved to greet the heroic sunset. Its boiling rivers flowed down the embroidered towels of peasant fields. The stillness grew pink. The earth lay like a cat's back, overgrown with a gleaming fur of grain. Crouched on the slope sat the muddy little village of Klekotov. Awaiting us past the top of the hill was a view of Brody, cadaverous and gap-toothed. But at Klekotov a shot burst loud in our faces. From behind a hut peered two Polish soldiers. Their horses were tied to posts. Already the enemy's light battery was briskly driving up the slope. Bullets threaded their way down the road.

"Go!" cried Afonka.

And we fled.

O Brody! The mummies of your crushed passions breathed their irresistible poison upon me. I already sense the deathly chill of your eye sockets filled with tears gone cold. And now—a jolting gallop bears me away from the chipped stones of your synagogues . . .

Brody, August 1920 (published 1923)

A Teaching on the *Tachanka*

Headquarters has sent me a driver, or, as we say here, a wagoner. Grishchuk is his surname. He is thirty-nine years old. His story is horrible.

He was in a German prison camp for five years, escaped a few months ago, crossed Lithuania, northwestern Russia, reached Volhynia, and in Belyov was caught by the world's most brainless mobilization commission and put to military service. To reach Kremenets district, where Grishchuk is from, it was only another fifty versts. In Kremenets district he has a wife and children. He hasn't been home in five years and two months. The mobilization commission made him my wagoner, and I ceased to be a pariah among the Cossacks.

I—master of a *tachanka* and the coachman in it. A *tachanka*! The word has come to form a triangle that epitomizes our ways: slaughter—*tachanka*—horse . . .

Thanks to the caprices of our civil strife, what had been a priest's or assessor's ordinary *britska* rose to the occasion, became a formidable and versatile combat vehicle, created a new strategy and new tactics, altered the very face of warfare, and gave birth to the heroes and geniuses of the *tachanka*. Such was Makhno, whom we suppressed, and who made the *tachanka* the axis of a mysterious and cunning strategy. Makhno did away with infantry, artillery, and even cavalry and replaced this cumbersome bulk with three hundred machine guns screwed onto *britska*s. Such was Makhno, manifold, like nature herself. Hay carts are prepared for battle and seize towns. A wedding procession approaches the local district council, opens concentrated fire, and a puny little priest unfurls a black flag of anarchy, orders the authorities to serve up the bourgeois, the proletariat, the music, and wine.

An army of *tachanka*s possesses untold possibilities of maneuver.

Budenny demonstrated this no worse than Makhno. To cut down such an army is difficult; to catch it, unthinkable. When the machine gun is hidden in a haystack and the *tachanka* stowed away in a peasant shed, they cease to be battle units. These buried positions, approximate but intangible figures, add up to the Ukrainian village of not long ago—savage, rebellious, and grasping.

Ammunition tucked away in every corner, Makhno can get an army like this ready for battle within an hour; it takes even less time to demobilize it.

With us, in Budenny's regular cavalry, the *tachanka* does not play such a predominant role. Still, all our machine-gun units go around on *britskas*. The Cossack's imagination distinguishes between two types of *tachanka*: the colonist type and the assessor's. And it's not merely their imagination, either, for the distinction is genuine.

Riding on the assessor's *britskas*, those ramshackle carriages made without love or inventiveness, you used to see wretched red-nosed officialdom, sleepy types rattling along the wheat-covered steppes of the Kuban, hurrying off to inquests and autopsies, while the colonist *tachanka*s came to us from the Samara and Volga-Ural regions, from the rich lands of the German colonies. The broad oak backrests of the colonist *tachanka* are decorated with cozy domestic motifs—bulging garlands of pink German flowers. The sturdy bottom is bound in iron. One is borne along upon unforgettable springs. I feel the warmth of many generations in these springs, now jolting over the old ruined roadways of Volhynia.

I experience the rapture of first possession. Every day after lunch we harness up. Grishchuk takes the horses out of the stable. They are improving day by day. I am proud and happy that I can already see a dull sheen on their groomed flanks. We rub down their swollen legs, trim their manes, cover their backs with a Cossack harness—a tangled web of fine cured straps—and pull out of the yard at a trot. Grishchuk sits sideways on the box; my own seat is padded with a flowery weave and hay that smells of perfume and tranquility. The tall wheels creak along the white grainy sand. Square patches of blooming poppies brighten the earth, the ruins of churches glow on the hillsides. High above the road, in a niche that a shell had smashed, stands a brown statue of Saint Ursula with round bare arms. And the narrow ancient letters weave a crooked chain upon the blackened gold of the pediment: "Glory to Jesus and His Blessed Mother."

Lifeless Jewish shtetls cling to the feet of Polish estates. A prophetic peacock shimmers on the brick walls, a dispassionate apparition against the blue expanse. Hidden away behind scattered shanties, a synagogue squats upon the barren soil, eyeless, dented, round like a Hasidic hat. Narrow-shouldered Jews stick out sadly at the intersections. And the image of southern Jews flares in my mind, jovial, potbellied, bubbly, like cheap wine. One cannot compare them to the bitter arrogance of these long and bony backs, the yellow and tragic beards. In these passionate features, hewn out of suffering, there is no fat and no warm pulsing of blood. The movement of the Galician and Volhynian Jew is uncontrolled, jerky, offensive to good taste, but the

A Teaching on the *Tachanka*   *203*

power of their grief is full of dark grandeur, and their secret contempt for the gentry is boundless. Watching them, I understood the smoldering history of these borderlands: the tales told of Talmudists who leased taverns, rabbis engaged in usury, young girls raped by Polish riflemen and over whom Polish magnates fought pistol duels.

(published 1923)

Dolgushov's Death

The pall of battle approached the town. At midday Korochaev flew past us in a black burka—the disgraced divchief four who fought single-handed, seeking death. He shouted to me as he rode past:

"Our communications got cut—Radziwillow and Brody under fire! . . ."

And he galloped off, fluttering, all black, his eyes like coals.

Across the board-flat plain, the brigades were regrouping. The sun rolled through the purple dust. In the ditches wounded men were having a bite to eat. Nurses lay on the grass, quietly singing. Afonka's scouts were scouring the fields for bodies and gear. Afonka rode past two paces from me and said without turning his head:

"Knocked the fat out of us, like two times two. I have a notion they'll sack the divchief. The troops have their doubts . . ."

The Poles reached the woods within three versts of us and posted their machine guns somewhere close. Bullets whine and wail. Their lament grows unbearable. Bullets riddle and dig into the ground, quivering with impatience. Vytyagaychenko, commander of the regiment, snoring in the baking sun, cried out in his sleep and woke up. He got on his horse and rode off to the forward squadron. His face was crumpled, lined with red streaks from his uncomfortable nap, and his pockets were full of plums.

"Son of a bitch," he said angrily, and spat a plum stone out of his mouth. "Bloody hassle. Get the flag out, Timoshka!"

"So we're going?" asked Timoshka, taking the shaft from his stirrup and unfurling a banner with a star and slogans from the Third International.

"There we'll see," said Vytyagaychenko and suddenly started shouting wildly, "Mount up, you girls! Squadron commanders, get the men together!"

Buglers sounded the alarm. The squadrons formed a column. A wounded man crawled out of a ditch and, shielding his eyes, said to Vytyagaychenko:

"Taras Grigoryevich, I'm speaking for the rest of us here. Looks like we're being left behind . . ."

"You'll fend them off," muttered Vytyagaychenko, rearing up on his horse.

"Got a sort of feeling we won't be fending off anybody, Taras Grigoryevich," said the wounded man after him.

"Quit moaning—don't suppose I'd leave you behind," Vytyagaychenko turned around and said, and then ordered the troops forward.

And that's when my friend Afonka's plaintive womanly voice rang out:

"No point going there at a trot, Taras Grigoryevich, there's five versts to cover. How will we fight if the horses are spent? What's the rush—you'll have time enough to tickle the Holy Virgin's pears."

"Forward walk!" commanded Vytyagaychenko without lifting his eyes.

The regiment rode off.

"If my notion about the divchief is correct," whispered Afonka, lingering for a moment, "if he gets sacked, then it's wash the withers and open the gates. Period."

Tears began streaming from his eyes. I stared at Afonka in amazement. He spun around, grabbed his hat, grunted, whooped, and sped off.

Grishchuk, with his stupid *tachanka*, and I as well—we stayed behind on our own till evening, bouncing between two walls of fire. The divisional staff had vanished. The other units wouldn't take us. The regiments entered Brody and were driven out by a counterattack. We drove up to the city cemetery. A Polish scout sprang out from behind the tombstones, aimed his rifle, and opened fire at us. Grishchuk turned us around. His *tachanka* shrieked on all four wheels.

"Grishchuk!" I cried through the whistling and the wind.

"Foolishness," he replied mournfully.

"This is the end," I shouted, in the grip of mortal passion, "the end, old boy!"

"Why do women bother?" he replied even more mournfully. "What's the point of matches and marriages and kin making merry at weddings . . ."

A pink tail flared across the sky and went out. The Milky Way moved between the stars.

"Makes me laugh," said Grishchuk sadly, pointing his whip at a man sitting by the roadside. "Makes me laugh, why women bother . . ."

The man sitting by the roadside was Dolgushov, a field telephonist. He sat staring at us with his legs splayed apart.

"That's it for me," he said when we had driven over to him. "I'm done for . . . Got it?"

"Got it," said Grishchuk, stopping the horses.

"You'll have to waste a cartridge on me," said Dolgushov.

He was sitting up against a tree. His boots were thrust wide apart. Without taking his eyes off me he carefully rolled up his shirt. His belly had been torn out, guts crawling to his knees, and you could see the heartbeats.

"The *szlachta* will come along and have some fun with me. Here are my papers. Write my mother, tell her how and what."

"No," I replied mutely and spurred my horse.

Dolgushov laid his blue palms on the ground and looked at them mistrustfully.

"Running away?" he muttered, sliding down. "That's it, run, you scum."

Perspiration crept over my body. The machine guns were pounding faster and faster, with hysterical insistence. Afonka Bida galloped over to us in a halo of sunset.

"Thrashing their hides!" he cried gaily. "What you got here, some kind of party?"

I showed him Dolgushov, and rode away.

They spoke briefly—I couldn't hear the words. Dolgushov gave his party membership book to the platoon commander, and Afonka tucked it away in his boot and shot Dolgushov in the mouth.

"Afonya," I said with a pathetic smile and rode up to the Cossack. "I just couldn't, see?"

"Get lost," he said, turning pale. "I'll kill you! Your kind with your glasses feel sorry for our brother like a cat's sorry for a mouse."

And he cocked his rifle.

I rode away at a walk, not turning around, the chill of death at my back.

"Whoa!" shouted Grishchuk behind me, "quit fooling!" and grabbed Afonka by the arm.

"Bloody lackey!" cried Afonka. "He won't get away from me . . ."

Grishchuk caught up to me at the turn in the road. Afonka was gone. He had gone the other way.

"There, you see, Grishchuk?" I said, "today I've lost Afonka, my first friend . . ."

Grishchuk took a shriveled apple from under his driver's seat.

"Eat," he said to me. "Please, eat . . ."

Brody, August 1920 (published 1923)

Brigcom 2

Budenny stood by a tree in silver-trimmed red trousers. Brigcom 2 had just been killed. The komandarm had named Kolesnikov to replace him.

An hour ago, Kolesnikov commanded a regiment. A week ago, Kolesnikov commanded a squadron.

The new brigcom was summoned to Budenny. The komandarm waited for him standing beside the tree. Kolesnikov arrived with Almazov, his commissar.

"The bastards are squeezing us," said the komandarm with his blinding smile. "We'll win or drop dead. No two ways. Understood?"

"Understood," replied Kolesnikov, eyes bulging.

"Run away and I'll have you shot," the komandarm said with a smile and turned his eyes to the chief of the Special Section.

"At your service," said the chief of the Special Section.

"Get rolling, Koleso!" some Cossack yelled cheerfully from the wings.

Budenny briskly turned on his heel and saluted the new brigcom. The latter spread five red, young fingers near the peak of his cap, broke into a sweat, and went off along a plowed path between two fields. The horses awaited him about a hundred *sazhen*s away. He walked with his head down, his long crooked legs slowly and agonizingly picking their way. The glow of sunset spilled over him, raspberry-colored and unreal, like impending death.

And then suddenly, across the sprawling earth, over the churned, yellow nakedness of the fields, we could see nothing but Kolesnikov's narrow back with his dangling arms and his sunken head in a gray cap.

An orderly brought him his horse.

He leaped into the saddle and galloped off to his brigade without looking back. The squadrons were waiting for him on the main road, the Brody high road.

A groaning "Hurrah!," rent by the wind, reached us at last.

I focused my binoculars and saw the brigcom twirling on his horse in columns of thick dust.

"Kolesnikov went in with the brigade," said an observer who was sitting in the tree above our heads.

"Very well," answered Budenny, lit a cigarette, and closed his eyes.

The "hurrah" faded away. The cannonade was extinguished. Useless shrapnel burst over the woods. And we could hear the great silence of slaughter.

"Tough kid," said Budenny as he got up. "Out for glory. And he'll find it."

And calling for horses he rode away to the place of battle. The staff followed him.

I got to see Kolesnikov again that very evening, only an hour after the Poles had been destroyed. He was riding by himself on a dun stallion at the head of his brigade, dreaming. His right arm hung in a sling. Ten paces behind him a Cossack cavalryman bore the unfurled banner. The first squadron was lazily singing bawdy songs. The brigade stretched on, dusty and endless like peasant carts on the way to a fair. Weary orchestras tootled at the rear.

In Kolesnikov's bearing that night I glimpsed the masterful indifference of a Tatar khan and could detect the training of the celebrated Kniga, the headstrong Pavlichenko, and the captivating Savitsky.

Brody, August 1920 (published 1923)

Sashka Christ

Sashka was his name, and they called him Christ because of his meekness. He was the communal shepherd in a Cossack settlement, and he had done no heavy work since about the age of fourteen, when he caught a foul disease. It all happened like this:

Tarakanych, Sashka's stepfather, had gone to spend the winter in Grozny and joined an artel there. The artel was made up of Ryazan muzhiks and it turned out well. Tarakanych did carpentry for them and found the work profitable. He couldn't keep up with all the work, so he wrote home for the boy to come and serve as his assistant: the settlement could manage well enough without Sashka through the winter. Sashka worked with his stepfather for a week. Then came Saturday, they took their rest, and sat down to have tea. It was October, but the air outside was mild. They opened the window and heated a second samovar. A beggar woman was traipsing around. She tapped on the window frame and said:

"Greetings, sojourners. Please consider my position."

"What sort of position?" asked Tarakanych. "Come in, little cripple."

The beggar scrabbled and then hopped into the room. She came over to the table and bowed low from the waist. Tarakanych seized her by the kerchief, pulled it off, and dug his fingers in her hair. The beggar's hair was gray, white, matted, and full of dust.

"Foo! Fine peasant brute, you are!" she said. "You're a regular circus . . . Please don't scorn an old lady like me," she whispered quick and clambered onto the bench.

Tarakanych lay with her and fooled around to his heart's content. The beggar kept tossing back her head and laughing.

"Raindrops falling on a dry old lady," she laughed. "I'll yield two hundred bushels an acre!"

She said this and saw Sashka, who was at the table drinking tea and wouldn't lift an eye to look at God's green earth.

"Your lad?" she asked Tarakanych.

"Sort of mine," answered Tarakanych. "The wife's."

"The wee boy's eyes are fit to burst," said the peasant woman. "Come over here."

Sashka went over to her—and caught a foul disease. But there was no thought of foul diseases then. Tarakanych gave the beggar some bones left over from lunch and a bright silver five piece.

"Polish it with sand, you woman of faith," said Tarakanych, "and it will look finer still. Lend it to the Lord God on a dark night and that five piece will shine instead of the moon."

The beggar woman wrapped her scarf on her head, took the bones, and left. And after two weeks it all became clear to the muzhiks. They suffered considerably from the foul disease and dragged on through the winter, treating themselves with herbs. When spring came, they returned to the settlement, back to their farmwork.

The settlement was nine versts from the railway. Tarakanych and Sashka went through the fields. The soil lay in its April dampness. Emeralds glimmered in the black furrows. Green shoots embroidered the ground in cunning stitches. And the earth smelled sour, like a soldier's wife at dawn. The first herds trickled down the barrows, foals played in the blue expanses of the horizon.

Tarakanych and Sashka followed barely noticeable paths.

"Let me go and be with the village shepherds, Tarakanych," said Sashka.

"What for?"

"I can't bear thinking how the shepherds live such splendid lives."

"I won't agree to it."

"For the love of God, let me go, Tarakanych," begged Sashka. "All the saints came from shepherds."

"Saint Sashka!" guffawed the stepfather. "Caught syphilis from the Mother of God!"

They passed the bend at Red Bridge, crossed the copse, the pasture, and came in sight of the cross on the settlement church.

The womenfolk were still digging in the gardens, while the Cossacks sat among the lilac bushes, drank vodka, and sang songs. Tarakanych's hut was still half a verst away.

"Pray God everything's all right," he said, crossing himself.

They went up to the hut and peered in at the little window. There was no one inside. Sashka's mother was in the shed milking the cow. The men crept up without a sound. Tarakanych started laughing and shouting behind the woman's back:

"Motya, Your Highness, get some supper for your visitors!"

The woman turned, starting shaking, ran out of the cowshed, and spun around the yard. Then she came back, cast herself on Tarakanych's chest, quivering.

"Look how naughty and uninviting you are," said Tarakanych, gently disengaging her. "Where are the kids?"

"They left the yard," said the woman, very white, and again she dashed about the yard and fell to the ground. "Oh, Alyoshenka," she cried wildly, "our babies left us feet first . . ."

Tarakanych waved his hand and went to the neighbors'. They told him that the week before God had taken his little boy and girl with typhus. Motya had written to him, but it seems he hadn't received the letters yet. Tarakanych returned to the hut. His wife was lighting the stove.

"You sure took care of things, Motya, nice and neat," he said. "I should tear you to pieces."

He sat down at the table and grieved—grieved on till bedtime, ate meat and drank vodka, and didn't tend to his work. He snored at the table, kept waking up, and then snoring again. Motya made a bed for herself and her husband, and a place for Sashka off to the side. Then she blew out the lamp and lay down with her husband. Sashka stirred on the hay in his corner, his eyes wide open, he couldn't sleep, and as if in a dream he saw the hut, a star in the window, the edge of the table, and the horse collars beneath his mother's bed. He was overcome by a violent vision, he gave himself over to his dream and rejoiced in it when he woke. Two silver cords appeared to him and twisted into a thick thread suspended from the sky, and a cradle hung down from them—a cradle of decorated rosewood. It swung high above the earth and far from the sky, and the silver cords swayed and sparkled. Sashka lay in the cradle, and the air caressed him. The air, loud as music, came from the fields, and a rainbow bloomed over the unripe grain.

Sashka rejoiced in his waking dream and kept closing his eyes so as not to see the horse collars under his mother's bed. Then he heard wheezing from Motya's bed and realized that Tarakanych was tumbling his mother.

"Tarakanych," he said in a loud voice, "I've got business with you."

"Business at night?" an angry Tarakanych shot back. "Go to sleep, you little bastard!"

"I swear on the Cross, there's business," said Sashka. "Come out into the yard."

And in the yard, beneath an undimmed star, Sashka said to his stepfather: "Don't hurt Mother, Tarakanych. You're tainted."

"And do you know about my temper?" said Tarakanych.

"I know about your temper, but did you look upon Mother's body? Her feet are clean, and her breast is clean. Don't hurt her, Tarakanych. We're tainted."

"Dear fellow," replied the stepfather, "keep clear of bloodshed and clear of my temper. Here's a twenty-kopeck piece—sleep it off and sober up."

"Twenty kopecks are no good to me," mumbled Sashka. "Let me go to the village shepherds."

"I won't agree to that," said Tarakanych.

"Let me go and be a shepherd," he mumbled, "or I'll make known to Mother the sort of folk we are. Why should she suffer, what with that body . . ."

Tarakanych turned around, went into the barn, and brought out a hatchet.

"Saint Sashka," he hissed. "No two ways about it. Going to chop you to bits, saint."

"You won't cut me down over a woman," the boy said in a barely audible voice, and leaned toward his stepfather. "You feel sorry for me—let me go and be a shepherd."

"May the joker take you!" cried Tarakanych, and threw down the hatchet. "All right, go be a shepherd."

He returned to the hut and passed the night with his wife.

That morning Sashka went to offer his services to the Cossacks, and from that day on he led the life of a communal shepherd. He became renowned throughout the area for his simple-hearted nature, was called Sashka Christ by the Cossacks, and remained a shepherd straight through until conscription. Old muzhiks, and the worst of them, too, would come to the pasture to wag their tongues with him, women would run to Sashka to recover from the thoughtless ways of their men, and they were never mad at him because of his love and because of his disease. Sashka was mobilized in the first year of the war. He fought for four years and returned to the settlement when the Whites were lording it over the place. He was urged to go to the Platov settlement, where a detachment was being formed against the Whites. Semyon Budenny, the former sergeant major, was in command of the detachment, and with him were his three brothers, Emilyan, Lukyan, and Denis. Sashka went to the Platov settlement, and there his fate was decided. He served in Budenny's regiment, in his brigade, in his division, and in the First Cavalry Army. He marched to free heroic Tsaritsyn, joined up with the Tenth Army under Voroshilov, fought at Voronezh, at Kastornaya, and at the General's Bridge on the Donets. During the Polish campaign he served on the supply convoy because he had been wounded and pronounced unfit for active duty.

That's how it all came to pass. I got to know Sashka Christ recently and moved my little trunk over to his cart. Often have we met the dawn and followed the setting sun. And whenever the course of battle thought to bring us together, we'd sit in the evening by the shimmering banked wall of a peasant hut, or make tea in a sooty kettle in the woods, or sleep side by side in freshly mown fields, hungry horses tethered to our legs.

(published 1924)

The Life Story of Pavlichenko, Matvei Rodionych

TO MITYA SCHMIDT, DIVCHIEF OF THE SECOND CAVALRY

Countrymen, comrades, my dear brothers! In the name of all mankind, learn the life story of the Red general, Matvei Pavlichenko. He was a herdsman, that general was, a herdsman on the Lidino estate, working for the master, Nikitinsky, and looking after the master's pigs, till life brought stripes to his epaulettes, and with those stripes our Matvei began to herd horned cattle. And who knows, if our Matvei, son of Rodion, had been born in Australia, then quite possibly, my friends, Matyushka might have risen to elephants, he'd have come to grazing elephants, but woe is me, one would never find elephants in our Stavropol district. I'll tell you straight, there's no animal bigger than a buffalo throughout the vast lands of our Stavropol. And a poor wretch wouldn't get no comfort out of buffaloes, it isn't any fun for a Russian just getting a laugh out of buffaloes; a horse—just give us poor orphans a horse on Judgment Day, when her soul tears past the pasture fence . . .

And so I look after my horned cattle, cows every which side of me, I'm stinking like a sliced udder shot through with milk, young bulls all around me, as one would expect, mousy little bulls gray in color. Sweet freedom all around me in the fields, grass rustling over the earth, heavens unfolding above like a multirow accordion—and the heavens in the Stavropol district can be deep blue, boys, deep blue. So that's how I grazed, nothing to do but blow my flute to keep the wind company, until an old man says to me:

"Go, Matvei," says he, "see Nastya."

"What for," says I, "or maybe you're having a laugh, old man?"

"Go," he says, "she wants you."

And so I go.

"Nastya," I say and blush black in the face. "Nastya," I say, "or maybe you're having a laugh?"

She won't hear me out, though, but takes off and runs away from me as fast as she can, and I run along with her till we get to the meadow, both of us red and dead out of breath.

"Matvei," says Nastya to me then, "three Sundays from last, during the spring fishing season and the fishermen went down to the river—you went with them, too, and hung your head. Why did you hang your head, Matvei, or was it some notion pressing on your heart? Answer me."

And I answer her:

"Nastya," I answer, "I've got no answer for you. My head isn't a rifle and it's got no front sight and no rear sight, but my heart you know well, Nastya, there isn't nothing in it—I suppose just milk shooting straight through it, an awful thing, how I stink of milk . . ."

But Nastya, I can see, starts cracking up at my words.

"Hand on a cross," she cracks up, laughing recklessly, laughing with all her might, across the whole wide steppe, like she was playing a drum, "hand on a cross, I see you making eyes at the young ladies."

And after we'd talked nonsense for a little while, we got married quick. And Nastya and I started living together how we knew how, and we sure knew how. We were hot all night, hot in winter, and all night long we went naked and rubbed our hides raw against each other. We lived well, like devils, right up until the old man comes to me a second time.

"Matvei," he says, "the master touched your wife all over, only recent like, and he'll get her, the master will."

But I say:

"No," I say, "do excuse me, old man, else I'll stitch you to this spot."

So, it goes without saying, the old man turns tail, and I covered twenty versts on foot that day, covered a good piece of ground on foot that day, and by evening turned up at the Lidino estate, at my merry master Nikitinsky's. He was sitting in the sitting room, the old granddad was, and he was taking apart three saddles: English, dragoon, and Cossack; and I stuck to his door like a burr, stuck there a wholesome hour, and all to no consequence. But then he cast his eyes my way.

"What is it you wish?" he asks.

"A reckoning."

"You've got designs on me?"

"No designs, just an open heart that wishes to . . ."

Here he turned his eyes away, turned from the highway to the alley, spread out raspberry saddlecloths on the floor, raspberrier than the tsar's own flags, those saddlecloths of his, then he got up, the geezer, and strutted about.

"Freedom for the free," he says to me and struts about. "I've crawled up all your Orthodox peasant mamas, you can have your reckoning, only the thing is, Matyushka, my little pal, don't you owe me a little certain something?"

"Hee-hee," I answer, "what a joker you are, really, God strike me down if you aren't a joker! Daresay, it's you that owes me compensation . . ."

"Compensation," my master grinds, and throws me to my knees and jerks his legs and stuffs me an earful of the Father, the Son, and the Holy Ghost. "Your compensation, but you forgot the yoke, that ox yoke of mine you broke last year—where is that yoke of mine?"

"I'll give you back the yoke," I reply to my master, and turn my simple eyes upon him and kneel before him lower than any earthly depth. "I'll give you back the yoke, only don't press me with debts, old fellow, just wait a bit."

And would you believe it, my Stavropol lads, my countrymen, comrades, my own dear brothers, it was five years that my master waited on my debts, for five lost years I was lost, till at last my little lost soul had a little visit from the year '18. It came along on lively stallions, on Kabardin horsies. It brought along a big wagon train and all sorts of songs. Eh, you, my sweet little '18! Can it be that we won't be going out with you no more, my very own flesh and blood, little '18? . . . We've spent your songs, drunk up your wine, decreed your truth—all that's left of you are your scribes. Eh, my sweetheart! Only it wasn't scribes that flew across the Kuban those days, setting the souls of generals free at a distance of one pace; back then it was Matvei Rodionych lying in blood outside Prikumsk, and the Lidino estate was only five versts from the last junction. Well, I went over by myself, without the detachment, and when I reached the sitting room, I entered politely. The local authorities was sitting there, in the sitting room, Nikitinsky carrying around tea and entertaining people, but when he saw me, his face fell, and I took off my Kuban hat to him.

"Greetings," I say to the people. "Greetings and kind regards. Shall you receive a guest, Master, or how will it be with us?"

"All will be calm with us, and honorable," one of them replies—by the way he talks I can tell he's a land surveyor—"all will be calm with us, and honorable, but it looks like you've galloped a good long way, Comrade Pavlichenko, for your countenance is streaked with dirt. Us local authorities dread such countenances—why is your countenance so?"

"It is so," I reply, "you local and cold-blooded authorities, because on my countenance one cheek has been burning for five years, burning in the trenches, burning for a woman, will burn on the Final Judgment itself. On the Final Judgment itself," I say, looking at Nikitinsky sort of cheerful, but by now he's got no eyes, only balls in the middle of his face, as if they had rolled these balls into position under his forehead, and with those crystal balls he was blinking at me, also sort of cheerful, but very dreadful.

"Matyusha," he says to me, "we used to know each other once upon a time, and now my wife, Nadezhda Vasilyevna, has lost her reason because of all the goings-on these days, and she used to be good to you, Nadezhda Vasilyevna was, and you, Matyusha, you used to respect her above the rest, and wouldn't you like to see her, now that she's lost her lights?"

"All right," I say, and we two go out into another room, and there he begins to touch my hands, my right hand, then my left.

"Matyusha," he says, "are you my fate or not?"

"No," I say, "and cut that talk. God ditched us lackeys. Our fate is late, our life is bait. So cut that talk and listen, if you like, to a letter from Lenin . . ."

"A letter for me, Nikitinsky?"

"To you," I say and take out my book of orders and open it at a blank page and read, though I can't read to save my life. " 'In the name of the people,' " I read, " 'and the establishment of a bright future, I order Pavlichenko, Matvei Rodionych, to deprive various people of life according to his discretion.' There," I say, "that's Lenin's letter for you . . ."

And he tells me, "No!"

"No," he says, "I know our life slumped over to the devil's side and that blood has become cheap in the Apostolic Russian Empire, but still, the blood you're owed—you'll get it all the same, and my death throes you'll forget all the same, so wouldn't it be better if I showed you a certain floorboard?"

"Show away," I say, "it might be better."

And again he and I went through rooms and down into the wine cellar, and there he pulled out a brick and found a coffer behind the brick. There were rings in that coffer, and necklaces, medals, and a holy image done in pearls. He threw it to me and froze.

"Yours," he says, "now you're in charge of the Nikitinsky icon, and now walk away, Matvei, back to your lair in Prikumsk."

And then I took him by the body, by the throat, by the hair.

"And what about my cheek?" I say. "What am I to do about my cheek, oh my brothers?"

And then he burst out laughing, much too loud, and stopped struggling.

"You jackal's conscience," he says, having stopped struggling. "I'm talking to you as I would to an officer of the Russian Empire, but you scoundrels were suckled by a she-wolf. Shoot me, son of a bitch!"

But I wasn't going to shoot him, I didn't owe him a shooting in any case, so I just dragged him upstairs into the parlor. There in the parlor was Nadezhda Vasilyevna, completely out of her mind, drawn saber in hand, walking back and forth and looking at herself in the mirror. And when I dragged Nikitinsky into the parlor, she ran and sat down in the armchair—she had a velvet crown trimmed with feathers—sat down in the armchair very brisk and alert and saluted me with the saber. And then I trampled my master Nikitinsky. I trampled on him for an hour or more than an hour, and in that time I got to know life in full. Shooting—I'll put it this way—only gets rid of a person, shooting is an act of mercy for him and for you it's too wicked easy, shooting won't get at the soul, to where it is in a person and how it shows itself. But, some of the times, I don't spare myself, some of the times, I trample an enemy for an hour or more than an hour, seeing as I wish to get to know life, this life that we live . . .

(published 1924)

The Cemetery in Kozin

A cemetery in a Jewish shtetl. Assyria and the mysterious decay of the East amid the overgrown weeds of the Volhynian plains.

Carved gray stones with inscriptions three centuries old. Crude impressions in high relief carved from granite. Depictions of lambs and fish over a dead man's head. Depictions of rabbis in fur hats. Rabbis with belts girt around their narrow loins. Below eyeless faces the rippling stone line of curly beards. To one side, beneath a lightning-shattered oak, stands the vault of Rabbi Azrael, slain by the Cossacks of Bogdan Khmelnitsky. Four generations lie buried in that resting place, humbler than a water carrier's dwelling, and the inscriptions, the moss-covered inscriptions, sing of them in an elaborate Bedouin prayer:

Azrael, son of Ananias, mouth of Jehovah.
Ilya, son of Azrael, mind locked in single combat with oblivion.
Wolf, son of Ilya, prince snatched from the Torah in his nineteenth
    spring.
Judah, son of Wolf, rabbi of Cracow and Prague.
O death, O covetous one, O greedy thief, why could you not have taken
    pity upon us, even once?

(published 1923)

Prishchepa

I'm on my way to Leshnev, where the divisional staff is quartered. My companion, as usual, is Prishchepa, a young Cossack from the Kuban—a tireless
scoundrel scrubbed out of the Communist Party, a future rag-and-bone man,
a careless syphilitic, and a carefree fraud. He wears a raspberry Circassian
coat of fine cloth and a downy Caucasian hood thrown back over his shoulders. On our journeys he would tell me about himself. I won't forget his
story.

A year ago Prishchepa ran away from the Whites. In response, they took
his parents hostage and killed them in a counterintelligence action. The
neighbors ransacked their belongings. When the Whites were driven out of
the Kuban, Prishchepa returned to his native settlement.

It was morning, daybreak, and a peasant slumber sighed in the acrid stuffi-
ness. Prishchepa hired an army cart and went about the settlement collecting
his phonographs, wooden kvass jugs, and the towels his mother had embroidered. He went out into the street in a black burka, a curved dagger at his
belt; the cart plodded along behind. Prishchepa went from one neighbor to
the next, trailing bloody footprints in his wake. In the huts where the Cossack found his mother's things or his father's pipe, he left old women pinned
to the wall, dogs hung above the wells, icons defiled with excrement. The
inhabitants smoked their pipes, watching his progress sullenly. The younger
Cossacks were scattered over the steppe, adding up the bill. The bill mounted,
and the settlement kept silent. When he was done, Prishchepa went back to
his despoiled ancestral home. He arranged the ruined furniture the way he
remembered it from childhood, and sent for vodka. He locked himself up in
the hut and drank for two days and nights, singing, weeping, and hacking at
the table with his saber.

On the third night the settlement saw smoke rising from Prishchepa's cottage. Torn, scorched, staggering, the Cossack led the cow out of the shed, put
his revolver in her mouth, and fired. The earth smoked beneath him, a blue
ring of flame flew out of the chimney and melted away, while in the stable
the young bull that had been left behind cried out. The fire shone bright as

Sunday. Then Prishchepa untied his horse, jumped in the saddle, threw a lock of his hair into the flames, and vanished.

Demidovka, July 1920 (published 1923)

The Story of a Horse

Savitsky, our divchief, once took a white stallion away from Khlebnikov, commander of the First Squadron. It was a splendid-looking horse, but its features were raw and always seemed a bit heavy to me. In exchange Khlebnikov received a little raven-black mare of decent breed and with a smooth trot. But he mistreated the mare, thirsting only for revenge, biding his time until his time came at last.

After our July battles turned out poorly, when Savitsky was replaced and sent back to the command reserves, Khlebnikov wrote to army headquarters applying for the horse to be returned to him. The chief of staff wrote his decision over the application, "The stallion in question to be returned to its prior status," and an exultant Khlebnikov rode a hundred versts to find Savitsky, who was then living in Radziwillow, a maimed little town resembling a bedraggled lady come down in the world. The former divchief lived alone, and the bootlickers from headquarters didn't recognize him anymore. The bootlickers fished for roast chicken in Budenny's smiles, like proper lackeys, and turned their backs upon the celebrated divchief.

Drenched in perfume and resembling Peter the Great, Savitsky lived in disgrace with Pavla, a Cossack woman he had taken away from a Jewish quartermaster, and with twenty thoroughbreds, which we considered to be his personal property. The sun in his yard strained and languished in blinding rays, the foals in his yard roughly sucked their dams, grooms with sweaty backs sifted oats on the faded winnows, and only Khlebnikov, wounded by truth and driven by vengeance, went straight to the barricaded yard.

"Are you acquainted with me?" he asked Savitsky, who was lying on hay.

"Could be I've seen you before," Savitsky yawned.

"Then take this resolution from the chief of staff," said Khlebnikov firmly, "and I must request that you, comrade in the reserve, should look upon me in an official capacity."

"Well, all right," Savitsky mumbled in a conciliatory tone, took the sheet of paper, and began to read it for an unusually long time. Then all of a sudden he called out to the Cossack woman, who was combing her hair in the shade of the porch awning.

"Pavla," he said, "Lord knows you've been combing your hair since morning . . . How about putting on the samovar?"

The Cossack woman put down her comb and, taking her hair into her hands, threw it back over her shoulder.

"All day long you've been pecking at me, Constantine Vasilyevich," she said, with a lazy and imperious grin, "first one thing, then another . . ."

She went over to the divchief, conveying her bosom on her high heels, a bosom that stirred like an animal in a sack.

"Pecking, all day long," the woman repeated, beaming, and buttoned the divchief's shirt over his chest.

"First one thing, then another!" laughed the divchief, rising, and putting his arms around Pavla's yielding shoulders, he suddenly turned a deathly chill face upon Khlebnikov.

"I'm still living, Khlebnikov," he said, clasping the Cossack woman. "My legs still walk, my ponies still prance, my hands will get you yet, and my gun grows warm against my flesh."

He took out the revolver that lay against his bare stomach and stepped toward the commander of the First Squadron.

The latter turned on his heel, spurs moaning, and left the yard like an orderly relaying an urgent message, and once again rode a hundred versts to find the chief of staff, but he was turned away.

"Your matter has been resolved, Commander," said the chief of staff. "I've returned your stallion, and I got enough complaints to handle without you . . ."

He wouldn't listen to Khlebnikov, and finally sent the truant commander back to his squadron. Khlebnikov vanished for an entire week. During that time we were sent to camp in the woods outside Dubno. We pitched our tents there and lived well. Khlebnikov, I remember, returned on a Sunday morning, on the twelfth. He demanded ink and a stack of paper from me. The Cossacks planed a tree stump for him, and on that stump he placed his revolver and the sheets of paper, and wrote till evening, scrawling through multiple pages.

"A regular Karl Marx," the squadron's military commissar said to him that evening. "What the hell are you writing there?"

"Describing various thoughts in accordance with my oath," replied Khlebnikov, and handed the commissar a declaration of his withdrawal from the Communist Party of the Bolsheviks.

"The Communist Party," read the declaration, "was founded, I believe, for the sake of unlimited joy and firm truth, and so it should also consider the little man. Now I will mention the white stallion that I took from some unbelievably reactionary peasants when it looked run-down, and many of my comrades had the nerve to laugh at its looks, but I had the strength to bear all their harsh laughter and—gritting my teeth for the common cause—I looked after the stallion until the desired change came, because I, comrades, am devoted to white horses and have given them what little strength I have left from the imperialist and civil wars, and such stallions feel my hand, and I can feel their unspoken wants as well and what they need, but the unjust raven-black mare is no use to me, I can't feel her and I can't stand her, as all the comrades will confirm, and things may come to grief. And seeing now how the party can't get me back my very own according to the resolution, I see no other way but to write this declaration with tears that are unfit for a soldier but flow unhindered and lash at my heart, slashing my heart till it bleeds . . ."

This and a good deal else was written in Khlebnikov's declaration. He spent the whole day writing it, and it was very long. The military commissar and I struggled with it for an hour and managed to get through the whole thing.

"Such a fool," said the commissar, tearing up the sheets. "Come by after supper, we'll have a talk."

"I don't need your talk," answered Khlebnikov, trembling. "You lost me, Commissar."

He stood at attention, shivering, hands to his trouser seams, looking around as if considering which way to run. The commissar came right up to him but wasn't quick enough. Khlebnikov cut and ran like mad.

"Lost me," he yelled wildly, and he climbed up onto the tree stump, tearing his jacket and scratching his chest.

"Kill me, Savitsky!" he cried, falling to the ground. "Kill me now!"

We dragged him into a tent, the Cossacks helped. We put on tea to boil and rolled him cigarettes. He smoked and kept trembling. Only toward evening did our commander calm down. He said no more about his raving declaration but went a week later to Rovno to be assessed by a medical board and was demobilized as unfit for service, since he had six wounds.

That was how we lost Khlebnikov. I was sad about it, because Khlebnikov was a quiet man who resembled me in character. He was the only man in the squadron who had a samovar. During lulls we used to drink hot tea together. And he would talk to me of women with such thoroughness that I was embarrassed and delighted to listen. This, I think, was because we were both shaken by the same passions. Both of us looked on the world as a meadow in May, a meadow traversed by women and horses.

Radziwillow, July 1920 (published 1923)

Konkin

We were making mincemeat of the *szlachta* down by Belaya Tserkov. Making mincemeat such that the trees bowed down. I caught a scratch somewhere that morning but still managed to get the job done, thanks very much. I remember daytime was getting close to night. I got knocked away from the brigcom with only five little Cossacks of the proletariat by my side. Everybody grabbing and hacking on one another, like a deacon with a deaconess, sap leaking out of me, front of my horse all wet . . . You get the picture.

Me and Spirka Zabuty got out of there and away from the woods, and lo and behold—the arithmetic improves. Three hundred *sazhen*s off, not more, we see either the staff or the convoy kicking up dust. If it's staff, good, if it's the convoy, even better. The boys were going around in such rags that their shirts didn't reach down to their puberty.

"Zabuty," I say to Spirka, "you and your mother this and that and the other, I say unto you as the speaker of record, that must be their staff heading out."

"Their staff, sure enough," says Spirka, "only there's two of us and eight of them."

"Let the wind blow, Spirka," I says, "I'll get their vestments dirty all the same. We'll die for a dill pickle and world revolution . . ."

And down we went. There were eight sabers. We picked two right off the vine with our rifles. Then I see Spirka taking a third "Dukhonin" into headquarters for a "document check," as we say. And I take aim at the big shot. Raspberry-red he was, boys, with a gold watch and chain. I had him cornered in a farm. The little farm was full of apple and cherry trees. My big shot's mount was like a merchant's daughter, but it was spent. Then Pan General drops the reins, aims his Mauser at me, and makes a hole in my leg.

"All right," I think, "you'll be mine yet, darling, you'll spread those legs . . ."

So I got to work and put two bullets in the little horse. I was sorry about the stallion. He was a little Bolshevik, a regular little Bolshevik that stallion was. He was red as a copper coin, had a tail like a bullet, and four well-strung legs. I thought, I'll take it alive to Lenin, but it didn't work out. I liquidated that pony. Down he went, like a bride, and my big shot fell out of the saddle. He tore off to the side but then turned around again and made another draft hole in my fine figure. So that means I've got three distinctions in action against the enemy.

"Jesus," I think, "he might just kill me accidental-like."

I galloped up to him, and he's drawn his sword, and tears were running down his cheeks, white tears, human milk.

"You'll get me the Order of the Red Banner," I shout. "Give up, Your Illustrious Highness, as I live and breathe! . . ."

"*Nie moge*, Pan," the old fellow answers. "You'll cut my throat."

Then up pops Spiridon, like a leaf in the grass. He's all in a lather, his eyes hanging from his mug by a thread.

"Vasya," he shouts to me, "you'll never believe how many people I've finished off! But that's a general you got there, he's got all the trimmings, I wouldn't mind finishing him off, too."

"Go to the Turk!" I say to Zabuty, getting mad now. "His trimmings have cost me blood."

And I got my mare to drive the general into a shed full of hay or something else. It was quiet in there and dark and cool.

"Pan," I say, "take it easy in your old age. Surrender, for the love of God, and we'll have a rest together."

But he's panting against the wall, wiping his forehead with red fingers.

"*Nie moge*," he says, "you'll cut my throat. I'll give my saber only to Budenny . . ."

Go and fetch him Budenny! How do you like that! I can see the old guy's a goner.

"Pan," I shout, wailing and grinding my teeth, "I'll give you my proletarian word that I'm the head chief in charge here. Don't look for trimmings on me, but I've got the title all right. Here's my title: musical comedian and salon ventriloquist from the town of Nizhny . . . Nizhny on the Volga River."

And a demon flew away with me. The general's eyes blinked like lanterns before me. A red sea parted before me. This was salt in the wound, for I could see that grandpa doesn't believe me. So I shut my mouth, boys, sucked in my belly the old way, our way, the warrior's way, the Nizhny way, and proved to the *szlachta* that I was a ventriloquist.

Then the old man went pale, clutched his heart, and sat down on the ground.

"Now do you believe Vaska the Comedian, Commissar of the Third Invincible Cavalry Brigade . . . ?"

"Commissar?" he cries.

"Commissar," I say.

"Communist?" he cries.

"Communist," I say.

"In my fatal hour," he cries, "as I draw my last breath, tell me, my Cossack friend, are you a Communist, or are you lying?"

"Communist," I say.

Then my grandpa sits on the ground and kisses some sort of amulet, breaks his saber in two, and lights two lamps in his eyes, two lanterns over the dark steppe.

"Forgive me," he says, "I can't surrender to a Communist," and shakes me by the hand. "Forgive me," says he, "and cut me down like a soldier."

This story was recounted to us once during a halt by Konkin, political commissar of the N—— Cavalry Brigade, thrice-decorated Cavalier of the Order of the Red Banner, who told it with his usual clowning.

"So what did you and the Pan agree to, Vaska?"

"What could he agree to? Full of honor and all. I even bowed to him again, but he was stubborn, the queer old bird. So we took what documents he had, took his Mauser, and took the saddle that's under me even now. And then I see all my strength is seeping out, I'm falling asleep like something awful, my boots are full of blood, I couldn't deal with him . . ."

"So then you took care of him, the old man?"

"Damn shame."

Dubno, August 1920 (published 1924)

Berestechko

We were on the march from Khotin to Berestechko. The troops were nodding off in their tall saddles. A song gurgled like a brook running dry. Monstrous corpses lay upon the thousand-year-old burial mounds. Muzhiks in white shirts doffed their caps before us. Divchief Pavlichenko's burka flew like a gloomy flag above the staff. His downy hood was thrown back across his burka, and his curved saber hung down at his side like it was glued there. Its handle was done in black ivory with magnificent carvings, and its case was kept by the orderlies leading the divchief's spare horses.

We rode past the Cossack burial mounds, past Bogdan Khmelnitsky's watchtower. From behind a headstone an old man crept out with a bandura and sang to us in a child's voice of the glory of the Cossacks of old. We listened to his songs in silence, then unfurled our banners and burst into Berestechko to the sounds of a thundering march. The inhabitants had put iron bars across their shutters, and silence, almighty silence, had ascended the shtetl's throne.

I ended up being quartered at the home of a red-haired widow who smelled of the grief of widowhood. I washed away the traces of the march and went out into the street. Notices had been posted up announcing that the divisional commissar, Vinogradov, would lecture that evening on the Second Congress of the Comintern. Right under my window a few Cossacks were trying to shoot an old silver-bearded Jew for espionage. The old man shrieked and struggled to get away. Then Kudrya from the machine gun detachment got hold of his head and tucked it under his arm. The Jew calmed down and spread his legs. With his right hand Kudrya drew his dagger and carefully cut the old man's throat, without splashing himself. Then he knocked at the closed window.

"If anyone is interested," he said, "come fetch him. Feel free."

The Cossacks turned a corner. I followed them and began to wander through Berestechko. There are mostly Jews here, but Russian townsfolk, tanners, have settled on the outskirts. They live cleanly, in little white houses with green shutters. Instead of vodka they drink beer or mead, grow tobacco in their little gardens, and smoke it in long curved pipes like Galician peasants.

Living next to three tribes, active and productive, has awakened in them that stubborn love of hard work that sometimes characterizes a Russian person when he is still free from lice, drink, and despair.

The everyday life of Berestechko was swept away, though it had been quite sturdy here. Offshoots of three centuries still sprouted in Volhynia with the warm decay of bygone days. With threads of profit the Jews here bound the Russian muzhik to the Polish *pan*, the Czech colonist to the Lodz factory. They were smugglers, the best on the border, and nearly always defenders of the faith. Hasidism kept that bustling population of hawkers, brokers, and tavern keepers in stifling captivity. Boys in gabardines still trod the age-old road to the Hasidic cheder, and just as before, old women still took young brides to see the tsaddik with frenzied prayers for fertility.

The Jews here live in spacious houses painted white or a pale, watery blue. The traditional squalor of this architecture goes back centuries. Behind the house there is always a shed that is two or sometimes even three stories tall. No sunshine ever penetrates them. They have these indescribably gloomy sheds instead of our yards. Secret passages lead to basements and stables. In wartime the inhabitants go down into these catacombs to escape bullets and pillage. Human waste and cow manure accumulate here for days. Horror and dismay fill the catacombs with the acrid stench and foul bite of excrement.

Berestechko reeks unremittingly even now—everyone smells of rotten herring. The shtetl stinks in anticipation of a new era, and instead of people there are only faded outlines of frontier misfortunes. I got tired of them by the end of the day, I walked past the edge of town, climbed a hill, and entered the despoiled castle of the Counts Raciborski, until recently the rulers of Berestechko.

The stillness of sunset turned the grass around the castle a pale blue. The moon, green as a lizard, rose over the pond. From my window I could see the estate of the Counts Raciborski—meadows and fields of hops, obscured by the undulant ribbons of twilight.

In that castle there used to live an insane, ninety-year-old countess, with her son. She used to plague him because he had produced no heir for their dying line, and—the muzhiks told me—she would beat him with a coachman's whip.

A meeting was being held in the square below. Peasants, Jews, and tanners from the outskirts had come. Vinogradov's voice burned with enthusiasm and his spurs rang out. He talked about the Second Congress of the Comintern, while I wandered past walls where nymphs with gouged-out eyes led a choral dance. Then in a well-trod corner I found a fragment of a letter yellow with age. In discolored ink was written, "Berestetchko, 1820. Paul, mon bien aimé, on dit que l'empereur Napoléon est mort, est-ce vrai? Moi, je me sens bien, les couches ont été faciles, notre petit héros achève sept semaines . . ."

Down below, the commissar will not be silenced. He is passionately persuading the bewildered townsfolk and the plundered Jews:

"You are in power. Everything that is here is yours. No more Pans. I will now proceed to the election of the Revolutionary Committee . . ."

Berestechko, August 1920 (published 1924)

Red Cavalry

Salt

Dear Comrade Editor. I want to write to you about the class unconscious-ness of certain women who are harmful to our cause. I put my hopes in you, that you who's traveled around our nation's fronts, which you have taken due note of, have not overlooked the stalwart station of Fastov, which lies a million thousand leagues away, in such and such a district in a distant land, I was there, of course, drank home-brewed beer—only wet my whiskers, not my lips. There's a lot you can write regarding this aforementioned station, but as they say in our humble abode—let's not drag the Lord's dirt around. That's why I am only going to write about what my own eyes saw firsthand.

It was a quiet and glorious little night seven days ago, when our well-deserved Red Cavalry transport train stopped there, loaded with fighters. All of us were burning to promote the common cause and were headed to Berdichev. Only thing is, we notice that our train can't manage to get a move on, our little rascal won't chug, and the fighters became all doubtful and ask-ing ourselves—why stop here now? And indeed, the stop turned out to be a huge deal in terms of the common cause, on account of the peddlers, those nasty villains among whom there was a countless force of the female sex, carrying on in an obnoxious manner with the railroad authorities. Recklessly they grabbed the handrails, the nasty villains, they scampered over the metal roofs, screwed around, made a muck, and each of them held in her hands a bag of the infamous contraband salt, up to five poods' worth. But the triumph of peddlerist capital did not last long. The initiative of the troopers who crept out of the train made it possible for the dishonored authority of the railroad personnel to breathe easy. Only those of the female sex with their bags of salt remained on the premises. Taking pity, the fighters let some of the women inside the heated cars, but others they didn't. That's how in our own railroad car of the Second Platoon two girls turned up, and then after the first bell here comes this impressive woman with a baby and says:

"Let me in, my gentle Cossack lads, the whole war I've been suffering at these train stations with a babe at my breast and now I just want to go and meet my husband, but because of the railroads you can't get anywhere these days—don't I deserve a bit of help from you, my Cossack lads?"

"As a matter of fact, woman," I say to her, "whatever the platoon agrees, that will be your fate." And, turning to the platoon, I prove to them that here is a woman who wishes to travel to meet her husband at an appointed place and that she in fact does have a child in her possession and so what's the decision then—should we let her in or not?

"Let her in," the boys yell. "Once we're done, she won't want her husband no more . . ."

"No," I say to the boys rather politely, "I beg your pardon, platoon, but I am surprised to hear such horse talk. Recall, platoon, your old lives and how you, too, were babes in your mother's arms, and so it seems to me that it won't do to talk that way . . ."

And the Cossacks, having talked it over among themselves, started saying how persuasive our Balmashev was, and so they let the woman onto the rail car, and she climbs aboard with gratitude. And every last one of them, each swearing by the truth of my words, tumbles over the other to make room for her, saying:

"Please sit down in that corner, woman, and be sweet to your babe the way mothers are, no one will touch you in that corner, and you will arrive untouched to your husband, as you wish, and we depend on your conscience to raise a change of guard for us, because what's old gets old and it looks like there's a shortage of youth. We've seen our share of grief, woman, both when we got drafted and then later in the extra service, we were crushed by hunger and burned by cold. But you, good woman, please sit here and don't worry about a thing . . ."

The third bell rang and the train shoved off. And the nice little night pitched its tent. And in that tent there were star lanterns. And the men remembered the Kuban night and the green Kuban star. And a tune flew up like a bird. While the wheels clattered and clattered . . .

Time passed, and when the night changed its guard and the red drummers welcomed the dawn on their red drums, then the Cossacks came up to me, seeing I was sitting there wide awake and none too pleased in the least.

"Balmashev," the Cossacks say to me, "why are you so awful displeased and sitting there wide awake?"

"I beg your most gracious pardon, fellow fighters, and I do apologize, but if I could just speak a few words with this citizen here . . ."

And quivering head to toe, I get up from my resting place where sleep has run off like a wolf from a pack of nasty hounds, and I walk up to her and take the baby out of her arms and rip off his diapers and rags, and in the diapers I see a nice fat little pood of salt.

"Well, here's an *inter*-resting kind of kid, comrades, it don't ask for titty and it don't wet your lap and it don't bother people when they sleep . . ."

"Forgive me, gentle Cossacks," the woman cut into our conversation rather cold-bloodily, "wasn't me that tricked you, it was my evil fate."

"Balmashev will forgive your evil fate," I tell the woman. "That doesn't cost Balmashev much—Balmashev sells the goods for what he paid for them. But address yourself to the Cossacks, woman, the Cossacks who held you up as a hardworking mother of the republic. Address yourself to these two girls who are crying at present for having suffered under us through last night. Address yourself to our wives on the wheat fields of the Kuban, who are wearing out their womanly strength without their husbands, and to the husbands, who are lonely, too, and who are wickedly forced against their will to have their way with the girls crossing their path . . . But you they didn't touch, even though, as a matter of fact, that's all you're good for. Address yourself to Rushah, crushed by pain . . ."

And she says to me:

"I've lost my salt anyways, so I'm not afraid of the truth. You don't care about Russia, it's those Yids Lenin and Trotsky that you're saving . . ."

"This conversation isn't about Yids, you despicable citizen. The Yids don't enter into it. And by the way, I don't know about Lenin, but Trotsky is the daring son of the governor of Tambov, who joined the working class, even though he came from different stock. Like prisoners sentenced to hard labor, they're dragging us out, Lenin and Trotsky are, to the free road of life, while you, foul citizen, are a worse counterrevolutionary than that White general waving his sharpest saber at us from his thousand-ruble horse. At least him you can see, that general there, from every road, and the working man has only one little dream—to chop him to bits. But you, dishonest citizen, with your *inter*-resting kids who don't ask for bread and don't need to crap, you we can't see, just like a flea, and so you grind on us, you grind and grind . . ."

And I frankly do admit that I threw that citizen off the moving train and derailed her, but she, heifer that she was, sat up, shook out her skirts, and went on her nasty way. And seeing this unharmed woman, with all Russia around her suffering untold and the peasant fields without an ear of grain, and the girls all dishonored, and the comrades, many of whom go to the front and few of whom return, I wanted to jump off the train and finish her off or die trying. But the Cossacks took pity on me and said:

"Get her with the rifle."

So I took the trusty rifle down from the wall and washed that disgrace from the face of the working land and the republic.

And we, the fighters of the Second Platoon, swear before you, dear Comrade Editor, and before all of you, dear comrades of the editorial office, that we will deal mercilessly with all the traitors who are dragging us into the ditch and want to turn back the stream and cover Russia with corpses and dead grass.

In the name of all the fighters of the Second Platoon

—Nikita Balmashev, soldier of the Revolution.
(published 1923)

Evening

O Charter of the RKP! You have laid headlong rails clean through the sour dough of our Russian tales. You have transformed three idle hearts, full of the passions of Ryazan Christs, into contributors for *The Red Cavalryman*, transformed them such that they write for our rollicking newspaper, full of swagger and crude fun.

Galin with the walleye, consumptive Slinkin, Sychev with the ulcerous gut—they wander the barren dust of the rear, ripping their leaflets of riot and fire clean through the ranks of our dashing Cossacks on furlough, the reserve swindlers known as Polish translators, the girls from Moscow sent to us to work as proofreaders on the Politsection train.

The newspaper appears only toward nightfall, laid like a dynamite fuse beneath the army. The slant-eyed lantern of the provincial sun dies down in the sky, the darting lights of the printing press blaze uncontrollably in their mechanical passion. Then, toward midnight, Galin gets down from the coach to shake off the bites of unrequited love for Irina, the washerwoman on our train.

"Last time," says Galin, narrow in the shoulders, pale and blind, "last time, Irina, we considered the execution of Bloody Nicholas by the Yekaterinburg proletariat. Now we move on to other tyrants who died like dogs. Peter III was strangled by Orlov, his wife's lover. Paul was torn to pieces by his courtiers and his own son. Nicholas the Rod poisoned himself, his son fell on March 1, and his grandson died of drink. You need to know about these things, Irina . . ."

And gazing at the washerwoman with naked eyes filled with adoration, Galin tirelessly ransacks the crypts of dead emperors. His slouching figure is bathed by the moon stuck in the sky like an impudent splinter, the printing presses clatter somewhere near him, and the wireless station glows with pure light. Rubbing up against the shoulder of Vasily the cook, Irina listens to the muffled and preposterous mutterings of love, stars trudge across the black seaweed of the sky above her, the washerwoman nods off, makes a cross over her thick mouth, and stares wide-eyed at Galin. Thus a young woman, gazing at a professor devoted to the quest for knowledge, longs for the inconvenience of conception.

Ham-faced Vasily yawns beside Irina. Like all cooks he looks down upon humanity. Cooks have much to do with the flesh of dead animals and the greed of living ones, so in politics they look for things that don't concern them. So, too, Vasily, that ham-faced conqueror. Pulling his trousers up to his nipples, he asked Galin about the civil lists of various kings, about the dowry for the tsar's daughters, and remarked with a yawn:

"It's nighttime, Irina. And we've got tomorrow ahead of us. Time to squash the fleas."

They've closed the kitchen door, leaving Galin alone with the moon, stuck there above like an impudent splinter. I sat in my eyeglasses across from the moon on the bank of a sleeping pond, boils on my neck and bandages on my legs. I was mulling over the class struggle in my muddled poetical brain when Galin approached with his gleaming walleyes.

"Galin," I said, overwhelmed by self-pity and loneliness, "I'm ill, looks like the end has come for me, and I'm so tired of life in our Red Cavalry . . ."

"You're a driveler," replied Galin, the watch on his thin wrist showing 1:00 A.M., "you're a driveler, and it's our fate to put up with you drivelers . . . The entire party goes around in aprons covered in blood and filth—we're cleaning the kernel out of the shell for you. Not long will pass and then you'll see those clean kernels and take your finger out of your nose and sing of the new life in no ordinary prose, but for now sit and be quiet, you driveler, and stop whimpering underfoot."

He came closer and fixed the bandages that had come loose on my mangy sores and tucked his head into his chicken chest. Night comforted us in our miseries, a light wind fanned us like a mother's skirt, and the grass below sparkled with freshness and moisture.

The rumbling machines of our train press gave a screech and went silent, dawn drew a streak along the edge of the earth, the kitchen door creaked open slightly. Four fat-heeled feet were thrust out into the cool, and we beheld Irina's amorous calves and Vasily's big toe with its crooked black nail.

"Vasilyok, my little cornflower," she whispered intimately in her faint Russian voice, "get out of my bunk, you rascal."

But Vasily just jerked his heel and drew closer.

"The Red Cavalry," Galin then said to me, "the Red Cavalry is a social focus produced by the Tseka of our party. The curving road of the Revolution has thrust to the fore the Cossack freemen, all of them steeped in many prejudices, but the nimble Tseka will guide and scrub them with a steel brush."

And Galin went on about the political education of the First Cavalry Army. He continued at length with dull and perfect clarity. His eyelid twitched over his walleye, and blood ran from his ragged palms.

Kovel, 1920 (published 1924)

Afonka Bida

We were fighting at Leshnev. The wall of enemy cavalry kept appearing everywhere. The coil of hard Polish strategy unwound with an ominous whistle. We were hard-pressed. For the first time in the whole campaign we felt on our back the devilish sharpness of flank attacks and breaks through in the rear—bites from the same weapon that had served us so well.

The front line at Leshnev was held by infantry. Blond and barefoot Volhynian muzhiks hunkered down in the crooked trenches. This infantry was taken from the plow just yesterday so that the Red Cavalry would have an infantry reserve. The peasants went willingly. They fought with the utmost diligence. Their snorting muzhik ferocity amazed even Budenny's men. Their hatred for the Polish landowners was made of inconspicuous but solid stuff.

During the second phase of the war, when our yelling and whooping no longer had any effect on the enemy's imagination and when mounted attacks became impossible against an entrenched opponent, this homemade infantry might have been invaluable to us. But our poverty prevailed. The peasants got one gun to share among three, and cartridges that did not fit the rifles. The venture had to be abandoned and this genuine people's militia was disbanded and sent home.

Now let us turn to the fighting at Leshnev. The foot soldiers were dug in three versts away from the shtetl. Before them went a slouching youth wearing eyeglasses. A sword dragged at his side. He shifted and lurched with a look of dissatisfaction, as if his boots were too tight. The peasants' ataman, elected and adored by them, was a Jew, a mope-eyed Jewish youth with the sallow and intense face of a Talmudist. In battle he displayed a watchful courage and sangfroid that resembled a dreamer's absentmindedness.

It was nearly three o'clock on a clear July day. A rainbow web of heat shimmered in the air. Behind the hilltops there glittered a festive streak of uniforms and horse manes streaming with ribbons. The youth gave the signal to make ready. Flopping in their bast shoes, the muzhiks ran to their positions and got ready. But the alarm turned out to be false. Onto the Leshnev high road rode Maslak's flamboyant squadrons. The horses, lean though still spirited, came along at a brisk walk. Magnificent standards fluttered in fiery pillars of dust above gilt staffs full of velvet tassels. The horsemen rode on majestically, cool and insolent. The ragged foot soldiers crept out of their ditches and gaped at the supple grace of this steady stream.

At the head of the regiment on a bandy-legged little steppe horse rode Brigcom Maslak, full of his own drunken blood and the rot of his greasy juices. His stomach rested like a large cat upon his silver-studded saddlebow. Catching sight of the foot soldiers, he went purple with glee and beckoned to the platoon leader, Afonka Bida. We called the platoon leader "Makhno" because of his resemblance to the Old Man. They exchanged whispers for a minute, the commander and Afonka. Then the platoon leader turned to the First Squadron, bent down, and in a low voice ordered, "Forward!" The Cossacks came to a trot. They spurred their horses and raced to the trenches, where the delighted foot soldiers were feasting their eyes on the display.

"Prepare for battle!" sang out Afonka's lugubrious voice, as though from afar.

Wheezing, coughing, and enjoying himself, Maslak rode off to the side, the Cossacks went on the attack. The poor foot soldiers tried to flee, but too late. The Cossacks' lashes were already descending upon their shredded rags. The horsemen rode around the field, twirling their whips with remarkable flair.

"What are you messing around for?" I yelled at Afonka.

"For laughs," he answered, fidgeting in the saddle and flushing out a lad who was hiding in the bushes.

"For laughs!" he cried, prodding the stunned fellow.

The sport came to an end when Maslak, mollified and majestic, waved his plump hand.

"Infantry, stay sharp!" Afonka shouted, smugly straightening his feeble body. "Now go catch fleas!"

Exchanging chuckles, the Cossacks re-formed their ranks. There was no trace of the foot soldiers. The trenches were empty. And only the slouching Jew still stood in the same place, attentively and haughtily surveying the Cossacks through his glasses.

Firing continued from the direction of Leshnev. The Poles were surrounding us. One could make out the isolated figures of mounted scouts through binoculars. They would gallop out of the shtetl and topple over like roly-poly dolls. Maslak gathered the squadron and positioned it along both sides of the road. The brilliant sky above Leshnev was unspeakably empty, as ever in the hour of peril. The Jew threw back his head and blew loud and mournfully on his metal whistle. And the infantry, that unrepeatable battered infantry, returned to their posts.

Bullets flew thick our way. The brigade staff came in the line of machine-gun fire. We bolted into the woods and began to scramble through the thicket on the right of the road. Bullet-pierced branches crackled above us. When we had made our way out of the bushes, the Cossacks weren't there. They were making their way back to Brody on the divchief's orders. Only the muzhiks remained, snarling the occasional shot out of their trenches, and Afonka, who had lagged behind and was now catching up with his platoon.

He rode at the very edge of the road, looking about him and sniffing the air. The gunfire slackened for a moment. The Cossack thought to take advantage of the lull and set off at a gallop. At that instant a bullet pierced the neck of his horse. Afonka rode about another hundred paces, and then, in our very midst, the horse abruptly bent its forelegs and collapsed to the ground.

Afonka slowly removed his crushed leg from the stirrup. He squatted and poked the wound with his bronzed finger. Then Bida straightened himself, and scanned the gleaming horizon in agony.

"Farewell, Stepan," he said in a wooden voice, stepping away from the dying animal and bowing to it from the waist. "How shall I go back to my sweet home without you? . . . What'll I do with your embroidered saddle? Farewell, Stepan!" he said again, louder, choking, squeaked like a mouse in a trap and broke into a howl. His seething cries reached our ears, and we saw him bowing manically, like a woman shrieking at church. "Well, I won't surrender to vile fate!" he shouted, removing his hands from his lifeless face. "Now I'll go and butcher that unspeakable *szlachta* without mercy. I'll cut them to the very heart, down to their very last breath and down to the last drop of the Virgin Mother's blood . . . I promise you, Stepan, I swear by my dear brothers from the settlement."

Afonka laid his face on the wound and was silent. Riveting its deep-violet, shining eyes on its master's face, the horse listened to Afonka's wheezing. It moved its drooping head about the ground in a gentle listlessness, while two streams of blood like ruby straps flowed down a chest lined with white muscles.

Afonka lay without stirring. Then Maslak, making his way through on his fat legs, went over to the horse, put his revolver in its ear, and fired. Afonka jumped and turned his pockmarked face upon Maslak.

"Take the harness, Afanasy," Maslak said tenderly, "go to your unit . . ."

And from the slope we could see Afonka bent beneath the weight of the saddle, his face raw and red like butchered meat, wandering off to his squadron, infinitely alone in the dry deserted dust of the day.

Late that evening I came across him on the convoy. He was sleeping in one of the carts with his stuff—swords, army jackets, and pierced gold coins—beside him. His blood-caked head with its twisted lifeless mouth lay as though crucified on the crook of the saddle. Nearby lay the harness of the dead horse, all the showy and complicated apparel of a Cossack racer—breastplates with black tassels, supple crupper straps studded with colorful stones, a bridle embossed with silver.

Darkness came down ever denser upon us. The convoy wound in a long file along the Brody high road; plain little stars rolled down the Milky Way, and distant villages flickered in the cool depths of the night. The deputy squadron commander Orlov and the long-whiskered Bitsenko sat in Afonka's cart and considered Afonka's sorrow.

"Brought the horse from home," said long-whiskered Bitsenko. "Where could you find another like it?"

"A horse is a friend," said Orlov.

"A horse is a father," sighed Bitsenko, "saves your life time and again. Bida will be lost without his horse."

But come morning Afonka had vanished. The fighting at Brody began and ended. Defeat gave way to transient victory—we saw a change of divchiefs, but still no Afonka. Only a terrible murmur across the countryside, the wicked and predatory trail of Afonka's plunder showed us his arduous path.

"He's looking for a horse," was what the squadron said about the platoon leader, and on those boundless evenings of our wanderings I heard more than a few tales of that savage and godforsaken "looking."

Men from other units ran across Afonka dozens of versts from our position. He would ambush straggling Polish horsemen or scour the woods in search of the horse droves hidden there by peasants. He went about setting fire to villages and shooting the Polish elders for concealing goods. Echoes of that ferocious single combat reached our ears, echoes of desperate and larcenous lone-wolf attacks upon the masses.

Another week passed. In our minds, the replacement of the divchief overshadowed the frail figure of Afonka and his flat Makhno-style seminarian curls. The bitter hatefulness of each day seared away the tales of Afonka's dark exploits, and we began to forget "Makhno." Then we heard a rumor that he'd been run through by Galician peasants somewhere in the woods. And so the day we entered Berestechko, Emelyan Budyak of the First Squadron went to the divchief to ask for Afonka's saddle and its yellow saddlecloth. Emelyan wanted to ride out on parade with a new saddle, but he didn't get the chance.

We entered Berestechko on the sixth of August. At the head of our division rode the Asiatic tunic and red Cossack coat of our new divchief. Lyovka, the crazed lackey, led the divchief's stud mare behind him. A battle march, full of sustained menace, flew along the flowery and impoverished streets. Decrepit blind alleys, a painted forest of rotted and trembling crossbeams had overrun the shtetl. Its core, eaten away by time, breathed its sad decay upon us. The smugglers and the pharisees had hidden themselves in their dark, spacious huts. Only Pan Ludomirski, the bell ringer in his green frock coat, met us at the church.

We had crossed the river and made our way to the settlement on the edge of town. We were approaching the priest's house when Afonka came round the corner on a tall gray stallion.

"Salutations!" he barked and, pushing the men aside, returned to his place in the ranks.

Maslak stared out into the colorless distance, and without turning around, he croaked:

"Where'd you get the horse?"

"It's my own," replied Afonka, rolled a cigarette, and closed it with a flick of the tongue.

The Cossacks rode up one after the other to greet him. Where his left eye had been, a monstrous pink swelling gaped on his charred face.

And on the following morning Bida went out on the town. In the church he smashed Saint Valentine's shrine and tried to play the organ. He wore a jacket cut from a blue rug with a lily stitched on the back, and his sweaty forelock was plastered down over the gouged-out eye.

After lunch he saddled his horse and fired his rifle at the shattered windows of the Raciborski castle. The Cossacks stood around him in a semicircle . . . They lifted the stallion's tail, felt its legs, and counted its teeth.

"A fine-looking mount," said Orlov the squadron commander's deputy.

"A proper horse," the long-whiskered Bitsenko approved.

(published 1924)

At Saint Valentine's

Our division occupied Berestechko yesterday evening. Headquarters was set up in the house of the priest Tuzinkiewicz. Tuzinkiewicz disguised himself as a woman and fled Berestechko before our troops entered town. All I know of him is that he bustled about with God for forty-five years in Berestechko and was a good priest. To make us understand this, the residents tell us that the Jews loved him. It was under Tuzinkiewicz that the ancient church was restored. The repairs were completed on the third centenary of the shrine. The bishop of Zhitomir arrived for the occasion. Prelates in silk cassocks led services in front of the church. Portly and gracious, they stood like bells in the dew-covered grass. Rivers of the faithful flowed from the neighboring villages. Peasants bent the knee and kissed the hands, and the heavens that day flared with clouds such as had never been seen before. Heavenly flags fluttered in honor of the ancient church. The bishop himself kissed Tuzinkiewicz on the brow and called him the father of Berestechko, *pater Béresteckea.*

I learned this story today in the morning at headquarters, when I was going through the report of our flank column that was scouting around Lvov, in the Radzichów district. I was reading through the papers, while the snoring of orderlies behind me bore witness to our eternal homelessness. The clerks, damp with insomnia, copied out orders for the division, ate cucumbers, and sneezed. By the time I was free it was already noon; I went over to the window and saw the cathedral of Berestechko—imposing and white. It gleamed in the cool sunlight like an enamel tower. Noontide lightning scintillated in its shining sides. Its convex lines began at the cupolas of ancient green and descended lightly to the ground. Pink veins smoldered in the white stone of the pediment, and at the very top were columns thin as candles.

I was amazed to hear the organ singing out, and that very moment an old woman with loose yellow hair appeared in the doorway of the staff quarters. She hobbled like a dog with a broken paw, reeling and stumbling to the ground. Her eyes were white with a damp film of blindness and splashed with tears. The sounds of the organ—at times ponderous, at time rushed—floated our way. Their flight was arduous, their trace resounded plaintively and long. The old woman wiped the tears away with her yellow hair, sat down on the floor, and began to kiss my boots at the knee. The organ grew still and then chortled on the bass notes. I grabbed the old woman by the hand and looked around. The clerks tapped away on their typewriters, the snoring of the orderlies grew in bounds, their sharp spurs cut into the felt beneath the velvet upholstery of the sofas. The old woman kissed my boots tenderly, embracing them as she would a baby. I took her outside and locked the door behind us. The church shimmered blindingly before us, like a stage set. The side gates were open, and horse skulls lay on the graves of Polish officers.

We ran into the yard, passed through a gloomy corridor, and ended up in a rectangular room attached to the altar. Sashka, a nurse of the 31st Regiment, had made herself at home there. She had torn the vestments and ripped out the silk from someone's garments. She was rummaging through silks that someone had thrown on the floor. The cadaverous aroma of brocade, scattered flowers, sweet decay, flooded her quivering nostrils, tickling and poisoning them. Then some Cossacks came into the room. They roared with laughter and grabbed at her breasts and stuck gilt canopy poles under her skirts. Kurdyukov the half-wit struck her across the nose with a censer, while Bitsenko tossed her onto the pile of fabric and sacred books. The Cossacks began uncovering Sashka's body, florid and strong smelling, like the meat of a freshly slaughtered cow, her overturned skirts revealed the legs of a squadron dame, shapely cast-iron legs, and Kurdyukov the half-wit mounted her and started to bounce as though in the saddle, pretending to satisfy his desires. She threw him off, smashed his head, and went for her bag. The Cossacks and I barely chased her away from the silks. Aiming her revolver at us, she backed away swaying, growling like an angry hound, and it was only then that we passed the altar and penetrated the church.

It was full of light, this church, full of dancing sunbeams, airy columns, a kind of breezy good cheer. How can I forget the picture hanging on the right side of the sanctuary, painted by Apolek? In that picture twelve rosy paters rocked the chubby infant Jesus in a ribbon-braided cradle. His toes are spread and his body is lacquered with the hot sweat of morning. The babe wriggles on his plump, dimpled back, the twelve apostles in cardinals' tiaras bent over the crib. Their faces are so closely shaven they look blue, and their flaming mantles bulge out over their bellies. The apostles' eyes twinkle with wisdom, determination, merriment, a wry smile drifts across the corners of their mouths, and their double chins sprout fiery little warts, raspberry-colored warts, like radishes in May.

In this Berestechko church there was a singular and alluring point of view upon the mortal sufferings of the sons of men. Saints in this temple went to their deaths with the charm of Italian singers, and the black hair of the executioners glistened like the beard of Holofernes. Right above the altar gates I beheld the sacrilegious likeness of John, also from Apolek's heretical and intoxicating brush. In this representation, the Baptist was beautiful in that reticent and equivocal manner for the sake of which kings' concubines would lose their half-lost honor and lavish life.

Driven out of my mind by memories of my fond dreams, of Apolek, I either did not notice the traces of destruction in the church or else they did not seem considerable to me. Only the shrine of Saint Valentine had been broken. Bits of moldy wadding were strewn beneath it, as well as the ridiculous bones of the saint, which looked more like chicken bones than anything else. And Afonka Bida was still playing the organ. He was drunk and wild and all cut up. It was only yesterday that he had returned with the horse seized from the peasants. He was stubbornly trying to pick his way through a march, and somebody was attempting to persuade him in a sleepy voice, "Drop it, Afonya. Let's get fed." But the Cossack wouldn't drop it, and Afonka's songs were many. Each sound was a song, and all the sounds were torn one from the other. The dense strains of a song would last a second, then give way to another. I listened and looked around—the traces of destruction did not seem considerable to me. Not so, thought Pan Ludomirski, bell ringer of Saint Valentine's church and husband of the blind old woman.

Ludomirski crawled out from someplace or other. He entered the church with even steps and bowed head. The old man did not dare throw a covering over the scattered relics, for a man of humble station may not handle sacred things. The bell ringer fell upon the pale-blue flagstones and raised his head, his blue nose rising above him like a flag above a corpse. His blue nose quivered above him, and at that instant the velvet curtain by the altar swayed and, quivering, slipped to the side. Deep in the niche, against a cloud-furrowed sky, ran a bearded figure in an orange robe—barefoot, with a torn and bloody mouth. A hoarse cry then pierced our ears. We retreated in disbelief before the face of horror—horror overtook and pinched our hearts with dead fingers. The man in the orange robe was being pursued and overtaken by hatred. His hand was bent to ward off the impending blow, and blood flowed carmine from that hand. A little Cossack lad standing next to me screamed, ducked, and fled, though there was nothing to run from, since the figure in the niche was only Jesus Christ—the most extraordinary image of God I had ever seen in my life.

Pan Ludomirski's Savior was a curly-headed little Yid with a ragged beard and a low, wrinkled forehead. His sunken cheeks were crimson-hued, thin red brows arched over his eyes closed in agony.

His mouth was torn like a horse's lip. His Polish robe was girt with a costly belt, and beneath the caftan writhed porcelain feet, painted, bare, and pierced with silver nails.

Pan Ludomirski stood in his green frock coat beneath the statue. He raised a withered hand and cursed us. The Cossacks gaped and hung their yellow tufts. In a thundering voice the bell ringer of Saint Valentine's anathematized us in the purest Latin. Then he turned his back upon us, fell on his knees, and clasped the Savior's legs.

Returning to headquarters, I wrote a report to the chief of the division concerning the outrage done to the religious feelings of the local population. The church was ordered closed, and the offenders subject to disciplinary action were to be brought before a military tribunal.

Berestechko, August 1920 (published 1924)

Squadron Commander Trunov

A t noon we brought to Sokal the bullet-riddled body of Trunov, commander of our squadron. He had been killed this morning in action against enemy aircraft. All the bullets had hit Trunov in the face, his cheeks were covered with wounds, his tongue torn away. We washed the dead man's face as best we could so that he wouldn't look so awful, we placed a Caucasian saddle at the head of the coffin, and dug him a grave in a place of honor—in the public gardens next to the cathedral in the center of town, right by the gates. Our mounted squadron, the regimental staff, and the divisional commissar showed up. And at two by the cathedral clock our rickety little cannon fired the first shot. It saluted the dead commander with all three of its ancient inches, a full salute, and then we carried the coffin to the open grave. The coffin lid was open, and the high noonday sun lit up the long corpse and its mouth stuffed with broken teeth, and the polished boots placed heel to heel as if standing for inspection.

"Men!" said Pugachov the regimental commander, looking at the corpse as he stood at the edge of the grave. "Men!" he said, trembling and straightening himself up with his arms stiff at his trouser seams, "we come to bury a world-class hero, Pasha Trunov, to give Pasha his final due."

And lifting his insomnia-scorched eyes to the sky, Pugachov shouted his way through a speech about the dead soldiers of the First Cavalry and about the proud phalanx beating the hammer of history upon the anvil of centuries to come. Pugachov shouted his speech at full volume, his grip tight on the hilt of his curved Chechen saber, digging his ragged boots with their silver spurs into the ground. After his speech the band played "The Internationale" and the Cossacks bade farewell to Pashka Trunov. The whole squadron leapt into the saddle and fired a volley in the air, our three incher sputtered forth a second time, and we sent three Cossacks to fetch a wreath. They dashed off, firing at full gallop, dropping out of their saddles, trick riding, and returned with fists full of red flowers. Pugachov scattered them on the coffin and we began to approach Trunov for the final kiss. My lips touched the gleaming forehead that lay below the saddle, and I left and went into the town, into Gothic Sokal in the blue dust and invincible Galician gloom.

A large square stretched to the left of the gardens—a square framed by ancient synagogues. Jews in ragged gabardines were arguing on that square, pulling and jostling one another in their incomprehensible blindness. The Orthodox party were extolling the teachings of Hadas the rabbi of Belz; for this they were attacked by Hasidim of moderate doctrine, disciples of the Husiatyn rabbi Judah. The Jews were arguing over the Kabbalah, making mention in their disputation of the name of Elijah the Gaon of Vilna and scourge of the Hasidim.

"Elijah!" they cried in contortions, their overgrown mouths agape.

Forgetting the war and the shooting, the Hasidim went so far as to defame the very name of Elijah, high priest of Vilna. And I, wallowing in sorrow over Trunov, I, too, went pushing and hollering among them to make myself feel better, until I saw before me a Galician, long and cadaverous like Don Quixote.

This Galician was dressed in a white linen shirt that came down to his toes. He was dressed as if for burial or communion, and he was pulling a disheveled little cow on a rope. Atop his gigantic torso there sat a tiny, nimble, shaved serpentine head; it swayed beneath a wide-brimmed hat of country straw. The pathetic little cow walked behind the Galician on its halter; he led it with an air of importance, the scaffold of his lengthy bones cleaving the brilliance of the blazing sky.

Solemnly he crossed the square and went down a winding lane all smoky with thick and nauseating vapors. In charred little houses, squalid kitchens, toiled Jewish women who looked like old Negroes, Jewesses with extravagant bosoms. The Galician went past them and stopped at the end of the lane by the facade of a battered building.

There, by the warped white pillars, a Gypsy blacksmith sat shoeing horses. The Gypsy was beating on the hooves with his hammer, shaking his greasy hair, whistling and smiling. Several Cossacks stood around him with their horses. My Galician went over to the blacksmith, silently handed him a dozen baked potatoes, and, paying no attention to anyone, turned around and left. I started to follow him, for I couldn't understand what sort of a person this was and what kind of life he led here in Sokal, but just at that moment I was stopped by a Cossack who was preparing his horse to get shod. The Cossack's last name was Seliverstov. He had left Makhno at some point and was in the 33rd Cav. Regiment.

"Lyutov," he said, shaking my hand, "you go after everybody; there's a devil in you, Lyutov—why'd you go and mess up Trunov this morning?"

And in dumb borrowed words Seliverstov started shouting some total nonsense about me beating up on my squadron commander, Trunov, that morning. Seliverstov rebuked me every which way, rebuked me in front of all the Cossacks, but his story didn't have a grain of truth in it. True, I had quarreled with Trunov that morning because Trunov was always getting endlessly tangled up with the prisoners—we quarreled, it's true, but Pashka is dead and there is no one to judge him on this earth, and I would be the last person to judge him. This is how we came to argue:

We had picked up today's prisoners at dawn, at Zawada station. There were ten of them. They were in their underclothes when we took them. A pile of clothes lay next to the Poles, a trick of theirs to make it impossible for us to distinguish the officers from the enlisted men by their uniforms. They had thrown off their clothes themselves, but this time Trunov made up his mind to get at the truth.

"Officers, step forward!" he commanded, approaching the prisoners, and took out his revolver.

Trunov had already been wounded in the head that morning—his head was bound with a rag, blood dripping down from it like rain off a rick.

"Officers, give it up!" he repeated, and began to push the Poles about with the butt of his revolver.

Then out of the pack stepped a skinny old man with big protruding bones on his back, yellow cheekbones, and a drooping mustache.

"Done, this war," said the old man with inexplicable delight in his mutilated Russian. "All officer run away. This war done . . ."

And the Pole stretched out his blue hands to the squadron commander.

"Five fingers," he said, sobbing and twisting his huge withered hand, "with this five fingers I raised my family . . ."

The old man gasped, swayed, poured forth tears of delight, and fell on his knees before Trunov, but Trunov pushed him aside with his sword.

"Your officers are scum," said the squadron commander. "Your officers threw off their clothes right here. If it fits—then curtains for you, so let's try it on."

And then the squadron commander picked out of the rag heap a cap with piping and placed it atop the old man.

"Just right," mumbled Trunov, moving closer and whispering, "just right," and stuck a sword into the prisoner's gullet. The old man fell, his legs started jerking, a foamy coral stream poured from his throat. Then Andryushka Vosmiletov, with his shiny earring and plump country neck, crept up to him. He undid the Pole's buttons, shook him a little, and started pulling the trousers off the dying man. He threw them over his saddle, grabbed another two uniforms from the heap, then rode away from us and started playing with his whip. The sun came out of the clouds at that moment. It swept and surrounded Andryushka's horse, its lively gait, and the carefree swing of its docked tail. Andryushka rode along the path to the woods where our wagons were—the drivers raved and whistled and made signs at Vosmiletov as though he were a deaf-mute.

The Cossack was already halfway there, but then Trunov suddenly fell to his knees and called after him in a raspy voice:

"Andrei," he cried, staring at the ground. "Andrei!" he repeated, not lifting his eyes from the ground, "our Soviet Republic is still alive, it's too soon to start carving it up, so drop the rags, Andrei."

But Vosmiletov didn't turn around. He rode on at his astonishing Cossack trot, and his little horse tossed its tail jauntily, as if waving us away.

"Treason!" muttered Trunov in astonishment. "Treason!" he said, quickly threw his rifle to his shoulder, and fired, missing in his haste. But this time Andrei stopped. He turned his horse around to face us, bouncing in the saddle like a woman, jerking his legs, his face red and angry.

"Listen here, countryman," he shouted, riding up to us and calming down at the sound of his own deep, powerful voice. "I should knock you and your mother upside the head, countryman . . . You pick up ten Poles and get hysterical, we picked up a hundred each and never sent for you. If you're really a worker, then mind your own work . . ."

And throwing the trousers and the two uniforms off the saddle, Andryushka grunted and turned away from the squadron commander to help me make out a list of the remaining prisoners. He busied himself beside me, his chuffing remarkably loud, and all that fuss of his was a burden to me. The prisoners wailed and fled from Andryushka, but he chased them and grabbed them up in his arms like a hunter grabs armfuls of reeds to get a good view of a flock flying riverward at dawn.

Dealing with the prisoners, I exhausted all the swearwords I knew and somehow managed to take down the names of eight men with their unit numbers and weapon types, and then I moved on to the ninth. This ninth was a young lad who looked like a German athlete from a good circus, a lad with a proud German chest and sideburns, wearing a serge waistcoat and Jaeger long-johns. He turned the two nipples on his high chest toward me, threw back his sweaty blond hair, and told me his unit. Then Andryushka grabbed him by the long-johns and asked sternly:

"Where'd you get the undies?"

"Mama knitted them," the prisoner replied and swayed.

"Your mama's got a factory," said Andryushka, still staring, and touched the Pole's well-kept nails with his pincushion fingertips. "Your mama's got a factory—nobody sewed nothing like this for our guys . . ."

He felt the Jaeger long-johns again and led the ninth prisoner by the arm over to the others whose names had already been taken. At that moment

I saw Trunov creeping from behind a knoll. Blood was dripping from the squadron commander's head like rain off a rick, his dirty bandage had come loose and was dangling down, he crept along on his belly holding a carbine in his hands. It was a Japanese carbine, lacquered and high velocity. From a distance of twenty paces Trunov blew the lad's skull to bits, showering my hands with the Pole's brains. Then Trunov expelled the spent cartridges and came over to me.

"Scratch one off," he said, pointing to the list.

"I'm not scratching anything off," I replied, shaking. "It's as though Trotsky's orders weren't written for you, Pavel."

"Scratch one off!" Trunov repeated and thrust a black finger at the sheet of paper.

"I'm not scratching anything off!" I shouted with all my might. "There were ten, now there's eight—they won't see who you are anymore at headquarters, Pashka."

"They'll see through this miserable life of ours," Trunov answered and began to move toward me through the smoke, all torn up and hoarse, but then he stopped, raised his gory head to the skies, and said with bitter reproach, "Buzz, buzz," he said, "and there's another come buzzing along."

And the squadron commander pointed out to us four specks in the sky, four bombers floating behind the shining swanlike clouds. They were planes belonging to Major Faunt-Le-Roy's combat squadron, great armored planes.

"Mount up!" the platoon leaders shouted, catching sight of them, and they led the squadrons off at a trot toward the woods, but Trunov did not ride off with his squadron. He stayed by the station building, pressed up against the wall and was silent. Andryushka Vosmiletov and two machine gunners, two barefoot fellows in raspberry breeches, stood beside him apprehensively.

"Thread your gun barrels neat, boys," Trunov said to them, and the blood began to drain from his face. "Here's a report to Pugachov from me."

And with his enormous peasant letters Trunov wrote on a piece of paper torn askew:

"Having to die on this date," he wrote, "I consider it my duty to fire a couple shots for the possible bringing down of the enemy, and at the same time pass on the command to Simon Golov, platoon leader . . ."

He sealed the letter, sat down on the ground, and strained to take off his boots.

"Use them," he said, handing over the report and the boots to the machine gunners, "use them, these are new boots."

"Take care, Commander," the machine gunners mumbled in reply, shifting from one foot to the other and hesitating to leave.

"And you take care of yourselves," said Trunov, "one way or another, kids . . . ," and went over to the machine gun that stood on a little mound beside the station sentry box. Andryushka Vosmiletov, the ragman, was waiting for him there.

"One way or another," Trunov said to him and began to level the machine gun. "Going to stick around with me, then, Andrei?"

"Motherloving Christ!" Andryushka replied fearfully, sobbed, went white, and burst out laughing. "Motherloving Christ and the whole goddamn motherloving processional!"

And he started to level the second machine gun at the airplanes.

But the planes kept flying more and more steeply over the station, fussily crackling on high, descending, tracing arcs, while the sun cast pink rays upon the yellow glint of their wings.

Meanwhile we—the Fourth Squadron—were sitting in the woods. There in the woods we awaited the end of the unequal combat between Pashka Trunov and the American, Major Reginald Faunt-Le-Roy. The major and his three bombers demonstrated their skill in this battle. They dropped to a height of three hundred meters and with their machine guns shot up Andryushka, then Trunov. None of our shots did the Americans any harm; the airplanes veered off without spotting the squadron hidden in the woods. So, after waiting half an hour, we were able to ride out and get the bodies. Andryushka Vosmiletov's body was taken by two relatives of his who served in our squadron, and Trunov, our late commander, was taken to Gothic Sokal and buried there in a place of honor—in one of the flower beds in the public gardens, in the center of the town.

(published 1925)

The Ivans

Deacon Ageyev had twice deserted from the front. For this he was turned over to the Moscow "branded" regiment. The commander in chief, Sergey Sergeyevich Kamenev, reviewed this regiment at Mozhaisk before it was sent into position.

"I don't need them," said the commander in chief, "send them back to Moscow to scrub latrines."

Somehow or other they knocked together a foot company out of these "branded" men. Among them was the deacon. He arrived at the Polish front and claimed to be deaf. Barsutsky, the medic from the first-aid unit, spent a week on him and couldn't dent the deacon's stubbornness.

"The hell with him, deaf and dumb," Barsutsky said to the nurse-orderly Soychenko. "Find a cart in the convoy, we'll send the deacon to Rovno for tests . . ."

Soychenko went and got three carts from the convoy: the driver of the first cart was Akinfiev.

"Ivan," Soychenko said to him, "you're going to take deaf and dumb here to Rovno."

"I'll take him," replied Akinfiev.

"And you'll bring me back a receipt . . ."

"Got it," said Akinfiev. "And what's the reason for his deafness?"

"Sad if I die, fine if it's the other guy," said Soychenko the nurse-orderly. "There's your reason. He's a freeloader, not deaf and dumb."

"I'll take him," Akinfiev said again, and followed after the other carts.

There were three carts gathered in front of the first-aid post. In the first one they put a nurse who was being sent to the rear, the second was for a Cossack suffering from inflammation of the kidneys, and Ivan Ageyev the deacon sat down in the third.

Having seen to everything, Soychenko called over to the medic.

"Our freeloader is all set," he said. "I put him in the Revolutionary Tribunal cart, receipt pending. They're heading out now . . ."

Barsutsky peered out the window, saw the carts, and dashed out of the house red and hatless.

"But you're liable to cut his throat!" he shouted to Akinfiev. "Put the deacon some other place."

"What other place?" the Cossacks standing around replied and burst out laughing. "Our Vanya will get him wherever . . ."

Akinfiev was standing by his horses, whip in hand. He took off his cap and said politely:

"Hello, Comrade Medic."

"Hello, friend," replied Barsutsky. "You know you're an animal—we got to put the deacon someplace else."

"I'd be interested to know," said the Cossack shrilly as his upper lip twitched, crawled, and quivered over his blinding white teeth, "I'd be interested to know whether or not it suits us, when the enemy oppresses us so unspeakably, when the enemy's knocking the very wind out of us, when he's hanging at our legs like lead and coiling like snakes around our arms, does it suit us to plug up our ears in such an hour of mortal peril?"

"Watch out, people, Vanya's standing up for the commissars!" shouted Korotkov, the driver of the first cart. "Watch out now!"

"Standing up?" muttered Barsutsky, turning away. "All of us are standing up. It's just that things have to be done according to regulation."

"But he can hear, this deaf comrade of ours!" Akinfiev cut in, rolled the whip in his fat fingers, laughed and winked at the deacon. The deacon was sitting in the cart, his great shoulders sagging, his head moving about.

"Well, God help you then," shouted the medic in despair. "But I hold you responsible for everything, Ivan."

"Agreed, I'll be responsible," Akinfiev said thoughtfully and bowed his head. "Sit comfortable," he said to the deacon without turning around, "even more comfortable," the Cossack repeated and gathered the reins in his hands.

The carts lined up and took off down the road, one after another. Korotkov rode in front, Akinfiev came third, whistling a tune and shaking reins. They covered fifteen versts like that, and toward evening they were thrown off course by a sudden flood of enemy activity.

On that day, July 22, the Poles mangled our rear with a swift maneuver, swept down on the shtetl of Kozin, and took many of the Eleventh Division prisoner. The squadrons of the Sixth Division were thrown into the Kozin area to counterattack. The lightning speed of their maneuvers cut off the convoys, the Revtribunal carts wandered two days and nights along the seething fringe of the battle, and it was only on the third night that they managed to strike out onto the road along which the rear staffs were evacuating. It was on that road that I, too, encountered them at midnight.

Numb with despair, I encountered them after a battle near Khotin. My horse had been killed in that battle near Khotin—Lavrik, my only solace on this earth. When I lost him, I got on an ambulance cart and picked up wounded till evening. Then all the uninjured men were thrown off the cart, and I was left all by myself beside a crumbling hovel. Night flew toward me on mettlesome horses. The deafening howl of the convoy filled the universe. The earth was lashed with shrieks, as the roads faded away. Stars crept forth from the cool belly of night, and deserted villages blazed on the horizon. Saddle on my shoulder, I went between churned-up fields and stopped where the path turned to attend to the call of nature. I relieved myself and was buttoning up my pants when I felt splashes on my hand. I lit my flashlight, looked around, and on the ground saw the corpse of a Pole drenched in my urine. It was pouring out of his mouth, splashing between his teeth, pooling in his empty eye sockets. A notebook and fragments of Piłsudski's proclamations lay strewn about the corpse. Recorded in the Pole's notebook were personal expenses, a schedule for the Cracow dramatic theater, and the birthday of a woman named Maria-Louisa. Using the proclamations of Commander in Chief Marshal Piłsudski, I wiped the stinking fluid off the skull of my unknown brother and went on, bent beneath the weight of the saddle.

Just then there was a groaning of wheels somewhere near me.

"Halt!" I shouted. "Who goes there?"

Night flew toward me on mettlesome horses, flames coiled high over the horizon.

"We're with the Revtribunal," came a voice smothered in darkness.

I ran forward and right into a wagon.

"They killed my horse," I said in an unusually loud voice, "Lavrik was his name."

Nobody replied. I climbed onto the cart, put my saddle under my head, fell asleep, and slept till dawn, warmed by the musty hay and the body of Ivan Akinfiev, who happened to be next to me. In the morning the Cossack woke up later than I did.

"It's getting on toward day, thank God," he said. He took a revolver out from under his little trunk and fired above the deacon's ear. The latter was sitting right in front of him, driving the horses. Above his enormous balding skull a gray hair fluttered. Akinfiev fired again above the other ear and put the revolver away in its holster.

"Good morning, Vanya!" he said to the deacon, grunting as he pulled on his boots. "How about a bite to eat?"

"Hey!" I cried. "What do you think you're doing?"

"Whatever I do is not enough," replied Akinfiev, getting out the food. "He's been faking on me three days now . . ."

Then Korotkov, whom I had known in the 31st Regiment, called over from the first cart and told the whole story of the deacon from the beginning. Akinfiev listened attentively, cupping his ear, then reached under a saddle and took out a roast ox leg. It was covered in sackcloth and straw.

The deacon climbed over to us from the driver's seat, cut up the green meat with a small knife, and handed everyone a piece. When breakfast was over, Akinfiev tied the ox leg up in a bag and tucked it away in the hay.

"Ivan," he said to Ageyev, "let's go and drive out the devil. Got to make a stop anyhow, water the horses . . ."

He took an ampoule of medicine and a Tarnovsky syringe from his pocket and handed them to the deacon. They got down from the cart and went off about twenty paces into a field.

"Nurse," cried Korotkov from the first cart, "reset your eyes for long range or you'll be blinded by Akinfiev's assets."

"Stick it up your assets, like I give a—," the woman muttered and turned away.

Akinfiev then rolled up his shirt. The deacon knelt before him and applied the syringe. Then he wiped the syringe with a rag and held it up to the light. Akinfiev pulled up his pants; seizing his moment, he went behind the deacon's back and once more fired a shot just above Ageyev's ear.

"Warmest regards, Vanya," he said, buttoning his pants.

The deacon put the ampoule down on the grass and rose from his knees. His wisp of hair flew up.

"I shall be judged by the highest judge," he said dully. "No one set you above me, Ivan . . ."

"Nowaday everbody judge everbody else," interrupted the driver of the second cart, who looked like a sprightly hunchback. "And judge to death, real simple."

"Or better still," Ageyev pronounced and straightened up, "kill me, Ivan . . ."

"Stop fooling, deacon," said Korotkov, a man I knew from before, as he went up to him. "Understand the sort of person you're riding with. Any other man would have trussed you like a duck without so much as a quack, but he's just fishing and learning the truth out of you, I'd defrock you myself . . ."

"Or better still," the deacon repeated obstinately and stepped forward, "kill me, Ivan."

"You'll kill yourself, you miserable wretch," replied Akinfiev, lisping and turning pale, "you'll dig your own hole and bury yourself in it . . ."

The Ivans

He waved his arms about, tore at his own collar, and fell to the ground in a fit.

"Eh, my own flesh and blood!" he cried wildly, and began pouring sand on his face, "eh, my own bitter flesh and blood, sweet Soviet power . . ."

"Ivan," Korotkov went over and gently put his hand on his shoulder, "take it easy, old friend, don't be sad. We should go, Ivan . . ."

Korotkov took a mouthful of water and sprayed it over Akinfiev, then carried him to the cart. The deacon sat down once again in the driver's seat, and we drove off.

It was no more than another two versts to the shtetl of Verby. Countless convoys had gathered there that morning. The Eleventh Division, the Fourteenth, and the Fourth were there. Jews in waistcoats with hunched shoulders stood in their doorways like plucked birds. Cossacks were going from yard to yard, collecting towels and eating unripe plums. As soon as we arrived, Akinfiev climbed into the hay and fell asleep, while I took a blanket from his cart and went to look for a place in the shade. But the fields on either side of the road were sown with excrement. A bearded fellow in copper-rimmed glasses and a Tyrolean hat who was reading a newspaper in a corner caught my glance and said:

"We call ourselves human beings but make filth worse than jackals. The earth is ashamed of us . . ."

And turning away he went on reading the paper through his enormous glasses.

I made for the patch of woods on the left and saw the deacon coming right up to me.

"Where are you off to, countryman?" Korotkov called out after him from the first cart.

"To relieve myself," muttered the deacon and caught at my hand and kissed it. "You're a kind gentleman," he whispered, grimacing, trembling, and gasping for breath. "When you have a minute, I beg you, please write to the town of Kasimov, let my wife have a cry over me . . ."

"Are you deaf, Father Deacon," I shouted at him point-blank, "or not?"

"Beg your pardon?" he said and bent his ear toward me. "Beg your pardon?"

"Are you deaf, Ageyev, or not?"

"Deaf, indeed," he said quickly. "The day before yesterday I had perfect hearing, but Comrade Akinfiev has injured my ears with his firing. They were supposed to deliver me to Rovno, Comrade Akinfiev was, but I don't reckon they will."

And falling to his knees the deacon crawled headfirst between the wagons, all tangled in his rumpled priest's hair. Then he rose from his knees, wriggled up through the reins, and went over to Korotkov. Korotkov poured him out some tobacco, and they rolled cigarettes and gave each other a light.

"Safer this way," said Korotkov, and cleared a space beside him.

The deacon sat down next to him, and they were silent.

Then Akinfiev woke up. He dumped the ox leg out of the sack, cut the green meat with a little knife, and gave everyone a piece. At the sight of this putrid leg I was overcome with weakness and despair and gave back my meat.

"Farewell, boys," I said, "good luck to you . . ."

"Farewell," said Korotkov.

I took the saddle from the cart and left, and as I left I could hear Ivan Akinfiev's never-ending muttering.

"Ivan," he was saying to the deacon, "you really messed up this time, Ivan. You ought to tremble at the sound of my name, but you went and got onto my cart. Maybe you could skip and jump before you met me, but now I'm going to desecrate you, I swear, Ivan, I am going to desecrate you . . ."

(published 1924)

The Story of a Horse, Continued

Four months ago Savitsky, our former divchief, took a white stallion away from Khlebnikov, commander of the First Squadron. Khlebnikov then left the army, and today Savitsky got a letter from him.

Khlebnikov to Savitsky:

". . . And I can't have any ill will toward Budenny's army anymore, I understand my sufferings inside that army and keep them in my heart more pure than a shrine. And to you, Comrade Savitsky, as a world-class hero, the laboring masses of the Vitebsk region, where I am now president of the Local Revolutionary Committee, send their proletarian cry: 'On with the World Revolution!' and hope that the white stallion may carry you long years along soft paths for the good of the freedom that we all love and the fraternal Republics, in which we ought to keep a specific eye on the local authorities and on district units in the administrative sense."

Savitsky to Khlebnikov:

"Faithful Comrade Khlebnikov! The letter that you wrote to me was very praiseworthy for the common cause, all the more so after your foolishness when you covered your eyes with your own hide and left our Communist Party of the Bolsheviks. Our Communist Party, Comrade Khlebnikov, is an iron band of fighting men that give their blood in the first rank, and when blood flows from iron, it's no joke, comrade, but a matter of victory or death. The same goes regarding the common cause, whose dawn I shall not live to see, as the fighting is heavy and I have to change commanders every two weeks. I've been fighting thirty days in the rearguard, covering the invincible First Cavalry Army, and I am at present under fire from enemy aircraft and artillery. They killed Tardy, killed Lukhmannikov, killed Lykoshenko, killed Gulevoy, killed Trunov, and there is no white stallion between my legs, so given our change of fortunes in the war don't expect to see your beloved Divchief Savitsky, Comrade Khlebnikov, but we shall meet again, to put it bluntly, in the Kingdom of Heaven, though they say that the old man in Heaven hasn't got a kingdom, but a regular whorehouse, and there's enough of the clap on earth already, so then again maybe we won't see each other. So farewell, Comrade Khlebnikov."

Galicia, September 1920 (published 1924)

The Widow

Shevelyov, the regimental commander, lies dying on an ambulance cart. A woman sits at his feet. Night, pierced by flashes of bombardment, arches out over the dying man. Lyovka, the divchief's driver, is warming food in a pot. Lyovka's forelock dangles over the fire, the fettered horses rustle in the bushes. Lyovka stirs the food with a twig and says to Shevelyov, stretched out on the ambulance cart:

"I worked in the town of Temryuk, my dear comrade, doing trick riding, and was a lightweight fighter, too. The little town was boring for the women there, of course—the little ladies would take one look at me and storm the walls: 'Lev Gavrilych, you won't say no to a snack à la carte. You won't regret any time lost for good . . .' Well, I go with one of them to the tavern. We order two portions of veal, get half a bottle, just sitting together real quiet, having a drink . . . Then I look and here comes some gentleman or other, dressed pretty nice and neat, only I notice that this individual's got ideas and looked like he had already knocked back a few.

" 'Excuse me,' he says, 'what's your nationality, anyway?'

" 'For what reason are you concerned with my nationality, mister?' I ask, 'especially when I'm in the company of a lady?'

"But he says:

" 'What kind of fighter are you?' he says. 'In French wrestling they'd knock a guy like you flat. Show me where you're from . . . !'

". . . On top of that, I hadn't even touched my food yet.

" 'Why are you—whatever your name is,' I says, 'why are you making up misunderstandings such that somebody's got to perish at this present time, in other words, to breathe their last?' Breathe their last . . ." Lyovka repeats excitedly, stretching his arms to the sky and wrapping himself in a halo of night. The implacable wind, the pure wind of night, sings, fills with ringing, and lulls the soul. Stars blaze in the dark like wedding rings, falling on Lyovka, getting tangled in his hair and doused in his bushy head.

"Lev," Shevelyov suddenly whispers to him with his blue lips, "come here. Whatever gold there is—that's for Sashka," says the wounded man, "the rings, the harness, all for her. We lived as best we knew how, I owe her that much. My clothes, the long-johns, the medal for selfless heroism, give those to my mother on the Terek. Send them with a letter and in the letter write, 'The commander sent regards, and don't cry. The hut is yours, old woman, go on living. Anyone bothers you, ride straight to Budenny and say, "I'm Shevelyov's mama."' I'll give my horse, Abramka, to the regiment, I'll turn over the horse so they can lay my soul to rest proper."

"I'll see to the horse," Lyovka mutters and waves his hands. "Sash," he yells to the woman, "did you hear what he said? Tell it to his face. Will you give the old woman what's hers, or won't you? "

"Up your mother five times over," Sasha replies and walks into the bushes, her back straight, like a blind man.

"Will you hand over the orphan's share?" Lyovka catches up and grabs her by the throat. "Say it in front of him!"

"I will. Let go!"

Having forced her to promise, Lyovka took the pot off the fire and began to pour the broth into the dying man's stiffened mouth. The sour cabbage soup dribbled down Shevelyov, and the spoon clinked against his gleaming dead teeth, and the bullets sang ever louder and more desolate in the thick expanses of the night.

"Hitting us good with those rifles, the scum," said Lyovka.

"Smart little lackeys," replied Shevelyov, "their machine guns are slicing us open on the right flank . . ."

And closing his eyes, solemnly, like a dead man laid out on a table, Shevelyov listened with his large waxen ears to the sounds of battle. Lyovka chewed meat beside him, crunching and panting. When he finished the meat, Lyovka licked his lips and dragged Sashka into a hollow.

"Sash," he said, trembling, belching, and wringing his hands, "God knows, we all sin before we begin . . . Live once, die once. Give it up, Sash, I'll pay you back, in blood if you like. His day is done, Sash, but God's days keep coming."

They sat down in the tall grass. The listless moon crawled out of the clouds and lingered on Sasha's bare knee.

"Warming yourselves," Shevelyov muttered, "meanwhile, look, they routed the Fourteenth Division."

Lyovka rustled and panted in the bushes. The misty moon traipsed along the sky like a beggar woman. Distant gunfire floated through the air. The feather grass rustled on the disturbed earth, and the stars of August fell among the blades.

Then Sasha returned to where she had been sitting before. She started changing the wounded man's bandages and raised a flashlight over the putrid wound.

"You'll be gone by tomorrow," she said, wiping the cool sweat from Shevelyov's sweating body. "You'll be gone by tomorrow, it's in your guts, death . . ."

That very instant a solid polyphonous blow shook the earth. Four fresh brigades, led into battle by the enemy's unified command, had fired the first shell over Busk, tearing apart our communications and lighting up the Bug watershed. Fires rose obediently on the horizon, the heavy birds of bombardment flew up out of the flames. Busk burned, and Lyovka, the stupefied lackey, went tearing through the woods in the reeling carriage that belonged to the divchief six. He tugged at the raspberry reins and knocked into tree stumps with its lacquered wheels. Shevelyov's ambulance cart charged after him, the attentive Sashka controlling the horses that bounded from the harness.

That's how they reached the edge of the woods where the first-aid post had been set up. Lyovka unharnessed the horses and went to the commanding officer to ask for a horsecloth. He went through the woods, which were cluttered with wagons. The bodies of ambulance men stuck out beneath the wagons, the fainthearted dawn beat its wings against their army sheepskins. The sleeping men's boots were thrown apart, their pupils rolling skyward, the black holes of their mouths askew.

The commanding officer found a horsecloth; Lyovka returned to Shevelyov, kissed him on the forehead, and covered him head to foot. Then Sasha came over to the cart. She tied a kerchief beneath her chin and shook the straw from her dress.

"Pavlik," she said, "my Jesus Christ." And she lay down sideways on the dead man, covering him with her extravagant body.

"It's killing her," Lyovka then said, "got to say, they lived good. Now she'll be bouncing under the whole squadron all over again. Tough."

And he drove on, to Busk, where the staff of the 6th Cav. Division was quartered.

There, ten versts from town, there was fighting with Savinkov's Cossacks. The traitors were under the command of Cossack Captain Yakovlev, who had gone over to the Poles. They fought like men. The divchief had been with the troops for a second day straight, and Lyovka, unable to find him at headquarters, went to his own hut, cleaned the horses, washed the carriage wheels, and lay down to sleep in a threshing shed. The barn was full of fresh hay, as incendiary as perfume. Lyovka slept his fill and then sat down to dinner. The lady of the house had cooked him some potatoes with sour milk. Lyovka was already sitting down to eat when the street resounded with the funereal wail of trumpets and the thunder of many hooves. The squadron proceeded with buglers and standards down the winding Galician street. Shevelyov's body, laid out on a gun carriage, was covered with banners. Sasha rode behind the coffin on Shevelyov's stallion; a Cossack song seeped from the ranks at the rear.

The squadron passed along the main street and turned off to the river. Then Lyovka, barefoot and capless, dashed after the retreating detachment and caught the squadron commander's horse by the reins.

Neither the divchief, who had stopped at the crossroads to salute the dead commander, nor his staff heard what Lyovka said to the squadron commander.

"Long-johns," the wind carried fragments of his words to us, "mother on the Terek," we heard Lyovka's disconnected cries. Without hearing him out to the end, the squadron commander jerked his reins free and pointed to Sashka. The woman shook her head and rode on. Then Lyovka jumped up onto her saddle, grabbed her by the hair, bent her head back, and smashed her in the face with his fist. Sasha wiped off the blood with the hem of her skirt and rode on. Lyovka dropped down from the saddle, threw back his forelock, and tied a red scarf around his hips. And the howling buglers led the squadron on to the gleaming streak of the Bug.

Soon after, he came back to us, Lyovka, the divchief's lackey, his eyes glowing, and shouted:

"I told her off proper. 'I'll send them to his mother,' she says, 'when the time comes. I'll keep his memory,' she says, 'remember it myself . . .' Well, remember then, and don't you forget, you piece of scum . . . Forget and we'll remind you another time. Forget a second time—we'll remind you a second time . . ."

Galicia, August 1920 (published 1923)

Zamoste

The divchief and his staff lay on a mown field three versts from Zamoste. The troops were to attack the town that night. Our orders were to spend the night in Zamoste, and the divchief awaited reports of victory.

It was raining. Over the flooded earth flew wind and darkness. All the stars were doused in ink-swollen clouds. The worn-out horses sighed and fidgeted in the dark. We had nothing to give them. I tied my horse's bridle to my foot, wrapped myself in my cloak, and lay down in a pit full of water. The sodden ground soothed and embraced me like a grave. The horse pulled at the bridle and dragged me by the foot. She discovered a tuft of grass and began to graze. Then I fell asleep and dreamed of a threshing barn blanketed with hay. Over the barn hummed the dusty gold of threshing. Sheaves of wheat flew across the sky, a July day was drawing toward evening, and goblets of sunset were tipped over the village.

I was stretched on a bed of silence, and the caress of hay on my nape was driving me mad. The barn doors opened with a screech. A woman dressed for a ball came near me. She freed her breast from the black lace of her bodice and brought it to me, carefully, like a wet nurse brings sustenance. She laid her breast against mine. An aching warmth shook the pillars of my soul, and drops of sweat, live, stirring sweat, seethed between our nipples.

"Margot," I wanted to shout, "the earth drags me on its string of sorrows like a stubborn dog, but nevertheless, I have seen you, Margot."

I wanted to shout this, but my jaws, suddenly frozen shut, would not open.

Then the woman pulled away from me and fell to her knees.

"Jesus," she said, "accept the soul of thy departed servant . . ."

She placed two worn five-coins on my eyelids and stuffed the orifice of my mouth with fragrant hay. A moan struggled vainly inside my clamped jaws, my fading pupils turned slowly beneath the copper coins, I could not open up my hands and . . . I awoke.

A muzhik with a matted beard lay before me. He had a rifle in his hands. The horse's back split the sky like a black crossbar. The tight noose of the bridle had caught my leg, which jutted straight up.

"Fell asleep, countryman," said the muzhik, his sleepless nocturnal eyes smiling. "Your horse pulled you half a verst."

I disentangled my leg from the strap and got up. My face had been shredded by weeds and was dripping blood.

There, only two paces away, was our front line. I could see the chimneys of Zamoste, the furtive lights in the folds of its ghetto and the watchtower with its broken lantern. Damp sunrise flowed over us like waves of chloroform. Green rockets soared above the Polish camp. They shuddered in the air, scattered like roses beneath the moon, and went out.

And through the silence I could hear the distant trace of groaning. The smoke of secret murder wandered among us.

"They're killing somebody," I said. "Who are they killing?"

"The Pole is worked up," the muzhik answered. "The Pole is slaughtering the Yids."

The muzhik moved his gun from his right hand to his left. His beard flopped over to the side, he looked at me with love and said:

"These nights on the line are long, no end to these nights. And a person starts wanting to talk to another person, but where do you find this other person, I'd like to know? . . ."

The muzhik made me light a cigarette from his.

"The Yid stands guilty before everybody, before ours and yours alike. After the war, only the smallest number of them will be left. How many Yids are there in the world anyway?"

"Ten million," I answered, putting the bridle on my horse.

"There'll be only two hundred thousand left," the muzhik cried out and touched my hand, afraid I would go. But I got into the saddle and galloped off to the place where headquarters was located.

The divchief was already preparing to leave. The orderlies stood at attention before him, sleeping as they stood. Dismounted squadrons crept over the wet slopes.

"They're putting the screws on," the divchief whispered and rode off.

We followed him along the road to Sitanets.

It started raining again. Dead mice floated on the roads. Autumn set its ambushes about our hearts, and trees like naked corpses set upright on their feet swayed at the crossroads.

We got to Sitanets in the morning. I was with Volkov, the staff quartermaster. He found us a free cottage at the edge of the village.

"Wine," I said to the lady of the house. "Wine, meat, and bread!"

The old woman sat on the floor, hand-feeding a calf hidden beneath the bed.

"*Nitz niema,*" she answered indifferently, "and I can't reckon a time I had a thing . . ."

I sat down at the table, took off my revolver, and fell asleep. A quarter of an hour later I opened my eyes and saw Volkov leaning over the windowsill. He was writing a letter to his fiancée.

"Most Esteemed Valya," he wrote, "might you remember me?"

I read the first line, then took matches out of my pocket and set fire to a pile of straw on the floor. The liberated flame flared and darted toward me. The old woman lay down with her chest on the fire and put it out.

"What are you doing, Pan?" she cried and stepped back in horror.

Volkov turned around, fixed his empty eyes upon her, and then returned to his letter.

"I'll burn you down, old lady," I muttered drowsily. "Burn you and your stolen calf."

"*Chekai!*" she cried in a high-pitched voice. She ran into the hall and returned with a jug of milk and some bread.

We had barely eaten half of it when shots began to crack in the yard. There were a great many of them. They kept on cracking for a long time and we got sick of them. We finished the milk, and Volkov went out into the yard to find out what was going on.

"I've saddled your horse," he said to me through the window. "Mine's been shot through, so there's no point. The Poles are posting machine guns at a hundred paces."

And so there was only one horse for two of us. She could barely get out of Sitanets. I sat in the saddle, and Volkov behind me.

The convoys rolled, roared, and sank in the mud. Morning oozed over us like chloroform oozes over a hospital table.

"Are you married, Lyutov?" Volkov suddenly asked behind me.

"My wife left me," I answered, dozed off for a few moments, and dreamed I was sleeping in a bed.

Silence.

Our horse staggers.

"Two more versts and that mare is done," says Volkov behind me.

Silence.

"We've lost the campaign," Volkov mutters and snores.

"Yes," I say.

Sokal, September 1920 (published 1924)

Treason

Comrade Investigator Burdenko. In regard to your question, my party number is twenty-four double zero, issued to Nikita Balmashev by the party committee of Krasnodar. My life story up to 1914 I will describe as domestic, where I was engaged with my parents in grain cultivation, and from grain cultivation I transferred to the ranks of the imperialists to defend Citizen Poincaré and the hangman of the German revolution Ebert-Noske, who, I presume, slept and had dreams about how to help out my native settlement of Saint Ivan in the Kuban region. And so my rope ran on until Comrade Lenin, along with Comrade Trotsky, turned my vicious bayonet aside toward designated guts and more suitable innards. From that time on I have been carrying number twenty-four double zero on the point of my clear-eyed bayonet, and it's rather shameful and just too ridiculous for me to hear such incomprehensible bunkum about the unknown N. Hospital from you, Comrade Investigator Burdenko. I couldn't give a flying fat one about that hospital, let alone shooting and going at it, which couldn't of happened anyway. All three of us wounded men—namely, trooper Golovitsyn, trooper Kustov, and I—all of us had a fever in the bones and didn't assault anything, but only wept in the square in our hospital bathrobes amid the free inhabitants, Jews by nationality. And as regards the three damaged windowpanes, which we damaged with an officer's revolver, I will cross my heart when I tell you those panes there did not correspond to their purpose, seeing as they were in the storeroom where they were not useful. And when Doctor Jawein saw our bitter shooting, he just smirked with various smiles, standing at the little window of his hospital, as the above-mentioned free Jews of the little town of Kozin can confirm. Regarding Doctor Jawein, I will also testify to the fact that he did sneer when us three wounded men—namely, trooper Golovitsyn, trooper Kustov, and I—first went in for treatment, and said to us straight off, much too rudely, "Each of you troopers go take a bath in the washroom, and drop your weapons and your clothes right this very minute—I'm afraid of infection, they'll have to be taken to the armory." Then, seeing that he was faced with an animal and not a human being, trooper Kustov stuck out his smashed leg and made an expression about what kind of infection could there be in a sharp Kuban saber, except for the enemies of our Revolution, and also that he was interested to learn about the armory, as to whether there was a party trooper in charge there or, on the contrary, only one of the nonparty masses. And then, it seems, Doctor Jawein noticed that we could understand well enough when there was treason. He turned his back on us and, without saying another word and again with various smiles, sent us into the ward, where we went limping on our smashed-up legs and waving our crippled arms and holding on to one another since the three of us are countrymen from the settlement of Saint Ivan—namely, Comrade Golovitsyn, Comrade Kustov, and me—we are countrymen with the same fate, and the one that got a torn-up leg holds on to his comrade's arm, and the one that lost an arm leans on his comrade's shoulder. In accordance with the order given, we went into the ward, where we were expecting to see cultural education and dedication to the cause, but would you be interested to know what we saw when we got to the ward? We saw Red Army men, exclusively infantry, sitting around on made beds, playing checkers, and tall nurses, all smooth, standing by the windows and doling out sympathy. When we saw this, we stopped in our tracks, thunderstruck.

"Done fighting, boys?" I exclaim to the wounded men.

"Done fighting," the wounded men reply and push their checkers that were made out of bread.

"It's early," I say to the wounded men, "you infantry are done fighting a bit early, seeing how the enemy tiptoes fifteen versts away from town and that you can read in the *Red Cavalryman* newspaper how our international situation is plain awful and there are dark clouds on the horizon." But my words bounced off the heroic infantry like sheep dung off a regimental drum, and all that came of our talk was the sisters of mercy led us to our bunks and began grinding their organ about surrendering weapons as though we were already defeated. They got Kustov worked up over this, I can't even tell you, and he began tearing at the wound situated on his left shoulder above his bloody proletarian soldier's heart. When they saw how tense he got, the nurses simmered down, but they simmered down only for the smallest amount of time, and then they started making a mockery again, in their nonparty lumpen way, and they started getting anyone who was up for it to try and pull the clothes out from under us as we slept or make us play theater roles for cultural-educational work in women's dress, which is not right.

Unmerciful nurses. On more than one occasion they tried sleeping powders on us to get the clothes, so we had to take turns and rest with one eye open, and when we had to go to the latrine, even only to make number one, we'd go in full uniform with revolvers. And when we had suffered like this a week and a day, we started raving, having visions, and finally, when we woke up on the accursed morning of August 4, we noticed a change in us, for we lay in robes with numbers on, like convicts, without weapons or the clothes woven by our mothers, frail old women in the Kuban . . . And we saw the sun was shining grand, while the trench infantry, in whose midst suffered three Red Horsemen, was fooliganizing us, and with them came the unmerciful nurses, who had poured us sleeping powder the night before, now shaking their young breasts and bringing us cocoa on saucers, and the cocoa had milk enough to drown in! Once the carousel got going, the infantry banged their crutches something horrible and pinched our sides like we was rented ladies, saying Budenny's First Cavalry was done fighting, too. But no, oh crazy-curly comrades who stuffed their monstrous bellies so that they play at night like machine guns: we weren't done fighting but only asked to be excused to relieve ourselves—the three of us went into the yard and from the yard we rushed out in a fever, our open wounds blue, to Citizen Boydermann, the local revolutionary committee chair, without whom, Comrade Investigator Burdenko, that little misunderstanding as regards the shooting possibly might not have come to pass, i.e., but for that revcom chair, because of whom we completely lost our heads. And though we have no solid evidence on Citizen Boydermann, still, right as we came in we observed he was an older citizen in a sheepskin, a Jew by nationality, sitting behind a desk, a desk stuffed with so many papers it was not pretty to look at . . . Citizen Boydermann looks about this way and then that way, and it's obvious he can't make out these papers at all, is fed up with these papers, all the more so since unknown but worthy fighting men come and threaten Citizen Boydermann over rations, shouting over the local workers warning of counterrevolution in the surrounding villages, and then up come regular workers from town who want to get married at the revcom quick as possible and no red tape. So we, too, raised our voices and explained about the case of treason at the hospital, but Citizen Boydermann only gaped at us and again looked this way, that way, and patted us on the back, which is really no kind of authority and is unworthy of authority—he didn't issue any resolution whatsoever and merely attested, "Comrade troopers, if you have any pity for Soviet authority, then leave these premises," to which we could not agree, i.e., to leave the premises, but insisted he present an official identity card, which not being presented, we went and lost our heads. And having lost them, we went out into the square in front of the hospital and disarmed the militia, consisting of one cavalryman, and—with tears in our eyes—breached three unfortunate windowpanes in the above-mentioned storeroom. Doctor Jawein made faces and chuckled at this inadmissible fact, and all this at a time when Comrade Kustov was to die of his illness in four days!

In his short Red life Comrade Kustov worried himself to no end about the treason winking at us from the window and mocking the rough proletariat, but the proletariat, comrades, knows that it's rough, we hurt on account of it, the soul burns and rips with fire the prison of the body and the jail of our hateful ribs . . .

Treason, I tell you, Comrade Investigator Burdenko, treason is laughing at us from the window, treason walks barefoot inside our house, treason carries her boots on her back so the floorboards don't creak in the house she's robbed . . . But we will rip out the floorboard that rises against our innocent roughhousing, and we'll fill those uncreaking boots with black blood . . .

(published 1924)

Chesniki

The Sixth Division was mustered in the woods outside the village of Chesniki, awaiting the signal to attack. But Pavlichenko, the divchief, was expecting the arrival of the Second Brigade and did not give the signal. Then Voroshilov rode up to him. He nudged him in the chest with his horse's muzzle and said:

"We're dawdling, comrade, dawdling."

"The Second Brigade," replied Pavlichenko in a dull voice, "in accordance with your orders, is moving at a trot to the scene of action."

"We're dawdling, Divchief Six, dawdling," said Voroshilov, yanking at his reins.

Pavlichenko took a step back.

"If you have any conscience," he shouted and wrung his raw fingers, "if you have any conscience, don't rush me, Comrade Voroshilov."

"Don't rush him," muttered Klim Voroshilov, member of the Revolutionary War Council, and closed his eyes. He sat on his horse, his eyes were half-closed, he kept silent, and his lips stirred. A Cossack in bast shoes and a derby hat looked at him in bewilderment. The army staff, strapping general staffers wearing pants redder than human blood, did squats behind his back and exchanged smiles. The galloping squadrons rustled like wind through the woods and splintered the branches. Voroshilov groomed his horse's mane with a Mauser.

"Komandarm," he shouted, turning to Budenny, "how about a parting word for the men. There he is standing on the hill, the Pole, standing just like a picture and having a laugh at you."

The Poles were indeed visible through binoculars. The army staff mounted up, and the Cossacks began to flow toward them from every corner.

Ivan Akinfiev, former driver for the Revtribunal, rode past and knocked into me with his stirrup.

"You're riding out there, Ivan?" I said to him. "But you've got no ribs . . ."

"Screw the ribs . . ." answered Akinfiev, who was sitting sideways on his horse. "Let me hear what the man has to say."

He rode ahead and right up against Budenny, who shuddered and quietly began to speak:

"Boys," said Budenny, "our situation is bad, got to step lively now, boys."

"Warsaw is ours!" shouted the Cossack in the bast shoes and derby, bulging his eyes and splitting the air with his sword.

"Warsaw is ours!" shouted Voroshilov, reared his horse up, and flew into the midst of the squadrons.

"Troopers and commanders," he said with passion, "in Moscow, in the ancient capital, an unprecedented regime is struggling. A government of workers and peasants, the first in the world, orders us, troopers and commanders, to attack the enemy and deliver victory."

"Ready swords . . . ," sang Pavlichenko's voice from afar behind the komandarm's back, and his protruding raspberry lips glittered with foam amid the ranks. The divchief's red Cossack coat was ripped, that beefy loathsome face of his contorted. With the blade of his priceless sword he saluted Voroshilov.

"In fulfillment of the revolutionary oath," said the divchief six, clearing his throat and looking around, "I report to the Revolutionary Soviet of the First Cavalry: the invincible Second Cavbrigade is moving at a trot to the scene of action."

"Go ahead," replied Voroshilov with a wave of his hand. He touched the reins, Budenny rode off beside him. They rode on tall chestnut mares, side by side, in identical tunics and gleaming trousers trimmed with silver. The men howled and followed them, and pale steel gleamed in the ichor of the autumn sun. But I heard no unanimity in that Cossack howl, and I went into the woods to await the attack, deep into the woods, to the relief station.

Two plump nurses in aprons had stretched out on the grass there. They nudged each other with their young breasts and then pushed each other away. They giggled in that lilting feminine way and winked at me from below, without blinking. They winked the way bare-legged village girls wink at a lickerish lad, village girls who squeal like coddled pups and spend nights in the yard nestling on languorous cushions of hay. A little ways off from the nurses lay a wounded and delirious Red Army man, and Styopka Duplishchev, a quarrelsome little Cossack, was currycombing Hurricane, a thoroughbred stallion that belonged to the divchief and that was descended from Lyulyusha, a record holder from Rostov. The wounded man rambled and reminisced about the town of Shuya, about a heifer and some kind of flax husks, while Duplishchev, drowning out his pathetic mutterings, sang a song about an orderly and a general's fat wife, singing louder and louder, waving the currycomb, and stroking the mount. But he was interrupted by Sashka—sturdy Sashka, girlfriend to all the squadrons. She rode up to the boy and jumped to the ground.

"We doing this or what?" said Sashka.

"Get lost," replied Duplishchev, turned his back on her, and started braiding ribbons in Hurricane's mane.

"Is that you talking, Styopka?" Sashka then said, "or is that a wax doll?"

"Get lost," repeated Styopka. "That's me talking."

He braided all the ribbons into the mane and suddenly shouted to me in despair:

"There now, Kirill Vasilich, look here at the outrage she's done me. A whole month I've had to put up with I don't know what from her. Wherever I turn there she is, wherever I go—she's a hedge in my path: let her use the stallion, let her use the stallion. Meantime, the divchief keeps scolding me on a daily basis, 'There'll be lots coming to you,' he says, 'asking for use of the stallion, but don't you let him loose till he's in his fourth year.'"

"I guess they only let you loose when you're fifteen," Sashka muttered and turned away, "only when you're fifteen, I guess, but you didn't say nothing then, you were just drooling bubbles . . ."

She went over to her mare, tightened the saddle girths, and got ready to ride.

The spurs on her shoes rattled, her fishnet stockings were spattered with mud and spiked with hay, her monstrous bosom swung around to her back.

"I did bring a ruble," said Sashka to no one, and put her spurred shoe in the stirrup. "Brought it, but looks like I'll have to take it back with me."

The woman took out two new half-rubles, jingled them on her palm, and tucked them away again in her bosom.

"We doing this or what?" said Duplishchev then, his eyes fixed on the silver, and he brought the stallion over.

Sashka picked out a slope on the glade and steadied her mare.

"Looks like you're the only one as walks the earth with a stallion," she said to Styopka, and began handling Hurricane. "It's just that my mare's been on the front, hasn't been covered for two years, so I figure might as well get a good bloodline if I can."

Sashka handled the stallion and then led her mare away.

"There we are, full of stuffing, little girl," she whispered and kissed the mare on her wet, piebald horse lips with their dangling strips of spit, rubbed up against its muzzle, and began listening attentively to the noise of hooves trampling through the woods.

"The Second Brigade is coming fast," she said sternly and turned to me. "Got to get moving, Lyutych."

"Coming or not," Duplishchev yelled, and the words caught in his throat, "where's the money, honey?"

"I got your money right here," Sasha muttered and leaped onto her mare.

I charged after her, and we moved off at a gallop. Duplishchev's roar resounded behind us, along with the faint crack of a gunshot.

"Now look here!" the little Cossack cried and dashed through the woods fast as he could.

The wind bounded through the branches like a frantic hare, the Second Brigade flew through the Galician oaks, the impassive dust of cannon fire rose above the ground like smoke above a peaceful cottage. And at the divchief's signal we moved on to the attack, the unforgettable attack at Chesniki.

(published 1924)

After the Battle

The story of my dispute with Akinfiev went like this.

The attack at Chesniki took place on the thirty-first. The squadrons were mustered in the woods near the village and, around six in the evening, threw themselves at the enemy. Our foe was waiting uphill three versts away. We galloped those three versts on horses that were utterly exhausted, and when we reached the top, we saw before us a wall of death composed of black uniforms and pale faces. These were the Cossacks who had deserted us at the beginning of the Polish battles, formed into a brigade by Captain Yakovlev. He had gathered his horsemen into a square formation and awaited us with saber bared. A gold tooth gleamed in his mouth, and his black beard lay on his chest like an icon upon a dead body. Hostile machine-gun fire tore into us at twenty paces, wounded men began falling among us. We trampled over them and clashed with the enemy, but his formation held firm, and we fled.

That was how the Savinkovists won a fleeting victory over the Sixth Division. They were victorious because they did not retreat before the streaming lava of our attacking squadrons. The captain stood firm that day, and it was we who fled, without staining our swords with the wretched blood of traitors.

Five thousand men, our whole division, swept down the slopes unpursued. The enemy remained on the hill. They couldn't believe their implausible victory and failed to chase us down. That was how we remained alive and were able to pour down without loss into the valley, where we were met by Vinogradov, political divchief of the Sixth. Vinogradov was whirling about on a fiery charger, sending the retreating Cossacks back to fight.

"Lyutov!" he yelled when he saw me, "turn the men back, blast your soul!"

Vinogradov struck his reeling stallion with the butt of his Mauser, shrieking and corralling the men. I got away from him and rode over to Gulimov, a Kirghiz, who was streaking along not far off.

"Go back up, Gulimov," I said, "turn the horse around . . ."

"Turn your own horse's ass," Gulimov replied, looking around. He looked around stealthily and fired a shot, singeing the hair above my ear.

"Turn you," he hissed, grabbed my shoulder with one hand, and began to draw his sword with the other. The sword stuck fast in its sheath, as the

Kirghiz quivered and looked around. He wrapped his arm around my shoulder and pressed his face close to mine.

"First you," he repeated softly, "mine right behind you . . ." He knocked me lightly on the chest with the drawn blade of his sword. Death was close and stifling and I felt sick, and with the palm of my hand I pushed away his face, hot like a stone in the sun, scratching him as deep as I could. Warm blood stirred beneath my nails, tickling them, and I rode away from Gulimov, panting as though I had been riding for hours. My horse, my tormented friend, walked on. I rode blindly, I rode not turning around until I met Vorobyov, commander of the First Squadron. Vorobyov was looking for his quartermasters and couldn't find them. We reached the village of Chesniki together and sat down on a bench with Akinfiev, former driver for the Revtribunal. Sashka, one of the nurses of the 31st Cav. Regiment, walked past, and two commanders sat down with us on the bench. The commanders were drowsy and silent—one of them, covered in contusions, was shaking his head uncontrollably, his eye blinking and rolling out. Sashka went off to let the hospital know about him and then came back dragging a horse by the reins. Her mare was pulling at the bit and slipping in the wet clay.

"Where you going, sailor?" Vorobyov asked the nurse. "Sit with us awhile, Sash."

"I'm not going to sit with you," replied Sasha, and struck her mare on the belly. "That I'm not."

"How's that, Sash?" cried Vorobyov, laughing. "Decided you won't take tea with the men no more?"

"Decided not to, not with you." The woman turned to the commander and flung the reins in disgust. "Decided I'll never drink tea with you, Vorobyov, because I saw all of you today, you heroes, and what I saw wasn't pretty, Commander."

"So you saw, and when you saw," Vorobyov grumbled, "you could have fired a shot yourself."

"Fired a shot?!" Sasha said in despair, and tore the hospital band from her sleeve. "I should shoot with this?"

Just then, Akinfiev, the former Revtribunal driver with whom I had accounts to settle, moved a little closer to us.

"You've got nothing to shoot with, Sashok," he said to reassure her. "Nobody's blaming you, I'm only blaming people that gets confused in the fight and doesn't put cartridges in their revolvers . . . You went into battle," Akinfiev suddenly started screaming at me, a spasm shooting across his face, "you went in and didn't load your gun. What would be the reason for that?"

"Drop it, Ivan," I said to Akinfiev, but he wouldn't let it go and came right up to me, all crooked, epileptic, ribs missing.

"The Pole goes at you, but you don't go at him," the Cossack muttered, twisting and turning his shattered hips. "What would be the reason for that?"

"The Pole goes at me," I replied brazenly, "but I don't go at him."

"So you're a Molokan?" Akinfiev hissed, stepping back.

"So I'm a Molokan," I said louder than before. "What do you want?"

"What I want is to know if you're in your right mind," cried Ivan, wildly triumphant. "You're in your right mind, all right, but I got a law about Molokans: you can dispense with them, they're God worshippers . . ."

A crowd gathered around as the Cossack wouldn't stop yelling about the Molokans. I tried to leave, but he caught up and punched me in the back.

"You didn't load your gun," Akinfiev whispered faintly right in my ear, and then got into it with me, trying to tear my mouth with his thumbs. "You treacherous God worshipper!"

He tugged and tore at my mouth—I shoved the epileptic and hit him in the face. Akinfiev fell sideways to the ground and began to bleed from his fall.

Then Sashka went over to him with her wobbling breasts. The woman threw water on Ivan, reached into his black mouth, and took out a long tooth that was swaying like a birch on a deserted highway.

"Strutting cocks," said Sashka, "all they want is to peck their faces off, but the things I seen today make me want to hide my eyes."

She said this full of sorrow and took the battered Akinfiev with her, and I slouched toward the village of Chesniki, slipping in the unrelenting rain of Galicia.

The village floated, growing swollen, crimson clay oozing from its dismal wounds. The first star glimmered above me and fell into clouds. Rain lashed the willows and spent itself. Evening flew skyward like a flock of birds, and darkness covered me in its watery wreath. I was exhausted and, bent beneath my funeral crown, I kept on, imploring fate to grant me the simplest of abilities—the ability to kill a human being.

Galicia, September 1920 (published 1924)

The Song

Quartered in the hamlet of Budyatichi, it was my fate to have a mean landlady. She was a widow, she was poor; I knocked many a lock off her larders without finding a single thing I could sink my teeth into.

I had to be clever, and so one day when I came home early, before dusk, I saw her closing the damper on an oven that was still warm. There was a smell of sour cabbage soup in the cottage, and maybe there was meat in that soup. I could sense meat in that soup of hers and laid my revolver on the table, but the old woman kept denying it, her face and her black fingers twitched in spasms, she darkened and glowered at me with fear and astonishing animosity. But nothing would have saved her, I'd have forced her with my revolver had I not been interrupted by Sashka Konyaev, otherwise known as Sashka Christ.

He came inside the hut with an accordion under his arm, his handsome legs flopping around in worn-out boots.

"Let's have a song," he said, looking at me with his eyes full of sleepy blue ice. "Let's have a song," said Sashka, sitting down on the bench and playing a prelude.

It seemed as though the wistful prelude came from afar—the Cossack broke off and pined with his blue eyes. He turned away from us and, knowing what I liked, began a song from the Kuban.

"Star of the fields," he sang, "star of the fields above my father's house, my mother's hand is full of sorrows . . ."

I love that song—my love for it reached the point of sublime and heartfelt ecstasy. Sashka knew this, because both of us, he and I, heard it for the first time in 1919 on the estuaries of the Don, by the Kagalnitskaya settlement.

A hunter who operated along the protected waters there had taught us that song. Fish spawn in those protected waters, and countless birds come there in flocks. The fish breed in the estuaries in such inexpressible abundance that they can be scooped out with ladles or simply by hand, and if an oar is put in the water it will stand on end—the fish take the oar and carry it away. We saw this ourselves, we will never forget those protected waters of Kagalnitskaya. All the authorities banned hunting there—and rightly so—but in 1919 there was heavy fighting along the estuaries, and Yakov the hunter, who conducted his unlawful business right in front of us, gave an accordion to Sashka Christ, our squadron singer, so that we'd look the other way. He taught Sashka his songs; many of them came from deep and ancient chants. We forgave the wily hunter everything, because we needed his songs: at that time no one could see an end to the war, and Sashka alone could strew our wearisome way with tunes and tears. Footsteps of blood marked our way. Song flew over these footsteps of ours. So it was in the Kuban and in the Green campaigns, so it was in Uralsk and in the foothills of the Caucasus, and so it is to this day. We need the songs, no one sees an end to the war, and Sashka Christ, our squadron singer, is not yet ripe for death.

So it was that evening, too, when I was cheated of my landlady's cabbage soup, that Sashka pacified me with that swaying, muffled voice of his.

"Star of the fields," he sang, "star of the fields above my father's house, my mother's hand is full of sorrows . . ."

And I listened to him, stretched out in the corner on a rotting mat. A dream ached in my bones, a dream shook the rotten hay beneath me, through its hot downpour I could scarcely make out the old woman resting her withered cheek on her hand. Drooping her flea-bitten head, she stood still by the wall and did not stir when Sashka was done playing. Sashka was done and put the accordion aside, he yawned and chuckled, as though waking from a long sleep, and then, noticing the desolation of the widow's hovel, he brushed the dirt from the bench and fetched a bucket of water.

"You see, sweetheart," the lady said to him, rubbing her back against the door and pointing at me, "your boss there came a little while ago, he yelled at me, stomped around, and broke the locks in my house and took out his gun. It's a sin before God, taking out a gun in front of me—I'm a woman, after all."

She rubbed her back against the door again and started covering her son with sheepskins.

Her son was snoring beneath the icon on a large bed littered with rags. He was a mute boy with a white, sagging, bloated head and the gigantic feet of a grown man. His mother wiped his dirty nose and returned to the table.

"Little lady," said Sashka to her then and touched her on the shoulder, "if you like, I can give you some attention."

But it was like the old woman didn't hear his words.

"Never seen no cabbage soup," she said, resting her cheek against her hand. "It's gone, my soup, people only show me guns, and when there does come along a good fellow I could make sweet to, I feel so sick there's no fun in sin even . . ."

She went on with her dreary grumbling and moved the mute boy closer to the wall, mumbling all the while. Sashka lay down with her on the ragged bed while I attempted to fall asleep and began making up dreams so as to fall asleep with good thoughts.

Sokal, August 1920 (published 1925)

Red Cavalry

The Rebbe's Son

...D o you remember Zhitomir, Vasily? Do you remember the River Teterev, Vasily, and that night when the Sabbath, the young Sabbath, crept along the sunset, crushing the stars beneath her little red heel?

The slender horn of the moon bathed its arrows in the dark waters of the Teterev. The comical Gedali, founder of the Fourth International, led us to Rebbe Motale Bratslavsky's for evening prayers. Comical Gedali shook the cock's feathers on his top hat in the red haze of evening. The predatory eyes of lighted candles blinked in the rebbe's room. Broad-shouldered Jews groaned dully, bent over prayer books, and the old jester of the Chernobyl tsaddiks jingled coppers in his frayed pocket . . .

. . . Do you remember that night, Vasily? Beyond the window, horses neighed and Cossacks shouted. The wasteland of war yawned beyond the window, and Rebbe Motale Bratslavsky prayed by the eastern wall, digging his emaciated fingers into his tallis. Then the curtain of the Ark was drawn aside, and in the funereal candlelight we saw the Torah scrolls sheathed in a garb of carmine velvet and pale-blue silk and, suspended above the scrolls, the lifeless, humble, lovely face of Ilya the rebbe's son, last prince of the dynasty . . .

And now, just the day before yesterday, Vasily, the regiments of the Twelfth Army opened the front at Kovel. The conqueror's bombardment thundered in contempt over the town. Our troops faltered and got mixed up. The Polit-section train started crawling away over the dead spine of the fields. And monstrous Russia, inconceivable, like a swarm of clothes lice, tramped in bast shoes on either side of the train cars. The typhoid muzhik mass rolled along behind the usual hump of a soldier's death. It jumped up onto the steps of our train and fell back, dislodged by the butts of our rifles. It sniffled, scrabbled, flowed in silence. And at the twelfth verst, when I had no potatoes left, I flung a pile of Trotsky's leaflets at them. But only one man among them stretched a filthy dead hand to catch a leaflet. And I recognized Ilya, son of the rebbe of Zhitomir. I recognized him at once, Vasily. And it was so heartrending to see a prince who had lost his pants and who was folded in two beneath his soldier's pack, that we broke the rules and pulled him up into our train car. His bare knees, useless as an old woman's, knocked against the rusty iron of the steps; two plump-breasted typists in sailor blouses dragged the long, timid body of the dying man along the floor. We laid him in a corner of the editorial office, on the floor. Cossacks in baggy red trousers fixed his fallen clothes. The girls, their plain, bandy cow legs planted on the floor, stared dully at his sexual organs, the withered, tender, curly virility of a wasted Semite. And I, who had seen him on one of my wandering nights, I began to pack into a little trunk the scattered belongings of the Red Army man Bratslavsky.

Everything was dumped together here—the directives of an agitator and the notes of a Jewish poet. Portraits of Lenin and Maimonides lay side by side. The knotted iron of Lenin's skull and the faded silk of Maimonides' portraits. A lock of woman's hair lay in a booklet of the resolutions of the Party's Sixth Congress, and the margins of Communist leaflets were crowded with crooked lines of ancient Hebrew verse. They fell upon me in a mean and dreary rain—pages of the Song of Songs and revolver cartridges. The sad rain of the sunset washed the dust in my hair, and I said to the youth dying on a wretched mattress in the corner:

"Four months ago, on a Friday evening, Gedali the junk dealer took me to see your father, Rebbe Motale, but you didn't belong to the party then, Bratslavsky . . ."

"I did belong to the party then," the boy answered, scratching at his chest and writhing in fever, "only I couldn't leave my mother behind."

"And now, Ilya?"

"In a revolution a mother is an incident," he whispered, more and more faintly. "My letter came up, the letter B, and the organization sent me to the front . . ."

"And you got to Kovel, Ilya?"

"I got to Kovel!" he cried in despair. "Damn kulaks opened up on us. I took over command of a scratch regiment, but too late . . . I didn't have enough artillery . . ."

He died before we reached Rovno. He died, the last of the princes, died among his poetry, phylacteries, and foot rags. We buried him at some forgotten station. And I—whose ancient body can scarce contain the storms of my imagination—it was I who received the last breath of my brother.

(published 1924)

RED
CAVALRY:
ADDITIONS

Argamak

decided to transfer to the front. The divchief frowned when he heard
about this.

"Where do you think you're going? You'll stand there with your lips hanging, get yourself clipped just like that."

I insisted. Not only that. My choice fell on the most active division, the
Sixth. I was attached to the 4th Squadron of the 23rd Cav. Regiment. The
squadron was commanded by a machinist from a Bryansk factory, Baulin,
a mere boy in years. In order to seem intimidating, he had grown out his
beard. Ashen tufts curled beneath his chin. In his twenty-two years Baulin
had never been flustered. This quality, characteristic of thousands of Baulins,
formed an important element in the victory of the Revolution. Baulin was
tough, of few words, stubborn. The path of his life had been decided. He had
no doubts about the correctness of this path. Deprivations came easy to him.
He could sleep sitting up. He would sleep pressing one hand in the other,
and would wake in such a way that you couldn't notice the transition from
slumber to wakefulness.

You could expect no mercy under Baulin's command. The beginning of
my service was marked by a rare omen of good fortune: I was given a horse.
There were no horses, not in the remount service nor among the peasants. I
was helped by circumstance. The Cossack Tikhomolov killed two captured
officers without permission. He had been entrusted to take them to brigade
headquarters—the officers might have had valuable information to impart.
Tikhomolov failed to get them there. They decided the Cossack should stand
trial before the Revtribunal, but then changed their minds. Squadron Commander Baulin imposed a more fearsome punishment than any tribunal. He
took away Tikhomolov's stallion, called Argamak, and sent the Cossack to
the convoy.

The torment I suffered with Argamak nearly exceeded the measure of
human endurance. Tikhomolov had brought the horse from home, on the
river Terek. It was trained for the Cossack trot, for the peculiar Cossack
gallop—dry, furious, abrupt. Argamak's stride was long, extended, stubborn.
With this devilish stride of his he would carry me away from the ranks, I

would lose the squadron, and, lacking any sense of direction, wander about for days looking for my unit, come within range of the enemy, spend the night in gullies, try to join up with other regiments, and get kicked out. My knowledge of horsemanship was limited to having served during the German war in the artillery division attached to the Fifteenth Infantry Division. Mostly this meant perching on an ammunition box—occasionally we would ride in a gun team. Nowhere did I have a chance to get used to the cruel, jolting trot of Argamak. Tikhomolov had passed on to his horse all the devils of his own downfall. I would wobble like a sack on the stallion's long, lean spine. I messed up his back. Sores appeared on it. Metallic flies gnawed at these sores. Bands of caked black blood girded the horse's belly. Because of incompetent shoeing Argamak began scalping his hooves, and his hind legs swelled up at the fetlock and grew to elephantine proportions. Argamak was becoming emaciated. His eyes were suffused with the peculiar fire of a tortured horse, the fire of hysteria and obstinacy. He wouldn't let himself be saddled.

"You've annihilated that horse, four-eyes," said the platoon commander.

In my presence the Cossacks kept silent, behind my back they were preparing themselves, as predators prepare in somnolent and insidious stillness. They didn't even ask me to write letters for them anymore . . .

The cavalry army captured Novograd-Volynsk. We had to cover sixty, eighty kilometers a day. We were approaching Rovno. No daytime breaks worth mentioning. Night after night I had the same dream. I am racing along at a trot on Argamak. Bonfires are burning on the side of the road. Cossacks are cooking their food. I ride past them, they don't look up at me. Some say hello, others pay no attention—they're not concerned with me. What does this mean? Their indifference means that there is nothing special about how I sit in the saddle—I ride like everybody else, there's nothing to see. I gallop on my way, happy as can be. My thirst for peace and happiness was not quenched when I was awake, so I would dream dreams.

There was no sign of Tikhomolov. He watched me from somewhere on the fringes of the march, from the lumbering appendages of wagons stuffed with rags.

The platoon commander once said to me:

"Pashka keeps pressing to know how you're making out . . ."

"What's he need me for?"

"Apparently, he needs you . . ."

"Could it be he thinks I wronged him?"

"Well, didn't you wrong him . . ."

Pashka's hatred reached me across rivers and forests. I would feel it on my skin and shiver. His bloodshot eyes were fixed upon my path.

"Why did you give me an enemy?" I asked Baulin.

The squadron commander rode past and yawned.

"That's not my trouble," he replied without turning around. "That's your trouble . . ."

Argamak's back would dry up a little and then open up again. I would put as many as three blankets under the saddle, but I couldn't sit right, and the scars wouldn't close. The knowledge that I was sitting on an open wound made me itch all over.

One Cossack in our platoon, Bizyukov by name, was Tikhomolov's countryman. He had known Pashka's father there on the Terek.

"His father, I mean Pashka's," Bizyukov once said to me, "breeds horses, fancies them . . . Hell of a rider, big old guy. He'll come out to the drove—he's going to pick a horse now . . . They bring them to him. He stands opposite the horse, legs wide, takes a good look . . . What's he want now? . . . Here's what: swings his big old fist, one knock between the eyes—no more horse. What for, Kalistrat, they say to him, why'd you finish off the creature? He says, my wicked fancy tells me that horse won't ride . . . Don't have a fancy for that horse. My fancy, he says, is something deadly. Hell of a rider, no question."

And so Argamak, left alive by Pashka's father, chosen by him, had fallen to me. Now what? I tried on a multitude of plans in my mind. It was the war that got me out of my troubles.

The cavalry army attacked Rovno. The town was taken. We spent two days there. Next night the Poles pushed us out. They had given battle in order to evacuate their retreating units. The maneuver worked. As cover the Poles had the benefit of a hurricane, cutting rain, a heavy summer thunderstorm, dumping torrents of black water upon the earth. We were cleared out of the town for twenty-four hours. In this night battle fell Dundich the Serb, bravest of men. In this battle Pashka Tikhomolov fought, too. The Poles went after his convoy. The place was flat and had no cover. Tikhomolov arranged his wagons in a battle order that only he could understand. No doubt the Romans had arranged their chariots that way. Pashka happened to have a machine gun. One must suppose he had stolen it and hidden it away just in case. With this machine gun Tikhomolov warded off the attack, saved the goods, and got the whole convoy out, save two carts whose horses had been shot.

"Why are you letting the men stew in their juices?" they asked Baulin at brigade headquarters a few days after the battle.

"If I'm letting them stew, must be a good reason . . ."

"Watch out, or you'll go too far . . ."

No amnesty for Pashka was announced, but we knew that he would be coming. He came wearing galoshes on his bare feet. His fingers were all cut up, ribbons of black gauze hung down from them. The ribbons dragged after him like a mantle. Pashka came to the village of Budyatichi, into the square in front of the Catholic church where our horses were tethered. Baulin was sitting on the steps of the church, steaming his feet in a tub. His toes were putrescent. They were pink, as iron is pink before tempering. Tufts of youthful straw-colored hair stuck to Baulin's forehead. The sun blazed on the bricks and tiles of the church. Bizyukov, standing next to the squadron commander, stuck a cigarette into the other's mouth and lit it. Tikhomolov, dragging his ragged mantle, went over to the hitching post. His galoshes slapped the ground. Argamak stretched out his long neck and neighed for his master, neighed soft and shrill, like a horse in the wilderness. On his back, the ichor twisted like lacework between strips of torn flesh. Pashka stood next to the horse. The filthy ribbons lay motionless on the ground.

"Like that, eh," said the Cossack, so low you could barely hear. I stepped forward.

"Let's make peace, Tikhomolov. I'm glad that you're getting the horse. I couldn't manage him. Let's make peace, eh?"

"Peace? It's not Easter yet, is it?" the platoon commander said, rolling a cigarette behind me. His wide trousers were loosened, his shirt unbuttoned on his bronze chest, he was resting on the steps of the church.

"Give him three Easter kisses, Pashka," mumbled Bizyukov, Tikhomolov's countryman, who had known Kalistrat, Pashka's father. "He wants to do the three kisses with you."

I was alone among these people, whose friendship I had not succeeded in gaining.

Pashka stood before the horse as if rooted to the ground. Argamak, breathing strong and free, stretched his muzzle toward him.

"Like that, eh," the Cossack repeated, abruptly turned to me, and said point-blank, "I won't be making peace with you."

Shuffling his galoshes, he started walking away along the parched chalky road, his bandages sweeping the dust of the village square. Argamak followed like a dog. The reins swayed beneath his muzzle, his long neck hung low. Baulin was still rubbing the reddish metallic rot of his feet in the tub.

"You gave me an enemy," I said to him. "And how was I to blame?"

The squadron commander looked up.

"Say more."

"I'll say more . . ."

"I see you," the commander interrupted me. "I see every bit of you . . . You strive to live without enemies. That's what it's all about for you—not having enemies."

"Give him three kisses," mumbled Bizyukov, turning away.

A spot of fire was printed on Baulin's forehead. His cheek twitched.

"You know what comes of that?" he said, his breathing out of control. "Boredom, that's what. Now get and go to your rag of a mother . . ."

I had to leave. I transferred to the 6th Squadron. There things went better. Whatever else may have happened, Argamak had taught me Tikhomolov's style of riding. Months passed. My dream came true. The Cossacks' eyes stopped following me and my horse.

1924–1930 (published 1932)

The Kiss

At the beginning of August, headquarters sent us to Budyatichi as part of a reorganization. Occupied by the Poles at the beginning of the war, it had soon been retaken by our forces. The brigade reached the shtetl by dawn; I got there toward noon. The best quarters had already been taken—I got the schoolmaster's place. In a low-ceilinged room, among tubs of fruit-bearing lemon trees, a paralyzed old man sat in an armchair. He wore a Tyrolean hat with a feather; his gray beard reached down to his chest, which was sprinkled with ash. Twitching his eyes, he was mumbling some sort of request. After I washed up, I left for headquarters and came back at night. My orderly, Mishka Surovtsev, a wily Orenburg Cossack, gave me a report on the situation: besides the paralyzed old man, the household consisted of his daughter, Elizaveta Alexeyevna Tomilina, and her five-year-old son, named Misha like Surovtsev; the daughter was the widow of an officer killed in the German war, conducted herself properly, but might, according to Surovtsev, make herself available to a decent person.

"It could be arranged," he said and went off to the kitchen and clattered with the dishes; the schoolmaster's daughter was helping him. As they prepared the meal, Surovtsev told her of my bravery, of how I had finished off two Polish officers in battle and how I was highly regarded by the Soviet leadership. Tomilina replied softly and full of hesitation.

"Where do you lie down to sleep?" Surovtsev asked as he left the kitchen. "Set yourself up a little closer, we're lively fellows."

He brought out an enormous pan of fried eggs and put it on the table.

"She wants to," he said, sitting down, "she just won't say it."

That very moment we heard muffled whispers, shuffling, a lumbering and surreptitious bustle in the house. We had hardly finished our food when the house was filled with a procession of old men on crutches and old women with their heads wrapped in shawls. They dragged little Misha's bed into the dining room by the lemon thicket near Grandfather's armchair. Our frail hosts, determined to defend Elizaveta Alexeyevna's honor, huddled together like a flock of sheep in bad weather, barricaded the door, and quietly played cards all night, whispering the stakes and hushing at the slightest rustle. I felt so awkward and embarrassed that I couldn't get to sleep on the other side of that door and could hardly wait until daybreak.

"For your information," I said when I ran into Tomilina in the hall, "for your information, I should tell you that I have a law degree, and one could say I'm something of an intellectual."

She stood before me numb with her arms dangling, an old-fashioned cloak flowing down her slim figure. She looked straight at me without blinking, tears shining in her widening blue eyes.

Two days later we became friends. The fear and ignorance that gripped the schoolmaster's family—soft and kindly people—was boundless. Polish officials had given them the notion that Russia had gone up in smoke and barbarism, like Rome in its day. A childlike and tentative joy filled them when I told them about Lenin, about Moscow, where the future is raging, about the Moscow Art Theatre. Evenings we'd receive twenty-two-year-old Bolshevik generals with messy red beards. We'd smoke Moscow cigarettes, eat meals that Elizaveta Alexeyevna made for us from army rations, and sing student songs. Leaning forward in his armchair, the paralytic would listen to us avidly, the Tyrolean hat trembling in time with our songs. Over the course of those days, the old man gave himself over to a roiling, vague, and sudden hope and, so as not to cloud his own happiness, did his best not to notice our bloodthirsty bravado and loudmouthed simplemindedness, which, in those days, accompanied our attempts to solve all the world's problems.

After the victory over the Poles—so the family council decided—the Tomilins would move to Moscow: we would get a celebrated professor to cure the old man, Elizaveta Alexeyevna would take courses at the university, and Mishka would go to the same school in Patriarch Ponds where his mother once studied. The future seemed indisputably ours, the war merely a roiling prologue to happiness, and happiness was the very essence of what we were about. All that was left to decide were the details, and we used to discuss them for nights on end, formidable nights, when candle stubs glowed, reflected in the cloudy bottles of our moonshine. The blossoming Elizaveta Alexeyevna was our speechless audience. I had never seen a creature so impulsive, free, and fearful. Sometimes in the evening, the wily Surovtsev would drive us in a wicker charabanc, requisitioned back in the Kuban, to a hilltop where the abandoned chateau of the princely Gonsiorowskis glimmered in the fire of the setting sun. The skinny but long and thoroughbred horses ran cheerfully at the end of their red reins; a carefree earring dangled from Surovtsev's ear, round towers rose above a moat overgrown with a yellow covering of flowers. The broken walls traced a long crooked line swollen with ruby blood, a rosehip bush hid its fruit, and a pale-blue step, the trace of a staircase once climbed by Polish kings, gleamed amid the brambles. Sitting on this step one evening, I drew Elizaveta Alexeyevna's head toward me and kissed her. She slowly pulled away, stood up, grasped the wall, and leaned against it. She stood there motionless, a fiery mote-flecked beam of light seethed around her blinded head, then she shuddered and raised her head as though she had heard something; her fingers pushed away from the wall; her steps swift and stumbling, Tomilina started to run down the hill. I called to her, there was no reply. Down below, ruddy Surovtsev was asleep stretched out in the wicker charabanc. That night, when everyone was sleeping, I crept to Elizaveta Alexeyevna's room. She was reading, holding the book at arm's length: the hand resting on the table seemed inanimate. When I knocked, Elizaveta Alexeyevna turned and got up.

"No," she said, gazing at me, "no, my dear," and wrapping her long bare arms around me, kissed me with a swelling, mute, and endless kiss.

The rattle of the phone in the neighboring room tore us apart. It was the staff adjutant.

"We're moving out," he said over the line. "Report to the brigade commander."

I ran out hatless, sorting my papers on the way. Horses were being led out of the yards, riders galloped past, yelling in the darkness. From the brigcom, who stood with a burka fastened around his shoulders, we learned that the Poles had just broken through our lines outside Lublin and that we'd been ordered to perform a flanking maneuver. Both regiments were to move out in an hour. The old man was awake now and watching me, worried, through the leaves of the lemon tree.

"Tell me you'll come back," he kept saying, and shaking his head.

Elizaveta Alexeyevna, throwing a fur jacket over her batiste nightgown, showed us out to the street. In the darkness an unseen squadron galloped madly past. On the edge of the fields I turned around—Tomilina was bending to straighten her boy's jacket, and the fitful light from the lamp on the windowsill flowed along her delicate, skeletal nape . . .

After a forced march of one hundred kilometers, we linked up with the 14th Cav. Division and retreated defensively. We slept in the saddle. Whenever we made camp, we'd fall to the ground dead asleep, and the horses, tugging at their bridles, would drag us sleeping through the mown fields. Autumn arrived, as did the mute Galician rain. Huddled into a silent and disheveled mass, we wove and went in circles, jumping right into the Poles' cinched satchel, and making our way out again. We lost all sense of time. As I was settling down for the night in a church at Tochenko, it didn't even occur to me that we were only nine versts from Budyatichi. It was Surovtsev who reminded me—we looked at each other.

"The main thing is the horses are spent," he chirped, "otherwise we could ride down."

"We can't," I said, "at night they'll notice."

And so off we went. We strapped a few goodies to our saddles: a sugar-loaf, a red fur pelisse, and a live two-week-old baby goat. Our route took us through a swaying, wet forest, a steel star wandered through the tall branches of oak. In less than an hour we had reached the shtetl, whose center had been burned down, clogged by trucks white with flour dust, gun carriages, and broken wheel shafts. Without dismounting I tapped on the familiar window—a white cloud passed across the room. Tomilina ran out onto the porch in the same batiste nightgown with its sagging lace. She took my hand in her hot fingers and brought me into the house. In the large room men's laundry was drying on the broken lemon trees, strangers slept on cots lined up without gaps, as in a hospital. Their dirty feet sticking out, mouths twisted and stiff, they cried out hoarsely in their sleep and took loud and greedy breaths. The house was occupied by our Spoils Commission, the Tomilins forced into a single room.

"When will you take us away from here?" Elizaveta Alexeyevna asked, clutching my hand.

The old man, now awake, was shaking his head. Little Misha, pressing the kid to his chest, was overcome with mute, delighted laughter. Looming above him pouting, Surovtsev shook spurs, pierced coins, a whistle on a yellow lanyard out of the pockets of his baggy Cossack pants. There was no place to hide in the house, now taken over by the Spoils Commission, and Tomilina and I went to the wooden annex where potatoes and beehive frames were stored for the winter. There, in that storage room, I realized how ineluctable and ruinous was the path begun with the kiss at the castle of the Gonsiorowsky princes.

Not long before dawn Surovtsev knocked on our door.

"When will you get us out of here?" said Elizaveta Alexeyevna, looking away.

I said nothing and went to the house to say good-bye to the old man.

"The main thing is there's no time," said Surovtsev, barring my path. "Saddle up, let's go."

He pushed me into the street and brought my horse. Tomilina gave me her chilled hand. She kept her head absolutely straight as she always did. The horses, having rested overnight, took off at a trot. Through the black tangle of oak rose a flaming sun. My soul overflowed with the glory of morning.

We came to a glade in the woods, I eased up on the horse, turned, and shouted to Surovtsev:

"Could've stayed longer . . . You rousted us early."

"Not early enough," he replied, drawing even with me and pushing the wet sparkling branches aside. "If it wasn't for the old man, I might've rousted you even sooner . . . But the old fellow just kept talking, got all worked up, groans and starts keeling over sideways . . . I get over to him and I look—dead, stick a fork in him . . ."

The woods receded. We came out onto a plowed field with no road. Surovtsev rose in the saddle, looked around, gave a whistle, sniffing out the right direction, and, when the air offered it to him, he leaned forward and galloped off.

We got there just in time. The squadron was waking up. The sun was warming up and promised a hot day ahead. That morning our brigade passed the former border of the Kingdom of Poland.

(published 1937)

CLOSINGS

Our Batko Makhno

The night before, six of Makhno's boys had raped the maidservant. When I learned about it in the morning, I decided to find out how a woman looked after being raped six times. I found her in the kitchen. She was washing clothes, bent over a tub. She was a fat one with blooming cheeks. Only an unhurried existence on the fruitful Ukrainian soil can imbue a Jewish girl with such bovine juices, impart such a greasy sheen to her face. The girl's legs, fat, brick-red, swollen like balloons, had a sickly-sweet stench like freshly sliced meat. And it seemed to me that of yesterday's maidenhood there remained only the cheeks, more swollen than usual, and the eyes, cast downward.

In the kitchen, aside from the maidservant, there was also a little Cossack called Kikin, our Batko Makhno's errand-boy. He was known at headquarters as a fool, and he thought nothing of walking on his hands at the most inappropriate moments. More than once I had found him looking in the mirror. Sticking out his leg in its torn trouser, he would wink at himself, slapping his bare boyish belly, sing battle songs, and twist his face into grimaces of triumph that made even him die of laughter. The lad's imagination worked in remarkably vivid ways. Today I again found him busy with a rather special project: he was gluing strips of gilt paper onto a German helmet.

"How many did you finish yesterday, Rukhlya?" he said and, screwing up his eyes, inspected his decorated helmet.

The girl said nothing.

"You did six," the boy went on, "but there are women that can do up to twenty. Our band of brothers had this one housewife in Krapivno, kept nailing and nailing her, until the boys gave up on it, though it's true she was fatter than you . . ."

"Go get some water," said the girl.

Kikin brought a pail of water from the courtyard. Shuffling his bare feet, he went over to the mirror, plopped the helmet with the golden streamers on his head, and closely examined his reflection. The image in the mirror absorbed him. Poking his fingers in his nostrils, the boy avidly watched how the shape of his nose changed under the pressure from inside.

"I'll be going on a mission." He turned to the Jewish girl. "Don't tell no one, Rukhlya. Stetsenko is taking me into the squadron. There at least you get a uniform, all honorable-like, and my comrades will be fighting men, not like this crew of ragpickers here. Yesterday, when they caught you, and I was holding you by the head, I said to Matvei Vasilyich, 'Look here, Matvei Vasilyich,' I said, 'now this is the fourth one already, and all I'm doing is holding her. You've had two goes, Matvei Vasilyich, but seeing as I'm not old enough and not in your unit, everyone thinks he can mistreat me.' I reckon you heard yourself what he said then, Rukhlya: 'Nobody's mistreating you, just let all the orderlies have a go, and then it'll be your turn.' So they let me have a go, sure, right. It was only when they was already dragging you into the woods that Matvei Vasilyich says to me, 'Go on, Kikin, if you want.' 'No, Matvei Vasilyich,' I say, 'I don't want to, not after Vasya's gone, and then cry about it the rest of my life.'"

Kikin snorted angrily and was silent. Shoeless, lanky, saddened, with his bare stomach and a gleaming helmet set on his strawlike hair, he lay down on the floor and stared into the distance

"People say all kinds of things about Makhno's men, about what heroes they are," he mumbled sullenly, "but you won't get your share with them, that's how they are, it seems each one got a stone in his chest."

The Jewish girl raised her blood-flushed face from the washtub, glanced at the boy, and walked out of the kitchen with the heavy stride of a cavalryman when he puts his numb legs on the ground after a long ride.

Left by himself, the boy cast a lonesome gaze around the kitchen, sighed, pressed his palms to the floor, threw his legs in the air, and, with his upturned heels perfectly still, quickly walked away on his hands.

1923 (published 1924)

The End of Saint Hypatius

Yesterday I was at the Ipatiev Monastery, and Father Illarion, last of the resident monks, showed me the home of the Romanov boyars.

The people of Moscow came here in 1613 to beg Mikhail Fyodorovich to be tsar.

I saw the trampled corner where Martha the Nun, mother of the tsar, used to say her prayers, her gloomy bedchamber, and the lookout tower from which she watched the wolf hunts in the woods of Kostroma.

Illarion and I passed over the rickety, snow-heaped bridges, shooed away the crows nesting in the boyars' chamber, and came to a church of indescribable beauty.

Ringed with a garland of snow, painted carmine and azure, it lay against the misty northern sky like a colorful woman's scarf adorned with Russian flowers.

The lines of its unpretentious cupolas were chaste, its pale-blue annexes were pot-bellied, and the patterned window frames shone in the sun with an unneeded radiance.

In this deserted church I came upon the iron gates donated by Ivan the Terrible, and I wandered looking at all the ancient icons, all the merciless shrines in their sepulchral decay.

The Blessed of the Lord—possessed naked men with rotted hips—writhed on the shabby walls, and next to them was the image of a Russian Mother of God: a thin peasant with knees spread apart and dangling breasts that looked like two spare green arms.

The ancient icons surrounded my carefree heart with the chill of their lifeless passions, and I barely escaped them, those coffin saints.

Their god lay in the church, ossified and clean as a body already washed at home but left unburied.

Only Father Illarion wandered among his corpses. He limped on his left leg, would keep nodding off, scratching his filthy beard, and I soon tired of him.

Then I threw open the gates of Ivan the Terrible and ran beneath the black arches out onto the square, and there the Volga flashed at me, shackled in ice.

The smoke of Kostroma rose and punched up through the snow; muzhiks clad in yellow halos of frost were hauling flour on sledges, and their draft horses drove their iron hooves into the ice.

Wreathed in hoarfrost and mist, the chestnut horses breathed noisily on the river, the pines flashed in the pink lightning of the north, and crowds, anonymous crowds of people, were crawling up the icy slopes.

A blistering wind blew upon them from the Volga, a multitude of peasant women fell through the snowdrifts and yet kept climbing higher, closing in on the monastery like besieging columns.

Loud female laughter thundered above the hill, samovar pipes and wash-tubs drove up the slope, boys' ice skates rasped as they turned.

The old crones were dragging a burden up the steep hill—the hill of Saint Hypatius—with infants asleep in their sleds, and they were walking white she-goats on leashes.

"Devils," I cried when I saw them and retreated before the unheard-of incursion. "I guess you're here to see Martha the Nun, to ask that her son Mikhail Romanov be made tsar?"

"May the joker take you!" a peasant woman answered me and stepped forward. "Why are you messing with us on the road? Are we supposed to have your kids or something?"

And packing herself onto her sled she drove into the monastery courtyard, almost knocking the dumbstruck Father Illarion off his legs. Into the cradle of the tsars of Muscovy she drove her washtubs, her geese, her hornless phonograph, and having given her name as Savicheva, demanded Number 19 of the episcopal chambers for herself.

And, to my surprise, Savicheva was given this apartment, and after her all the rest were given quarters.

That's when it was explained to me that the Union of Textile Workers had rebuilt forty apartments in the burned-out structure for the workers of the Kostroma United Flax Manufactory, and that today they were being moved into the monastery.

Father Illarion stood at the gate, counting all the goats and transplants; then he invited me to tea and silently placed on the table cups he had stolen in the courtyard when the dishes of the Romanov boyars were being taken to the museum.

From these cups we drank tea till the sweat came, while the bare legs of peasant women plodded past me on the windowsills: they were washing the panes in their new quarters.

Then smoke began to billow from every chimney, an unfamiliar rooster flew up onto the tomb of Father Sionius the abbot, right on cue, and started squawking, somebody's accordion, having wheezed through an introduction, launched into a tender song, and some little old lady we hadn't seen before wearing a peasant caftan poked her head into Father Illarion's cell to borrow a pinch of salt for her sour cabbage soup.

It was already evening when the little old lady came to visit; scarlet clouds heaved above the Volga, the thermometer on the wall outside showed forty below, gigantic bonfires flared and died away on the river—and an irrepressible young man was still stubbornly trying to climb up the frozen ladder to the crossbar above the gate, climbing up there to hang up a tiny lantern and a signboard emblazoned with a multitude of letters: U.S.S.R. and R.S.F.S.R., and the emblem of the Textile Union, and a hammer and sickle, and a woman standing at a loom streaming with rays of light in every direction.

(published 1924)

Dante Street

Between five and seven our Hotel Danton was lifted aloft by the groans of love. Specialists were at work in their rooms. Having arrived in France convinced that the nation had gone to seed, I was not a little surprised by such effort. In our country, a woman is not kindled to such white heat, far from it. My neighbor, Jean Biénal, once said to me:

"*Mon vieux,* in the thousand years of our history we have invented Woman, Cuisine, and Books. This no one can deny."

In the matter of getting to know about France, Jean Biénal, dealer in used cars, did more for me than the books I read and the towns I visited. At our first meeting he asked me about the restaurant, café, and brothel I went to. My reply horrified him.

"On va refaire votre vie."

And so we did. We started dining at a tavern where cattle dealers and wine merchants took their meals—opposite les Halles aux vins.

Country girls in slippers would serve us lobster in red sauce, roast hare stuffed with garlic and truffles, wine unobtainable anywhere else. Biénal did the ordering, I did the paying, but I paid only what the French pay. It wasn't cheap, but it was the correct price. And I paid the same price at the brothel near the Gare St-Lazare patronized by a number of senators. It cost Biénal more trouble to introduce me to the residents of this house than if I had wanted to attend a session of parliament when a minister was being ousted. We used to finish the evening at the Porte Maillot in a café frequented by boxing promoters and race-car drivers. My mentor belonged to the half of the country that sells automobiles; the other half exchanges them. He was an agent for Renault and did most of his business with Romanian dealers, the dirtiest dealers of all. In his free time Biénal would teach me the art of buying a used car. The way to do it, according to him, was to go to the Riviera toward the end of the season when the English went home, abandoning in their garages cars driven only two or three months. Biénal himself used to ride around in a battered Renault that he drove as a Samoyed drives his sled dogs. On Sundays we would go a hundred and twenty kilometers in a peeling Renault to Rouen to eat duck prepared in its own blood, as they do it there. We would be accompanied by Germaine, who sold gloves in a shop on the rue Royale. Wednesday and Sunday were their days together. She would arrive at five o'clock. A moment later their room would resound with growls, the thud of falling bodies, cries of fright, followed by the woman's tender agonies:

"Oh, Jean . . ."

I used to calculate it myself: so, Germaine has gone inside now, closed the door behind her, they've kissed each other hello, she's taken off her hat and gloves and put them on the table, and according to my calculations they had no time left. There was no time left to undress. Without uttering a single word they were already bouncing in their sheets like rabbits. After some groaning, they'd be dying with laughter, prattling on about their affairs. Of this I knew all that could be known by a neighbor who lives on the other side of a plank partition. Germaine had disagreements with Monsieur Henriche, manager of the glove shop. Her parents lived in Tours, and she would go stay with them. One Saturday she bought herself a fur boa, another Saturday she saw *La bohème* at the Grand Opera. Monsieur Henriche made his saleswomen wear sleek tailleurs. Monsieur Henriche had Anglicized Germaine, turning her into one of those businesswomen, flat-bosomed, brisk, tightly wound, painted in flaming brown makeup, but her full ankle, her rapid throaty laughter, the gaze of her keen and flashing eyes, and that agonizing groan—oh, Jean!—all this still belonged to Biénal.

Through the smoke and gold of the Parisian evening Germaine's strong slender body surged along before us; she would throw back her head in laughter and press her nimble rosy fingers to her breast. My heart would grow warm during those hours. There is no solitude more hopeless than solitude in Paris.

For all those who come from afar this town is a form of exile, and it had occurred to me that our need for Germaine was greater than Biénal's. With this in mind I left for Marseille. There I caught a glimpse of my native land—Odessa—as it could have become in twenty years had previous possibilities remained unobstructed, I caught a glimpse of the unrealized future of our streets, embankments, and ships.

After a month in Marseille I returned to Paris. I waited for Wednesday, to hear Germaine's voice.

Wednesday came and went, and no one disturbed the silence behind the wall. Biénal had changed his day. On Thursday I heard a woman's voice at the customary five o'clock. Biénal gave his visitor time to take off her hat and gloves. Germaine had changed her day, and she had also changed her voice. No longer was there a jerky, pleading "oh, Jean . . ." and then silence, the terrible silence of someone else's happiness. Now this was replaced by a hoarse domestic bustle, by guttural exclamations. The new Germaine grated her teeth, plumped down on the couch, and in the intervals held forth in a thick drawling voice. She said nothing of Monsieur Henriche, and having growled till seven o'clock, prepared to depart. I half opened the door to get a glimpse of her and saw coming along the corridor a mulatto with a cockscomb of horsehair and large sagging breasts jutting out. The mulatto, shuffling her feet in their worn and heelless slippers, passed along the corridor. I knocked on Biénal's door. He was sprawled on the bed in his shirtsleeves, wrinkled, gray, wearing threadbare socks.

"*Mon vieux*, have you quit Germaine?"

"Cette femme est folle," he replied shuddering. "The simple fact that on this earth there is winter and summer, a beginning and an end, that after winter comes summer and then the other way around—this does not concern Mademoiselle Germaine, that's not her tune . . . She piles a burden on your back and insists that you bear it . . . where to? No one knows except Mademoiselle Germaine."

Biénal sat up in bed, rumpled trousers around his noodle legs, his pale scalp glimmering through matted hair; the triangle of his mustache twitched. A liter of four-franc Mâcon cured my friend. Over dessert he shrugged and said, responding to his own thoughts:

"There's more to life than everlasting love—there are also Romanians, promissory notes, men who go bankrupt, busted automobiles. *Oh, j'en ai plein le dos . . .*"

Over a glass of cognac at the Café de Paris he cheered up. We were sitting on the terrace beneath a white tent. It had wide stripes flowing across. Crowds mingled with the electric stars and flowed along the pavement. Opposite us there stopped a car stretched long as a mine shaft, and from it emerged an Englishman and a woman in a sable cape. Her unnaturally elongated body, with its shiny little porcelain head, floated past us on a warm cloud of perfume and fur. When he saw her, Biénal lurched, put out his leg in its shabby trouser, and winked as one winks at girls from the rue de la Gaîté. The woman smiled with the corner of her carmine mouth, tilted her tightly drawn pink head ever so subtly, swaying and dragging her serpentine body until she disappeared. The stiff Englishman went click-clacking after her.

"Ah, canaille!" said Biénal after them. "A couple of years ago she was satisfied with an aperitif . . ."

We parted late. I told myself that on Saturday I would go to Germaine's, invite her to the theater, go with her to Chartres if she wanted, but it turned out that I saw them—Biénal and his ex-girlfriend—earlier than that. On the evening of the following day there were police at the Hotel Danton, and their blue cloaks swung wide through our vestibule. They let me pass after ascertaining that I was one of Madame Truffaut's lodgers. I found gendarmes outside my room. Biénal's door had been thrown open. Biénal lay on the floor in a pool of blood, his eyes glazed and half-closed. The stamp of street death congealed upon. He'd been stabbed to death, my friend Biénal, no two ways about it. Dressed in a tailleur and a narrow little hat, Germaine was sitting at the table. She greeted me and bowed her head, and the feather on her hat bowed, too . . .

All this took place at six in the evening, the hour of love; in each room there was a woman. Before leaving—half-dressed, stockings up to their thighs like medieval pages—they were hastily applying rouge and black lip liner around their mouths. Doors were open, men in unlaced shoes lined the corridor. In the room occupied by a wrinkled Italian racing cyclist, a barefoot girl was weeping into a pillow. I went down to tell Madame Truffaut. The girl's mother sold newspapers on boulevard St-Michel. At the front desk the old women from our street, Dante Street, had already gathered: greengrocers and concierges, vendors of roast chestnuts and fried potatoes, fleshy mounds of twisted goiters, bewhiskered heavy breathers with cataracts and purple blotches.

"Voilà qui n'est pas gai," I said when I came in, "quel malheur!"

"C'est l'amour, monsieur . . . Elle l'aimait . . ."

Madame Truffaut's lilac bosom was pouring out of her bodice, her elephant legs bestrode the room, her eyes flashed.

"L'amore," echoed Signora Rocca, who kept a restaurant on Dante Street. "Dio castiga quelli, chi non conoscono l'amore . . ."

The old ladies huddled together, murmuring all at once. Their pocked cheeks were ablaze, eyes rolling out of their sockets.

"L'amour," repeated Madame Truffaut, coming toward me, "c'est une grosse affaire, l'amour."

There was honking in the street. Capable hands bore the murdered man downstairs. He had become a mere number, my friend Biénal, had lost his name in the ebb and flow of Paris. Signora Rocca went over to the window and looked at the corpse. She was pregnant, her belly stuck out alarmingly, silk covered her protuding hips, the sun passed across her puffy yellow face and her soft yellow hair.

"Dio," affirmed Signora Rocca, "tu non perdoni quelli, chi non ama . . ."

Darkness descended over the frayed lattice of the Latin Quarter, stunted crowds scuttled into its folds, hot garlic breath wafted from its courtyards.

Dusk covered the house of Madame Truffaut, its Gothic facade with two windows, traces of turrets, curls of petrified ivy.

A century and a half ago Danton lived here. From his window he could see the Conciergerie, the bridges cast lightly across the Seine, an assortment of blind hovels pressed close against the river, the same breath wafting up to him. Rusted rafters and tavern signs, creaking in the wind.

(published 1934)

The Trial (from a Notebook)

Madame Blanchard, sixty-one years old, met the former lieutenant colonel Ivan Nedachin in a café on the boulevard des Italiens. They fell in love. Their love had more sensibility than sense. Three months later the lieutenant colonel ran off with the stocks and valuables that Madame Blanchard had entrusted him to take to a jeweler on the rue de la Paix to be appraised.

"Accès de folie, passagère," is how the doctor described Madame Blanchard's fit.

When she came to, the old woman confessed to her daughter-in-law. The daughter informed the police. Nedachin was arrested in Montparnasse at a wine cellar where Moscow Gypsies sang. In jail, Nedachin turned yellow and flabby. He was tried in Room 14 at the criminal court. First there was a traffic case, then the sixteen-year-old Raymond Lepique came before the court for shooting his lover out of jealousy. After the boy came the lieutenant colonel. The gendarmes shoved him out into the light, just as the *Ursus* was once shoved out into the Roman Circus. Inside the courtroom, Frenchmen in ill-tailored suits were shouting at one another, duly painted women fanned their tear-stained faces. Before them, up behind the bench, beneath the marble crest of the Republic sat a red-cheeked man with Gallic whiskers in a toga and a little hat.

"Eh bien, Nedatchine," he said when he saw the accused, "eh bien, mon ami." And he spilled his rapid lisping speech upon the shuddering lieutenant colonel.

"A descendant of the noble Nedatchine line," the presiding judge proclaimed, "you, my friend, are inscribed in the heraldic books of Tambov Province . . . An officer of the tsar's army, you emigrated along with Wrangel and became a policeman in Zagreb . . . Disagreements over a question of state versus private property," the judge continued in his resonant voice, the tip of his lacquered shoe darting in and out of robes, "these disagreements, my friend, forced you to depart from the hospitable kingdom of the Yugoslavs and to set your sights on Paris . . . In Paris . . ." Here the judge scanned the document lying before him, "in Paris, my friend, the taxi exam proved to be a fortress you could not conquer . . . So then you deployed all your unspent reserve forces on Madame Blanchard, who is absent from these proceedings."

The foreign words poured down on Nedachin like a summer rain. Helpless, gigantic, his arms hanging down—he towered above the crowd like a sad animal from another world.

"Voyons," said the judge unexpectedly, "I see that the daughter-in-law of the esteemed Madame Blanchard is present."

A plump, neckless woman, resembling a fish stuffed in a frock coat, scuttled over to the witness stand with her head bowed. Panting and raising her stubby arms to the sky, she began listing the names of the stocks stolen from Madame Blanchard.

"Thank you, madame," the judge interrupted her and nodded to a lean man with a well-bred sunken face sitting to his left.

Rising slightly, the prosecutor muttered a few words through his teeth and sat down, clasping his hands in their broad sleeves. After him came the defense counsel, a naturalized Kiev Jew. He sounded offended, as if he were arguing with someone, and began shouting about the veritable Golgotha undergone by Russian officers. Slurred French words came crumbling out of his mouth, and toward the end of his speech they began to sound like Yiddish. For several moments, the presiding judge looked on silently at the defense attorney with a blank expression, then suddenly turned right to a shriveled old man in a toga and a little hat, and then swung the other way to an identical old man sitting on his left.

"Ten years, my friend," the presiding judge said softly as he nodded at Nedachin and quickly caught the new case file that the clerk had flicked in his direction.

Nedachin stood at attention, perfectly still. His colorless eyes were blinking, sweat formed on his narrow forehead.

"T'a encaisse dix ans," said the gendarme standing behind him, "c'est fini, mon vieux." And prodding gently with his fists, the gendarme nudged the convicted man out the door.

(published 1938)

The *Ivan & Marya*

S ergey Vasilyevich Malyshev, who later became chairman of the Nizhni Novgorod Fair Committee, organized the first produce expedition in our country in the summer of 1918. With Lenin's approval he loaded several trains with goods that were needed by peasants and took them along the Volga to trade for grain.

I ended up being a clerk on this expedition. We chose the Novo-Nikolaev district in Samara Province as our area of operations. According to expert calculations, this district could, under proper management, feed the entire Moscow region.

Not far from Saratov, at the river station of Uvek, the goods were loaded onto a barge. The hold of this barge had been converted into a makeshift department store. Between the curved ribs of the floating warehouse we nailed up portraits of Lenin and Marx, wreathed them in ears of grain, stocked the shelves with printed cotton, scythes, nails, leather; nor did we lack accordions and balalaikas.

Also there, in Uvek, we were reinforced by a tug, the *Ivan Tupitsyn*, named after a Volga merchant to whom it once belonged. The "headquarters"— Malyshev with his assistants and cashiers—was set up on the steamer. The guards and the clerks were quartered on the barge, under canopies.

It took us a week to load. Then one morning in July the *Ivan Tupitsyn*, belching greasy clouds of smoke, towed us up the Volga to Baronsk. The Germans called it Katharinenstadt. It was now the capital of the Volga German region, a beautiful area inhabited by manly folk sparing of words.

The steppe near Baronsk is covered with heavy golden wheat such as you find only in Canada. It is littered with sunflower crowns and oily clods of black soil. From Petersburg—licked clean by granite fire—we had been transported to a kind of Russian, and thus even more improbable, California. A pound of grain cost sixty kopecks in our California, and not ten rubles as in the north. We threw ourselves on the bread with a ferocity now impossible to convey; we plunged our chiseled canines into the cobwebs of dough. For two weeks after our arrival we were drunk with blissful indigestion. The blood now coursing through our veins, it seemed to me, had the taste and color of raspberry jam.

Malyshev had calculated correctly: trade was brisk. From every corner of the steppe slow streams of carts made their way to the riverbank. The sun slid over the backs of well-fed horses. The sun gilded the tops of hills of wheat. Wagons descended in a thousand dots down to the Volga. By the horses strode giants in woolen jerseys, descendants of the Dutch farmers settled on plots along the Volga in Catherine's day. Their faces were the same as they had been in Saardam and Haarlem. Under the patriarchal moss of their eyebrows, inside the fishnets of leathery wrinkles glistened drops of faded turquoise. The smoke from their pipes melted in the pale-blue lightning stretching over the steppe. The colonists climbed slowly up the gangplank onto the barge; their wooden clogs clamored like bells of composure and resolve. Old women in starched bonnets and long brown cloaks picked out the merchandise. The purchases were loaded onto the wagons. Local painters had sprinkled armfuls of wildflowers and pink bull snouts along the sides of these carts. Their exteriors were usually painted a deep shade of blue. Waxen apples and plums kissed by sunbeams glowed inside of them.

They arrived on camels from distant lands. The beasts settled down along the riverbank, presiding over the horizon with their drooping humps. Our trade would finish toward evening. The shop would lock up; the guards, all of them invalids, and the salesmen would strip and jump overboard into the Volga, aflame with the sunset. Across the distant steppe stretched red waves of wheat, walls of sunset crumbled in the sky. When the workers of the Produce Expedition to the Province of Samara (this is what we were called in official documents) went for a swim, it presented an unusual spectacle. The cripples sent muddy pink fountains shooting out of the water. The guards were one-legged or were missing an arm or an eye. They would link up in twos in order to swim. Two men with two legs between them would beat the water with their stumps, muddy streams stretched and swirled between their bodies. Grunting and snorting, the cripples would tumble onto the shore; they'd frolic and shake their stumps at the streaming heavens, bury themselves in the sand, and wrestle, kneading each other's severed limbs. After swimming we would go to Karl Biedermeier's tavern for dinner. This dinner crowned our days. Two waitresses with blood-brick hands, Augusta and Anna, would serve us ground cutlets—russet cobblestones trembling beneath streams of scalding butter and piled with stacks of roast potatoes. To flavor this mountain village of food they added onion and garlic. Jars of pickles were set before us. Through the little round windows cut high near the ceiling, the smoke of sunset drifted from the market square. The pickles stewed in the crimson mist and smelled like the seashore. We drank cider with our meat. Residents of Peski and Okhta, denizens of suburbs frozen yellow with piss, on each evening we felt afresh like conquerors. The little windows, carved into walls blackened by centuries, resembled portholes. Through them glimmered a little courtyard, divinely clean, a little German courtyard with rosebushes and wisteria and the violet abyss of the open stable. Cloaked old women on the porch knitted stockings fit for Gulliver. Herds were returning from the pastures. Augusta and Anna would sit down by the cows on milking stools. The cows' rainbow eyes glimmered in the dusk. It seemed like there was no war on earth and never had been. And yet the front of the Ural Cossacks lay twenty versts from Baronsk. Karl Biedermeier would never guess that the civil war was rolling toward his home.

At night I would return to our quarters in the hold with Seletsky, another clerk like me. He'd start to sing along the way. Heads in nightcaps would poke themselves out of lancet windows. The moonlight drained down red canals of tiles. The muffled barking of dogs rose above the Russian Zaandam. Augusta and Anna, frozen in place, listened to Seletsky's singing. His bass voice carried us away to the steppe, to the Gothic palisade of the granaries. Moonbeams trembled on the river, the darkness held on lightly; it retreated to the sandy banks; luminous worms wriggled in a torn net.

Seletsky's voice was of unnatural power. A great tower of a lad, he was one of those provincial Chaliapins who, to our good fortune, are sown throughout the Russian land in great number. He had the same face as Chaliapin— like a cross between a Scottish coachman and a nobleman from the time of Catherine the Great. He was simpleminded, unlike his divine prototype, but his voice, spreading boundless and deadly, filled the soul with the sweetness of self-destruction and Gypsy oblivion. He preferred convict songs to Italian arias. It was from Seletsky that I heard for the first time Grechaninov's "Death." Dread, implacable, passionate, it soared through the night above the dark waters:

> . . . She won't forget, she'll come and caress;
> She will embrace, with a love that's endless—
> And put a heavy bridal crown upon your head.

The song flows through this fleeting husk called man. It washes everything away and to everything gives life.

The front was twenty versts away. The Ural Cossacks, having linked up with Major Voženílek's Czech battalion, were attempting to drive the scattered Red detachments from Nikolaevsk. To the north, from Samara, the forces of the Komuch—the Committee of Members of the Constituent Assembly—were advancing. Our disorganized and undisciplined units regrouped on the left bank. Muravyov had just betrayed us. Vatsetis was appointed Soviet commander in chief.

Weapons were being brought to the front from Saratov. Once or maybe twice a week the pink-and-white steamboat *Ivan & Marya* pulled into the Baronsk pier. It was transporting rifles and ammunition. The ship's deck would be littered with crates on which skulls were stenciled, and beneath the skulls the inscription LETHAL.

The ship's captain was Korostelyov, an emaciated alcoholic with limp, flaxen hair. Korostelyov was an escape artist, an unsettled soul, a drifter. He had sailed the White Sea, walked across Russia, served time in prison and in monastic obedience.

On our way back from Biedermeier's we always used to drop in on him if we saw the lights of the *Ivan & Marya* from the pier. One night, having drawn level with the granaries, with that magical string of deep-blue and brown castles, we saw a torch blazing high in the sky. Seletsky and I were returning in that softened and impassioned condition produced by this unusual part of the country, by our youth, by the night, by the melting rings of fire on the river.

The Volga rolled by in silence. There were no lights on the *Ivan & Marya*, the hulk of the vessel lay deadly dark, only the torch tore up into the sky above. The flame smoked and flapped above the mast. Seletsky was singing, his pale face thrown back. He walked to the water's edge, and then broke off. We went up the ramp, which was completely unguarded. The deck was littered with crates and gun wheels. I pushed the door of the captain's cabin, it swung open. On the soaked table there was a tin lantern burning without the glass hood. The metal around the wick was melting. The windows had been nailed up with humpbacked boards. From the gas cans strewn under the table came a sulfurous draft of moonshine. Korostelyov sat on the floor in a sackcloth shirt amid green streams of vomit. His matted monkish hair stood around his face. Korostelyov stared up from the floor at his commissar, Larson the Latvian. The latter had a copy of *Pravda* in a yellow cardboard cover and was reading it by the light of the sinuous kerosene flame.

"So that's how you are," said Korostelyov from the floor. "Go on with what you were saying . . . Torture us, if you want . . ."

"Why should I talk?" Larson retorted, turning his back and shielding himself with his cardboard. "Better I should listen to you."

On the velvet couch, dangling his legs, sat a redheaded muzhik.

"Lisei," Korostelyov said to him, "vodka."

"All gone," replied Lisei, "and nowhere to get any . . ."

Larson pushed his cardboard aside and started chortling all of a sudden, like a drum roll:

"A citizen of Russia requires drink," said the Latvian with an accent. "The soul of this citizen of Russia has at last come undone, but over here it's dry as a bone . . . So why call it the Volga, then? . . ."

Korostelyov stretched out his thin childlike neck, splayed his legs in their sackcloth trousers across the floor. His eyes were full of plaintive bewilderment, then there was a glint in them.

"Torture us," he said almost inaudibly and stretched out his neck, "torture us, Karl . . ."

Lisei folded his chubby hands and looked sideways at the Latvian.

"Look at him, knocking the Volga like that . . . No, comrade, don't you knock our Volga, don't you insult it. You know how our song goes: 'Mother Volga, queen of rivers . . .'"

Seletsky and I were still standing by the door. I kept thinking of beating a retreat.

"Now, I cannot understand in any way at all," Larson addressed us, apparently continuing an earlier argument, "and perhaps the comrades could explain to me, how it can be that reinforced concrete is worse than birch and aspen, and dirigibles worse than the crap in Kaluga."

Lisei twisted his head in its padded collar. His legs didn't reach the floor, he was weaving an invisible net with his chubby fingers pressed to his belly.

"What do you know about Kaluga, friend?" he asked soothingly. "In Kaluga, I can tell you, you will find an illustrious people: a splendid people, if you want to know."

"Vodka," pronounced Korostelyov from the floor.

Larson again threw back his porcine head and burst out laughing.

"A cup for me, a cup for you," he mumbled, pulling the cardboard toward him. "Possibly maybe . . ."

Roiling sweat beat against his brow, oily streams of fire swam in the tangled mat of his colorless hair.

"Possibly maybe," he snorted again, "a cup for you, a cup for me."

Korostelyov felt around himself with his fingers. He began to crawl, hauling himself forward with his hands, dragging his skeletal frame in its sackcloth shirt.

"Don't you dare torture Russia, Karl," he hissed, when he had crawled over to the Latvian, hit him in the face with the tuft of his hand, and started squealing and pounding on him.

The Latvian puffed himself up and gazed haughtily at all of us over eyeglasses that had slipped down his nose. Then he wrapped his fingers around the silken river of Korostelyov's hair and mashed him face-first into the floor. He picked him up and dropped him again.

"Take that," said Larson abruptly and shoved the bony body away. "There's more where that came from."

Korostelyov, pushing himself up on his palms, got up on all fours like a dog. Blood poured from his nostrils, his eyes were squinting. They twitched, then he jerked and crawled under the table, howling.

"Russia," he pronounced under the table and started flailing, "Russia . . ."

The spades of his bare feet lurched and stretched. Only one word—like a hoot or a moan—could be made out in his screeching.

"Russia," he howled, with his arms outstretched and thrashing his head.

Redheaded Lisei sat on the velvet couch.

"They got going around noon," he said to me and Seletsky, "thrashing over Rushah, full of pity over Rushah . . ."

"Vodka," said Korostelyov firmly from beneath the table. He crawled out and stood himself up—his hair had mopped up the puddle of blood and now hung across his cheek.

"Where's the vodka, Lisei?"

"The vodka, my friend, is at Voznesenskoye, forty versts away—forty versts by water, fifty versts by land, however you like. There's a church there, must be moonshine, too. Do what they like, the Germans can't stop it."

Korostelyov turned around and went out on his straight stork legs.

"We're from Kaluga," Larson shouted out of nowhere.

"No respect for Kaluga," sighed Lisei, "do what you will . . . But me, I've been there, in Kaluga. An elegant people dwells there, an illustrious people . . ."

Outside, orders were shouted, the anchor rattled, up went the anchor. Lisei's eyebrows rose.

"Are you going to Voznesenskoye, perchance?"

Larson cackled, his head thrown back. I ran out of the cabin. Korostelyov stood barefoot on the captain's bridge. There was a brazen glint of moonlight on his torn-up face. The gangway dropped to the shore. Sailors went around pulling in the ropes.

"Dmitry Alexeyevich," Seletsky shouted up to him, "could you let us off, what've we got to do with this?"

The engines exploded and shifted to a disjointed sputter. The paddle wheel dug into the water. A rotten plank on the pier splintered softly. The *Ivan & Marya* turned its prow about.

"Let's go," said Lisei, emerging onto the deck. "Let's go to Voznesenskoye for some moonshine."

As the paddle twirled, the *Ivan & Marya* gained speed. The engine cultivated a greasy clank, a rustling, a whistling, like wind. We flew through the darkness, cutting corners, kicking aside beacons, spar buoys, and red lights.

The water foamed under the paddles, streaming behind like the gilded wing of a bird. The moon burrowed into the black whirlpools. "The fairway of the Volga is tortuous," I recalled a phrase from a schoolbook, "it abounds in shoals . . ." Korostelyov kept shifting around the captain's bridge. His gleaming blue skin was stretched tight on his cheekbones.

"Full steam," he said into the speaking tube.

"This is full steam," a muffled invisible voice replied.

"Give me more."

Silence below.

"The engine will blow," the voice replied, after a pause. The torch was blown off from the masthead and dragged over a rolling wave. The steamer reeled; an explosion shuddered down the hull. We were flying through darkness, headlong. Onshore a rocket flared up, and we were hit by a three-inch gun. A shell whistled between the masts. The cook's boy, hauling a samovar on the deck, raised his head. The samovar slipped from his hands, tumbled down the stairs, cracked open, and a gleaming stream shot down the dirty steps. The cook's boy grinned, crouched down on the steps, and passed out. From his mouth came the ghastly scent of moonshine. Below, among the greased cylinders, the stokers, stripped to the waist, were yelling, waving their arms about, falling to the floor. Their distorted faces were reflected in the pearly glow of the shafts. The crew of the *Ivan & Marya* were drunk. Only the helmsman stood firm at his wheel. He turned when he saw me.

"Yid," the helmsman said to me, "what'll happen to the children?"

"What children?"

"The children aren't learning," said the helmsman, spinning his wheel. "The children will become thieves . . ."

He brought his lead-blue cheekbones close to me and ground his teeth. His jaws grated like millstones. The teeth, it seemed, were being ground to sand.

"I'll chew you up . . ."

I backed away from him. Lisei was passing along the deck.

"What's going to happen, Lisei?"

"He'll just have to get us there," said the red-haired muzhik and sat down on a bench to rest.

He was put ashore at Voznesenskoye. There was no "church" to be found there, no lights, no carousel. The gently sloping bank was dark beneath a low canopy of sky. Lisei was swallowed by the darkness. There had been no sign of him for more than an hour when he surfaced right at the water's edge carrying gas cans. He was escorted by a pockmarked peasant woman, handsome as a horse. An ill-fitting child's blouse pushed her breasts together. Some kind of dwarf in a pointy cotton hat and tiny little boots, his mouth yawning wide, stood there, too, and watched us load.

"It's plum," said Lisei, setting the cans on the table. "The absolute plummest moonshine there is."

And then our spectral ship resumed its course. We reached Baronsk by dawn. The river stretched limitless. Water trickled down the bank like satin-blue shadow. Pink sunlight struck the fog that hung on clumps of brush. The dark painted walls of the granaries, their slender spires turned slowly and began to float toward us. We approached Baronsk in full song. Seletsky had cleared his throat with a bottle of the absolute plummest and let it loose. He worked in a bit of everything: Mussorgsky's "Flea," Mephistopheles' glee, and the demented miller's aria that goes, "I'm no miller—a raven am I . . ."

The barefoot Korostelyov was leaning back over the railing of the captain's bridge. His head swayed, his eyes were closed, his gashed face was thrown up to the sky, a vague childish smile wandered over it. He came to as we slowed down.

"Alyosha," said Korostelyov into the speaking tube, "full steam."

And we collided into the pier at full speed. The plank we had crushed when we left was now pulverized. They cut the engines just in time.

"Told you he'd bring us back," said Lisei, appearing next to me. "And you, my friend, was all concerned."

Onshore, Chapayev's *tachanka*s were already lined up. Rainbow stripes darkened and cooled on the bank just abandoned by the water. The pier was littered with ammunition crates dumped on previous arrivals. On one of the crates, sitting in a Caucasian fur cap and an unbelted shirt, was Makeyev, commander of one of Chapayev's detachments. Korostelyov went over to him, his arms spread wide.

"I did it again, Kostya, made a fool of myself," he said with his childish smile. "Used up all the fuel . . ."

Makeyev sat sideways on the crate, tufts of his cap hung around the brow-less yellow arches of his eyes. A Mauser with an unpainted handle lay on his knees. He fired without turning around, and missed.

"Hey hey, now now," babbled Korostelyov, radiant. "Getting all mad at me like that . . ." He spread his skinny arms even wider. "Hey hey, now now . . ."

Makeyev sprang up, spun around, and fired all the rounds in his Mauser. The shots rang out in rapid succession. Korostelyov wanted to say something else but didn't have time, sighed, and fell to his knees. He sank to the wheel rims of the *tachanka*, his face was blown apart, the milky plates of his skull were stuck to the rims. Makeyev, bending over, was trying to clear the last round that got jammed in the chamber.

"They had their little joke," he said, surveying the Red Army men and all the rest of us who had gathered around the gangway.

Lisei crouched and sidled over with a horsecloth and covered Korostelyov, stretched out long as a tree. On the steamer, the occasional shot could be heard. The Chapayev boys ran around the deck arresting the crew. The peasant woman, palm on her pockmarked face, gazed at the shore with her squinting, unseeing eyes.

"I'll give you an eyeful," Makeyev said to her, "I'll teach you to waste fuel."

The sailors were brought ashore one by one. Behind the granaries they were met by the Germans shaken from their houses. Karl Biedermeier stood among his countrymen. War had come to his doorstep.

That day we had a lot of work to do. The large village of Friedenthal had come to trade for goods. A chain of camels lay down by the water. In the distance, on the black-and-white tintype of the horizon, windmills began to turn.

By dinnertime we had dumped the Friedenthal grain into the barge; toward evening Malyshev sent for me. He was washing up on the deck of the *Tupitsyn*. An invalid with a pinned-up sleeve was pouring water for him from a pitcher. Malyshev snorted, grunted, put his cheeks under the stream. Drying himself with a towel, he said to his helpmate, apparently continuing an ongoing conversation:

"And that's as it should be. You may be a jolly good fellow three times over, been to the monasteries, and sailed the White Sea, and you may be a real desperado—but when it comes to fuel, for goodness' sake, don't go wasting fuel . . ."

Malyshev and I went into the cabin. There I surrounded myself with stacks of financial statements and started taking down a telegram to Ilyich:

"Moscow. The Kremlin. To Lenin."

In the telegram we reported the first shipments of wheat to the proletariat of Petersburg and Moscow, two trainloads with twenty thousand poods of grain in each.

1920–1925 (published 1932)

Crude

...L ots of news, as always. Shabsovich got a prize for oil cracking, walks around in fancy foreign labels, the bosses got promoted. When people found out about the appointment, everyone saw the light: he's a big boy now. That's why I stopped going out with him. The "big boy" now thinks he knows a mighty truth concealed from us ordinary mortals and has become so one hundred percent and orthodox (ortho*box*, as Kharchenko says) that he won't budge. When we ran into each other a couple of days ago, he asked me why I didn't congratulate him. I replied, "Who should be congratulated—you or the Soviet government? . . ." He got the message, swerved, and said, "Give me a call . . ." Right away, his better half got wind of this. Yesterday I get a call: "Klavdyusha, we've got connections with the Municipal Commerce Authority, in case you need any undergarments . . ." I replied that I hoped to live to see the World Revolution on my own clothes ration . . .

And now about me. As you already know, I'm manager of the Petro Syndicate. They wanted me for a while, but I kept turning them down. My reasons: I don't know how to push paper, and besides, I wanted to enroll at the Industrial Academy. The question came before the bureau four times, eventually I had to accept, and now I've got no regrets. From where I am, I get a clear picture of the entire enterprise, managed to get a couple things done, organized an expedition to our part of Sakhalin, intensified our prospecting, and I deal a lot with the Petroleum Institute. Zinaida is with me. She's doing well, expecting a baby soon, had lots of detours and dead ends . . . Zinaida told her Max Alexandrovich (Max and Moritz, I call him) about her pregnancy pretty late, in the fourth month. He pretended to be thrilled, planted an icy kiss on her forehead, and then made it clear that he was on the verge of a great scientific discovery, that his thoughts were far from quotidian existence, that he couldn't imagine anyone more unsuited to family life than he, Max Alexandrovich Sholomovich, but that, of course, he would absolutely not hesitate to give everything up, and so on, and so on, and so on . . . Zinaida, being a woman of the twentieth century, burst into tears, but kept it together. She couldn't sleep all night, gasping, craning her neck. At the crack of dawn, her hair uncombed, looking frightful in her old skirt, she ran to the Metallurgical Institute, begged him to forget what had happened yesterday—she'll get rid of the child but shall never forgive a world that could let this happen . . . All of this happening right in the hallway of the Metallurgical Institute, people everywhere. Max and Moritz blushes and blenches and mumbles:

"We should give each other a call, get together . . ."

Zinaida didn't wait to hear the rest, rushed back to me, and declared:

"I'm not going to work tomorrow!"

I blew up, saw no need to restrain myself, and told her off like the Levites of old. Just think, the girl's in her thirties, no great beauty, a good man would hardly blow his nose on her, and here comes this Max and Moritz (and it wasn't even her he was after but her race, her aristocratic forebears), gets herself knocked up by him—so keep it, raise it. Jewish half-castes turn out quite well, as we know—look at the specimen Anya produced—and when should you have a kid if not now, when the abdominal muscles still work and when you can still nurse the thing?! Her answer is always the same: "I can't bear my child to have no father"—in other words, we're still in the nineteenth century, General Papa will emerge from his study with an icon and curse her (or is it without an icon—I don't know how they used to curse), the maids will cart the infant off to the foundling home or to a wet nurse in the countryside.

"That's bunk, Zinaida," I say to her, "bygone days, bygone ways—we'll make do without Max and Moritz. I know these Jews and their sense of family—he'll come back on his own, running like a pig on a leash . . ."

I wasn't done talking when they called me to a meeting. At that time the question of Victor Andreyevich had to be resolved. And now we had to deal with the Central Committee's decision that, instead of the former version of the Five-Year Plan, oil extraction should be increased to forty million tons in 1932. The details were entrusted to the planners—in other words, Victor Andreyevich. He shuts himself up in his office, then calls me in and shows me a letter. Addressed to the Presidium of the Supreme Economic Council. The contents: I divest myself of responsibility for the planning department. I regard the figure of forty million tons to be arbitrary. More than a third must be found in unprospected regions, which means carving up the bearskin not just before the bear is killed but before it's been tracked. What's more, from the three cracking plants operating today we are, according to the new plan, jumping to a hundred twenty in the last year of the plan. And all this with a shortage of metal, and the fact that we have yet to achieve a state-of-the-art cracking process. The letter concluded as follows: like any mortal, I am all for high rates of production, but I have a responsibility, and so on and so forth . . . I read it. He asks:

"Should I send it or not?"

I say:

"Victor Andreyevich, your reasons and your whole attitude are unacceptable to me, but I don't think I have the right to advise you to conceal your views . . ."

So he sent the letter. The Supreme Economic Council hit the roof. They called a meeting. Bagrinovsky came from the council. They tacked a map of the Soviet Union to the wall showing the new oil fields, with pipelines for crude and refined petroleum; as Bagrinovsky put it:

"A country with a brand-new circulatory system."

At the meeting, young engineers of the "omnivorous" sort demanded that Victor Andreyevich be brought to his knees. I took the floor, went on forty-five minutes. "Though I do not doubt the knowledge and good intentions of Professor Klossovsky and even revere him, we reject this fetishism of numbers to which he is captive"—that's the idea I was defending.

"Let us reject the multiplication table as a guide to statecraft. If we had gone only by the raw numbers, would we be able to say that we'd fulfill the Five-Year Plan for crude-oil production in two and a half years? If we had gone only by the raw numbers, would we be able to say that as of 1931 we would increase our exports ninefold and become second only to the United States?"

Muradyan spoke after me, criticizing the proposed route of the Caspian-Moscow pipeline. Victor Andreyevich was silently taking notes. His cheeks had an elderly blush, a blush of venous blood. I felt sorry for him, didn't stay to the end, and went back to my quarters. Zinaida was still sitting in the study, her hands clasped.

"So are you going to have the child," I asked, "or not?"

She looks and does not see, wobbling her head she speaks and the words have no sound.

"There are two of us, Klavdyusha," she says, "me and my grief, stuck like a hump on my back . . . And how quickly one forgets—already I can't even remember how people live without misery . . ."

She says this, her nose poking out more than usual and quite red, her muzhik cheekbones (aristocrats sometimes have cheekbones like that) jutting out. I think, Max and Moritz wouldn't be so hot for you if he saw you like this. I started shouting and drove her to the kitchen to peel potatoes . . . And don't laugh—if you come, I'll make you peel potatoes, too. They gave us such tight schedules for planning the Orsky Factory that the design department and the draftsmen sit there working day and night; for dinner Vasilisa makes them potatoes and herring, fries an omelet—and the trumpets sound anew . . . So anyway, off she goes to the kitchen. A minute later I hear a scream. I come running—my Zinaida's on the floor, no pulse, eyes rolled back . . . Can't even describe what an awful time we had with her—Victor Andreyevich, Vasilisa, and I. We sent for the doctor. She came to in the night, touched my hand—you know Zina, how incredibly tender she can be. I could see everything in her had burned away over the course of those hours and everything was born anew . . . There was no time to lose.

"Zinyusha," I say, "we'll get Rosa Mikhaylovna on the phone (she's still our court councillor in such matters) and tell her you changed your mind and you're not coming. Can I call her?"

She gave me a sign—yes, go ahead. On the sofa next to her sat Victor Andreyevich, still feeling her pulse. I went out, and I could hear him saying:

"I am sixty-five, Zinyusha, each day my shadow grows fainter on the ground. I am a scientist, an elderly man, and now God (it's always God!) has so arranged things that the last five years of my life are to coincide with this—well, you know what I'm talking about—this Five-Year Plan. Until the day I die I'll have no time to catch my breath, to think of myself. And if my daughter didn't come by in the evening and pat me on the shoulder, if my sons didn't write me letters, I would be more sad than I can say. Have the child, Zinyusha, and Klavdia Pavlovna and I will look after it."

The old man is still mumbling, I call up Rosa Mikhaylovna and tell her, well, Rosa Mikhaylovna, my sweetheart, I know Murasheva promised to come tomorrow, but she changed her mind . . . I hear a bright voice on the telephone:

"That's brilliant, changed her mind, absolutely wonderful!"

Our court councillor is ever the same: pink silk blouse, English skirt, curled hair, freshly showered, always exercising, boys flirting with her.

Then I telephoned Mironchik to bring a car, he had enough tact not to come in a Ford but brought the Packard. We took Zinaida home, I tucked her in nice and warm, and made tea. We slept together—shed a few tears, remembered things best forgotten, talked everything over, mingling our tears, and fell asleep. My "devil" sat quietly at work, translating a technical book from the German. You wouldn't recognize the "devil" now, Dasha—he's all meek, hunched up, and quiet. I'm worried about it . . . All day he slaves away at the State Planning Commission, evenings he's doing his translations.

"Zinaida's keeping the baby," I tell him. "What should we call the boy?" (Nobody imagines it could be a girl.) We decided on Ivan—there are enough Yuris and Leonids already . . . I bet he'll be an obnoxious youngster with sharp teeth, teeth enough for sixty mouths. We've certainly made enough gasoline for him; he'll be driving his girlfriends to Yalta or Batum—not like us, who only get to go to Sparrow Hills. Good-bye, Dasha. The "devil" will write you separately. How are things with you?

Klavdia

P.S. I'm scribbling this at work, there's a racket upstairs, plaster falling from the ceiling. Our building, it turns out, constructed quite soundly by the firm of Scrape and Collapse, is still standing, and they're adding four more stories to the original four. Moscow is all torn up—trenches, pipes, bricks all over the place, streetcar lines all tangled, foreign machines flailing their trunks everywhere, ramming and rattling, everything smells like tar, smoke heaving like a house on fire. Yesterday I saw this young fellow on Varvarskaya Square . . . Big broad face, red shaved head gleaming, no belt on his peasant tunic, sandals on his bare feet. The two of us were hopping from one foothold to another, hill to hill, crawling out and then falling back in . . .

"This is what the thick of battle is like," he says to me. "The real front line's in Moscow now, miss, that's the real war."

He had a big kind face, smiling like a child. I can still picture him . . .

(published 1934)

Sulak

In 1922, Gulay's band was crushed in the Vinnytsa district. His chief of staff had been Adrian Sulak, a village schoolmaster. He had managed to escape across the border into Galicia, where the papers soon reported his death. Six years after these reports we learned that Sulak was alive and hiding in the Ukraine. Chernyshev and I were assigned to find him. Carrying work orders as livestock technicians in our pockets, we set off for Khoshchevatoe, where Sulak was from. The chair of the village soviet turned out to be a demobilized Red Army man, a plain, decent sort.

"You wouldn't part with a jug of milk around here," he told us, "in Khoshchevatoe they eat people alive . . ."

As we began to inquire about a place to stay, Chernyshev brought the conversation around to Sulak's cottage.

"You could," said the chairman, "the widow's there."

He took us to the edge of the village to a house with a tin roof. A dwarf of a woman in a loose white blouse sat by the hearth before a pile of cloth. Two crop-haired boys in orphanage jackets were bent over a book. There was an infant with a pasty swollen head sleeping in a cradle. Everything was cold and clean, like a monastery.

"Kharitina Terentievna," the chairman said hesitantly, "I'd like to lodge these good people here with you."

The woman showed us around the cottage and returned to her pile.

"The widow won't turn you away," the chairman said when we were outside, "her situation is such that . . ."

He looked around and then told us that Sulak served with the Yellow-Blues at one point and then switched over to the Pope of Rome.

"The husband's with the Pope of Rome," said Chernyshev, "but the wife has a new kid each year . . ."

"Plain as life," the chairman replied and picked up a horseshoe he saw on the road, "don't look at that widow like she's too small, she's got milk enough for five. Other women come to borrow her milk."

At home the chairman made us an omelet with fatback and put out some vodka. Once he was drunk, he climbed into bed atop the stove. From there we heard whispers, a child crying.

"Hannochko, I swear to you," our host was muttering, "I swear to you, tomorrow I'll go to the schoolmistress . . ."

"Quite the discussion," cried Chernyshev, lying next to me, "people are trying to sleep down here . . ."

The disheveled chairman looked down from the stove; his shirt was undone, his bare legs dangled.

"The teacher gave them coneys to breed at school," he explained apologetically, "she gave them a doe coney but no buck . . . The doe coney waited and waited, then, come spring—well, plain as life, she sprung for the woods. Hannochko," the chairman suddenly cried out, turning to the girl, "tomorrow I'll go to the schoolmistress, I'll get you a pair, we'll make a cage for them . . ."

The father and daughter discussed this for some time over the stove—he kept crying out "Hannochko," and at last fell asleep. Chernyshev was tossing and turning on the hay beside me.

"Come on," he said.

We got up. The moon glowed in the clear, cloudless sky. The spring ice had sealed the puddles. Sulak's garden, overgrown with weeds, was full of bare stems of corn and bits of scrap metal. A stable stood next to the garden; rustling could be heard inside, light flickered through the cracks in the boards. Chernyshev crept up to the gates, leaned against them, and the bolt gave way. We entered and saw an open pit in the middle of the stable with a man sitting at the bottom. The dwarf stood in her white blouse at the edge of the pit with a bowl of borsht in her hands.

"Hello, Adrian," said Chernyshev, "ready for supper? . . ."

The dwarf dropped the bowl, threw herself on me, and bit my hand. Her teeth clamped down, she was shaking and moaning. A gunshot came from the pit.

"Adrian," Chernyshev said as he took cover, "we need you alive . . ."

Below, Sulak was busy with the bolt of his gun, the bolt clicked.

"We're trying to talk to you like a human being here," said Chernyshev and fired.

Sulak fell against the chiseled yellow wall, groping at it, blood pouring from his mouth and ears, and then collapsed.

Chernyshev stayed with the body. I ran to get the chairman. We took away the slain man that same night. The boys walked alongside Chernyshev on the wet, faintly glistening road. The dead man's feet, in their Polish, hobnailed shoes, stuck out of the cart. The dwarf sat frozen by her husband's head. In the darkling light of the moon, her face looked metallic with its warped bones. A child was sleeping on her tiny knees.

"A regular dairy," Chernyshev suddenly said, making his way down the road, "I'll show you milk."

(published 1937)

Gapa Guzhva

Over the course of Butter Week in 1930 they put on six weddings in Velikaya Krinitsa. The carousing reached a level of rowdiness not seen in a long time. Customs of old were reborn. The father of one groom got drunk and insisted he be allowed to try out the bride—a practice abandoned in Velikaya Krinitsa some twenty years before. The father-in-law had already unwound his sash and thrown it to the ground. The bride, weak with laughter, tugged the old man by the beard. He puffed up his chest and came at her, guffawing and stomping his boots. In any case, the old man had no cause for alarm. Of the six bedsheets raised over the huts, only two were wet with nuptial blood—turns out the other brides hadn't gone on midnight strolls for nothing. A Red Army man, home on furlough, got ahold of one of the sheets, and Gapa Guzhva climbed after the other one. Bashing men on the head as she made her way through, she hopped onto the roof and began scrambling up the pole. It sagged and swayed under her weight. Gapa tore down the red rag and slid down the pole. On the flat part of the roof stood a table and stool, and on the table were a half liter of vodka and slices of cold meat. Gapa tipped the bottle into her mouth; with her free hand she was waving the sheet like a flag. Down below, the crowd crashed and danced. Gapa's stool kept slipping, creaking and coming apart underneath her. Herdsmen from Berezan, driving their oxen to Kiev, stared at the woman drinking vodka high above beneath the very sky.

"A woman?" the wedding guests replied to them, "nah, our widow's a devil . . ."

Gapa chucked bread, twigs, and plates from the roof. Having polished off the vodka, she smashed the bottle on the chimney ledge. The muzhiks below roared in approval. The widow jumped to the ground, untied the shag-bellied mare slumbering by the picket fence, and galloped off to get wine. She returned with flasks all over her like a Circassian bandoliered with cartridges. The mare was breathing heavily, rearing its head; her foal-heavy stomach sagged and swelled, her eyes trembled with an equine madness.

The wedding guests danced holding handkerchiefs, their eyes lowered and feet shuffling in place. Only Gapa let herself go like a city girl. She was dancing with her lover, Grishka Savchenko. They grappled like wrestlers; tore at each other's shoulders with stubborn animosity; fell to the ground with a rattling drumbeat of boots, as if someone had knocked them over.

It was the third day of weddings in Velikaya Krinitsa. The groomsmen, smeared with soot and wearing their sheepskins inside out, banged stove lids and ran around the village. Bonfires were lit right on the street. Mummers with painted horns jumped over them. They'd harness horses to washtubs, drag them over knolls, and gallop through the fire. Muzhiks dropped to the ground, overtaken by sleep. Housewives tossed broken dishes out into their backyards. The newlyweds had washed their feet and climbed atop their tall beds, and only Gapa was still dancing by herself in an empty shed. She was whirling around with her hair loose and a gaff in her hand. Her tar-covered club pounded the walls. The blows shook the structure and left black, sticky wounds.

"Ain't we deadly," Gapa whispered, twirling the gaff.

Straw and planks of wood rained down on the woman, the walls collapsing. She danced with her hair loose amid the ruins, amid the din and dust of splintering pickets, flying wood rot, and snapping planks. Her red-collared boots spun through the wreckage and stomped to the rhythm.

Night descended. Bonfires waned in their thawed-out pits. The shed lay in a disheveled heap on the hill. Across the road, a ragged little flame began smoking inside the village council hall. Gapa flung away the gaff and started running down the street.

"Ivashko," she shouted, bursting into the village council, "come out with us to drink our lives away . . ."

Ivashko was the representative of the Regional Collectivization Commission. It had been two months since he began his discussions with Velikaya Krinitsa. Resting his arms on the desk, Ivashko sat before a crumpled, chewed-up heap of papers. The skin around his temples was creased, sickly cat's eyes sagged in his skull. Two bare arcs protruded pink above them.

"Don't disdain our peasant ways," Gapa shouted and stamped her foot.

"I'm not disdaining nothing," Ivashko said sullenly, "it's just that it wouldn't be prudent for me to go out with you."

Gapa paraded before him, stomping and waving her arms.

"Come break bread with us," the woman said, "we'll be at your service, Deputy, only tomorrow, not today . . ."

Ivashko shook his head.

"Wouldn't be prudent for me to break bread with you," he said, "after all, what kind of people are you? . . . You all go around barking at dogs—I've lost eight kilos because of you . . ."

He chewed with his lips and closed his eyes a little. He reached out and groped around his desk for a canvas briefcase. He rose and lurched to the door chest first, dragging his feet as if he were walking in his sleep.

"He's pure gold, that citizen," Kharchenko the secretary said as Ivashko left, "he's a man of great integrity, it's just that Velikaya Krinitsa treated him rough . . ."

An ashen forelock hovered above Kharchenko's pimples and button nose. He was reading a newspaper, his feet hoisted on a bench.

"Just wait till that judge comes down from Voronkov," said Kharchenko, turning over a page, "then they'll remember."

Gapa pulled a pouch of sunflower seeds from under her skirt.

"How come all you remember is your job, Mr. Secretary?" she said. "How come you're afraid of death? . . . Since when does a muzhik refuse to drop dead? . . ."

Out in the street, a black swollen sky churned around the belfry; the wet huts slouched and slithered. The struggling stars were etched above them, the wind crept below.

From the front porch of her hut Gapa could hear the mumbling mono-tone of a rasping, unfamiliar voice. A wanderer looking for a place to spend the night sat on the stove with her legs tucked beneath her. The holy corner was braided in raspberry strands of light from the icon lamps. The tidy hut was draped in absolute quiet; the walls and partitions smelled of apples and alcohol. Gapa's large-lipped daughters stared up and down at the beggar. The girls were overgrown with short horselike hair, their lips were turned out, their narrow foreheads had a greasy, lifeless sheen.

"Tell me some lies, Granny Rakhivna," Gapa said leaning against the wall, "I do like listening to some lies . . ."

Sitting up beneath the ceiling, Rakhivna fixed her hair into braided rows along her little head. Her washed and disfigured feet were resting on the edge of the stove.

"Three patriarchs are reckoned in this world," said the old woman, lower-ing her crumpled face. "The Moscow Patriarch is imprisoned by our rulers, the Jerusalem Patriarch is with the Turks, so that means all Christendom is governed by the Patriarch of Antioch . . . He's sent forty Greek priests to the Ukraine to curse all the churches that had bells removed by the rulers . . . The Greek priests passed through Kholodny Yar, people seen them in Ostro-gradsk, by Forgiveness Sunday they'll be here in Velikaya Krinitsa . . ."

Rakhivna closed her eyes and fell silent. The icon lamps lit the arches of her feet.

"The Voronkov judge," the old woman said as she came to, "he collec-tivized Voronkov in a single day. He took nine squires and put them in a cold cell . . . The next morning it was their lot to be marched off to Sakhalin. But listen, my daughter, in every place that people live, Christ abides in glory . . . The nine squires spend the night in the cold cell, guard comes to get them . . . Guard unlocks the jailhouse door, in the full morning light, there's nine masters swinging from the rafters on their own belts . . ."

Rakhivna fussed for a long while before she lay down. Sorting through her scraps, she whispered with her God as you would with your old man lying next to you on the stove, then all at once her breath came soft. Another woman's husband, Grishka Savchenko, slept below on a bench. He lay curled up on the very edge as though he'd been run over, waistcoat riding up over his arched back, his head wedged into a pillow.

"That's muzhik loving for you." Gapa gave him a shake and began shoving him about. "I know all about that muzhik loving . . . Look how you turn your muzzle away from the wife, doing that little shuffle you do . . . But this ain't your house, this ain't Odarka's . . ."

Half the night they rolled around on the bench in the dark, their lips clenched, their arms reaching out through the darkness. Gapa's braid went flying across the pillow. Come dawn, Grishka sat up all of a sudden, groaned, and fell back to sleep with a grin on his face. Gapa could see the brown shoulders of her daughters, low-browed, big-lipped, black-breasted.

"Like camels," she thought, "where did they come from? . . ."

Darkness stirred outside the oak window frame. The dawn revealed a violet streak in the clouds. Gapa came out into the yard. The wind grasped at her like ice-cold river water. She harnessed and loaded sacks of wheat onto the sled—over the holidays everybody had run out of flour. The road wound its way through the fog, through the mists of dawn.

It took them till the next evening to finish up at the mill. It snowed all day. Back at the village, through a solid wall of sleet, snub-legged Yushko Trofim emerged before Gapa wearing a soaking-wet floppy-eared hat. His shoulders heaved and sank beneath a snowy ocean.

"Woke up, I see," he muttered, approaching the sled, and lifted his black bony face.

"What's that supposed to mean? . . ." Gapa pulled up on the reins.

"Last night all the bosses came down," said Trofim, "packed up that granny of yours real proper . . . The head of the collectivization committee came, local party secretary, too . . . They took Ivashko and put the Voronkov judge in his place . . .

Trofim's mustache bobbed up and down like walrus whiskers, wiggling with snowflakes. Gapa shook the reins and then tugged them again.

"But, Trofim, why the granny? . . ."

Yushko stopped, cupped his hands to his mouth, and shouted from a distance through the howling snow.

"Looks like she was agitating about the end of the world . . ."

He limped away, and soon his broad back disappeared in the sky that blended into the earth.

As she pulled up to her house, Gapa tapped on the window with her whip. Her daughters were loitering around the table in their shawls and shoes, like guests at a get-together.

"Ma," said the oldest, unloading the sacks, "Odarka came while you were out and took Grishka home . . ."

The girls set the table, prepared a samovar. Gapa ate and went to the village council. There, on benches along the walls, the old men of the village of Velikaya Krinitsa sat in silence. The window, shattered during earlier disputes, was covered with a sheet of plywood, the lamp glass had been wiped, a poster nailed to the pockmarked wall: NO SMOKING PLEASE. The Voronkov judge was reading at the desk with his shoulders hunched. He was reading a book containing the minutes of the Velikaya Krinitsa village council; the collar of his drab little coat was turned up. Sitting beside him, Secretary Kharchenko was writing up an indictment of his village. He was filling out columns with all the crimes, failures to deliver, penalties, all injuries evident or concealed. When he arrived in the village, Oslomovsky, the judge from Voronkov, declined to call meetings or convene a general assembly of citizens as commissioners before him had done; he made no speeches and simply asked for a list of anyone with unmet quotas, former traders, inventories of their property, crops, and farms.

Velikaya Krinitsa sat on the benches in silence. The scrape and hiss of Kharchenko's pen bustled in the stillness. There was a momentary stir when Gapa entered the council hall. Party chief Evdokim Nazarenko perked up when he saw her.

"Now here's our top party asset, Comrade Judge," Evdokim snickered and rubbed his hands, "our widow's ruined all the boys . . ."

Gapa stood by the door, screwing up her eyes. A grimace touched Osmolovsky's lips, wrinkles appeared on his narrow nose. He nodded and said, "Good day."

"She was the first one to sign up for the *kolgosp*," Evdokim gushed, trying to chase the clouds away, "then some good people had a talk with her and she signed out . . ."

Gapa didn't budge. Her face flushed brick-red.

". . . And good people say," she proclaimed in her low, ringing voice, "they say that on the *kolgosp* all the people will be sleeping under one blanket . . ."

The eyes in her impassive face were laughing.

"But I'm opposed to sleeping in a heap, we like sleeping two by two, and we like our *horilka*, goddamn it . . ."

The muzhiks started laughing and stopped abruptly. Gapa screwed up her eyes. The judge raised his sore eyes and nodded at her. He hunched even lower, put his head in his thin reddish hands, and plunged back into the minutes of Velikaya Krinitsa. Gapa turned to go, her stately back flashed before those who stayed behind.

Out in the yard on wet planks, his knees apart, sat Grandpa Abram, overgrown with proud flesh. Yellow locks of hair fell to his shoulders.

"What is it, Grandpa?" Gapa asked.

"Makes me sad," said the old man.

Back home, her daughters had already gone to bed. Late at night, inside the hut of Komsomol member Nestor Tyagay across the road, a mercurial tongue of light came on. Osmolovsky had arrived at his assigned quarters. The judge had taken off and thrown his sheepskin coat on the bench—supper awaited him, a bowl of sour milk and a crust of bread with an onion. He took off his glasses and pressed his palms to his aching eyes, this judge who was known in these parts as Two Hundred Sixteen Percent. That was how much grain he had managed to procure in the rebellious village of Voronkov. Secrets, songs, folk beliefs adorned Osmolovsky's percentage.

He chewed his bread and onion and spread out a copy of *Pravda*, instructions from the District Committee, and reports from the People's Commissariat for Collectivization. It was late, past one in the morning, when his door opened and a woman with a shawl across her shoulders stepped inside.

"Judge," said Gapa, "what'll happen to the whores? . . ."

"Won't be any need for them."

"Will whores be able to make a living or not?"

"They will," said the judge, "but another way, better."

The woman stared blankly into a corner. She touched the coin necklace on her breast.

"Thanks for your words . . ."

Her necklace jingled. Gapa left, shutting the door behind her.

The piercing, raging night threw itself upon her, thickets of mist, humps of ice with sparks of black. Clouds grew light as they swept low. Silence lay prostrate over Velikaya Krinitsa, over the flat, sepulchral, icy wasteland of the village night.

Spring 1930 (published 1931)

Kolyvushka

Four men came into Ivan Kolyvushka's yard: Ivashko, representative of the Regional Collectivization Commission; Evdokim Nazarenko, head of the village council; Zhitnyak, chairman of the newly formed kolkhoz; and Adrian Morinets. Adrian moved like a tower that had come to life and begun to walk. Clutching a collapsible canvas briefcase against his hip, Ivashko ran past the barns and burst into the cottage. Ivan's wife and two daughters were sitting by the window spinning thread on blackened spindles. In their long sleeveless gowns, scarves on their heads, and their clean bare little feet, they looked like nuns. Between the towels and cheap mirrors hung photographs of imperial ensigns, schoolmistresses, and townsfolk at the dacha. Ivan followed his guests inside and took off his hat.

"How much tax does he pay?" Ivashko asked as he spun around.

Evdokim had his hands in his pockets and was looking at the twirling wheel of the spindle.

Ivashko snorted when he learned that Kolyvushka paid two hundred sixteen rubles.

"That's the best he can do? . . ."

"Looks like . . ."

Zhitnyak stretched his dry lips across his face; Evdokim kept staring at the spindle. Standing at the doorway, Kolyvushka winked at his wife; she took out a receipt tucked behind an icon and gave it to Ivashko.

"And the seed fund? . . ." Ivashko asked abruptly, fidgeting impatiently with his foot, digging it into the floorboards.

Evdokim raised his eyes and looked around the house.

"As far as this farm goes," said Evdokim, "everything has been handed over, Comrade Chairman . . . As far as this farm goes, it couldn't be that there's anything that hasn't been handed over . . ."

The whitewashed walls converged in a cozy low cupola above the guests. The flowers in the lamp glasses, the plain cupboards, the polished benches—everything reflected an excruciating neatness. Ivashko bolted toward the door with his rickety briefcase.

"Comrade Chairman." Kolyvushka ran after him, "will I get instructions or what? . . ."

"You'll get notification," cried Ivashko, his arms dangling, and rushed off.

Adrian Morinets, inhumanly massive, moved along behind him. Tymysh, the cheerful bailiff, flashed through the gate after Ivashko. With his long legs Tymysh tested the mud of the village street.

"What is all this, Tymysh? . . ." Ivan called him over and grabbed his sleeve. The cheerful beanpole of a bailiff bent down and opened his jaw, stuffed with a raspberry-colored tongue and set with pearls.

"They're confiscating your house . . ."

"And what about me? . . ."

"You're being expelled . . ."

And Tymysh darted away on his cranelike legs to catch up to his superiors.

In Ivan's yard there was a horse standing in its harness. Its red reins lay thrown across sacks of wheat. Beside a crooked lime tree in the middle of the yard there stood a stump with an axe sticking out of it. Ivan put his hand on his hat, pushed it back, and sat down. The mare dragged the sledge over to him, stuck out her tongue, and folded it into a little spout. The horse was heavy with foal, and her belly was thoroughly distended. Playfully, she nuzzled and nibbled at the shoulder of her master's padded coat. Ivan stared down at his feet. Trampled snow rippled around the stump. Kolyvushka slumped over and pulled out the axe, raised and held it aloft for a moment, and then struck the horse on the forehead. One of her ears jerked up, the other twitched and fell; the mare moaned and bolted. The sledge turned over, casting sinuous stripes of wheat across the snow. The horse reared up high and threw her head back. She got tangled in the teeth of the harrow next to the barn. Her eyes bulged beneath a streaming veil of blood. She squealed plaintively. The foal turned inside her, a vein swelled across her abdomen.

"Forgive me," said Ivan, reaching out to her, "forgive me, my sweet little girl . . ."

The palm of his hand was spread open. The horse's ear was limp, her eyes squinted as circles of blood glistened around them, the neck formed a straight line with the muzzle. Her upper lip curled in despair. She pulled at the breech band and lurched, dragging the stuttering harrow. Ivan brought the axe behind his back. The blow landed between the eyes, the foal turned again inside the fallen animal. Circling the yard, Ivan went to the barn and rolled out the winnower. He swung slow and wide, smashing the machine, twisting the axe in the delicate lacework of the wheels and drum. His wife appeared on the porch in her long sleeveless gown.

"Mother," Ivan heard a voice far away, "Mother, he's destroying everything . . ."

The door opened; an old woman in sackcloth trousers came out of the house leaning on a stick. Yellow hair clung to the hollows of her cheeks, a shirt hung like a shroud over her flat body. The old woman stepped onto the snow in her shaggy stockings.

"Butcher!" she said to her son, taking away his axe. "What about your father? What about your brothers, slaving away like convicts?"

Neighbors were gathering in the yard. Muzhiks stood in a semicircle looking away. Some woman burst through and started shrieking.

"Enough, you wretch," her husband said to her.

Ivan stood against a wall. The rattling of his breath could be heard throughout the yard. It sounded like he was engaged in heavy labor, pulling in air and pushing it out again.

Kolyvushka's uncle Terenty ran around the gate, trying to lock it.

"I'm a human being," Ivan suddenly declared to everyone around him, "I am a human being, a peasant . . . You've never seen a human being before? . . ."

Terenty, pushing and crouching, chased the neighbors away. The gates creaked shut. They opened again that evening. A sleigh emerged with difficulty through the gate, rumbling and packed with possessions. The women sat perched atop the bundles like frozen birds. A cow walked along with a rope tied to its horns. The procession skirted the edge of the village and sank into the flat snowy waste beyond. Out there, the wind, billowing in blue waves, moaned and crushed everything from below. The sky behind them was like tin, braided with a gleaming diamond net.

Kolyvushka, staring straight ahead, walked down the street to the village council. A meeting of the new kolkhoz, "Rebirth," was taking place there. The hunchbacked Zhitnyak was sprawled behind the table.

"This change in our way of life—what is it, exactly, this change?"

The hunchback pressed his hands to his body before once again launching them into the air.

"Fellow villagers, we are moving into dairy and garden production, and this is of enormous significance . . . Our fathers and grandfathers trampled on a buried treasure with their boots, and now we're digging it up. And isn't it a disgrace, isn't it a scandal that, only sixty-odd versts from the main town, we haven't been farming scientifically? Our eyes were shut, we were running away, running from ourselves . . . What's sixty versts, after all—does anyone know? Around here that's an hour's time, but even that little hour is our own precious human property . . ."

The village council door opened. Kolyvushka walked over to the wall in his molded half coat and his tall hat. Ivashko's fingers jumped and burrowed into his stack of papers.

"Those without assigned voting rights," he said, looking down at his papers, "are asked to leave the meeting . . ."

Emerald streams of sunset poured through the dirty windowpanes. In the twilight of the village hut, sparks gleamed faintly through the damp smoke of shag tobacco. Ivan removed his hat, his crown of black hair falling loose.

He went over to the table where the committee sat: a farmhand named Ivga Movchan, the village council chief, Evdokim, and the taciturn Adrian Morinets.

"Everybody," said Kolyvushka as he put a bundle of keys on the table, "everybody, I'm quitting you all . . ."

The iron rattled and lay on the blackened boards. Adrian's distorted face emerged from the shadows.

"Where will you go, Ivan? . . ."

"People won't have me, maybe the earth will . . ."

Ivan tiptoed out with his head down.

"He's doing a number," Ivashko shrieked as soon as the door closed behind him, "a provocation . . . He went to get the sawed-off, he's not going anywhere except to get a sawed-off shotgun."

Ivashko banged his fist on the table. His lips were bursting with words about panic and the need to keep calm. Again Adrian's face loomed from a dark corner.

"No," he said out of the darkness, "likely not his shotgun, Chairman."

"I propose . . ." Ivashko shouted.

It was proposed that a guard be posted at Kolyvushka's house. Tymysh the bailiff was selected for the job. Grimacing, he brought a bentwood chair out onto the porch, collapsed in it, propped his shotgun and his truncheon at his feet. From the height of the porch, from the height of his village throne, Tymysh hollered at the girls, whistled, howled, and tapped his shotgun. The night was lilac, heavy, like a semiprecious stone. It was streaked with veins of frozen streams; a star descended into a well of black clouds.

In the morning, Tymysh reported that there were no incidents. Ivan spent the night with Grandpa Abram, an old man overgrown with proud flesh.

In the evening, Abram dragged himself to the well.

"What for, Grandpa Abram? . . ."

"For the samovar," said the old man.

They slept late. Smoke began to rise from the other houses; their door was still shut.

"He's vanished," Ivashko said at the kolkhoz meeting, "are we going to cry about it? . . . What say you, villagers? . . ."

His sharp quivering elbows splayed across the table, Zhitnyak was writing down the particulars of horses confiscated by the collective. His hump cast a trembling shadow.

"What else can we shove down our throats," Zhitnyak ranted as he wrote, "we need everything you can imagine now . . . We need artificial sprinklers, we need mechanical plows, tractors, pumps . . . Villagers, we are insatiable . . . Our whole country is insatiable . . ."

All the horses logged by Zhitnyak were bay and piebald, with names like Boy and Missy. Zhitnyak made the owners sign next to their last names.

He was interrupted by a distant, muffled stomping . . . A tidal wave crested and crashed over Velikaya Staritsa. A crowd surged along the broken street. Legless cripples rolled before it. An unseen banner hovered over the crowd. When they reached the village council, they slowed down and closed ranks. A circle took shape in their midst, a circle of ruffled snow, a clearing like the one left for a priest during a processional. In that circle stood Kolyvushka with his shirt untucked beneath his vest, his head all white. Night had silvered his gypsy crown, not a black hair was left. Snowflakes, like feeble birds carried by the wind, drifted beneath the warming sky. An old man with broken legs who had pushed his way through stared greedily at Kolyvushka's white hair.

"Tell us, Ivan," the old man declared, raising his arms, "tell the people what's in your heart . . ."

"Where are you chasing me, everyone," whispered Kolyvushka, looking around, "where will I go . . . I was born here among you . . ."

A grumbling crept through the ranks. Morinets elbowed his way to the front.

"Let him be," the cry caught fast in his mighty body, his deep voice trembling, "let him be . . . Whose share is he going to eat, anyway?"

"My own," Zhitnyak said and started laughing. Shuffling his feet, he went up to Kolyvushka and winked at him.

"Last night I slept with a woman," said the hunchback, "when we got up she made pancakes and we stuffed ourselves like wild hogs, farted up a storm, she and I . . ."

The hunchback suddenly broke off and stopped laughing, the blood drained from his face.

"You've come to put us up against a wall," he said softly now, "you've come to lord it over us with that white head of yours, make us suffer—only we won't suffer, Vanya . . . Right now we're sick of suffering."

The hunchback came closer on his thin, bandy legs. There was something whistling in him, like a bird.

"You ought to be killed," the idea came to him, "I'll get my gun and exterminate you."

His face became radiant, he gave Kolyvushka's hand a gleeful pat, and ran to the house to get Tymysh's shotgun. Kolyvushka swayed and then set off. The silver curl of his head disappeared down the swirling lane between the huts. At first he stumbled, then his feet became more certain. He turned onto the road to Ksenevka. No one has seen him in Velikaya Staritsa since.

Spring 1930 (published 1963)

NOTES

Odessa

5 **Kamennoostrovsky Prospect**   Known as the Gallery of Art Nouveau because of its period buildings, Kamennoostrovsky Prospect was, in the words of Osip Mandelstam, "one of the lightest and most irresponsible streets of Petersburg . . . Kamennoostrovsky: a feather-brained young man with starch in his only two stone shirts and a sea breeze in his streetcar-filled head. It is a young dandy out of work, carrying its houses under its arm like an idle fop returning with his airy bundle from the laundress" (Osip Mandelstam, *The Egyptian Stamp*, in *The Noise of Time*, trans. Clarence Brown [Evanston, Ill.: Northwestern University Press, 2002], 140).

5 *qui sait?*   French, "Who knows?"

5 **Isa Kremer**   A Russian Jewish soprano, Isa Kremer (1885–1956) moved to Odessa when she was twelve and began writing revolutionary poetry for a local paper. After studying opera in Milan, she went on to become a star of classical and popular song, singing in many languages, including Yiddish. She eventually moved to the United States and then settled in Argentina.

5 *quand même et malgré tout*   French, "all the same and despite everything."

6 **Utochkin**   The pioneering Russian aviator Sergei Utochkin (1876–1915) was born in Odessa. In 1929, fellow Odessan Yuri Olesha wrote that Utochkin "was considered a freak. He was a figure of fun. It's unclear why that was. He was one of the first to ride a bicycle, a motorcycle, an automobile, one of the first to fly. People laughed. He crashed flying between Petersburg and Moscow. People laughed. He was a champion, but in Odessa they thought he was the town madman" (my translation. English may be found in Yuri Olesha, "The Chain," in *Envy and Other Works*, trans. Andrew R. McAndrew [New York: Norton, 1981], 128).

6 **Black Hundreds**   A Russian ultranationalist movement of the early twentieth century consisting of landowners, clergy, government officials, and conservative intellectuals that became notorious for inciting pogroms against Jews.

7 **"The Nose," "The Overcoat," "The Portrait," and "Diary of a Madman"** The narrator lists four titles from Nikolai Gogol's Petersburg tales, as well as their best-known hero (Akaky Akakievich Bashmachkin, from "The Overcoat"), before mentioning Gritsko and Taras, characters from Gogol's earlier Ukrainian stories. Father Matvei Konstantinovsky (1791–1857) was a conservative religious fanatic under whose influence Gogol starved himself to death in 1852. Babel's suggestion is that the earlier, "southern" provincial Gogol was ultimately eclipsed by the gloomy "northern" Petersburg Gogol.

7 **As for Maupassant** Here, as in the story "Guy de Maupassant," the narrator refers to Maupassant's brief story "The Confession," which is arguably more a satire about the hard-boiled frugality of Norman farmers than it is about sex and sunshine. Céleste, a peasant girl, decides one day to accept Polyte's standing offer to do "a dance for two without music" because she is shocked to realize how much she has paid him over the past two years to drive her to the market. The story is framed as Céleste's confession to her mother, who stops beating her to ask, " 'Have you told him about the baby?' 'No, of course not.' 'Why haven't you told him?' 'Because very likely he'd have made me pay for all the free rides!' The old woman pondered awhile, then picked up her milk pails. 'Come on, get up, and try to walk home,' she said, and, after a pause, continued: 'And don't tell him as long as he doesn't notice anything, and we'll make six or eight months' fares out of him.' And Céleste, who had risen, still crying, disheveled, and swollen around the eyes, started off again with dragging steps, murmuring, 'Of course I won't say'" ("Confessing," in Henri Rene Albert Guy de Maupassant, *Complete Short Stories*, vol. 2 [London: Cassell, 1970], 431).

8 **Cross of the Holy Sophia** The Holy Sophia (Hagia Sophia, or "Holy Wisdom") cathedral served as the seat of the Orthodox Patriarchate of Constantinople from 537 until 1453, when it was converted to a mosque by the Ottomans. It became a museum in 1935. Many Russians—notably, including Dostoevsky—believed that it was Russia's messianic destiny, as the last remaining Christian empire, or "Third Rome," to retake Constantinople from the Muslim Turks.

Shabbos Nahamu

This story is from the Hershele cycle. Hershele Ostropolyer (1770?–1810) was a legendary Hasidic trickster based on an actual person, a ritual slaughterer who became a wanderer after his jokes offended community leaders in Ostropol, Poland. Hershele eventually found refuge as the court jester of Barukh ben Yechiel Tulchiner of Mezhbizh, the depressed grandson of the Baal Shem Tov, the founder of Hasidism. Babel based his story on one of the many popular Yiddish tales about Hershele. He refers to Hershele in one of the *Red Cavalry* stories ("The Rebbe") and in an entry in the *1920 Diary* in which he gazes at the faces in a synagogue in Dubno "and thinks of Hershele" (July 23). The first Sabbath after the fast day of Tisha b'Av is referred to in Hebrew as Shabbos Nahamu, meaning "Sabbath of Comfort." Tisha b'Av commemorates the destruction of the First Temple by the Babylonians in 586 B.C.E. and of the Second Temple by the Romans in 70 C.E., both events believed to have occurred on the ninth day of the Hebrew month of Av. Shabbos Nahamu is therefore a relief from mourning, deriving its name from Isaiah 40:1, which is read on this Sabbath: "Nahamu, nahamu, ami" ("Comfort ye, comfort ye my people"). This is often the first weekend on which observant Jews will travel, after the three-week period of mourning that precedes Tisha b'Av.

9   **Gapka**   A stereotypical Ukrainian name for a country girl. For example, see the servant Gapka in Nikolai Gogol's story "How Ivan Ivanovich Quarreled with Ivan Nikiforovich." The American equivalent would be something like "Mary Jane."

9   **there is a** *pan*   *Pan* and *pani* are, respectively, male and female honorific forms of address in Polish, reserved in the past for members of the *szlachta*, or Polish aristocracy.

10   **muzhiks**   Depending on the context, the term *muzhik* can mean a Russian peasant, male servant, manly person, husband, man, or guy. Here (and generally anywhere else it is used in English) it refers to a Russian peasant. See Michele A. Berdy, "A Muzhik for All Seasons," *Moscow Times*, December 10, 2010, http://www.themoscowtimes.com/opinion/article/a-muzhik-for-all-seasons/426008.html.

10   **about five versts**   A verst is an obsolete Russian unit of measurement equal to one kilometer.

12   **in all their robes and caftans**   The "robes and caftans" are *kuntush* and *chuham*, or, in Polish, *kontusz* and *żupan*, the chief components of the traditional dress of the male Polish aristocracy, who adopted these "eastern" garments as part of an ideology of "Sarmatism"—the belief that Polish nobles were descended from ancient Sarmatians who invaded and ruled the Slavic tribes before the sixth century.

Elya Isaakovich and Margarita Prokofyevna
Babel claims he was charged with pornography for this story. His trial was set for March 1917, but the February Revolution intervened.

15 **he'd be sent out with the convicts**   Jewish residence in the Russian Empire was heavily though inconsistently restricted to the Pale of Settlement in the west and southwest. Exceptions were made for merchants of the First Guild (the wealthiest variety and their servants), artisans, military veterans, doctors, pharmacists, midwives, prostitutes, and university students. Hershkovich evidently lacks a permit to stay in Orel, and vagrancy was once punishable by hard labor in Siberia.

15 **five poods**   A pood, roughly thirty-six pounds, consisted of forty funts and was an old Russian unit of measurement replaced by the metric system in 1924. Margarita weighs four poods, thirty funts, or almost 174 pounds.

17 **Moldavanka**   A largely Jewish, working-class Odessa neighborhood at the time, the Moldavanka began as a Moldavian (Romanian) settlement just outside Odessa in the early nineteenth century. By the early twentieth century, it had become the city's seedy industrial backyard.

17 **sit on the correspondence copybook**   Merchants were required to keep copies of all business correspondence in a copybook. Presumably, Hershkovich asks Margarita to sit on the book to blot the wet ink.

Through a Crack
This story was first published in 1917, with a note that it had been rejected by the imperial censor in 1916.

The Sin of Jesus
29 **Forgiveness Sunday**   In the Orthodox Christian calendar, Forgiveness Sunday concludes the revelry of Butter Week, commemorates the Expulsion from Eden, and liturgically inaugurates the Great Lent with Christ's words, "If you forgive men their trespasses, your heavenly Father will also forgive you, but if you forgive not men their trespasses, neither will your Father forgive your trespasses" (Mark 6:14–15). See also the note on "Forgiveness Sunday" attached to "Gapa Guzhva."

29 **Madrid and Louvre**   A famous Moscow hotel before the Bolshevik Revolution, the Madrid and Louvre was popular with actors, writers, and artists.

30 a Jaeger jersey German naturalist and hygienist Gustav Jaeger (1832–1917) advocated the wearing of rough fabrics, such as wool, close to the skin and inspired the creation of the Jaeger clothing brand.

Line and Color

33 **Alexander Fyodorovich Kerensky** Alexander Fyodorovich Kerensky (1881–1970) was a moderate socialist statesman who led the Provisional Government after the February 1917 Revolution, first as minister of justice, then minister of war, and finally as minister-chairman before he was overthrown by the Bolsheviks in the October 1917 Revolution. He spent the remainder of his life in exile, dying in New York City at the age of eighty-nine. In 1916, Kerensky would have been a deputy in the Russian imperial Duma, where he was a parliamentary leader of the socialist opposition to the tsar's government.

33 **Turkestan** The western part of this central Asian historical region was conquered by Russia in the late nineteenth century. Kerensky spent his youth in Russian Turkestan, an area comprising present-day Uzbekistan, Turkmenistan, Russian Tatarstan, Tajikistan, and Kyrgyzstan.

33 **Grand Duke Pyotr Nikolaevich** Grand Duke Pyotr Nikolaevich (1864–1931) was the grandson of Tsar Nicholas I. Babel offers an entirely fictitious biography for him, albeit one loosely inspired by the life of Pyotr's father, Grand Duke Nikolai Nikolaevich (1831–1891), who, having gone mad when an oral cancer spread to his brain, was sent away to Crimea.

33 **Helsingfors** Helsingfors is the Swedish name for Helsinki; Finland was part of the Russian Empire from 1809 to 1917.

33 **Fröken Kirsti** Babel uses *Fröken*, Swedish for "Miss," although Nikkelson is Norwegian with a Danish name. Parts of Denmark and Norway had been under Swedish control in the early modern period.

34 **the Klyazma** A river in central Russia that became a popular summer destination in the nineteenth century.

34 **master of our destinies** In June 1917, Kerensky attempted a renewed offensive against the Germans to honor Russia's commitments to the Allies—which enraged many workers and soldiers in Petrograd, resulting in the violent demonstrations of the "July Days." According to Kerensky's biographer Richard Abraham, Babel went for a walk with Kerensky at Bad Grankulla, a resort outside Helsinki (then called Helsingfors), in December 1916. Kerensky did in fact wear glasses but had left them "at home for reasons of vanity." Abraham

argues that Kerensky was no less potent an analyst of political reality than Lenin or Trotsky (with his famous spectacles), but that the Bolsheviks prevailed because of "the correlation of social forces" (Richard Abraham, *Alexander Kerensky: The First Love of the Revolution* [New York: Columbia University Press, 1990], 117). In June 1917, Trotsky's faction (the Mezhraiontsy, or "Interdistrictites," social democrats who straddled the Menshevik and Bolshevik positions) had not yet formally joined the Bolsheviks, as it would over the two months that followed.

Bagrat-Ogly and the Eyes of His Bull

In 1922, to improve his health and earn money, Babel traveled to Georgia and Caucasia (and in particular the Muslim region of Abkhazia), where he experimented with an Orientalist style. This story is a result.

35 **"Allah il Allah"** Mangling of the Arabic *la ilaha illallah*, "There is no God but Allah."

36 **Bay of Trebizond** A Black Sea port in northeastern Turkey located along the historical Silk Road, Trebizond is now known as Trabzon.

36 **feluccas** Wooden sailing vessels that typically ferry ten passengers through protected waters, such as rivers and bays.

My First Advance

The author dated this story 1922–1928. It was submitted and rejected in 1933 and published posthumously (along with "Froim the Rook" and "Kolyvushka") in New York in 1963. A shorter version of this story, called "Information," was published in a Soviet English-language journal in 1937. According to Antonina Pirozhkova, Babel attributed the plot to the journalist P. I. Staritsyn, who had "gone to a prostitute, gotten undressed, and, glimpsing himself in the mirror, he saw that he resembled 'an overwrought pink swine.' Disgusted, he quickly dressed, told the woman he was a boy with the Armenians [a catamite, in other words], and left. Sometime later he was on a tram when he saw this woman at a stop along the way . . . She called out to him: 'Greetings, little sister'" (*Babel*, 4:454).

38 **to write worse than Lev Tolstoy** In an interview from 1937, Babel stated, "As I read [Tolstoy's novella] *Hadji-Murad* again, I thought: this is the man one should learn from. Here the electric charge went from the earth, through the hands, straight to the paper, with no insulation,

quite mercilessly stripping off any and all outer layers with a sense of truth—a truth, furthermore, which was clothed in dress both transparent and beautiful" (Isaac Babel, *You Must Know Everything: Stories, 1915–1937*, ed. Nathalie Babel, trans. Max Hayward [New York: Dell, 1970], 213).

38 **"Whither goest thou, pilgrim?"**   Literally, "To what Palestines?"—an archaic Russian expression wherein the plural "Palestines" means "corners of the earth."

40 **Golovin's novel about the life of the boyars**   Possibly a novel about contemporary (not boyar) court life by Konstantin Fyodorovich Golovin (1843–1913), who published under the pseudonym K. Orlovsky. The phrase could also mean "a novel about the life of the boyar Golovin." Fyodor Golovin (1650–1706) was a favorite of Peter the Great's and was known as the last of the boyars and the first Russian prime minister, though I know of no novel about him published before 1934. A different general, Evgeny Golovin, fought the Chechens in the mid-nineteenth century; Golovinsky Prospect, where Vera lives, was named after him. It is the main thoroughfare of the New Town built in Tiflis (now known as Tbilisi, the capital of Georgia) during the early Russian imperial period in the nineteenth century and was eventually renamed after Rustaveli, the thirteenth-century poet who wrote the Georgian national epic *Knight in the Panther Skin*. Golovin—from the word *golova*, or "head"—is also the surname of Lev Tolstoy's protagonist in *Ivan Ilyich*.

Guy de Maupassant

44 **the winter of 1916**   In 1916 Babel enrolled as a law student at the Petrograd Psycho-Neurological Institute, which would have meant a residence permit and thus no need for a forged passport. This was also when he befriended Gorky, who would publish several of his stories.

44 **Blasco Ibáñez**   Vicente Blasco Ibáñez (1867–1928) was a Spanish Republican politician, a journalist, and a best-selling novelist, whose books—which often inspired Hollywood films—were popular in Russia at the time.

46 **"An Idyll"**   The action of Maupassant's "Idylle" (1884) takes place toward dusk (not noon) on a train from Genoa (not Nice) to Marseille. Babel published a Russian translation of the story in 1926–1927.

48 *L'Aveu*   See the note concerning Maupassant's "The Confession" attached to "Odessa."

49 **night had slipped** The Russian *podlozhil pod* (literally, "placed under") can mean to line or bolster (as with a pillow), to add (as in wood to a fire), place as an obstacle, to place furtively, or to play a trick. "Slipped" retains some of that ambiguity.

49 **the 1624 edition** In 1624 the Portuguese Inquisition censored a passage in Cervantes's *Don Quixote* (part 1, chapter 26) in which the hero fashions a rosary out of his torn shirttail.

49 **a dedication to the duc de Broglie** Most likely Jacques-Victor-Albert, fourth duc de Broglie (1821–1901), a French monarchist politician, diplomat, and writer, whose 1882 speech is the basis for a fictional one given by Comte de Lambert-Sarrazin in a parliamentary scene in Maupassant's *Bel-Ami*.

49 **crawled about on all fours and ate his own excrement** Babel means Laure Le Poittevin. Elif Batuman has noted that "according to contemporary Babel scholarship, 'neither Maynial nor any other biographer has Maupassant walking on all fours or eating his own excrement'; the image appears to be borrowed from either [Zola's] *Nana* (Count Muffat crawls at Nana's feet, thinking of saints who 'eat their own excrement') or *Madame Bovary* (a reference to Voltaire on his deathbed, 'devouring his own excrement') . . . Babel mentions neither Voltaire nor Zola nor Flaubert—except to claim that Maupassant's mother is Flaubert's cousin: a false rumor explicitly controverted by Maynial" (Elif Batuman, "Babel in California," *n+1*, no. 2 [Spring 2005]: 79).

49 *va s'animaliser* The French that Babel uses would be more accurately translated as "Mr. de Maupassant *is becoming* an animal." The quote does not actually come from a medical chart but is a bastardized version of an entry in Edmond de Goncourt's diary, as cited in Édouard Maynial, *La Vie et l'Œuvre de Guy de Maupassant* (Paris: Société de Mercure de France, 1907), 282: Goncourt writes that Maupassant's Dr. Blanche, whom he had met in a salon, "laisse entendre qu'il Maupassant est en train de *s'animaliser*" (suggests that Maupassant is in the process of becoming an animal).

The Road

51 **began bombing the city** The Eastern Front of World War I collapsed after the Bolsheviks overthrew Kerensky's Provisional Government (which had attempted a disastrous offensive against the Germans in July) and declared Russia's withdrawal from the war. Mikhail Artemyevich Muravyov (1880–1918) led Red Guard units against the

Central Rada of Ukraine in January 1918 and, by early February, had taken Kiev from the Ukrainian Central Council government; cruelty characterized his takeover of Kiev. Hearing of the Left Socialist Revolutionary uprising against the Bolsheviks in early July, he left the front open, allowing the Whites to take Simbirsk, only to be captured by the Bolsheviks and shot trying to draw a gun.

51 **the "complex method" of teaching** As Carol Avins pointed out to me, the "complex method" was associated with the Dewey-inspired psychologist and educational reformer Pavel Blonsky (1884–1941) and involved active, theme- and project-based experiential learning. It was adopted by the Soviets in the early 1920s.

51 **Lunacharsky** Anatoly Lunacharsky (1875–1933) was the first Soviet commissar of enlightenment (from 1918 to 1929), responsible for education and culture. He instituted Soviet censorship, while protecting many of the writers and artists of the Russian avant-garde during his tenure.

51 *treyf* Yiddish for nonkosher food.

52 **"Ankloyf, Chaim . . ."** Yiddish, "Run, Chaim." The stereotypically Jewish name Chaim also means "life" in Hebrew.

52 **that nation of yours** The medical orderly is evidently a Ukrainian nationalist, opposed to the Marxist internationalism that would serve as a pretext for Soviet expansion into the western areas of the former Russian Empire. Like many anti-Communists at the time (and, for that matter, today), he conflates the Bolsheviks with the Jews. In fact, according to Liliana Riga, ethnic Russians formed the largest contingent in the early Soviet leadership, while Latvians were overrepresented by a factor of 7:1, and Jews, Georgians, and Armenians 4:1 (Liliana Riga, *The Bolsheviks and the Russian Empire* [New York: Cambridge University Press, 2012], 16). And as Vadim Abramov has noted, although Jews, as a formerly oppressed Russian imperial minority, were deemed trustworthy in the early years of Communist rule, their number in the secret police never exceeded 9 percent (Vadim Abramov, *Evreyi v KGB* [Moscow: Yauza Press, 2005], 8).

53 **The Cheka was set up at Number 2** Operating between 1917 and 1926, the Cheka (Emergency Committee) was the first of a series of Soviet secret police and political security organizations (including the OGPU, NKVD, MGB, and the better-known KGB). Soviet and Russian security agents are still sometimes referred to as Chekists. Gorokhovaya 2 is now the location of the Museum of the History of Political Police and Organs of State Security.

53 **Anichkov Palace** The Anichkov Palace became the Petersburg residence of Tsar Alexander III, his wife, Maria Fyodorovna, and their children, including the last Russian tsar, Nicholas II. Nicholas II's mother, after becoming dowager empress, continued to have right of residence in the palace until the February Revolution. After the revolution the Ministry of Provisions moved there.

53 **Yehuda Halevi** Yehuda Halevi (1075–1141) was a Spanish Jewish physician, poet, and philosopher. In 1140, moved by religious conviction, he decided to travel to the Crusader kingdom of Jerusalem. Greeted by friends in Egypt, according to the *Jewish Encyclopedia* (New York: Funk and Wagnalls, 1906), "he resisted the temptation to remain there, and started on the tedious land route trodden of old by the Israelitish wanderers in the desert . . . It is related that as he came near Jerusalem, overpowered by the sight of the Holy City, he sang his most beautiful elegy, the celebrated 'Zionide,' 'Zion ha-lo Tish'ali' [Zion, thou art anxious for thy captives]. At that instant he was ridden down and killed by an Arab, who dashed forth from a gate" (347). As Vladimir Khazan and Lev Usyskin have noted, there are a great many resonances between Halevi's last days, his "Ode to Zion," and Babel's story.

54 **Anichkov Bridge** The Anichkov Bridge, along which Nevsky Prospect crosses the Fontanka River, is the most famous bridge in Petersburg thanks largely to its four statues, *The Horse Tamers*, designed by the Russian sculptor (of Baltic German origin) Baron Peter Klodt von Jürgensburg. One of the statues depicts a tamer about to be trampled by a horse—not unlike the aforementioned Yehuda Halevi.

54 **about nine poods** Approximately 325 pounds. Tsar Alexander III (1845–1894) was indeed rotund.

55 **Sultan Abdul-Hamid** Abdülhamid II (1842–1918) was the thirty-fourth sultan of the Ottoman Empire and the last to wield autocratic control over the crumbling Turkish state. He was deposed by the Young Turks in 1909.

55 **"À sa majesté, l'Empereur de toutes les Russies"** French, "To His Majesty, emperor of all the Russias."

55 **Maria Fyodorovna's library . . . her sister, the queen of England** Maria Fyodorovna (1847–1928), christened Dagmar, was a Danish princess who became empress of Russia when she married Alexander III of Russia. She was the sister of Britain's Queen Alexandra and of King George I of Greece. Her son was the last Russian tsar, Nicholas II, whom she outlived by ten years, to the end refusing to believe he and his family had been murdered by the Bolsheviks in 1918.

55   **a talk with Uritsky**   Mikhail (born Moisey) Uritsky (1873–1918) was the chief of the Petrograd Cheka (Bolshevik secret police). He was assassinated the same day that Fanya Kaplan tried to kill Lenin—events that served as the pretext for the Red Terror that would claim perhaps more than a hundred thousand political and "class" enemies during the Russian Civil War. Uritsky's assassin, a poet and socialist cadet named Leonid Kannegisser (1896–1918)—whose father was a mechanical engineer and the head of Russia's largest shipyards in Nikolaev (where Babel had grown up)—apparently acted because Uritsky had executed his lover and fellow officer Viktor Pereltsveig. Kannegisser's publisher, Mark Aldanov (Landau), claimed that Uritsky's assassination was intended to restore the "good name of the Russian Jews."

56   **translating testimony given by diplomats, provacateurs, and spies**   Although there is no documentary evidence to confirm that Babel worked for the Cheka, it is possible that he did interpretation and translation for the organization in 1918—albeit an odd and perhaps unlikely activity given that Babel was publishing stories in opposition (non-Bolshevik) journals at that time. However, in 1930, when Babel published this story, he had been falsely accused of making anti-Soviet comments to an émigré journalist while traveling in Europe, and so it would have suited him to emphasize or even invent this connection to the Cheka. Moreover, as Janneke van de Stadt has noted, Babel told the anti-Stalin Marxist émigré Boris Souvarine that there were valuable literary works in the Cheka archives, which contained the confessions that educated "diplomats, provacateurs, and spies" were required to write upon arrest—many of which made for good fiction as the victims attempted to invent autobiographies they thought might please the secret police. Van de Stadt suggests that this is also what Babel was attempting to do in this story. See Janneke van de Stadt, "Two Tales of One City: Isaac Babel, Fellow Traveling, and the End of NEP," *The NEP Era: Soviet Russia 1921–1928* 6 (2012): 1–25, and Cristina Vatulescu, *Police Aesthetics: Literature, Film, and the Secret Police in Soviet Times* (Stanford, Calif.: Stanford University Press, 2010), 41.

Childhood. At Grandmother's

61   **Turgenev's *First Love***   One of Turgenev's finest novellas, whose title Babel borrowed for one of his own childhood tales, "First Love" (1860) contains a scene in which the uncomprehending sixteen-year-old hero, Vladimir, spies his father lashing Zinaida's arm (not her cheek). She

kisses the welt, whereupon the father rushes into her house. Later, Vladimir has a dream in which his father lashes Zinaida across the forehead. Vladimir was infatuated with Zinaida, his "first love." But as he narrates his tale, years after his father's early death, he is filled with the retrospective understanding that his first love was never his nor even his first, and, instead of feeling Oedipal resentment for his father, Vladimir is filled with a muted sense that his first, true, and unfulfilled love was between him and his father, whose demise seems connected to Zinaida's. Why is young Babel so transfixed by this story? Perhaps because it depicts violence as intoxicating, vaguely intertwined with love, not as an expression of freedom or will but of beautiful tragedy, hopelessness, illness turned inward by intellectual introspection, turned outward by the likes of Benya Krik.

63 **"You must know everything."**   This is the title selected for this story in Max Hayward's early English translation and, indeed, for the collection (edited by Nathalie Babel) where it was published. Jonathan Brent has pointed out to me that these words contain an echo of two passages in *From the Fair: The Autobiography of Sholom Aleichem*, trans. Curt Leviant, (New York: Viking, 1985): (1) ". . . was there a connection between fiddling and knowledge? Well, there was a connection. . . . Along with other subjects, like German or French for a child of a good family. No one expected any practical benefit from it, but if you came from a good home . . . , you had to know everything" (168); (2) " 'as soon as the doorbell rings, grab the thickest book you can find, immerse yourself in it, and rub your forehead. Don't dare let a client slip out of your hands until you've squeezed him dry. And remember, there is nothing under the sun to which you'll admit 'I don't know'—because you know everything!'" (270)

63 **beneath seven seals**   A Russian fairy-tale formula.

63 **Saratov, November 12, 1915**   The Kiev Commercial Institute, where Babel was enrolled from 1911 to 1916, was evacuated to Saratov at the beginning of World War I.

The Story of My Dovecot

64 **the town of Nikolaev**   Nikolaev, or Mykolaiv, as it is now known in Ukrainian, is about a hundred and thirty kilometers east of Odessa. Babel (born Bobel) and his family moved here from the seedy Jewish working-class Moldavanka district of Odessa several months after he was born, in 1894. Babel was denied admission to the preparatory

class of the Count Witte Commercial School (not the gymnasium) in Nikolaev "for lack of vacancies" in 1903 (not 1904) and enrolled in its first grade in 1904 (not 1905). At the end of 1905, Babel left Nikolaev to live in Odessa with his aunts. According to Antonina Pirozhkova's account, Babel told her that even his childhood stories were not auto-biographical, that he used his own name as a shortcut in order to avoid describing the narrator's appearance and background. At the same time, it is clear that the narrator strives for a kind of documentary effect in these stories. See Pirozhkova, "Years at His Side (1932–1939) and Beyond," *Canadian Slavonic Papers / Revue Canadienne des Slavistes* 36, no. 1/2, Centenary of Isaak Babel (March–June 1994): 169–240 (205).

64 **Now, after two decades . . . scared I was.** Omitted in later editions.

64 **less than 5's** Five is the highest grade, an A.

64 **a mere five percent** It was, in fact, 10 percent, and the Jewish quota was 50 percent at the commercial school the author actually attended.

64 **Khariton Ephrussi** The Ephrussis were a well-known Jewish grain, oil, and banking dynasty, initially based in Odessa. Charles Ephrussi (1849–1905), art historian and proprietor of the *Gazette des Beaux-Arts*, was an inspiration for Charles Swann in Marcel Proust's *À la recherche du temps perdu*. Edmund de Waal's *The Hare with Amber Eyes* offers a history of the Ephrussis, but lists no Khariton in de Waal's family tree.

65 **an unrivaled 5-plus** Literally, "five with a little cross," in other words, an A+.

65 **Our little town . . . a father to me.** Omitted in later editions.

65 **who do no heavy labor, an inoffensive** Omitted in later editions.

65 **assistant curator Pyatnitsky** The Russian word *pyat'* means "five."

66 **Belaya Tserkov** City in central Ukraine in the Kiev district.

67 **Polish Uprising of 1861** Also known as the January Uprising, the Polish Uprising was preceded by demonstrations in Congress Poland against conscription into the Russian Army, followed by an Imperial decree of martial law in 1861 and an insurrection that began in January 1863 and was put down by 1865.

68 **had defeated Goliath** See 1 Samuel 17. Of course, David was not yet king when he challenged Goliath on King Saul's behalf.

68 **even mother had a drop of wine** In earlier editions, "even mother drank until she was drunk."

68 **Hunters Square** I.e., the bird market. However, there was no Hunters Square (Okhotinskaya) in Nikolaev; that was in Odessa. There is a kind of blurring of verisimilitude in this "autobiographical" tale. Moreover, October 20, 1905—one of the dates on which pogroms

swept Nikolaev, Odessa, and other towns across the Ukraine after the granting of the Manifesto on the Improvement of the State Order on October 17—was a Thursday, not a Sunday.

68 **unexpected obstacles** An earlier version has "sudden troubles blocked my way."

71 **Son of Man** In Christian scriptures, Jesus refers to himself as the "Son of Man" more often than the "Son of God." Makarenko uses the former term to connote his own evidently Christlike suffering as someone who is missing out on the best loot from the pogrom.

71 **the startails** The narrator names the breed of pigeons here for the first time: *turmany*. Most likely these are Rzhev Startailed Turmans, a Russian breed said to have been developed in Afghanistan and brought to Moscow as spoils of war from Turkish-held cities in Ukraine around 940 C.E.

71 **He swung and struck me with the palm clutching the bird** An earlier edition telegraphs the graphic description to come: "He swung and struck me, close-palmed, the dove cracked on my temple."

71 **a great steed** An earlier version has "a lame and vigorous steed."

72 **a procession with the cross** The Black Hundreds would often incite a pogrom with a religious procession.

First Love

74 **Japanese War** The narrator is referring to the Russo-Japanese War (1904–1905), which was fought between the Russian and Japanese Empires in Manchuria and Korea and resulted in a humiliating defeat for Russia—a defeat that exacerbated domestic problems for Tsar Nicholas II.

74 **In her jubilant eyes** Replaced in later editions with "I saw in them . . ."

75 **"I was tormented by unbridled fantasies"; "only in children these feelings are more secretive, exalted, ardent"** These phrases are omitted in later editions.

75 **the pogrom against the Jews that broke out in 1905** In the aftermath of the failed 1905 Revolution, 3,000 Jews were massacred in 690 pogroms across the western Russian Empire; 800 were killed in Odessa alone. In Nikolaev, Babel's family had taken refuge with their gentile neighbors, and their property was spared.

75 **quickly looked around** Later editions have "turned away," a less sexually furtive gesture.

75 **"Look here," he said** An earlier edition has instead " 'Babel.' "

76 **the Molokans** A pacifist nonconformist Spiritual Christian sect with Judaizing tendencies that arose in the seventeenth century, the Molokans took their name from the Russian word for "milk," which they drank during the fast days of Lent, when Russian Orthodox practice abjures meat and milk. Old Believers separated after 1666 from the official Russian Orthodox Church as a protest against Patriarch Nikon's reforms, and they continue liturgical practices that the church maintained before the implementation of these reforms. In the late modern period many Russian Old Believer merchant families were more open to industrial innovation, which may be why Vlasov confuses them with wealthy Jews (who adhere to the Torah, or the "Old Testament").

76 **and its thick, patient, hairy muzzle** Omitted in later editions.

76 **and trembled out of love for me** Omitted in later editions.

77 **flush with unforgiving winter glee, like a rich girl at the skating rink** Omitted in later editions.

78 **shammes** A synagogue sexton.

78 **tsar's manifesto of October 17** The October Manifesto, or the Manifesto on the Improvement of the State Order, promised basic civil rights and an elected assembly or Duma. It represented Tsar Nicholas II's reluctant concession to the unrest of 1905, and was soon followed by reaction, pogroms, repression, and martial law.

78 **Father's face . . . come to grief.** Omitted in later editions.

79 **His failing eyes were ringed with tears.** Omitted in later editions.

79 **rolling in my own green vomit** Omitted in later editions.

79 **try to bear it, my poor Babel** Omitted in later editions.

79 **I tossed on the bed . . . straight from the heart.** Omitted in later editions.

79 **"This disorder . . . affects only women."** Omitted in later editions.

80 **And now . . . terrible decline.** Omitted in later editions.

Awakening

81 **From Odessa came Mischa Elman, . . . Zagursky** Zagursky was based on the famous music teacher Pyotr Stolyarsky (1871–1944), a family friend who taught Babel and went on to teach the great violinist David Oistrakh. Leopold Auer (1845–1930), a converted Hungarian Jew, was a renowned violinist and professor at the St. Petersburg Conservatory. Mischa Elman (1891–1967), Efrem Zimbalist (1890–1985),

and Jascha Heifetz (1901–1987) were among the most acclaimed violinists of the twentieth century; Ossip Gabrilowitsch (1878–1936) was a noted pianist, conductor, and composer who was married to Mark Twain's daughter.

81 **what a Gobelin was, why the Jacobins betrayed Robespierre** A Gobelin is a decorative tapestry, named after the Gobelins Manufactory in Paris. Maximilien Robespierre (1758–1794) was a French Revolutionary Jacobin elected to the nine-member Committee of Public Safety in 1793, formally inaugurating the Reign of Terror; he was executed by his fellow Jacobins a year later, accused of behaving like a dictator after he led a festival inaugurating his deist Cult of the Supreme Being. See, in this collection, "In the Basement," which makes reference to Spinoza (viewed as a precursor of deism) and Julius Caesar (like Robespierre, betrayed by his allies, who accused him of aspiring to dictatorship).

83 **Benvenuto Cellini** An Italian goldsmith, sculptor, draftsman, soldier, musician, and artist, Benvenuto Cellini (1500–1571) wrote an important and very colorful autobiography, full of grandiose boasts and supernatural tales. His life was the inspiration for other creative works, including a novel by Alexandre Dumas père and an opera by Berlioz.

85 **De Ribas** Deribasovskaya, or De Ribas Street, is named after José de Ribas (1749–1800), a Spanish officer in Russian service, who helped build Odessa, served as its first mayor, and lived on that street.

85 **There was nowhere to run.** Omitted in later editions.

85 **Cadet Corps** An exclusive academy that trained children of the nobility—which would certainly not include the narrator—for service as officers in the tsar's army.

In the Basement

88 **My report card consisted of 3-minuses.** A 3-minus, like a C-minus, is a nominally passing grade, unlike a 2, which is a failing grade (D).

92 **He was shouting his usual repertoire.** Omitted in later editions.

93 **Serenity and determination took hold of me.** Omitted in later editions.

94 **I let her have them.** Omitted in later editions.

Di Grasso

95 **Anselmi and Tito Ruffo** Baritone Tito Ruffo (1877–1953) and tenor Giuseppe Anselmi (1876–1929) were Italian opera stars.

95 **Chaliapin**   Feodor Chaliapin (1873–1938) was a bass vocalist and well-known Russian opera singer of the early twentieth century. He did not return to Russia after 1921.

96 **the most remarkable actor of the century**   Di Grasso is based on the Sicilian actor Giovanni Grasso, "Senior" (1873–1930), who toured Russia when Babel would have been fourteen. Gregory Freidin identifies the play described here as *Maria Rosa* by Catalan dramatist Ángel Guimerá, who reworked it for Grasso with the new title *Feodalesimo*, which was reviewed by a Petersburg critic in 1909; see Gregory Freidin, "Fat Tuesday in Odessa: Isaac Babel's 'Di Grasso' as Testament and Manifesto," *Russian Review* 40, no. 2 (April 1981): 119–21. Babel's childhood notebook contains a record of his visit to Grasso's company: in December 1908, he watched *Maḷia* by Luigi Capuana and *La morte civile* by Paolo Giacometti. Babel might also have seen Cecil B. DeMille's 1916 silent film version of *Maria Rosa*—or perhaps another Sicilian love-and-revenge melodrama, Mario Gargiulo's 1924 screen adaptation of Giovanni Verga's *Cavalleria rusticana*, in which Grasso himself plays Alfio, the avenging everyman (in this case a carter, not a shepherd).

96 *The Outlaw*   Paulo Giacometti's drama *La morte civile* (1861).

The King

101 **Benya Krik**   Babel's Odessa Jewish gangster-hero Benya Krik ("Benya the Scream") is based on Mishka the Jap (Moisey Vinnitsky, 1891–1919), a real-life Odessa Jewish gangster and revolutionary who formed his own Red Army regiment, which was active until he was ambushed and killed in an arrest attempt by the Cheka in 1919.

102 **Sender Eichbaum, the King's son-in-law**   As Freidin notes, Eichbaum the dairyman (and reluctant father-in-law) is surely an homage to Sholom Aleichem's famous Tevye the Dairyman (*Isaac Babel's Selected Writings*, 262n).

103 **the Sixteenth Station**   A picturesque resort area of Odessa, also known as the Sixteenth Station of the Great Fountain and the Gold Coast.

104 *treyf*   Opposite of kosher.

104 **That's what . . . deafening din.**   Not included in the earliest edition (1921).

104 **"Bitter!"**   *Gor'ko!* is a traditional drunken chant at Russian wedding parties, imploring the bride and groom to kiss to "sweeten" the otherwise "bitter" mood.

105 **He was giggling like a bashful schoolgirl.**   Omitted in later editions.

How It Was Done in Odessa

Gregory Freidin notes that the title of this story alludes to the Formalist critic Boris Eikhenbaum's famous 1919 essay "How Gogol's Overcoat Was Made": "Babel ironically matches Eikhenbaum's view of how Russian literature 'was made' in St. Petersburg with his own—the way things were done in Odessa" (Freidin in *Isaac Babel's Selected Writings*, 266n). Russian uses the same verb, *delat'*, for "to do" and "to make"—a word that also evokes a perennial Russian political question *chto delat'?*, "What is to be done?" This was the title of Nikolai Cherneshevsky's 1863 political novel, which was parodied by Dostoevsky in *Notes from Underground* and inspired Vladimir Lenin's own 1902 pamphlet with the same title.

107   **Arye Leib . . . Froim the Rook**   A few words about names: Froim the Rook (*grach*, a type of crow, *Corvus frugilegus*) is also called Froim Shtern in "Justice in Brackets." Arye-Leib: Arye means "lion" in Hebrew and Leib is "lion" in Yiddish. Krik means "yell"; Byk means "bull"; Moiseyka is "little Moses"; Shimshon is Hebrew for Samson.

107   **autumn in your heart**   Jonathan Brent has pointed out to me that this famous line may be an echo of the following passage from Sholom Aleichem's story "A Daughter's Grave," found in *The Old Country*, trans. Julius and Frances Butwin (New York: Crown, 1946): "In your heart you feel autumn. And you're longing, you're longing for home . . ." (403).

111   *Laugh, Clown*   Reference is to the opera *Pagliacci* [Clowns] by Ruggero Leoncavallo, 1892. The narrator conflates its famous aria with the title of the opera: see below.

111   *karbovanets*   Ukrainian name for the Russian imperial ruble.

112   **"Laugh, clown!"**   "Ridi, Pagliaccio!": "Laugh, Pagliaccio, at your broken love! / Laugh at the grief that poisons your heart!" From "Vesti la giubba" ("Put on the Costume"), a famous tenor aria in *Pagliacci*. The aria is sung at the conclusion of the first act, when Canio discovers his wife's infidelity but must nevertheless prepare for his performance as Pagliaccio the clown because the show must go on.

The Father

115   **that self-serving, weak-sighted little town**   Omitted in later editions.

115   *zrazy*   Roulades stuffed with rice or kasha.

116   **They both walked past Baska . . . They walked past her**   Omitted in later editions.

116   **five poods plus a couple funts**   In other words, more than 180 pounds.

118 **with terrible calm** Omitted in later editions.
118 **with terrible calm** Again, omitted in later editions.
121 **outside her locked door, two hours** Omitted in later editions.
121 **"they are but straw that burns"** Compare to Isaiah 47:14: "Look, they are no better than straw that the fire burns."

Justice in Brackets

123 **Seryozhka Utochkin** Sergei Utochkin (1876–1915) was a pioneering Russian aviator from Odessa who was also among the first to race bicycles, motorcycles, and automobiles. The narrator implies that the daredevil Utochkin would have run him down in his car. See note above for "Odessa."
125 *Und damit Punktum* "And that was that."

Lyubka the Cossack

128 **Lyubka Schneiweiss** *Schneiweiss* means "snow-white" in Yiddish.
129 *The Miracles and the Heart of the Baal-Shem* The Baal Shem Tov (Master of the Good Name) was the title—often abbreviated as Besht—given to Israel ben Eliezer (1698–1760), founder of the Hasidic movement. He was popularly known as a miracle worker, though Hasidic Jews prefer to emphasize his role as a spiritual master and guide. Pesya-Mindl is perhaps reading some version of his legendary biography *Praises of the Besht*.

Sunset

133 **the Yiddish for "dove"** In the original, "In Russian, Tabl means 'dove.'" In fact, the Yiddish for "dove" is *Toiba*, and the Yiddish for "devil" is *Teivel*.
136 **an exclusive engagement** "Exclusive engagement" is my attempt at *perekidki* (literally, "crossovers" or "passes"), which, as Galya Diment explained to me, is a kind of underworld reception where stolen goods would be "passed." Grisha Freidin, however, told me that this is actually an ironic metaphorical contrast and that *perekidki* is instead an innocent game in which people of all ages stand in a circle tossing a ball (or some other object) back and forth; since only the person with the ball knows whom it will be thrown to next, the game lends itself to displays of flirtation when boys and girls are throwing the ball to one another.

My earlier variant was "a game of circle dodge." Other possible meanings of *perekidki*: a fit of hysterics, overthrowings, a card hustler's tricks, and juggling between two or more jugglers. At the very least, "an exclusive engagement" wouldn't necessarily *exclude* any of these activities. (Earlier published translations render *perekidki* as "a game" or "a wake," which must be a transposition of *pannikhida*, the Eastern Orthodox funeral service.)

136 **like people go to Fairground Square on Easter Monday** The original, *kak idut na Yarmarochknuyu ploshchad' vo vtoroi den' Paskhi*, has typically been rendered as "like people go to the market square (or fair) on the second day of Passover." Paskha refers to both Easter and Passover, but, even though the action is set in the largely Jewish Moldavanka, the reference here is to Fairground Square, a specific street in the Peresyp factory district, a largely Russian working class neighborhood. The day after Russian Orthodox Easter Sunday, as Barbara Henry explained to me, was a festive day that would herald the end of Lent, with the reopening of theaters, processions, and drunken displays, including Petrushka (Punch and Judy) shows in public squares.

141 **here is a Jew** The manuscript of this story—first published after Babel's death in the newspaper *Literaturnaya Rossiya*, no. 47, in 1964— is cut off here. The lines that follow were taken from the last scene of the play *Sunset* (1926–1928) and inserted by the editors since they appear right after the same word in the play.

Froim the Rook

144 **the colonialist forces** A reference to French, Polish, and Greek troops—Allied Forces of World War I—that occupied Odessa in December 1918 to help General Denikin's anti-Bolshevik White Volunteer Army, which was evacuated from Crimea on Allied ships after its defeat by the Soviets in 1920.

146 **contempt for his fellow man** The Russian phrase is a direct borrowing from Proverbs 11:12.

The End of the Poorhouse

147 **Café Fanconi** A posh Odessa café.

147 **"From earth you came and to earth you shall return."** Genesis 3:19.

147 *tachanka* A horse-drawn chaise mounted with a heavy machine gun.

147 **RSDLP of the Bolsheviks** The Russian Social Democratic Labor Party was a revolutionary socialist political party formed in 1898 to unite the various revolutionary organizations of the Russian Empire into one party. In 1903 it split into "Majority" (Bolshevik) and "Minority" (Menshevik) factions. The former—which was always, in fact, a minority faction—became the Communist Party of the Soviet Union.

147 **Sonya Yanovskaya** A mathematician, historian, and Red Army commissar, Sofya Yanovskaya (1896–1966) described herself as a friend of Isaac Babel. See Boris Rosenfeld, "Reminiscences of S. A. Yanovskaya," *Modern Logic* 6, no. 2 (January 1996): 74.

150 **great numbers of Tatars are mad with hunger** From 1921 to 1922, two million Soviet Tatars died of famine as a result of War Communism.

150 **shell-shocked outside Rostov** There was an operation against Denikin's White forces at Rostov in January 1920.

151 **"El moley rachim"** "El maley rachamim," "God, full of mercy," a Hebrew (Ashkenazi) funeral prayer.

151 **"Hevel havolim"** . . . **Kuloi hevel** Hebrew, *Havel havalim hakol havel*: "Vanity of vanities, all is vanity" (Ecclesiastes 1:2). *Havel* can also be translated as "breath," and it is the name of Cain's brother, Abel, whose life endures not much longer than a breath in Genesis 4.

152 **Khadjibey** Existing from the thirteenth through the eighteenth century, Khadjibey was a Crimean Tatar settlement and later an Ottoman Turkish fortress. It was captured by Russia in 1792 and became the site of Odessa by decree of Catherine the Great in 1794.

153 **the plague mound** Burial place for the victims of the 1812 plague.

Karl-Yankel

Freidin notes that this story reflects "Babel's own personal drama of the adoption of his son Mikhail by Tamara Kashirina's new husband, Babel's old friend and fellow writer Vsevelod Ivanov" (*Isaac Babel's Selected Writings*, 305n1).

156 **You couldn't find** . . . Post-1932 editions omit from "You couldn't find . . ." to "There were three of them."

156 **The blacksmith's wife** . . . **teachings of Hasidism.** Omitted in post-1932 editions.

156 **Primakov** A Red Army commander who participated in the assault on the Winter Palace during the Bolshevik coup in 1917, Vitaly Primakov

(1897–1937) formed the first Red Cossack Regiment in 1918; he was executed during the Great Purge.

157 **divcom** *Komdiv*, or divisional commander, was a rank instituted after 1924. Post-1932 editions omit "and later, when the division was expanded into a corps, he became a divcom."

157 **that unexpected breed of Jewish warriors, raiders, and partisans.** An earlier version has "that breed—conspicuously unexpected and vivid—of Jewish . . ."

157 **Duc de Richelieu** Armand-Emmanuel du Plessis, fifth duke of Richelieu (1766–1822), was a French royalist statesman who was appointed governor of Odessa in 1803 by Tsar Alexander I. During the eleven years of his administration, the city became the third most populous in the Russian Empire.

158 **in the service of a cult** An earlier version has "priest" instead of "cult."

158 **The shaggy nut . . . contracted implausibly.** Omitted in later editions.

158 **He pressed Naftula even more fiercely.** Omitted in later editions.

159 **oilcake** Also known as press cake, oilcake is the solids that remain after an agricultural product is pressed to extract the liquids—most commonly used for animal feed or fertilizer.

161 **door to the red corner** Formerly a "holy corner" reserved for Orthodox icons, the "red corner" in Soviet buildings was a common area, often a reading room with Communist books and portraits of Lenin and other Communist "saints."

161 **Kirghiz** The Kirghiz are a Turkic people, predominantly Muslim, who trace their origins to western Mongolia.

The Crossing of the Zbruch

Historically, Budenny's capture of Novograd-Volynsk took place on June 27, 1920, at the Sluch River (which runs through the town), not the Zbruch, which is several hundred kilometers to the southwest. There are two possible reasons for Babel's invocation of the wrong river, aside from an unlikely phonetic confusion or the more likely intentional misdirection: (1) the Zbruch marked the boundary between the Austro-Hungarian and Russian Empires between 1815 and 1918 and was the intended border between Poland and Ukraine after the short-lived Polish-Ukrainian alliance of 1920; (2) the river is the namesake of the phallic, four-faced Zbruch idol, discovered on its banks in 1848 and thought to represent Svetovid, the Slavic god of war, fertility, and abundance. Novograd-Volynsk is a small Ukrainian city that had a large Jewish population (50 percent) during the early twentieth century. In 1919, troops loyal to Symon Petliura's anti-Bolshevik Ukrainian government slaughtered a thousand of the city's Jews.

165 **The divchief six** Babel uses Soviet military acronyms here and elsewhere: divchief six (*nachdiv shest*) is the chief of the Sixth Division, and a brigcom (*kombrig*) is a brigade commander. I have tried, where possible, to devise legible English equivalents for them. Through most of *Red Cavalry*, the divchief six is Savitsky, a character based on Semyon Timoshenko (1895–1970), born in the Odessa region, commander of the Sixth Division of the First Cavalry Army (November 1919–August 1920). Timoshenko makes another notable literary cameo in Primo Levi's account of his liberation from Auschwitz: in 1945, Marshal Timoshenko traveled alone to review the recovery camp in Starye Dorogi where Auschwitz survivors recuperated after their liberation. Levi describes how the extremely tall Timoshenko "unfolded himself from a tiny Fiat 500A Topolino" to promise the liberated survivors they would soon begin their final journey home. He asked the Italians to sing "O Sole Mio," which they tearfully did. On September 15, they began their journey home. See Levi, *If This Is a Man; The Truce*, trans. Stuart Woolf (London: Abacus, 2013), 350.

165 **the legendary high road** Omitted in later editions.

165 **Peaceful Volhynia** Volhynia is a region straddling Poland, Ukraine, and Belarus that was annexed by the Russian Empire during the third partition of the Polish-Lithuanian Commonwealth in 1795.

165 **Eastertime** The Russian (as well as Greek, Latin, and Aramaic) word for "Easter," used here, is Paskha, which can also mean Passover (Pesach in Hebrew), the term more recent translations of this story use. I remain convinced, however, that "Eastertime" better accords with the overall impact of this first story in *Red Cavalry*, in which the narrator wishes to screen his Jewish identity behind a series of military, lyrical, and ethnographic masks. See Mark Halperin, "Translation as Interpretation: Two Translations of a Story from Isaac Babel's *Red Cavalry*" (paper presented at the Third International Conference: Odessa and Jewish Civilization, Odessa, November, 2004. Accessed here: http://www.migdal.org.ua/migdal/events/science-confs/3/5850/print/).

165 **circus Japanese** In the nineteenth century, most Europeans who actually saw a Japanese did so at the circus, since the first groups of Japanese to be allowed to travel abroad after centuries of national seclusion were circus troupes.

The Church at Novograd

169 **faithless monk**   Compare with Afonka's description of Lyutov himself in "Dolgushov's Death," included in this collection.

170 **Rzecz Pospolita**   Traditional name of the Polish state since the sixteenth century, usually referred to in Polish as Rzeczpospolita Polska: *rzecz* (thing) and *pospolita* (common), meaning a commonwealth or republic.

170 **Józef Piłsudski**   Józef Piłsudski (1867–1935) was the Polish statesman most responsible for the creation in 1918 of the Polish Second Republic, which he led in various capacities until 1935. Babel describes finding Piłsudski's proclamations in his *1920 Diary* (July 16): "A moving proclamation. 'Our graves are white with the bones of five generations of warriors . . .'"

170 **Prince Radziwiłł . . . Prince Sapieha**   Radziwiłł and Sapieha are two old aristocratic Polish families. Prince Janusz Franciszek Radziwiłł (1880–1967) was a conservative politician in the Second Polish Republic and a supporter of Józef Piłsudski; Prince Eustachy Sapieha (1881–1963) was a Polish minister of foreign affairs who served in the cavalry during the Polish-Soviet War.

A Letter

172 **Budenny**   Semyon Budenny (1883–1973) served as commander (*komandarm*) of the First Cavalry Army in 1919 and 1920 and was made a marshal of the Soviet Union in 1935. Although he grew up in the Don Cossack region, his family were not Cossacks but poor Russian peasants who settled among them (*inogorodnie*), as were the majority (perhaps more than 60 percent) of the so-called Cossacks in the Red Cavalry. In 1924, Budenny publicly took issue with Babel's fictional portrayal of the Red Cavalry. See Stephen Brown, "Communists and the Red Cavalry," 89.

172 *szlachta*   Polish nobility.

172 **scalping his hooves**   *zasekaetsya*, referring to interference between the front and hind hooves of a galloping horse.

Chief of the Remount Service

For Babel's description of the colorful Dyakov and his work in the Remount Service, see *1920 Diary*, July 13 and 16.

176　**"Blessings from the nun for honest whores and everyone!"**　Dyakov's absurd greeting literally means: "To all honest whores/wretches, blessings from the mother superior!" I tried to capture the theatrical and sacrilegious near-rhymes of the original, earlier variants being: "Mother Superior, bless the inferior," and "Blessings and trumpets to all honest strumpets!"

Pan Apolek

179　*zrazy*　Roulades stuffed with rice or kasha.

180　**a war that was merciless like a Jesuit's passion**　Omitted in post-1930 editions.

181　**like blossoms in a tropical garden**　Omitted in post-1930 editions.

181　**Pan Scribe**　Apolek calls Lyutov Pan Pisar, which means "Mr. Writer" in Russian, "Mr. Clerk" in Polish, and —as Amelia Glaser has pointed out (*Jews and Ukrainians in Russia's Literary Borderlands*, 163)—"Mr. Chancellor" in Ukrainian, each reflecting a different aspect of Lyutov's identity as an artist, scrivener-witness, and occupying Red Cavalryman.

182　**"O *ten chlovek!*"**　Transliterated Polish (*ten człowiek*), "that fellow."

182　**shifty-eyed**　Omitted in later editions.

183　**"hidden by the priests"**　Louis Iribarne argues that Apolek—who has ministered for a Christlike thirty years as a church painter—implies that he himself is the "offspring of the union between Christ and Deborah." Iribarne notes that Apolek's "sacrilegious tale may be read as an allegory on the artist in the world," an allegory that suggests that "man is still worthy of art if for no other reason than he is man" (Iribarne, 63).

183　*Tso vy muvite?*　Transliterated Polish (*Co wy mówicie?*), "What are you saying?"

183　*Tak, tak*　Polish, "Yes, yes."

The Sun of Italy

185　**My soul . . . haze in July.**　Omitted in later editions. The story is dated June 1920, not July. And again, it is the Sluch, not the Zbruch, that flows through Novograd-Volynsk. The Russian word for "lady" here is *baba*, which, depending on context, could mean woman, peasant woman, grandma, wench, broad, old hag, or sissy. In 1924, Budenny publicly accused Babel of *"babizm"*—that is, unheroic and effeminate conduct—for his unflattering portrayal of the Red Cavalry in his stories.

185   **ennui**   The word used here is *toska*, which Nabokov defines as follows: "At its deepest and most painful, it is a sensation of great spiritual
anguish, often without any specific cause. At less morbid levels it is a
dull ache of the soul, a longing with nothing to long for, a sick pining, a
vague restlessness, mental throes, yearning. In particular cases it may be
the desire for somebody or something specific, nostalgia, love-sickness.
At the lowest level it grades into ennui, boredom." See Nabokov in
Aleksandr Pushkin, *Eugene Onegin: Commentary and Index*, trans.
Vladimir Nabokov (Princeton, N.J.: Princeton University Press, 1964),
vol. 2, p. 141.

185   **My vague stupor . . . a shedding snake.**   Omitted in later editions.

186   **Makhno . . . Volin**   Nestor Makhno (1888–1934), nicknamed "Batko,"
or "Little Father," was a Ukrainian anarchist guerrilla leader who fought
twice alongside the Bolsheviks until they turned against him after the
defeat of the White Army in November 1920. He is credited with the
introduction of the *tachanka*, a horse-drawn chaise mounted with a
heavy machine gun. Volin—born Vsevolod Eikhenbaum (1882–1945),
brother of the critic Boris Eikhenbaum—was a Russian Jewish anarchist intellectual who fled the Soviet Union in 1921, as did Makhno.

186   **the long snake of**   Omitted in later editions.

186   **self-proclaimed Tsekists . . . "made in" Kharkov**   Tseka is an abbre-
viation for the Central Committee of the Communist Party, the key
decision-making body of the Soviet Union until it was eclipsed by the
smaller Politburo under Stalin; *tsekh* means "guild": Sidorov is making
a pun. Kharkov (now Kharkiv) was the capital of Soviet Ukraine from
1917 to 1934. The phrase "made in" appears in English in the original—in the 1920s many Bolsheviks looked to the United States as a
model of rapid modernization and institutional rationalization, which
Sidorov mocks as lacking revolutionary spirit.

186   **Narkomindel**   Acronym for the Soviet Ministry of Foreign Affairs.

187   **King Victor Emmanuel**   King Victor Emmanuel III (1869–1947; r.
1900–1946), Italian monarch.

Gedali

The source material for both "Gedali" and "The Rebbe" may be found in
Babel's *1920 Diary* (Zhitomir, June 3).

189   **Ibn Ezra**   Born in Muslim Spain, Abraham ibn Ezra (1089–1167) was
an illustrious Jewish poet, philosopher, scientist, and biblical exegete.

189 **On such evenings . . . melancholy of memories!** These two sentences are missing in later editions.

189 **a shy star** While this may be a reference to the Star of David, the star reappears throughout the story as a herald of the Jewish Sabbath, which begins Friday at sundown. However, as Babel would no doubt have known, a star traditionally marks not the beginning of the Sabbath but rather its end—when three stars are visible about forty minutes after sunset on Saturday. The confusion is perhaps deliberate, since the Sabbath, in kabbalistic thought, represents a weekly moment of redeemed or messianic time. In the apocalyptic context of the Bolshevik Revolution—which followed its own "star"—the Sabbath seems to wane as it begins.

189 **Dickens, where was your ghost** See Charles Dickens' *The Old Curiosity Shop* (1841), which follows the tragic life of the orphan Nell Trent and her grandfather, who both live in a curiosities shop in London. Babel describes the shopkeeper "philosopher" of Zhitomir and his "unimaginable shop" in his *1920 Diary* (June 3).

190 **Rashi's commentaries and the books of Maimonides** Rashi is an acronym for Shlomo Yitzchaki (1040–1105), a medieval French rabbi and the author of comprehensive commentaries on the Talmud and the Hebrew Bible. Moses Maimonides (1135–1204) was a Sephardic rabbi, philosopher, physician, and scholar who sought to reconcile the Jewish faith with Aristotelianism and to codify Jewish law.

190 **the International** The Second Congress of the Third Communist International met from July 19 to August 7, 1920. The opening session was held in Petrograd with subsequent sessions in Moscow and was attended by more than two hundred delegates, who represented workers' organizations from thirty-seven countries. Lenin spoke at the opening session, and his speech was published in *Pravda* on July 20. As Gregory Freidin has noted (*Isaac Babel's Selected Writings*, 113n), there was a large map on display in the main congress hall showing the progress of the Red Army's march on Warsaw. After the Soviet defeat in Poland in August 1920, the Comintern became an instrument of Moscow's activities abroad.

My First Goose

192 **the raspberry of his tilted cap** The color raspberry (*malina, malinovoi*) appears throughout Babel's work, and it is also a common color on Cossack flags and standards. In Russian slang, *malina* can refer to a criminal union, a thieves' hideout, or a honey trap.

192 **"Speak!" he shouted . . . of the division.** Replaced in later editions with "I gave him the paper ordering my assignment to the divisional staff."

193 **the Second Congress of the Comintern** See the note on "the International" attached to "Gedali."

The Rebbe

197 **raging winds of history** "Raging" is omitted in later editions. The imagery here suggests several Jewish matriarchal traditions: (1) Rachel in Jeremiah 31, mourning as the Israelites are cast into exile: "Thus saith the LORD; A voice was heard in Ramah, lamentation, and bitter weeping; Rachel weeping for her children refused to be comforted for her children, because they were not. Thus saith the LORD; Refrain thy voice from weeping, and thine eyes from tears: for thy work shall be rewarded, saith the LORD; and they shall come again from the land of the enemy. And there is hope in thine end, saith the LORD, that thy children shall come again to their own border" (Jer. 31:15–17); (2) Miriam, who rescued her brother Moses by floating him down the Nile, has been traditionally associated with water in the wilderness: "And Miriam died there . . . And there was no water for the congregation" (Num. 20:1); (3) The kabbalistic concept of Shekhinah—a feminine aspect of the divinity, representing God's presence in the creation itself—was said to have accompanied the Israelites into exile and was expected to be reunited with God in messianic times.

197 *khokhlushki* From *khokhol*, a pejorative Russian and Polish term for ethnic Ukrainians, deriving from the stereotypical Ukrainian Cossack style of haircut that features a forelock of hair sprouting from the top or the front of an otherwise closely shaved head.

197 **a sable hat and a white robe cinched with a cord** Traditional Hasidic garb, although a white robe would generally be worn only by a Hasidic leader. The cord reinforces the division between lower and higher (more spiritual) bodily functions and would be worn during prayer.

197 **"A God-fearing town"** A deeply ironic description of Odessa, which was considered a godless town by more traditional, provincial Jews. Two old Yiddish sayings convey this view: (1) Seven miles around Odessa burn the fires of hell; (2) To live like God in Odessa (a rich, worldly, hedonistic city). Babel records the basis for this conversation in the *1920 Diary* (June 3).

197 **Hersh of Ostropol** See the first note attached to "Shabbos Nahamu."

198 **Who hath chosen us** The line about chosenness is in the Friday night *kiddush*, or blessing over the wine, not in the *motzi*, or blessing over the bread.

The Way to Brody

200 **untold hives** The word "untold" is omitted in later editions. See *1920 Diary*, August 4, where Babel mentions searching beehives.

200 **sky-blue earth** The poem "I Go Out on the Road Alone" by Mikhail Lermontov contains the following line: "The earth sleeps in its sky-blue radiance." The poem may be found in *From the Ends to the Beginning: A Bilingual Anthology of Russian Verse*, edited by Ilya Kutik and Andrew Wachtel, trans. Tatiana Tulchinsky, Andrew Wachtel, and Gwenan Wilbur. http://max.mmlc.northwestern.edu/mdenner/Demo/texts/road_alone.html.

200 **And so I forced . . . to my sorrows.** Omitted in later editions.

200 **and even Grishchuk . . . to the side** Omitted in later editions.

201 **Day of the Beheading** The Beheading of Saint John the Baptist is a holy day observed (usually on August 29) by various Christian churches to commemorate the martyrdom of John, who was beheaded on the orders of Herod Antipas in response to the vengeful request of his stepdaughter, Salome, and her mother, Herodias. John had declared Herodias's marriage to Herod unlawful.

201 **the heroic sunset** The word "heroic" is omitted in later editions.

A Teaching on the *Tachanka*

202 **His story is horrible.** Omitted in later editions. In his *1920 Diary*, July 23, Babel notes: "Grishchuk is only 50 versts away from home. He doesn't run away."

202 **slaughter—*tachanka*—horse** In post-1936 editions, the word "blood" appears instead of "horse."

202 **whom we suppressed** Omitted in later editions.

203 **the assessor's** The assessor was something like a rural magistrate or a justice of the peace in prerevolutionary Russia. German colonists had been settling in the Russian Empire since the late seventeenth century, peaking at almost two and a half million by 1914. Many of the German colonists in Volhynia (Ukraine) were Mennonites, who were often raided by Makhno's forces.

203 **Saint Ursula** Legendary fourth-century Romano-British saint said to have perished along with her eleven thousand virgin handmaidens in Cologne at the hands of the Huns.

Dolgushov's Death

205 **burka** Unlike the outer garment worn by many observant Muslim women, here the burka refers to a felt overcoat traditionally worn by men in the Caucusus and adopted by Russian cavalry, including Cossacks; they were sewn with high, squared-off shoulders, producing a distinctive high-shouldered silhouette.

207 **"Please, eat . . ."** The 1925 edition of the story ends with "And I accepted Grishchuk's charity, the charity of a simple man, and ate his apple with sadness and reverence."

Brigcom 2

209 **Budenny stood by a tree** See note on Budenny above in "A Letter."

209 **Koleso** *Koleso* means "wheel," a bad pun on Kolesnikov.

209 **a hundred *sazhen*s** A *sazhen* is a Russian unit of measurement equal to seven feet that became obsolete when the Soviet Union adopted the metric system in 1924.

209 **columns of thick dust** Pre-1931 editions have "pale-blue" instead of "thick."

210 **"Very well" . . . closed his eyes.** In place of this sentence the first edition (1923) has the following:

> And in that instant, the first Polish shell traced its howling flight above us.
> "They're going at a trot," said the observer.
> "Very well," Budenny replied, lit a cigarette, and closed his eyes. The hurrah was barely audible, receding from us like gentle song.
> "Going at full gallop," said the observer, stirring the branches. Budenny smoked and did not open his eyes.
> The cannonade fumed, expanded, flashed lightning, beclouded the vault of heaven, hammering it with blows and thunder.
> "The brigade is attacking the enemy," the observer sang out above.

210 **the celebrated Kniga, the headstrong Pavlichenko, and the captivating Savitsky** Vasily Kniga (1883–1961) commanded the First Brigade

of the Sixth Division of the First Cavalry Army. Matvei Pavlichenko is based on Iosif Apanasenko (1890–1943), commander of the Sixth Division of the First Cavalry Army (August–October 1920); like Kniga, Pavlichenko hailed from the Stavropol region. Kniga and Apanasenko were temporarily relieved of command for failing to stop their division's three-week mutiny in September and October 1920 as the Polish war came to an end, an uprising that began with the killing of a commissar (who had shot a cavalryman in defense of a Jewish family) and continued with widespread looting and violence against Communists and Jewish civilians. Savitsky is based on Semyon Timoshenko (1895–1970). See note to "The Life Story of Pavlichenko, Matvei Rodionych."

Sashka Christ

211 **Tarakanych . . . joined an artel**   *Tarakan* means cockroach in Russian; so *Tarakanych* sounds like "Cockroachson." An artel was a semiformal craft or artisan work cooperative, often temporary or seasonal, that existed in Russia and the Soviet Union from the 1860s through the 1950s.

211 **and fooled around to his heart's content**   Omitted in later editions.

214 **Sashka went to the Platov settlement . . . under Voroshilov**   Platov was Budenny's native settlement and where he formed his detachment. Tsaritsyn (later Stalingrad and Volgograd) was the site of an important Bolshevik victory (under the command of Stalin and Voroshilov) against besieging White Cossack forces. Kliment Voroshilov (1881–1969) was the political commissar of the First Cavalry Army, sharing authority with the *komandarm* (Budenny). A close associate of Stalin's, Voroshilov was a member of the Tseka (Central Committee of the Communist Party) and later the Politburo and served as people's commissar for military and naval affairs and chairman of the Revolutionary Military Council of the USSR until 1934; he was named a marshal of the Soviet Union the following year. Thanks to Voroshilov's blunders during the German invasion of the Soviet Union in 1941, Krushchev declared him the "biggest bag of shit in the army."

The Life Story of Pavlichenko, Matvei Rodionych

Matvei Rodionych Pavlichenko was based on Iosif Rodionovich Apanasenko, a commander about whom Babel wrote in his *1920 Diary* (August 18), "Apanasenko's irritability, his swearing—is this what's meant by strength of will? . . . Must penetrate the soul of the fighting man, I'm penetrating, it's all horrible, wild beasts with principles . . . I hate life, murderers, it's unbearable, baseness and crime . . . The military commissar and I ride along the line begging the men not to massacre prisoners. Apanasenko washes his hands of it . . . Apanasenko—don't waste cartridges, stick them. That's what Apanasenko always says—stick the nurse, stick the Poles . . . Lvov's defenses—professors, women, adolescents. Apanasenko will massacre them, he hates the intelligentsia, and it goes deep, he wants a government of peasants and Cossacks, aristocratic in its own peculiar way." See note to "Brigcom 2."

216 **To Mitya Schmidt** The dedication to Babel's friend Dmitri Schmidt—a decorated Jewish Red Cavalry commander who was among the first generals to perish in Stalin's purges in 1937—appeared in early versions of this story.

218 **the year '18** After the October 1917 Revolution, Russia fought a civil war (1918–1922) that pitted the Bolshevik Red Army against the anti-Bolshevik White Army—with involvement by the peasant Green guerrillas, Makhno's anarchist Black Army, a Socialist Revolutionary-led peasant Blue Army, and foreign armies from thirteen different countries.

The Cemetery in Kozin

223 **the Cossacks of Bogdan Khmelnitsky** Bogdan Khmelnitsky (1595–1657) was the hetman of the Zaporozhian Host of the Crown of the Kingdom of Poland in the Polish-Lithuanian Commonwealth, in what is now Ukraine. He led an uprising against the commonwealth and its magnates (1648–1654), resulting in the creation of a Ukrainian Cossack state. In 1654, he concluded the Treaty of Pereyaslav, which led to the eventual absorption of Ukraine by the Russian Empire by 1775. Tens of thousands of Jews—many of whom served as leaseholders for absentee Polish lords—were killed during Khmelnitsky's uprising, with a total of a hundred thousand killed by 1667 during two subsequent wars. Babel's *1920 Diary* contains several descriptions of Jewish cemeteries (July 18, 21, and 24).

Prishchepa

Babel discusses Prishchepa at some length in his *1920 Diary*: "Argument between a Jewish youth and Prishchepa . . . Prishchepa is offensively dumb, he talks of religion in ancient times, mixes up Christianity and Paganism, his main point, in ancient times there was the commune, needless to say nothing but rubbish." The diary portrays Prishchepa as an antisemitic lout who forces his Jewish hosts to cook on a Sabbath before the fast day of Tisha b'Av (the ninth of the month of Av, a day of mourning for the destruction of the First and Second Temples in Jerusalem) and who presses a young Jewish woman: "He wants to go to bed, spend some time with her, she is tormented, who understands her soul better than I? He: We'll write to each other. I wonder with a heavy heart: surely she won't. Prishchepa tells me she wants to (with him they all want to). I remember that he probably had syphilis; I wonder: was he cured? The girl, later: I'll scream" (July 24).

The Story of a Horse

226 **Savitsky . . . Khlebnikov** This story was first published in 1923 with the real names of the officers upon whom Savitsky and Khlebnikov are based—Timoshenko and Melnikov. Babel removed their names and apologized to both men after Melnikov wrote to complain to one of Babel's editors that the letter with his resignation from the Communist Party, quoted in the story, never existed, as he never resigned from the party. Efraim Sicher writes that Melnikov "thanked Babel for his story," confirmed that Timoshenko did take his white horse, and noted that there were other negative aspects of the Red Cavalry—such as the looting of Rovno—that Babel did not mention. See Sicher, " 'The Jewish Cossack': Isaac Babel in the First Red Cavalry," *Studies in Contemporary Jewry: An Annual IV: The Jews and the European Crisis 1914–21* (New York: Oxford, 1988), 133n16.

228 **And he would . . . was because** Omitted in post-1930 editions.

Konkin

229 **for a "document check"** An expression used during the Russian Civil War meaning "to summarily execute." Nikolai Dukhonin (1876–1917) became the de facto supreme commander of the Russian Army after the Bolshevik takeover of Kerensky's Provisional Government in Petrograd. After surrendering to the Bolsheviks in Mogilev, he was killed by Red Army troops, who then used his naked body for target practice. The root of his name is the word *dukh*, or "soul."

230 **"Nie moge"** Polish, "I can't."

Berestechko

232 **Its handle . . . spare horses.** Omitted in later editions. In still later editions, the phrase "like it was glued there" is also omitted.

232 **the divisional commissar, Vinogradov, . . . Second Congress** In his *1920 Diary*, Babel refers to a divisional commissar named Vinokurov: "Meeting in the castle park, the Jews of Berestechko, stupid Vinokurov, kids running around, selection of the Revolutionary Committee, Jews twisting their beards, Jewesses listening to tales of paradise in Russia, the international situation, the uprising in India" (August 7). "Vinokurov—typical military commissar, sticks to his own line, wants to fix the 6th Division, the struggle with the guerilla mentality, slow-witted, bores me with his speeches, rude sometimes, uses the familiar 'you' with everyone" (August 13). For more on the Second Congress, see the note on "the International" attached to "Gedali."

233 **the Hasidic cheder . . . see the tsaddik** Once common throughout eastern Europe, a cheder is a traditional Jewish elementary school, usually held in the home of the teacher, or *melamed*, where the basic elements of the Hebrew language, scripture, and Jewish practice are taught. Hasidic tsaddiks or holy men were often associated with miracles.

233 **"Berestechko, 1820 . . ."** "Berestechko, 1820. Paul, my beloved, they say that Emperor Napoléon is dead, is it true? I feel well, the birth was easy, our little hero is seven weeks old . . ." Part of this letter, as well as much of the other source material for this story, appears in Babel's *1920 Diary*, August 7.

Salt

235 **Dear Comrade Editor** The letter—an example of framed, orally inflected *skaz* narration—opens with set formulas typically employed by Russian folk storytellers.

235 **pood** equivalent to roughly thirty-six pounds.

237 **under us** Omitted in later editions.

237 **those Yids Lenin and Trotsky** "Lenin and Trotsky" is omitted in later editions, as is the passage "And by the way . . . road of life." Lenin, who was largely of Russian, German, and Swedish lineage, was often derided as a Jew by anti-Bolsheviks, and it seems many Cossacks believed this; ironically, the fact that his maternal grandfather was Jewish was concealed in Soviet archives until 1992. Trotsky (born Lev Bronshtein) was the son of Jewish farmers in Ukraine. It is unclear why the narrator invokes

Tambov Province in his strange "biography" of Trotsky. One possible point of reference is Alexander Antonov (1889–1922), a Socialist Revolutionary (SR) who had grown up in Tambov and was freed in 1917 by the February Revolution from a twenty-year prison sentence for robbing a train. Antonov returned to Tambov and became a district police official under the Provisional Government. He left this post in April 1918 and went underground, organizing an armed guerrilla group to resist the new Communist government, until he was killed in a firefight with the Cheka in 1922. Another point of reference might be Maria Spiridonova, another SR from Tambov, convicted of assassinating a Tambov provincial councillor and imperial security chief in 1906; she alleged that after her arrest she was tortured and raped on a train by a Cossack commander, who would himself be assassinated several months later.

Evening

239 **RKP** Russian Communist Party.

239 **Bloody Nicholas . . . died of drink** "Bloody" Nicholas II, who had abdicated the throne in 1917, was killed along with his family by the Bolsheviks in 1918. Peter III was replaced by his wife, Catherine (II) the Great. Catherine's son Paul was replaced by his own son Alexander I in 1801. Nicholas I—known as Nikolai Palkin, or "the rod," because of his introduction of flogging into the army—died of pneumonia after refusing treatment in 1855, though there were rumors he committed suicide because of Russia's defeat in the Crimean War. Nicholas I's son, Tsar Alexander II, was assassinated by the radical "People's Will" in 1881; his grandson Alexander III was rumored to be an alcoholic.

239 **Thus a young woman . . . inconvenience of conception.** Omitted in early and later editions.

240 **that ham-faced conqueror** Omitted in later editions.

240 **The entire party . . . blood and filth** Omitted in later editions.

240 **Vasilyok** Vasilyok is a diminutive for Vasily and also means "cornflower."

240 **her faint Russian voice** "Russian" is omitted in later editions.

Afonka Bida

241 **ataman** Cossack chief or hetman.

241 **Maslak's flamboyant squadrons** Babel added a note here: "Maslakov, commander of the First Brigade of the Fourth Division, an incorrigible guerrilla who soon betrayed the Soviets." Gregory Maslakov

(1877–1921) was indeed among the Red Cavalry commanders who mutinied in 1921 (after being denied permission to move their troops out of a famine zone), joining forces with anti-Bolshevik dissidents Makhno and Antonov.

242 **their shredded rags**   The Russian word for "rags" here is *svitki*, which can also mean "scrolls," offering an interesting resonance with the infantry's bookish Jewish commander.

243 **like a woman shrieking at church**   The Russian word for "shrieker" is *klikusha*. For more on this phenomenon, see Dostoevsky's *The Brothers Karamazov* (trans. Pevear and Volokhonsky, [New York: Farrar, Straus, and Giroux, 1990], 13–14): "a terrible woman's disease that seems to occur predominantly in our Russia, . . . a testimony to the hard lot of our peasant women, caused by exhausting work too soon after difficult, improper birth-giving without any medical help, and, besides that, by desperate grief, beatings, and so on, which the nature of many women, after all, as the general examples show, cannot endure." Such women, "taken to the Sunday liturgy, . . . would screech or bark like dogs so that the whole church could hear, but when the chalice was brought out, and they were led up to the chalice, the 'demonic possession' would immediately cease and the sick ones would always calm down for a time."

244 **In our minds . . . seminarian curls.**   Omitted in later editions.

At Saint Valentine's

247 **She had torn . . . from someone's garments.**   Omitted in later editions.

247 **and grabbed at . . . sacred books.**   Omitted in later editions.

247 **She threw him off, smashed his head . . . penetrated the church.** Replaced in later editions with "She threw him off and rushed to the door. And it was only then that we passed the altar and penetrated the church."

248 **like the beard of Holofernes**   In the Book of Judith, the Babylonian king Nebuchadnezzar II (634–562 B.C.E.) sent his general Holofernes to punish the nations of the west that did not support his reign. When he besieged the city of Bethulia, Judith, a beautiful Hebrew widow, entered Holofernes's camp, seduced him, and beheaded him while he was drunk. Judith's execution of Holofernes was a popular subject for Renaissance painters (and for such writers as Chaucer and Dante), alongside the subject of Salome and John the Baptist.

248 **Driven out of my mind . . . of Apolek**   Omitted in later editions.

248 **We retreated . . . with dead fingers.**   Omitted in later editions.

248 **little Yid**   Later editions have "Jew" instead of "little Yid."
249 **I wrote a report...population.**   See Isaac Babel, *1920 Diary*, August 7.

Squadron Commander Trunov

251 **in their incomprehensible blindness**   Omitted in later editions.
251 **Hadas the rabbi of Belz . . . Husiatyn rabbi Judah . . . Elijah the Gaon
     of Vilna**   Belz and Husiatyn are eastern Ukrainian towns less than two
     hundred miles from Sokal. Both towns were known for their Hasidic
     dynasties, although neither Hadas nor Judah are identifiable as Belzer
     or Husiatyner rebbes. Elijah ben Shlomo Zalman, the Gaon (genius)
     of Vilna (1720–1797), was one of the most important rabbinic authori-
     ties and Talmudic commentators since the medieval period; he was also
     a bitter opponent of the Hasidic movement, urging excommunication
     for anyone in Vilnius who would not recant Hasidism. Kabbalah is
     a Jewish esoteric mode of thought, commentary, and practice. Start-
     ing in the eighteenth century, Hasidism, with its notions of mystical
     leadership by charismatic rebbes, popularized Kabbalah (which literally
     means "to receive [tradition]") as a kind of social mysticism for the
     whole Jewish community. See Isaac Babel, *1920 Diary*, August 26.
251 **"Elijah!" . . . mouths agape.**   Omitted in later editions.
251 **for I couldn't understand . . . in Sokal**   Omitted in later editions.
253 **and all that fuss of his was a burden to me**   Omitted in later editions.
253 **proud German chest . . . Jaeger long-johns**   See note on *Jaeger* in "Sin
     of Jesus." In later editions, the word "proud" was replaced with "white."
254 **Trotsky's orders**   The narrator is referring to Trotsky's order forbid-
     ding the murder of prisoners of war. Trotsky's name does not appear in
     post-1933 editions.
254 **Major Faunt-Le-Roy's combat squadron**   Colonel Cedric Errol
     Fauntleroy (1891–1973), whom Lyutov calls Major Reginald Faunt-
     Le-Roy, was an American pilot who volunteered in the Polish Air
     Force during the Polish-Soviet War of 1919–1921 as part of the
     Kościuszko Squadron along with twenty other American pilots.
     Among them was the squadron's organizer, Captain Merian Cooper,
     who would go on to a career in the film industry, most notably as the
     maker of *King Kong*. (See Elif Batuman's "Babel in California" for a
     discussion of the Trunov-*Kong* connection.) Cooper was shot down,
     captured by the Red Cavalry, and spent nine months as a POW. He
     pretended to be a conscripted corporal named Frank Mosher—he
     chose a Jewish-sounding name because he assumed most Bolsheviks

were Jews—and was interviewed by Isaac Babel, as noted in the *1920 Diary* (July 14). Babel mentions that "Mosher" pretended to be interested in Bolshevism. Cooper escaped from the Soviet Union in April 1921, making his way to Latvia. The air squadron was named after Polish patriot Tadeusz Kościuszko, who fought on the American side in the American Revolution and led the Poles' unsuccessful revolt against the Russian Empire in 1794.

255   **Trunov, our late commander**   In an obituary titled "We Need More Trunovs!" that Babel wrote for the actual Trunov (whose first name was Konstantin, not Pavel) in the August 13, 1920, edition of the *Red Cavalryman*, he notes that Trunov died by a Polish officer's bullet and not in "unequal combat" with an American bomber in Sokal.

The Ivans

Babel's story about two opposed Ivans seems to be an ironic invocation of Gogol's "How Ivan Ivanovich Quarreled with Ivan Nikiforovich," in which an absurd and interminably litigious dispute between two neighbors is sparked when one Ivan calls the other a "goose"—another odd connection to a different *Red Cavalry* story.

256   **Sergey Sergeyevich Kamenev**   Kamenev (1881–1936) was commander in chief of the Soviet Armed Forces from 1919 to 1924.

256   **a freeloader**   The men call the deacon a *farmazovshchik*, which literally means "freemason" but is also used to describe a freethinker, malingerer, or freeloader.

258   **Lavrik . . . this earth**   Omitted in later editions.

259   **Tarnovsky syringe**   Used for injecting medicine to treat syphilis and named after the eminent venereologist V. M. Tarnovsky (1837–1906). Babel notes in his *1920 Diary* that syphilis was rampant among Red Cavalry troops (July 28).

The Widow

265   **hadn't even touched my food yet**   The slang here is *ne rubayu*, which might also mean "I don't get it."

266   **rustled and panted in the bushes**   The sexual interlude between Sasha and Lyovka is missing in later editions.

267   **first shell over Busk . . . the Bug watershed**   Busk is a town in the L'viv region of western Ukraine. The Bug River (pronounced *boog*), which

forms part of the present-day border between Poland and Ukraine, was often considered the boundary between Orthodox Christian and Catholic regions.

267 **Savinkov's Cossacks** Boris Savinkov (1879–1925) was a writer and a leader of the Socialist Revolutionary Party, which carried out several assassinations of key Russian imperial officials under his operational command in 1904 and 1905. After the February Revolution in 1917, Savinkov joined the Provisional Government; he became a counter-revolutionary after the Bolshevik takeover and eventually went to Warsaw, where he led a Russian political organization responsible for forming several infantry and cavalry units made up of Red Army POWs that fought on the Polish side. This explains why the narrator calls Yakovlev's men *savinkovtsy*. After the war ended, in 1921, Poland expelled Savinkov to avoid spoiling relations with the Soviets. Savinkov was arrested trying to infiltrate the Soviet Union in 1924; he died in 1925—either as a suicide or, as Stalin reportedly claimed, from being thrown out the window of Moscow's Lubyanka Prison, where Babel would be held in 1939. (Stalin allegedly made this claim in the 1950s to his secret police, chiding them for being too humane in their interrogation of political prisoners.)

267 **Cossack Captain Yakovlev** Yesual (a Cossack rank roughly equivalent to captain or major, derived from the Turkic word for "chief") Vadim Yakovlev was a Russian World War I officer who commanded a Cossack brigade in General Anton Denikin's White Army in Ukraine, joined the Red Cavalry upon Denikin's defeat in 1919 to command the Third Don Cossack Cavalry Brigade, and switched again in late May 1920 to the Polish side, where he would command the roughly seventeen hundred men of the Free Cossack Brigade as a colonel. Yakovlev's troops were notorious for their pillaging of Ukrainian and Belarusian towns and for anti-Jewish pogroms in the early 1920s. After the cease-fire agreement in late 1920, Yakovlev signed an alliance with the exiled government of the Ukrainian People's Republic and decided to continue the struggle against the Reds. His forces were quickly defeated and forced back to Polish-held territory. Yakovlev would remain the brigade's commander until it was disbanded in 1923. Babel's *1920 Diary* contains the following entry: "Rumor of atrocities. I walk into town. Indescribable terror and despair. They tell me all about it. Privately, indoors, they're afraid the Poles may come back. Captain Yakovlev's Cossacks were here yesterday. A pogrom. The family of David Zyz, in people's homes, a naked, barely breathing prophet of an old man,

an old woman butchered, a child with fingers chopped off, many people still breathing, stench of blood, everything turned upside down, chaos, a mother sitting over her butchered son, an old woman lying twisted up like a pretzel, four people in one hovel, filth, blood under a black beard, just lying there in their blood" (Isaac Babel, *1920 Diary*, August 8).

268 **Lyovka, the divchief's lackey** Omitted in later editions.

Zamoste

270 **doused in ink-swollen clouds** Earlier editions have "smothered" instead of "doused."

270 **live, stirring sweat** Not included in earlier editions.

270 **"Margot," I wanted to shout** Since there is no Margot anywhere else in *Red Cavalry*, Babel is probably alluding to Alexandre Dumas père's 1845 novel *La Reine Margot*, a fictionalized account of the events surrounding Margaret's marriage to the French king Henry of Navarre in 1572, and perhaps to Goethe's Gretchen in *Faust*. See also Babel's early story "Elya Isaakovich and Margarita Prokofyevna," included in this collection, in which a prostitute named Margarita accepts five rubles from Elya to shelter in her room for the night.

270 **my leg, which jutted straight up** Compare this language with the narrator's description of Savitsky at the beginning of "My First Goose," included in this volume.

271 **Ten million** In 1920 there were almost 10 million Jews in Europe and 14 million worldwide. About 100,000 Jews were killed in pogroms (estimates range from 70,000 to 250,000) during the Russian Civil War and Polish-Soviet War period of 1918 to 1921. The muzhik sounds more unambiguously antisemitic in most translations: "The Yids are to blame for everything, on our side and yours." But the grammar is less direct, in a way that Russian manages—oddly echoing the famous credo in *The Brothers Karamazov*: "vsiakii iz nas pred vsemi vo vsem vinovat, a ya bolee vsekh" ("Each of us is guilty before everyone in everything, but I more than everyone"). It is also tricky to identify this muzhik. Some critics assume he is a Pole, since he situates himself and Lyutov on opposite sides, but his speech is not tagged with the usual "Pan" prefixes one finds in Babel's Polish characters. Efraim Sicher identifies him as a Bolshevik, but then why would he say "ours and yours," implying that he's not on Lyutov's side? He certainly sounds like a Russian. But perhaps the muzhik is more an allegorical figure in this

story. He is genuinely and desperately lonely and is therefore weirdly sweet to Lyutov, probably not realizing Lyutov is a Jew. So, on one level the genocidal small talk is a repulsive pretext for redemption through human dialogue—literally repulsive, as Lyutov flees. But it also echoes the observations of such writers as Israel Zangwill, who said that during this period, "It is as Bolsheviks that the Jews of South Russia have been massacred by armies of Petlyura [the Ukrainian nationalist], though the armies of Sokolow have massacred them as partisans of Petlyura, the armies of [anarchist] Makhno as bourgeois capitalists, the armies of Grigoriev as communists, and the armies of Denikin at once as Bolsheviks, capitalists and Ukrainian nationalists. It is Aesop's old fable [about the lamb and the wolf, who will always come up with an excuse to eat the lamb]" (Nora Levin, *The Jews in the Soviet Union since 1917: Paradox of Survival*, vol. 1 [New York: NYU Press, 1990], 43). In other words, the classic pogromist dynamics of this contested border region, visible starting in the early modern period, would become amplified exponentially as it became the friction zone not just between competing nationalisms (in which the Jewish presence was generally understood as a "problem") but ultimately between competing totalitarian utopias, one racial, the other based on class. As non-Aryan petty tradesmen, Jews were of no use to Nazis and not much use (qua Jews) to the Communists, either. "The Yid stands guilty before everybody," as the muzhik says. On the one hand, during long nights standing vigil, "a person starts wanting to talk to another person"; on the other hand, the other person is to blame for everything—and for my loneliness most of all.

272 "*Nitz niema*" Russian transliteration of Polish *Nic niema*, "There's nothing."

272 "*Chekai!*" Transliteration of Polish *Czekaj!*, "Wait!"

Treason

275 **Citizen Poincaré . . . Ebert-Noske** Raymond Poincaré (1860–1934), president of France, supported the Whites against the Bolsheviks in the Russian Civil War and—thanks to German and Soviet propaganda in the 1920s—was scapegoated along with Nicholas II as an instigator of World War I. Moderate socialists Friedrich Ebert (1871–1925) and Gustav Noske (1868–1946) cooperated with the army and Freikorps paramilitary forces to suppress the leftist Spartacist uprising in Germany (1919).

275 **couldn't give a flying fat one** Later editions omit the vulgar language and have instead "As for that hospital, I didn't shoot at it . . ."

278 **the jail of our hateful ribs** Omitted in later editions.

278 **But we will . . . black blood** This sentence was included only in one version of this story published in 1926.

Chesniki

281 **The army staff . . . exchanged smiles.** This sentence was struck (likely censored) from later editions of *Red Cavalry*.

281 **"Komandarm," he shouted, turning to Budenny** An early version has "then he turned to Budenny and fired in the air."

282 **Two plump nurses . . . from the nurses** Struck (likely censored) from later editions of *Red Cavalry*.

282 **a lickerish lad** My attempt at *peresykhayushchii paren'*—previously translated as "parched lad" or "lad with his tongue hanging out." In Russian, the more common expression is *on po nei sokhnet*—"he's drying out over her"—i.e., horny. Because Babel uses an unusual form of the idiom and because I wanted to retain the alliteration, I opted for "lickerish," an archaic version of "lecherous."

283 **Kirill Vasilich** The narrator's full name is Kirill Vasilevich Lyutov, the name Babel used when he served with the Red Cavalry. "Vasilich" is an informal contraction of the patronymic. Later in this story, Sashka calls Lyutov "Lyutych," an even more casual distortion of, in this instance, his last name.

After the Battle

287 **"So you're a Molokan?"** The Molokans, a pacifist nonconformist Spiritual Christian sect with Judaizing tendencies that arose in the seventeenth century, took their name from the Russian word for "milk," which they drank during the fast days of Lent when Russian Orthodox practice abjures meat and milk.

The Song

288 **my love for it reached the point of sublime and heartfelt ecstasy** Omitted in later editions.

289 **the Green campaigns** The Green guerrillas, active between 1917 and 1922, were deserters from the imperial and Soviet armies who hid in

forests and operated against White and Red forces. They were less an organized army than spontaneous manifestations of peasant discontent and resistance.

289 **"Little lady . . . some attention."** Omitted in earlier editions.

The Rebbe's Son

291 **Do you remember Zhitomir, Vasily?** There is no "Vasily" accompanying Lyutov in the two stories set in Zhitomir, "Gedali" and "The Rebbe," although Lyutov's own patronymic is Vasilevich. I would suggest that this figure is a lyrical and ethical "secret addressee"—to borrow from Osip Mandelstam's essay "On the Addressee," in *Critical Prose and Letters*, trans. J. G. Harris and C. Link (Ann Arbor, Mich.: Ardis, 1990), 68. Or, as Sasha Senderovich has argued, he is the invocation of a ghostly ideal reader whom Lyutov needs as a witness in this story ("The Hershele Maze," 253–54).

291 **the Fourth International** "Fourth International" is the narrator's term for Gedali's unattainable "International of Kind People." (Eventually, in 1938, Trotsky and his supporters, expelled from the Soviet Union, did organize a Fourth International in France.) See also the note on "the International" attached to "Gedali."

291 **the old jester . . . his frayed pocket** See "The Rebbe" for the first appearance of the jester. Observant Jews may not handle money on the Sabbath. A tsaddik, or "righteous one," is a term used to describe a Hasidic leader or holy man.

291 **Rebbe Motale . . . last prince of the dynasty** Taking things somewhat nonsequentially here, "Ilya" is the Russian form of Elijah, the prophet associated with the coming of the messiah in Jewish tradition. "Bratslavsky" refers to the Hasidic movement of Rebbe Nachman of Bratslav (1772–1810), whose successor was never named and whose sect is therefore sometimes referred to as the dead Hasidim. In other words, neither Rebbe Motale nor his son Ilya can be a "prince" of the Bratslav line. Moreover, Babel conflates them with a completely different Hasidic line, the Twersky dynasty of Chernobyl (not Zhitomir). The "jester of the Chernobyl tsaddiks" is Reb Mordkhe in "The Rebbe"—possibly an oblique and travestied reference to Rebbe Mordechai Twersky (1770–1837), known as the Maggid of Chernobyl and reputed in Hasidic thought to be the sustainer in his generation of all the Nistarim or Lamed Vav, the thirty-six hidden tsaddiks, whose role, according to the Talmud and later mystical literature, is to

justify the purpose of humanity in the eyes of God. The Torah scrolls (Pentateuch) are removed from the Ark and read during Saturday morning Sabbath services, not Friday evening (Kabbalat Shabbat) as depicted here. A tallis is a Jewish prayer shawl worn over the outer clothes during the morning prayers and during all prayers on Yom Kippur; it is also used as part of a funeral shroud in traditional burials of Jewish men.

291 **Trotsky's leaflets** Trotsky's name is removed in post-1930 editions.

292 **a little trunk** As Sasha Senderovich has significantly pointed out, this is Lyutov's *own* trunk, not Ilya's ("The Hershele Maze," 250–51).

292 **the Party's Sixth Congress** The Sixth Congress of the Russian Social Democratic Labor Party (Bolsheviks) in Petrograd, July 26 through August 3, 1917, took place shortly after demonstrations for the overthrow of Kerensky's Provisional Government and the subsequent order to arrest Bolshevik leaders that had forced Lenin into hiding. In what would come to serve as a prelude to the October Revolution, the delegates declared that Lenin (elected chair in absentia) should not appear in court to face charges and that the peaceful phase of the revolution was over since power had passed into the hands of the counterrevolutionary bourgeoisie. During this congress, Leon Trotsky's Menshevik dissident faction formally joined the Bolsheviks.

292 **"Damn kulaks"** *Kulak*—literally, "fist," thus "tightfisted"—was a pejorative term for a rich peasant, considered a class enemy ("bloodsuckers") by the Bolsheviks. Before the Bolshevik Revolution, kulak referred to the roughly 20 percent of peasants who came to own land as a result of Russian prime minister Stolypin's 1906 agrarian reforms. Robert Conquest has noted, "The land of the landlords had been spontaneously seized by the peasantry in 1917–18. A small class of richer peasants with around fifty to eighty acres had then been expropriated by the Bolsheviks. Thereafter a Marxist conception of class struggle led to an almost totally imaginary class categorization being inflicted in the villages, where peasants with a couple of cows or five or six acres more than their neighbors were now being labeled 'kulaks,' and a class war against them declared" (*Reflections on a Ravaged Century* [New York: Norton, 2000], 93–94). During the "dekulakization" campaign of the 1930s, the average value of goods confiscated from so-called kulaks was $90–$210 (Robert Conquest, *The Harvest of Sorrow: Soviet Collectivization and the Terror-Famine* [New York: Oxford University Press, 1987], 118). Anywhere from seven hundred thousand to six million perished after Stalin ordered kulaks to be eliminated as a class.

292 **phylacteries** Tefillin or phylacteries are small boxes containing parchments with Torah verses (Exod. 13:11–16, Deut. 6:4–9 and 11:13–21), attached by long leather straps to the forehead and left arm by observant Jews (traditionally men) typically during weekday morning services to serve as reminders of the Exodus from Egypt and the receipt of the Law at Sinai. They are worn in such a way as to direct the heart, mind, hand, and eyes away from earthly and toward spiritual matters.

Argamak

"Argamak" was first published in 1932. It was dated 1924–1930 and footnoted as an "unpublished chapter of *Red Cavalry*." In 1933, it became the concluding chapter of *Red Cavalry*. "Argamak" means "sacred horse"; it is a Russian term for a prized central Asian (Turkmen) breed known as Akhal-Teke. Although this story is placed at the end of the *Red Cavalry* cycle, it is out of chronological order, since the action begins before the beginning of the cycle; it presents an alternative narrative of the campaign.

298 **cruel, jolting trot** An earlier edition had the word *zhosktii* (stiff, firm) instead of *zhestokii* (cruel).

299 **"Don't have a fancy for that horse."** The word *fancy* in this paragraph is my translation of *okhota*, which can mean both "hunt" and, in this case, "liking, appetite, fancy." Several earlier translations assume Pashka's father, Kalistrat, was breeding horses for the hunt.

299 **Dundich the Serb** The Serb Oleko Dundich (1897–1920) was a legendary Red Cavalry commander.

300 **the three kisses** A Russian Orthodox Easter tradition—one of the possible origins of the socialist fraternal kiss—in which one person would greet another with three kisses on the cheek and the words "Christ is risen!" The person receiving the greeting would respond, "Verily he has risen." It is also a gesture of reconciliation, as in this context. Interestingly, if "Argamak" is to be understood as the conclusion or postscript to *Red Cavalry*, then both the first and last stories are suffused with a curious paschal motif, though the action takes place in the summer, not spring. Eastertime was often the occasion for accusations of blood libel and pogroms against Jews (as proverbial "Christ-killers") throughout much of European and Russian history. Christians would "forgive" winter for the sake of spring, forgive each other, engage in wild and sanctioned acts of carnival—but all such practices relied

on the idea of the Jew as standing outside these acts of communal sublimation.

300 **"Say more." . . . "I'll say more . . ."**   Omitted in later editions.

The Kiss

Published in 1937, this story was never included in *Red Cavalry*, although it is set in the Soviet-Polish campaign—in the same town mentioned in "The Song" and "Argamak."

303 **Patriarch Ponds**   Elegant residential neighborhood in downtown Moscow.

The End of Saint Hypatius

Saint Hypatius (*Ipatiev* in Russian) the Wonderworker was the bishop of Gangra in Asia Minor. In 326 c.e., he was attacked on the road by followers of the schismatics Novatus and Felicissimus and thrown into a swamp. A woman among the attackers struck him on the head with a stone, killing him. She soon went mad, began hitting herself with the same stone, and was healed only after they took her to the saint's burial place.

311 **in 1613 . . . woods of Kostroma**   In 1613, after a fifteen-year interregnum known as the Time of Troubles—marked by a famine that killed millions, civil war, pretender tsars ("False Dmitris"), and invasions by Sweden and the Polish-Lithuanian Commonwealth—the Great National Assembly of the boyars (*zemsky sobor*) asked the sixteen-year-old Mikhail Fyodorovich Romanov (1596–1645) to be tsar. His parents, Fyodor (Patriarch Philaret) and Xenia Shestova (the "great nun" Martha), were boyars who had been forced into monastic life by the late Boris Godunov. During this period, Mikhail and his mother had taken refuge in the Ipatiev (Hypatian) monastery at Kostroma, a city two hundred miles northeast of Moscow. Curiously, the Romanov dynasty that began at the Ipatiev Monastery in Kostroma ended when the family was murdered in the basement of the Ipatiev House (named after the engineer who owned it) in Yekaterinburg.

311 **I barely escaped them, those coffin saints**   Compare this language to the last lines of "The Way to Brody" in Red Cavalry.

311 **limped on his left leg**   Interestingly, Mikhail Romanov likewise had a progressive leg injury. In the popular Christian imagination, Satan limped on his left side—the consequence of his fall from heaven. In

Dostoevsky's *Brothers Karamazov*, at the end of the "Grand Inquisitor" chapter, Alyosha notices that his brother Ivan swayed as he walked, and that his right shoulder appeared lower than his left.

313 **having wheezed through an introduction** Appears in the first publication (1924) and is omitted in 1927.

313 **U.S.S.R. and R.S.F.S.R.** Union of Soviet Socialist Republics, more commonly known as the Soviet Union, of which the Russian Soviet Federative Socialist Republic was the largest "republic."

Dante Street

314 **"On va refaire votre vie."** French, "We must remake your life."

314 **duck prepared in its own blood** *Canard à la presse*, a dish developed in the nineteenth century. A duck, preferably from Rouen, is asphyxiated to retain the blood. The duck is then partially roasted, its liver ground and seasoned and the legs and breast removed. The remaining carcass is then put in a special press to extract blood and other juices. The extract is thickened and flavored with the duck's liver, butter, and cognac, and then combined with the breast to finish cooking.

315 **sleek tailleurs** An English women's business suit.

315 **There I caught a glimpse . . . and ships.** This sentence, omitted from the published version, was found in the typed manuscript at the Russian State Archive of Literature and Art (see Babel, 1996, II, 310).

316 **"Cette femme est folle"** "This woman is crazy."

316 **"*Oh, j'en ai plein le dos . . .*"** "Oh, I've got enough to worry about."

316 **"Ah, canaille!"** "Ah, scoundrel!"

317 **The stamp of street death** In some later editions (such as the 1966 *Izbrannoe*) the word "stamp" (*pechat'*) is replaced with "sorrow" (*pechal'*).

317 **"Voilà qui n'est pas gai . . . quel malheur!"** "Here's an unhappy one . . . how awful!"

317 **"C'est l'amour, monsieur . . . Elle l'aimait . . ."** "That's love, monsieur . . . She loved him."

317 **"L'amore . . . Dio castiga quelli, chi non conoscono l'amore . . ."** Italian, "Love . . . God punishes those who do not know love."

317 **"L'amour . . . c'est une grosse affaire, l'amour."** "Love . . . is a great matter, love."

317 **"Dio . . . tu non perdoni quelli, chi non ama . . ."** Italian, "God . . . you do not forgive those who do not love."

318 **Danton lived here** Georges-Jacques Danton (1759–1794) was a leading figure in the French Revolution and the first president of the

Committee of Public Safety. A moderating influence on the Jacobins, he was guillotined by the advocates of revolutionary terror after allegations of financial corruption and collusion with foreign powers.

The Trial (from a Notebook)

319 "Accès de folie, passagère" "A temporary fit of insanity."

319 *Ursus* Babel uses the Latin word for "bear."

319 "eh bien, mon ami" "Well, now, my friend."

319 along with Wrangel Baron Pyotr Nikolayevich Wrangel (1878–1928) was an officer in the Imperial Russian Army and later commanding general of the anti-Bolshevik White Army in southern Russia in the later stages of the Russian Civil War. After their defeat by the Red Army, Wrangel and his officers made their way to Yugoslavia, where, in 1924, he established the Russian All-Military Union, an organization established to fight for the preservation and unity of all White forces living abroad.

320 "Voyons" "See here."

320 "T'a encaisse dix ans . . . c'est fini, mon vieux." "You got ten years . . . it's all over, pal."

The *Ivan & Marya*

The barge in this story, the *Ivan-da-Marya*, is named after a wildflower, *Melampyrum nemorosum*, known in English as the wood cow wheat. It has yellow blossoms and new leaves that are blue or purple before they turn green, giving the species the appearance of having two different flowers on the same stem. The Swedish common name for the plant—*natt och dag*, "night and day"—likewise captures this duality.

321 Sergey Vasilyevich Malyshev . . . to trade for grain. S. V. Malyshev (1877–1938) was a writer and Soviet economic administrator known as the red merchant. The trade described here was not the norm for the War Communism of 1918–1921, during which all surplus grain was confiscated by the Soviet military to feed the cities and the Red Army. Babel took part in Malyshev's Volga expedition in July and August 1918. Malyshev would become a prominent figure during the economic liberalization—the New Economic Policy, or NEP—of 1921–1928; the market fair of Nizhni Novgorod became an NEP showcase under

his aegis. Malyshev was confined to bed during his last years and, by one account, died in Moscow. According to an execution list, however, he was shot near Gorky in 1938. In 1928, after the peasants held back their grain hoping for prices to rise, Stalin scrapped the small-scale private enterprise of NEP in favor of the command economy of the Five-Year Plan and a policy of rural collectivization that would outstrip War Communism in brutality.

322 **Saardam and Haarlem** Dutch towns. Saardam, later known as Zaandam or Zaanstadt, was where Tsar Peter the Great lived during his time working as a common shipwright in the Netherlands in 1697.

323 **the Committee of Members of the Constituent Assembly** The Komuch was a democratic counterrevolutionary government—consisting largely of Socialist Revolutionaries—formed on June 8, 1918, after the Czechoslovak Legion had occupied the city of Samara. The Komuch was dissolved in November 1918, after Admiral Alexander Kolchak's takeover of the White Forces following a British-sponsored coup.

324 **Muravyov . . . Vatsetis** See note on Muravyov in "The Road." Jukums Vācietis (1873–1938) was a Latvian Soviet military commander who led the Eastern Front from July through September 1918 and became the first commander in chief of the Red Army in September 1918. He perished in the Great Purges.

326 **the Germans can't stop it** Most of the Volga Germans were Mennonites who abstained from drink, but the presence of an Orthodox church in Voznesenskoye meant there were Russians (and therefore vodka) there.

328 **Mussorgsky's "Flea" . . . demented miller's aria** Modest Mussorgsky (1839–1881) wrote "Mephistopheles' Song of the Flea" in 1879 for a tour of the Russian south, shortly before he died. The text is taken from scene 5, part 1 of Goethe's *Faust* and concerns a story about a king who lavishes extravagant attention on a flea in his court. The song—which achieved fame thanks to Chaliapin's recordings—has a famous refrain consisting of the devil's laughter. Chaliapin was also known for his rendition of the miller's aria in Alexander Dargomyzhsky's opera *Rusalka* (1856), based on Pushkin's dramatic poem. The miller goes mad from grief after his daughter is seduced by a prince, drowns herself, and turns into a water nymph (*rusalka*).

329 **telegram to Ilyich** Lenin, in other words—"Ilyich" is Vladimir Ilyich Lenin's patronymic.

Crude

330 **oil cracking**   The Russian term "cracking" is a borrowing from English. It refers to the process of breaking down the complex molecules in crude oil into refined petroleum products. Crude oil had become the Soviet Union's most important export by 1928.

330 **our part of Sakhalin**   From 1925 to 1945, the Soviet Union controlled the northern three-fifths of Sakhalin Island; Japan had sovereignty over the southern portion.

330 **Max and Moritz**   *Max and Moritz (A Story of Seven Boyish Pranks)* is a popular German illustrated story written in verse by Wilhelm Busch and published in 1865. Max and Moritz's "pranks" are quite gruesome and full of dark humor.

331 **I know these Jews . . .** This sentence, omitted from the published version, appears in the typewritten manuscript at the Russian State Archive of Literature and Art (Babel, 1996, II, 309).

331 **forty million tons**   In response to rapidly growing demand for petroleum products on the foreign and domestic markets, Soviet agencies repeatedly amended the 1928 Five-Year Plan production goals almost every year. In 1932, for example, the target for 1932–1933 was reset from 24 to 46 million tons—a goal that would not be reached until the 1950s, despite the use of forced labor from the gulags and exchanges of expertise with Western oil companies. See Vagit Alekperov, *Oil of Russia: Past, Present, and Future*, trans. Paul B. Gallagher and Thomas D. Hedden (Minneapolis: East View Press, 2011).

332 **she speaks and the words have no sound**   See Matthew 13:13: "This is why I speak to them in parables: 'Though they look, they do not see; though they hear, they do not listen.'" See also Ezekiel 12:2, Jeremiah 5:21, Isaiah 42:20, as well as 1 Samuel 1:13: "Hannah was praying in her heart, and her lips were moving but her voice was not heard. Eli thought she was drunk." The ironic biblical diction seems strikingly Aesopian here.

333 **Then I telephoned Mironchik . . .** This sentence, omitted from the published version, appears in the typewritten manuscript at the Russian State Archive of Literature and Art (Babel, 1996, II, 309).

334 **Sparrow Hills**   A scenic spot in Moscow that offers a panoramic view of the city. The Black Sea resort towns of Yalta (in Crimea) and Batum (now known as Batumi, the capital of Adjara, an autonomous republic in southwest Georgia) are, in contrast, considerably more exotic.

334 **constructed quite soundly by the firm of Scrape and Collapse**   This phrase, omitted from the published version, appears in the typewritten

manuscript at the Russian State Archive of Literature and Art (Babel, 1996, II, 309).

Sulak

335 **Gulay's band . . . the Vinnytsa district** Vinnytsa is in west-central Ukraine. General Diomed P. Gulay served in the Ukrainian anti-Bolshevik army and was an official of the Ukrainian anti-Bolshevik regime from 1917 to 1919. He eventually became a public figure active in anti-Communist émigré circles. In 1951, three men from the Organization of Ukrainian Nationalists attempted and failed to assassinate Gulay in a displaced persons camp in Germany, where he had been put in charge of the so-called Ukrainian Liberation Movement, an umbrella group of Ukrainian parties in exile that was collaborating with anti-Stalinist Russian nationalists organized by the American Committee for the Liberation of Peoples of Russia. See *The Ukrainian Weekly* 20, no. 17 (April 28, 1952).

335 **Sulak served . . . Pope of Rome** Blue and yellow were the colors of the Ukrainian nationalists, who were typically Orthodox Christian; the implication is that Sulak left them to serve with the Poles, who are Roman Catholic.

336 **bed atop the stove** A traditional Russian or Ukrainian peasant cottage or hut would have a large earthen stove with an extended platform atop which people could sleep and keep warm.

336 **gave them coneys** The word used here for "coney"—or European rabbit—is the Belorussian *trus*, which means "coward" in Russian and Ukrainian.

Gapa Guzhva

This story was published with the following subtitle: "First chapter from the book *Velikaya Krinitsa*." The stories "Gapa Guzhva" and "Kolyvushka" are the only extant sections of Babel's projected book about the collectivization of agriculture.

338 **Butter Week** Maslenitsa (here Maslenaya) takes place before the start of Russian Orthodox Lent and has roots in a Slavic pagan folk tradition that originally marked the end of winter and the beginning of spring. Like Mardi Gras, it involves feasting and revelry before the Lenten fast, with blini (fried in butter) as the food of choice.

340 **Forgiveness Sunday** In the Orthodox Christian calendar, Forgiveness Sunday concludes the revelry of Butter Week, commemorates the Expulsion from Eden, and liturgically inaugurates the Great Lent with Christ's words, "If you forgive men their trespasses, your heavenly Father will also forgive you, but if you forgive not men their trespasses, neither will your Father forgive your trespasses" (Mark 6:14–15). On Sunday evening, at the culmination of Butter Week, the mascot Lady Maslenitsa—a brightly dressed straw effigy, once known as Kostroma (a fertility goddess whose name derives from the Russian word for "bonfire")—is stripped of her finery and burned. Any remaining blini are also thrown on the fire, and Lady Maslenitsa's ashes are buried in the snow as a fertility rite. During the Soviet period Maslenitsa was suppressed; celebrations resumed during glasnost in the late 1980s.

342 **to sign up for the *kolgosp*** *Kolgosp* is the Ukrainian contraction for a Soviet collective farm (*kolkhoz* in Russian). Collective farms formed gradually alongside state farms (sovkhozes) during the early years of Soviet rule, under the influence of propaganda workers. The collective farms that emerged after Stalin ordered the brutal forced collectivization of agriculture in 1928 were cooperatives in name only and soon resembled state farms.

343 *horilka* The word for this Ukrainian liquor, similar to vodka, is from the root meaning "to burn."

343 **proud flesh** Literally, "wild flesh" in Russian. Proud flesh refers to an excessive growth of granulation tissue in a wound.

343 **the coin necklace on her breast** Gapa is wearing a *monisto*, a peasant necklace with coins and other beads.

Kolyvuskha

344 **kolkhoz** See the note on *kolgosp* attached to "Gapa Guzhva." It is curious that here—in a collectivization story about the same village with several of the same characters as in "Gapa Guzhva"—Babel uses the Russian contraction kolkhoz instead of the Ukrainian *kolgosp*.

348 **Velikaya Staritsa** A village outside Kiev that Babel actually visited to observe Soviet agricultural collectivization, Velikaya Staritsa appears under the fictional name Velikaya Krinitsa in "Gapa Guzhva."

Babel, Isaac. *Babel: Collected Stories*. Translated by David McDuff. London: Penguin Classics, 1994.

———. *The Collected Stories*. Translated by Walter Morison. New York: Meridian, 1955.

———. *Detstvo i drugie rasskazy*. Edited by Efraim Sicher. Jerusalem: Biblioteka Aliya, 1979.

———. *Isaac Babel's Selected Writings*. Translated by Peter Constantine. Edited by Gregory Freidin. New York: Norton, 2007.

———. *Isaac Babel: The Lonely Years 1925–1939: Unpubished Stories and Private Correspondence*. Translated by Andrew MacAndrew and Max Hayward. Edited by Nathalie Babel. Lincoln, Mass.: Verba Mundi, 1995.

———. *Izbrannoe*. Kemerovo: Kemerovskoe Knizhnoe Izdatelstvo, 1966.

———. *Konarmiya*. Edited by Christopher Luck. Russian Text Series. London: Bristol Classical Press, 2001.

———. *1920 Diary*. Translated by H. T. Willetts. Edited by Carol Avins. New Haven, Conn.: Yale University Press, 1995.

———. *Red Cavalry*. Translated by Nadia Helstein. New York: Knopf, 1929.

———. *Sobranie sochinenii v chetyrekh tomakh*. Edited by I. N. Sukhikh. Moscow: Vremia, 2006.

———. *Sochineniia v dvukh tomakh*. Edited by I. Shurygina. Moscow: Terra, 1996.

———. *You Must Know Everything: Stories, 1915–1937*. Edited by Nathalie Babel. Translated by Max Hayward. New York: Dell, 1970.

Batuman, Elif. "Babel in California." *n+1*, no. 2 (Spring 2005): 22–68.

Brent, Jonathan. *Inside the Stalin Archives: Discovering the New Russia*. New York: Atlas, 2008.

Brown, Stephen. "Communists and the Red Cavalry: The Political Education of the Konarmiia in the Russian Civil War, 1918–20." *Slavonic and East European Review* 73, no. 1 (January 1995): 82–99.

Freidin, Gregory, ed. *The Enigma of Isaac Babel: Biography, History, Context*. Stanford, Calif.: Stanford University Press; 2009.

———. "Fat Tuesday in Odessa: Isaac Babel's 'Di Grasso' as Testament and Manifesto." *Russian Review* 40, no. 2 (April 1981), 101–21.

Glaser, Amelia M. *Jews and Ukrainians in Russia's Literary Borderlands: From the Shtetl Fair to the Petersburg Bookshop*. Evanston, Ill.: Northwestern University Press, 2012.

Iribarne, Louis. "Babel's *Red Cavalry* as a Baroque Novel." *Contemporary Literature* 14, no. 2 (Winter 1973): 58–77.

McSmith, Andy. *Fear and the Muse Kept Watch: The Russian Masters—from Akhmatova and Pasternak to Shostakovich and Eisenstein—Under Stalin*. New York: The New Press, 2015.

Pirozhkova, A. N. *At His Side: The Last Years of Isaac Babel*. Translated by A. Frydman and R. Busch. South Royalton, Vt.: Steerforth Press, 1996.

Senderovich, Sasha. "The Hershele Maze: Isaac Babel and His Ghost Reader." In *Arguing the Modern Jewish Canon: Essays on Literature and Culture in Honor of Ruth R. Wisse*, edited by Justin D. Cammy, Dara Horn, Alyssa Quint, and Rachel Rubenstein, 233–54. Cambridge, Mass.: Harvard University Press, 2007.

Sergay, Timothy D. "Isaac Babel's Life in English: The Norton *Complete Babel* Reconsidered." *Translation and Literature* 15, no. 2 (Autumn 2006): 238–53.

Shklovsky, Victor. "I. Babel: A Critical Romance." In *Isaac Babel*, edited by Harold Bloom, 9–14. New York: Chelsea House, 1987.

Sicher, Efraim. *Babel' in Context: A Study in Cultural Identity*. Boston: Academic Studies Press, 2012.

Stanton, Rebecca Jane. *Isaac Babel and the Self-Invention of Odessan Modernism*. Evanston, Ill.: Northwestern University Press, 2012.

Timmer, Charles. "Translation and Censorship." In *Miscellanea Slavica: To Honour the Memory of Jan M. Meijer*, edited by B. J. Amsenga et al., 443–68. Amsterdam: Rodopi, 1983.

Trilling, Lionel. Introduction to *The Collected Stories*, by Isaac Babel. Translated by Walter Morison. New York: Meridian, 1955.

van de Stadt, Janneke. "Two Tales of One City: Isaac Babel, Fellow Traveling, and the End of NEP." *The NEP Era: Soviet Russia 1921–1928* 6 (2012): 1–25.

Vinokur, Val. "Morality and Orality in Isaac Babel's *Red Cavalry*." *Massachusetts Review* 45, no. 4 (Winter 2004/2005): 674–95.

———. "Roth, Babel, and a Question of Blood." *Zeek.net* (February, 2008) www.zeek.net/802vinokur.

———. *The Trace of Judaism: Dostoevsky, Babel, Mandelstam, Levinas*. Evanston, Ill.: Northwestern University Press, 2008.